THE LIGHTHOUSE

THE LIGHTHOUSE

by

M.A. Lanham

 PAROLA
PRESS

THE LIGHTHOUSE

by

M.A. Lanham

>☀< PAROLA
🗼 PRESS

This is a work of fiction. Names, characters, places, and incidents either are
the product of the author's imagination or are used fictionally, and any
resemblance to actual persons, living or dad, businesses, companies, events,
or locales is entirely incidental.

ISBN-13: 978-1-62225-6808 hardcover
ISBN-13: 978-1-62225-6815 paperback
ISBN-13: 978-1-62225-6822 eBook

First Edition: October 2024

Printed in the United States of America

10 9 8 7 6 5 4 3 2 1

Cover Design: A.R. Redington
Author Photo: Arpit Mehta

M.A. Lanham is the nom de plume of an Amazon #1 bestselling, award-
nominated author of novels, short stories, and more in diverse genres.
Lanham lives in small town Kansas with his wife, two kids, two dogs and
two cats, making up stories and dreaming dreams, and hopes to never stop.
Find him online at www.malanham.com.

For M,

who brought me love and music again

CHAPTER 1

JACK PACE'S NIGHTMARES always started the same way. The '98 Toyota Camry's radio was too loud. Abby grimaced as the song finished and Caroline stopped belting the latest K-Pop hit from the back. She reached down to lower the volume.

"Again, mommy!" Caroline cheered. It was a conversation they seemed to repeat day after day.

"On the way home, baby," Abby said gently as she reached up and tucked a loose strand of her brunette hair back behind her ear. "Mommy needs a break."

"Awwwww," Caroline whined, making a sad face.

Abby laughed and shook her head. "It's not going to work. You sing that song a hundred times a day already. You'll survive giving your mama a break."

Caroline frowned and bulged her upper lip in a pouty expression, but Abby wouldn't budge, so moments later, her daughter sighed and grinned, her hand reaching for the silver plastic tiara resting atop her head. "Mommy, do I make a good princess?"

"The best," Abby said and meant it.

Abby slowed the car to a stop at a stop sign and waited to

turn left off Belmont Boulevard onto South Ohio Street. Ah, Salina. The only home she'd ever known. It was small, and she'd wanted desperately to get out when she was a teenager but now all her best memories, and everyone she loved was here. What else could a woman want? She'd told Jack those very words more than once.

The trees looked great with their reddish orange and yellow Fall colors. Soon, the leaves would begin to fall as the weather went from pleasant to cold with the approach of Winter. A mother robin flew down from its nest to peck at worms in the grass, the movement of her babies' heads barely visible above the walls of the nest as they chirped and called.

As Abby waited for several cars to pass, she glanced in the rearview mirror at her daughter. Seven years old going on twenty—or at least it seemed like it at certain moments. Wisdom from the mouths of babes, her mother would say. While Caroline was all girl with her blonde curls and spunky, giggly personality, sometimes the things she said just hit home as beyond her years. The flowery scent of her daughter's Disney Princess Perfume drifted to the front and tickled her nose.

Jack had objected at first when her parents gifted it the past Christmas. "She's too young for makeup!"

Abby agreed about makeup but this was a child's perfume, hardly as potent as the adult kind. It smelled, at best, like a scent a teenager might wear. Caroline play-acted at being older. To Abby, that was normal. As a little girl Abby had liked imagining herself as older too. Perfume was not makeup, as she'd made sure Jack understood. In the end, they'd struck a deal with Caroline: she could wear the perfume but no makeup until she was thirteen. Period. But Jack wondered if that agreement would last that long.

"Mommy, were you a princess when you met daddy?" Caroline asked, her blonde head bobbing in excitement, pigtails bouncing on either side. It was a question their daughter asked Jack, too, whenever they were alone on a drive. Oh to be a child and live in a world of fairy tales again.

2

Abby smiled. "No, but I felt like I was meeting a prince."

"Really? Daddy was a prince? Did he have a white horse?"

Abby laughed then slowly accelerated as she took advantage of the opportunity to turn and headed north on South Ohio, moving right into the outside lane which connected to the parking lot at their destination. Dillons, their local grocery chain, lay a few blocks ahead on the right. "No, babe. No white horse," Abby said, pausing a moment as she pondered how to answer. "Oh but the way he looked at me... It made me feel so special."

"Really? How did he look at you, mommy?" Caroline asked.

Just that morning, he'd come up and wrapped his arms around Abby from behind. As always, her cheeks reddened and her body responded at the touch of his body to hers. He'd leaned over and kissed her cheek. She'd reached back and caressed his hair, then rested her open palm against the side of his face. "I'm grateful every moment," he'd said as he spun her around and they kissed again.

"Ewwww, gross," Caroline whined, making a face as she all but danced into the kitchen and interrupted them. "Too much love."

"I can never have too much love for my girls." Jack smiled, his eyes locked on Abby's.

"I hope your day goes well," she'd said as she pulled away and stepped to the counter to fix their daughter's breakfast. "It sounds stressful."

"Nah, Barry Kline is a bit of a micromanager, but it's early enough the changes he wants aren't going to necessitate a lot of adjustments," Jack had said. "The toughest part is listening to him bitch. The rest is easy."

"Ummmmm," Caroline scolded. "Language, daddy."

"Sorry, pumpkin," he'd said and kissed his daughter on the head as he sneakily reached down to tickle her. For the next few moments, they'd dissolved into silliness as Caroline screamed and made to escape but Jack kept after her—another morning ritual Abby secretly adored. After a few seconds, Abby arrived to set a plate of scrambled eggs and bacon in front of their daughter and shoo Jack away.

Jack's cell phone beeped as a text message arrived. He read it quickly and grimaced as he skidded back loudly in his chair and stood. "Crap! Barry moved the meeting up. I'm late!"

"But you promised you'd have time to eat with us," Abby had objected, frustrated. He'd promised to make time this morning. These were the kind of promises he always struggled with. It had been the source of several fights over the years

Noting Abby's frown, Jack leaned and kissed Caroline on the forehead then turned and kissed Abby on the cheek, his hand caressing her cheek. "I love you," he'd said, meaning them both. But his eyes had added "I'm so sorry" just for her. And she knew he always meant it. Somehow they'd get through this.

"We love you, too," Abby and Caroline said together, their daughter adding "daddy" to the phrase, and then he'd run out the door.

He got the call thirty minutes later when he was hurrying down the hall to the conference room for the meeting with Barry and the client. He almost ignored it until he saw "Emergency Services" scrolling across the caller ID.

"Mister Pace, I'm very sorry to bother you, but there's been an accident," the 911 operator said in a voice that was way too calm and gentle for what she was about say. Forever after, he couldn't remember her exact words. What he could remember was falling to his knees in the hallway and the feeling as if someone had slammed into his chest, pushing all the air out. Something about a truck barreling through the intersection. The big industrial kind—the kind the Toyota was no match for.

And then time stopped. His world ended. Everything that mattered gone in a flash. As usual, he awoke gasping, his heart pounding and jagged pain throughout his body. Why? Why God, why?! his internal voice always demanded. And for the thousandth time he echoed back, I'd trade places with them in a minute. It should have been me. And then dissolved into sobbing as coworkers rushed toward him with concerned looks, asking what was wrong.

CHAPTER 2

TWO DAYS LATER, the restaurant was a gem, the blind date sitting across the table, a horror show, and Jack wondered how in the world he'd let his younger sister, Josie, talk him into this.

"What part of mineral water with lemon did you not understand?!" his date scolded, glaring at the waitress who had brought her a Dasani with lemon included, not a mineral water with a slice of lemon on the rim as she'd asked. Of course, Jack wondered how a slice of lemon was supposed to actually fit on the rim of a bottled water, but his date, Linda's, instructions had been quite explicit.

"The lemon is included," the waitress explained, her eyes strained as she lost patience. "We ran out of lemons. The owner sent someone to the market." Glasses clinked and silverware dinged against plates around them as the other diners enjoyed their meals, oblivious to the "lemon crisis" occurring in their midst.

Linda crinkled her nose with distaste. "It's not the same thing," she strained to read the waitress's name tag, "Sarah." Linda wasn't even his type. She was in many ways the opposite of Abby—short blond hair, pale white skin, almost six foot, whereas Abby was a tanned auburn-haired beauty of five feet three. But most of all, Linda was very outgoing and type A. Abby had been introverted and gentle, the perfect wife and mother. Jack couldn't imagine living with this woman in a house.

"It's the best I could do, I'm sorry," Sarah replied. "I'll bring you another in a few minutes when John gets back from the market." Sarah looked about fifteen, though Jack was pretty sure she had to be a bit older to work in a place serving alcohol. She was pretty, blonde, not too much make-up—reminding him of how he'd imagined his nine-year-old daughter Caroline might grow up to look one day.

Linda scowled. "Who runs out of lemons on a Friday night?!" She looked at Jack. "The talk was this is a classy place, but I'm not seeing it."

As far as Salina went, The Scheme was classy. But it was a pizza joint, not fine dining. Founded in the late eighties by one of Jack's parents' neighbors, The Scheme was downtown on North 7th Street, its red canopy a local landmark. The interior had dark wooden tables, and a bar with classic gold-embossed chandeliers overhead that left all the right shadows. Soft eighties music played from speakers overhead, taking Jack back to his first time here during high school with his family. He didn't glance around the crowded dining room—it usually was—afraid of seeing someone he knew from his job at Kline Architects, instead staring at the painting of a scene from a Marilyn Monroe movie that hung on the wall above a nearby table.

He blushed, turning to Sarah, and sighed. "I'm so sorry."

"What are you apologizing to her for? I'm the one who was wronged," Linda snapped, expanding her glare to include him.

"My four-year-old daughter has better manners," Sarah said, finally fed up, as she shot Jack a look of thanks.

"My nine-year-old, too," Jack agreed, then winced as he thought of Abby and Caroline. They'd been dead a year now, and he mourned them every day. Why did he still think of them as if they were alive at home, waiting for him? Why was he even here?

Linda grunted. "My brother said your daughter had died.

Did he lie to me? I hate kids!"

Jack just scooted back from the table and motioned to Sarah. "Check please. We're leaving."

"What?! I want my water!" Linda protested.

"It's three dollars for the water, and your soda's on the house," Sarah said and smiled.

Jack handed her cash, including a tip equal to the bill, and headed for the door. "You can find your own ride home," he said, slapping another twenty down on the counter in front of Linda then kept right on walking.

"OH MY GOD!" his sister Josie exclaimed as he related the story to her an hour later on the phone. "What the hell was Ben thinking?" Linda's brother, who worked in the office next to Jack's at Kline, had set up the date.

"I don't know, but that was the worst one yet," Jack growled. "I wish everyone would just stop trying to set me up and leave me be." He ran a hand through his hair and leaned back on the sofa, groaning, then took a big sip from the Budweiser he'd opened as soon as he walked through the door.

"We just want you to be happy," Josie reminded him.

"I don't know if I can be without Abby and Caroline," he said for not the first time. "They're the loves of my life, and they were stolen from me. You can't fix that. So please stop trying."

He could almost hear Josie throwing up her hands. "I get that, and yet I refuse to believe Abby would want you to stay at home like a hermit. She'd want you to move on, and at least get out and live, Jack."

"I will when I'm ready," Jack snapped. "This is not when."

It was Josie's turn to sigh. "I gotta get the boys to bed. I'm sorry it went badly. I'll call you tomorrow, 'kay?"

He grunted. "Good night, sis."

"I love you," she said as she hung up the phone.

The accident, on what Jack Pace had come to call "the day that changed everything," came out of nowhere like most of them do. And even today, a year later, most of it was still a blur. He'd laughed and joked with them both like always that morning, snuggling both his wife and daughter—one of his favorite ways to start any day. He'd been preparing for an important new client all week and had to miss Caroline's dance recital and their meals together, but that day he'd promised to make time, and he did... until Barry texted. He'd moved the meeting up last minute at the client's request, and Jack had to rush out the door. He'd seen Abby's displeasure on her face. He'd kissed his wife and daughter and apologized, but even as he headed for the door, he knew it would take more to make it up to Abby. He'd let her down. And he'd fully intended to come home early that night and take a day off the next Monday so they could have his full attention for the next three days. When the police called two hours later, nothing was the same anymore—his job, the house, food... everything—and he doubted it would ever be the same again. Time stopped that day his life ended.

He had been smitten the first time he set eyes on Abby in her Roosevelt Lincoln Junior High School cheerleader outfit—her long, smooth tan legs sending thoughts through his adolescent hormone-ridden brain that would have made him blush if anyone could hear them. He admired her curves, especially the curve of her breasts and that small patch of cleavage the sweater she wore on top revealed every time she did a dance move or bent to twirl or spin. She had beautiful, long auburn locks, and that adorable smile. Jack had never met a girl who'd had such an effect on him. He literally had to remind himself to breathe whenever he looked at her, and that one time when her bright blue eyes caught his... he was pretty sure his heart had stopped, frozen in time, for at least a minute or two. Neither the fact that he was still alive or that the idea defied the laws of physiology didn't change his mind.

It was love at first sight. But it had taken him a while to not only win her over but be ready for their relationship. He was a bumbling, pimpled, geeky ball of hormones, a farm boy, and she was the popular, sophisticated girl from the Hill, where all the wealthy families lived. Abby had been friendly but kept her distance. Jack had never worked so hard in his life as he did winning her over. And by the time they reached high school, they were inseparable.

Abby Brown, she was the one for Jack Pace for sure. And from that day on, his whole life had been about winning her over, and then keeping her happy, no matter what it took. She was the only woman he'd ever loved. And as far as he could imagine, the only woman he ever would. That she loved him back was the greatest gift he'd ever been given, because Jack knew he didn't deserve her, and she'd put up with her share of frustration from him over the years as he tried to find balance between work and home—something he was bad at from years of working ever spare hour helping his parents on the farm. Work was their life back then, and they'd engrained that work ethic in their children, but Abby's dad had come home every night for dinner and family time, despite his well-paying job and great success. That was her role model and had set her expectations. She loved Jack and he loved her, but Abby wanted a husband who made time for his family like her father had, especially after Caroline was born. Jack's career was ever rising and with it, new demands on his time. He did his best, but he knew it had never been enough.

Abby had followed Jack to Lawrence to attend the University of Kansas where he majored in architecture while she studied history. They'd married at First Baptist Church in Salina a week after his graduation, then returned to Lawrence where he'd interned with a local firm until she graduated a year later. Jack accepted the job back in Salina with a firm owned by friend of his father's, and the years before the birth of their daughter had been like an extended honeymoon. Abby took a job teaching history as an adjunct at Kansas Wesleyan, and outside work, they pretty much spent all their time together. With the exception of a few close friends they occasionally spent time with, there was no one else they wanted to be with, and that didn't change for the twelve years before the accident.

The second love of his life, after Abby of course, had been their daughter, Caroline. For seven glorious years before the accident, their life had been as close to perfect as Jack had ever imagined life could be. Not really perfect, but damn close, and he couldn't have asked for a better daughter. She had all the good qualities of her mother, and few of Jack's faults, thank God.

But then that day came. The accident. The hospital. A walking nightmare.

The other driver was a man named Mitchell Bass. He drove a red Chevy Silverado 5500 Crew Cab platform truck bearing the emblem of his employers—Zimmer Industrial. He'd been checking something on the clipboard beside him and failed to stop at what he presumed was a yellow light. When Abby crossed the intersection under a green light, he T-boned her white Toyota Corolla square on the driver's side at a mere thirty-five miles per hour, a mistake that took all of five seconds to destroy everything that had ever mattered to Jack Pace. Bass walked away with a few cuts and scrapes. And for the first nine months after the accident, Jack had thought about killing him every single day.

"Just get up and breathe," Josie and others had told him. "That's your only job right now. It'll take a while, but you know Abby wouldn't want you doing anything to seek revenge. She'd want you to go on, try to find a way to carry on somehow."

He'd listened in silence usually, but most of the times it was because he was fighting the urge to laugh in their face and scream, "What do I have to live for?! I've lost everything! And that bastard doesn't deserve to live for taking it from me!"

The accident occurred at eight-thirty a.m., and Jack had been in a meeting for thirty minutes already. Abby died instantly, the car crushed so quickly it was almost a Z when the emergency crews used the jaws of life to extract her and Caroline, only to rush them to Asbury Hospital downtown. Caroline survived the crash, though critical and in a coma. Jack had never prayed or cried so hard in all his life as he did those two days. Josie and Abby's parents, Grace and Paul, did their best to keep him comfort, offering what comfort and conversation they could, but Jack was like a zombie—reliving over and over all the moments he'd missed from meals to school events, the recitals, and the second honeymoon he'd promised Abby for over a decade. He'd made lots of promises how they'd do it one day when things slowed down, only life never did, and now all he wanted was his life rewound to that terrible morning like it never happened. He hoped Abby's two surgeries would bring her back to him, but she died three days later, leaving Jack to sleep in a chair next to Caroline's bed, squeezing her tiny, precious hand as if it was keeping them both breathing. But Caroline herself had finally succumbed to her injuries the following Friday, and his family was gone forever.

Jack kept it together as best he could, making funeral arrangements, notifying his family and hers, and hosting everyone as they gathered for the funeral a week later at First Baptist, presided over by Pastor Jim Owen, a family friend. The church called in a "Celebration of Life," but Jack could think of nothing to celebrate. He made it through somehow, and as the guests went home, her parents and his—Ken and May Pace—and his sister Josie turned the donated casseroles, the spiral ham, the trays of dinner rolls, three cherry dump cakes, and the reams of noodle salad into freezer-trays-for-one his mother said should feed him for six months. Each kissed him good-bye while Jack held to Josie's sleeve, willing her at least to stay. Abby's mother, Gloria, lingered long enough in front of Abby's closet that she had to be led outside crying into a sweater she'd given her late daughter for Christmas. Each voice flew away with the prevailing winds blowing over Kansas until the house fell silent, leaving Jack alone with hundreds of cards and letters from friends and strangers expressing condolences and sympathies for loss of two people most of them barely knew.

Jack's fall into darkness pressed him into an obsequious square of deep overwhelming sadness, sliced up by a pain that haunted his every waking hour. Missing both of them seeped into his sedated sleep where he relived the accident and its aftermath over and over again. The nightmares began a week after the funeral. Perhaps it was a result of so much speculation and discussion with family during the wake about what Abby's and Caroline's final moments might have been like. Or perhaps he bore some guilt in how he might have rearranged their morning to keep them out of the path of Bass. To Jack, it hardly mattered. There was one thing they all had in common: they were all torture. Who would enjoy reliving their great loves' final moments over and over again—in various scenarios—with no way to distinguish between fantasy and truth? For all Jack knew, it was all fiction—the product of his warped, guilt-ridden mind. Yet it seemed so real when Caroline and Abby were crying out to him for help while he went on at work oblivious, never helping or even being aware of their need for him. He hadn't been aware, he feared, and he became tortured by the fear he'd been a bad husband and father, one who wasn't there when he should have been. A man who had the wrong priorities—too focused on work and not what really mattered.

In the end, he just wanted it to stop. And yet he didn't. At least this way they visited him every night. He heard their voices, their laughs, saw them happy in the moments leading up to their deaths—animated and whole just as they were in life. If that was the only way he could see them, he didn't want to give it up, did he? If nightmares were the price, he'd gladly bear it. Whatever it took to keep the memories of who they were and what they had together alive. He lived in a constant state as if a vise were pressing on the sides of his chest, permanently squeezing it tight. It was a feeling he'd learned to live with and figured would never go away. This was his life now.

HE AWOKE THE morning after the bad date at The Scheme, from yet another night terror that left him gasping to breathe as he always did after reliving the accident. He hadn't been there, and other than traffic cam footage and security footage from the Dillon's Supermarket, like the police, he'd only picked over eyewitness testimony from Bass and other drivers to fill in what happened. For obvious reasons, he refused to rely on Bass' word. Although he'd been tested on site for drugs and alcohol and a lab had cleared him, Jack didn't care. He'd be damned if he let the man who'd murdered his family—stolen them from him—be the narrator of their final moments.

Over the next few months, there were three more failed dates—three more blind dates, two of them just as horrible, and one with a woman who felt more like a friend than anyone he could get serious about. The most horrible had been at Guiterrez Mexican Restaurant, one of his and Abby's favorites—his date's choice, not his, because too many memories. He'd gotten along with the date, Erin, just fine but there was no passion. Then he'd looked across the dining room to see Abby's parents, Grace and Paul, staring at him. The final straw. He wound up excusing himself to go over and apologize to them, and then, when he got back to the table, he told Erin something had come up and left cash on the table, offering her a ride home and food to go. She had accepted, totally confused, and he'd never seen heard from her again. He'd insisted from then on that everyone to stop setting him up. But his aunt and a couple co-workers weren't easily discouraged, so finally, he began wondering if he might actually have to move away to escape, to just get some peace.

At first, he'd started looking at job and real estate listings out of idle curiosity. But as time went on, he became more and more intrigued with the idea of starting over in a new place. Yes, Salina was home. He'd lived there since he was six except for his college years. He knew its every nook and cranny almost everyone who lived there it seemed—he'd dated enough of them, right? This is where his memories of Abby and Caroline were strongest—their stuff, their favorite places, the world they'd shared—could he really leave that behind? Then again, the memories were his wherever he went, and after taking a couple of business trips, and then a week-long vacation spent in Colorado with his sister's family hiking the Rockies, he realized he'd never leave them behind, so why did he have to feel stuck in the same place? Maybe a fresh start somewhere new was exactly what he needed. He'd always mourn them, but he didn't have to wallow in it. Maybe he could find some place isolated enough that he wouldn't be surrounded by people. That would ease the pressure and allow him to escape the most painful reminders he encountered almost daily.

They'd been gone eighteen months now, and he wasn't sure he could ever move on, but that didn't mean he enjoyed the daggers of pain that struck every nerve each time he passed the Southgate Dillon's Supermarket or Salina Central High School where he'd met Abby, or her parents' house, or any of a dozen other places seared with memories of time spent together. No, a fresh start was sounding better and better the longer he considered it, and one day, he spotted the job at a remote lighthouse in Florida. That night, when he went over to Josie's house for dinner—a weekly tradition since the accident—he asked his sister about it to see how she'd react.

"Well, isolation's what you're after, right?" his sister, Josie, asked when he told her about it as he helped her with the dinner dishes.

"Yeah," he said.

"You should check out Kansas City or Chicago, see how you like it," she said, handing him another pan to scrub as she continued rinsing plates and silver before loading them into the dishwasher. She said it more than once every time they'd talked since the accident.

"You know how much I hate cities," Jack reminded her yet again.

"Live in the suburbs like we did," Josie said. "It's almost like a small town."

"Yeah, sure," he said, not really believing her. Usually she argued, offering examples, but this time she let it go. "You went there to start a family and for Andy's career. I don't need that." Josie and Andy were also high school sweethearts who'd met their senior year and fallen hard, getting engaged just after Christmas and planning a wedding right after graduation. Though their parents had worried a little, especially their mother, May, Josie and Andy had moved off to Chicago that July to seek the bigger life together they'd always dreamed of and only come back when Andy's company downsized him, leaving them forced to start over again on a much lower budget.

"Yeah but people move to cities for lots of reasons," Josie countered. "They're crowded, for one. And they're busy. Easy place to get lost in the crowd if that's what you want. Or you can meet more and interesting people from all over the world. A lot better dating pool than what we have around here."

He rolled his eyes. "For God's sake, you know that's the last thing I want."

She chuckled and offered a shrug. "Just pointing out options, bro."

He finished scrubbing the pan and handed it to her. She accepted it and placed it precisely along one side of the lower rack of the dishwasher, then said, "Well, maybe this is your opportunity."

"Opportunity?"

"To downsize. Get rid of some things that remind you of what you lost. I mean, do you really need a little girl's bedroom set? What about Abby's old clothes or Caroline's toys?" Josie suggested.

He sighed. "But that's theirs," he said. He'd locked most of it away in a spare room he refused to enter since a month after the accident, but could he really bear to be without it?

"It'll cost a lot to move everything," Josie said. "Do you even know if the new place has room for it? Besides, you said you wanted a simpler life."

"You're the one who wanted a simpler life," Jack reminded

17

her. "That's why you moved back to Grandma's house, remember?" Their grandma had left it to May in her will when she'd died two summers before Andy lost his job. May had been about to sell it when Josie and Andy found themselves needing to relocate and start over, so she'd gifted it to them, and they'd lived there ever since.

"But Florida is so far away," Josie said, shifting him back onto the topic of his own career change decision. "And the job—lighthouse keeper—it's so random. How'd you even find that? I didn't think they had lighthouse keepers anymore."

"Well, in the U.S, no. This is a rare exception, but in Canada and other places around the world, they're still quite active," Jack said, having done a bit of research. "The Keys look beautiful, and I probably would never spend the money on real estate in a place like that, but the house comes with the job. I'd live in the lighthouse. And you know I like the outdoors."

"It's a big pay cut from architecture," Josie said. "You spent all those years getting a degree and building your reputation. Can you really leave that behind like it's nothing?"

"I can always come back to it," Jack argued. "Anyway, utilities are included with the house, I don't have a family to support. The salary's more than sufficient for my needs."

"But it's on some small island. I know you want privacy but do you really want to be that alone?" From the way she scrunched up her face when she said, Jack knew Josie had a hard time imagining such a life. But for Jack, the isolation was one of the job's biggest appeals. Moving his possessions would get a big complicated, with only private boats to ferry things over. And he'd have to find somewhere to park his car safely on the main island for when he needed it. But…there were really nice advantages. "No one trying to set me up on blind dates every other day. Limited space, so people can't just surprise visit me. I have to get permission from the Coast Guard and only a few at a time. No more finicky or demanding clients." He ticked them off on his fingers as he said them, smiling at the thought, especially of the last.

"Well, it sounds crazy to me, Jack, and you know the kids and I will miss you like crazy," Josie said as she finished loading and bent over to retrieve a pod of dishwashing soap from a box under the sink. She deposited it in the soap holder of the dishwasher and slid the door shut, then closed the outside door as her eyes met his. "But it's your life. If you're really that unhappy, and this is what you need, you know I'll always support you."

"Thanks," Jack smiled and hugged her.

In truth, Jack had already called and been interviewed over the phone twice. His future boss, Warren Gregg, was an interesting older man and Coast Guard veteran with a million fascinating and entertaining stories, and Jack would be working alone there except for days off, so except for the a few scattered tourists, he knew he'd have the time he craved to just mourn in peace and figure out what the future held if anything. No matter what he got out of it, at least he'd have peace from everyone trying to push a future on him he didn't want.

The following day, he'd gone to Barry's office and quit. He put the house on the market and held a garage sale. He needed a clean break and moving all their stuff made little sense, especially when all it did was remind him of his heartache and loss. He kept a few little reminders, like Caroline's Disney Princess perfume, and the engagement and wedding rings he'd given Abby. Most of the rest sold so quickly, he didn't have time for regret. He had to get away from this town and these people, and especially the memory of Michael Bass and the accident. Oh, it'd be with him the rest of his life wherever he went, but that didn't mean he needed constant reminders. He no longer wanted revenge. He supposed that was progress, but as for the rest he needed to start over. Afterward, his head was spinning and he was terrified he'd made the wrong choice. How much did their possessions have to do with the strength of his memories? But those possessions were gone. and there was no going back. He was headed to Florida to start a new life, and he could only hope and pray that somehow it would be the right choice.

CHAPTER 3

O N A TUESDAY morning four months after the disastrous blind date with Linda, Jack woke up to unfamiliar surroundings at a Holiday Inn in downtown Islamorada in the Florida Keys. He was in the rightmost of two queen beds covered by cheap tropical bedspreads with lamps modeled after coconuts, wicker furniture that looked like it belonged beside a pool or on a beach, and a seashell themed waste can. The two paintings in the room were both ocean scenes. He'd slept in the bed closest to the air conditioner because the humidity had him soaked just on the walk from the Jeep to the room. Then there was the smell—an unbalanced cocktail of pleasant and unpleasant. The briny marine smell of the ocean combined with the distinct crispness of pine trees, and an underlying offensive punch to the nostrils of methane from the swamps. Definitely not in Kansas anymore. The walls were pastels right out of Miami Vice, and a small round table next to an entertainment center with a large flatscreen TV, DVD player, and remote he'd never touched, held the Floridian-type welcome brochures, area tour books of attractions, and the hotel guidebook with information on room service and other amenities. He rolled over and flipped on the coconut lamp hung above the nightstand separating the beds, blinking as he checked his watch.

5 a.m.

He had to be at the pier to catch a boat for work at 6:30 to start his first day at the lighthouse, so he had just enough time to shower and grab a bite from the hotel's continental breakfast setup before he headed there. He took a deep breath and sat up, yawning, then stood and walked over to the window, cracking the curtains and looking outside across Overseas Highway toward the Atlantic Ocean half a mile away. Seabirds playfully soared and dove in arcs and loops, as the sun reflected off the peaceful early morning waves. A year ago he'd never have imagined finding himself here. It was like the edge of the world. A different world from the one he'd always known in Central Kansas.

He released the curtains, letting them close, to head for the bathroom. And yet every time he got in the shower, he scrubbed himself all over multiple times, hoping the pain and sorrow would wash away with the sweat and grime, but it never did. Somehow, this time though, he found his hope renewed every time he stepped naked under the warm shower stream. Today was the first day of his new life at San Jose Island as the lighthouse keeper. Why was he trying to wash away the pain or the memories? Instead, he would carry them like a banner to honor the ones he loved and always would. Cristof's Key was a private island, its only occupant the lighthouse which was mostly automated and served as a caretaker's house. The light itself was run by computers down below. Jack would be in charge of checking its systems, making occasional adjustments, and maintaining the building and island by himself—its only occupant. No clients. No coworkers. No relatives with blind dates to set him up with—the perfect place for a broken man wanting to start over and be left alone.

He finished his shower and slipped into his brown polo shirt and pressed Khaki pants. It had been ages since Jack had ironed anything. Almost back to his college days. When the uniform had arrived in the mail, it had come already pressed and this was his second time putting it on. He wondered if his ironing would be up to standards the next time he washed it, and missed Abby. He then slid on his belt and reached for his boots. The belt and boots were matching black leather, and the belt had pouches for a flashlight, pliers, two screwdrivers—one each Phillips and standard head—and a clip for his keys. The flashlight was one Caroline had given him as a gift the previous Christmas—a first responder issue with an extra strong beam and multiple settings but also sturdy casing that could take a beating. She'd seen her father break so many cheap flashlights over the years that it had become a joke between them. When he opened it, she'd said she wanted to give him something that would remind him of her and last. Like her memory, he added to himself and suddenly felt sad.

When he'd finished putting it all on, he looked at himself in the mirror assessing. He looked pretty good for a man who felt barely alive. "Not bad, Jack, not bad," he mumbled. The irony was only his new supervisor, Warren Gregg, and a few people at the hotel would see him.

He combed his hair and put on some hairspray then as an afterthought reached for some cologne. He'd rarely worn any in the year since Abby had passed, and her favorite—Paço Rabanne—had been in a box in the closet he'd let Josie donate to Goodwill. He couldn't bear that reminder. Instead, he used a new bottle of something called Passion Josie had given him before he left Salina—part of his fresh start, Josie had said. It smelled alright, he supposed, and he applied it conservatively. "Just enough to smell civilized," as their mother always said.

And then he was ready. He packed up his bag and dopp kit, tossed them in the closet, then sat at the mirror and stared at himself. Who was the man in the keeper's uniform with the Coast Guard crest on the shoulder and right front pocket? The bags under his eyes and even the way he combed his hair left him indifferent. That's just how it was for him. This was his life now, and he had to keep going, though he sometimes wondered why. He closed his eyes and took a deep breath, then rose from the chair and headed for the continental breakfast bar in the lobby.

JACK LEFT HIS Jeep at the Holiday Inn and took an Uber to the public pier where a jetty boat chartered by the Coast Guard waited to take him over to San Jose Island. The boat captain who met him at the pier, Bert, informed him he provided regular ferry service much of the time, but had a special contract with the Coast Guard. The jetty boat's proportions, though small, were not too tiny; an enclosed cabin contained two raised stools facing the control and communications panel operated by the captain and his second crew member. A large rail of multiple tiers top deck protected passengers assembled on benches lining the aft end of the boat. Those remaining lined up, their backs against the sides of the cabin or scattered around the front.

The engine ripped and off they headed in the direction of the Teatable Key Reef Channel passing parked yachts and sailboats and other vessels lining the docks near the jetty stop. As he looked around, Jack realized this was what most people would call a tropical paradise—with its mile of palm tree lined beaches, docks, and piers, endless sunshine, and endless blue skies. And the views were stunning. Way different from the wheat and corn fields, dirty and clay, and endless prairies back home. The temperatures were different, too. It was sixty-five degrees when he stepped out the door, and the predicted high was in the mid-seventies. Back home, most March days started in the thirties and though they got occasional sixties, most March days topped out in the forties and fifties.

A narrow channel moved between two sections of reef and even looking down off the side of the jetty, thousands of fish of all shapes, sizes, and colors zipped around like it was their own little kingdom. The ocean breeze on his face soothed his skin like an air shower cleansing him all over again. The ocean and reefs stretched ahead as far as the eye could see, though it was only a few minutes until they reached the end of the channel and where scattered smaller islands lay in the distance ahead. Fishing boats and sail boats dotted his vision as the ferry traversed its well-worn route, until five minutes later, he could see the object of all his thoughts and hopes for escape—the tall white lighthouse gleaming in the distance. Its red-and-white-striped tower rose like a sentinel overlooking the water and other small islands around it. This was to be his new home, and what a stunning sight it made across the open expanse of water. At the moment, all he could make out were the edges of the island and the tower rising from their midst, but as the boat drew closer, he made out a few smaller structures at its base, though not well, but he'd soon come to know more about them than almost anyone on Earth.

The undisturbed natural beach stretched out like an oasis and at its end away from the lighthouse, he began to make out the wood poles and planks of a pier. For a moment, his eyes just soaked it all in, his emotions mixed. He'd never been here before and probably only a few thousand tourists had been in a hundred years. But the keepers numbered less than thirty. Only new memories and a new life awaited him there—memories and life he'd live entirely without his wife and daughter, and at that thought, his breath caught in his throat for a moment, until he forced himself to take a deep breath. This is what you wanted, remember? No turning back. And yet he wished his heart could feel as certain about it as his head.

As the jetty slowed and moved alongside the pier, two pelicans dove down to the water and arced back up bearing their morning fish, soaring gracefully on the wind as Jack watched them with jealous admiration. Oh to fly on the wind without a seeming care in the world. Shaking it off he looked around, examining what he could see now of the island up close. Except for the Coast Guard golf cart waiting for him with his new boss, the beach was barren as far as he could see. It stretched over twenty miles to the north, a vast strip of wet sand covered with scattered clumps of Sargasso Weed and other seaweeds, and numerous seashells of all shapes and sizes. A stirring among the passengers caused him to stand and lean against the rail as Bert brought the boat to a stop beside the pier.

Only two signs of life marked the island—an old, dilapidated lifeguard stand about twenty-five yards down the beach, and the tall, striped, Cristof's Lighthouse, built in the 1930s and named after the original discoverer or an early resident—no one was sure which—sitting above the vegetation line off the beach, less than a mile from the pier where the jetty boat was dropping him off. As he stepped onto the pier, Jack spotted crabs and other small animals moving among the weeds and shells. Abby would have loved this, he thought and flashed back to the first time they'd seen a lighthouse together on their honeymoon when they'd visited South Texas.

"So romantic," Abby said. "Like something out of stories."

"Lighthouses have that effect on people, I suppose."

"You suppose?" she teased him as he came up behind and pressed against her, wrapping her in his arms as he bent to kiss her neck. "You're really sweeping me off my feet, babe."

Jack laughed. "I like it, too, but I hadn't thought of it as romantic."

Abby smiled. "Well, I like to think of every moment I spend with you as romantic."

Jack started feeling guilty then. He'd missed the mark on that one. It was one of the many times Abby reminded him how the world appeared through her eyes and her invitations to share the view. Looking back, he wished he'd paid more attention so as not to miss such moments. But then, covering, he'd turned her head gently and kissed her passionately. "I love you, too," he'd replied.

Jarring him back to the present, Bert handed him his shoulder bag and called past him to the man waiting on shore in the golf cart, "Need anything, Warren?"

The Coast Guard supervisor shook his head and waved, calling back, "Not at the moment, Bert. Thanks. Ask me a little later this morning, when you're on another run."

Jack strode quickly along the pier and onto the sand and stopped. It was like a virgin paradise just waiting to be explored—the kind he'd dreamed about as a kid when he and Josie and the neighbor boys had played pirates or castaways. Sheer beauty and wondrous nature unfolded everywhere he looked, and amidst the wonder, he had to remind himself to breathe once or twice. I really get to live here? How could a cursed man like him have gotten so lucky? Yeah, it wasn't Kansas. The humidity and heat would definitely take getting used to, but if this was his view every day, he could get over that. More magically, everywhere he looked he pictured Abby and Caroline—frolicking in the sand, laughing, running, playing—all scenes of joy from his memory set in this new place where they'd never been and never would be. His heart raced as a surge of warmth built within.

And then he heard a familiar voice, "Good luck." And he blinked, coming back to the present as Bert waved to them both then pushed off again for Islamorada, leaving Jack to stroll up the pier alone toward Warren Gregg, who smiled, waiting patiently. Medium height with grey hair and warm brown eyes, his new boss looked like a friendly grandfather type. He wore the official white shirt over blue pants uniform of the Coast Guard, the shirt bearing patches and pins representing his years of service and various citations. A gentle breeze flicked through the hair on his forehead as he sat in his cart.

"I hope you like peace and quiet," Warren commented as Jack drew nearer to him. "You'll have that and to spare out here."

Jack grunted. "Exactly what I need." And he somehow knew it was for certain in that moment.

Warren smiled and motioned for Jack to take the passenger seat as he slid back behind the wheel. Once Jack had settled, he took off along the top edge of the beach just below the vegetation line, moving at decent speed for a golf cart. Pelicans and gulls circled and swooped over the water, a few landing on the beach to grab crabs or other small animal life in their bills.

"It's peaceful but ruthless," Warren commented, while a gull tore a crab into edible bits. "You have to take care of yourself."

"Yeah, I can handle that," Jack replied as the same breeze assaulted his nose from the smell of wet seaweed and dead fish. There was a time when he couldn't have imagined being alone or ever wanting to, but that was before. Now, he craved it.

Warren turned left slightly and angled up off the sand onto a dirt path that followed the vegetation line toward the lighthouse, growing bigger as they neared it.

Jack could make out its wider base alongside a few side buildings, each of them painted white to match the main structural shaft. "What is it, about fifteen hundred feet from the water?"

Warren agreed by nodding. "These islands are geographically young by comparison with most land around here," he said, informing him. "But Cristof's Key is also pure, almost untouched by comparison with the others. It's a reminder of what these islands should look like if we left them alone or at least took proper care of them."

Jack envied the place. How freeing it must be to be untouched. Human beings didn't have that option. "Don't tourists come here?" he asked. "The public beaches are so close."

"Occasionally we get a few outliers, but since they have to bring everything they need with them, not many want to make the effort."

"So we chase them off?" Jack asked, hoping the answer didn't involve his duties.

"Up to you, but if they leave a mess, you'll have to clean it up, so use your best judgment," Warren said, pointing out a leftover lunch sack he drove past to grab and sack in a trash bag.

Just what Jack wanted, to be the beach cop for a bunch of tourists. But he held his tongue. He didn't hate people. They just complicated life in ways he preferred to do without. Time would tell. "No one else lives here?" he asked instead, knowing what he'd been told but curious given the beauty and proximity to the main island.

"Oh, probably at some point long ago in the past," Warren said. "There're remnants of a couple old foundations on the other side of the island, but not anymore. I'm sure you're aware you've got her all to yourself."

Warren slowed the cart as they neared the lighthouse and a dirt path leading up to it. "Can I ask you a question?"

"Sure."

"What's a thirty-eight-year-old successful architect from Kansas doing giving up a high paying job for a career in public service on a small, private island to live alone?" Warren asked, eyes locked on Jack's as the cart slowed to a stop.

Jack's chest felt heavy, his stomach roiling. So much for his new boss not asking the one question Jack didn't want to answer. "Is that so odd?"

Warren grunted. "Considering most of our applicants were fresh out of college?"

Jack got the gist, and said, "I just wanted a change."

Warren raised an eyebrow and continued watching him, clearly waiting for more.

"I need a fresh start," Jack added, fumbling for words. "Somewhere new. And the money is not what matters. I need peace. And this seems like the perfect place for that."

Warren pursed his lips, cocking his head slightly as he considered it. "Okay, well, that depends on you."

Jack took a slow breath and shrugged.

"Can whatever brought you here be so easily escaped?" Warren added.

Jack looked away, shoulders sinking again as he leaned back against the passenger seat of the cart. "I really hope so," he almost whispered.

Without further word, Warren got the car moving again,

29

turning left onto the path and accelerated again. "Here she is, home sweet home."

It'll never really be home, Jack thought. Not without Caroline and Abby. But it was definitely a nice place to start over. He'd take it a day at a time without others telling him how he should act or think or what he should want.

The lighthouse base was a rectangular building about twenty feet high with white walls and a black tiled roof. Rising from the north end was the round tower itself which rose some additional 230 or so feet, Jack guessed, and narrowed as it went until the lantern room at the top, covered by another black tiled roof, was its narrowest point. There were three smaller buildings—one to the north and two to the west of the main lighthouse itself. Storage perhaps? A garage for the cart? It looked about the right size. Surely Warren wouldn't leave him without some form of transportation to get himself and his maintenance tools and equipment around the island, right? He'd find out soon enough. All three had solar panels on their roofs.

Warren pulled the cart to stop beside the lighthouse's south end where a hand painted wooden sign read, "Cristof's Lighthouse, U.S. Coast Guard." The door beside it was black with a glass screen door over it. Warren turned off the engine and climbed out as Jack grabbed his bag off the back seat and followed.

"Well, let me take you inside then we'll do the grand tour, okay?" Warren said. "When's your moving truck arrive?"

"Two days supposedly."

Warren paused, considering. "Depending on how much you're bringing, we'll have to rent a boat or two and load it up to haul stuff over. There are wagons and a flatbed in the garage we can use. Make a regular train out of it."

"Okay," Jack said, looking forward to settling in. He pictured a trail of boxes floating along the channel through the reefs, headed for the island. He could relax better once he'd made the lighthouse his own.

Warren opened the screen door and slid a key into the lock of the main door, turning the knob and pushing the door open. A large map of the island hung framed on one wall with various labels and flags highlighting the landmarks. The rest of the room had walls covered with maps and Coast Guard paperwork—everything from notices about various new regulations to a list of rules and the standard workplace notices required by Federal and State laws. A long table against one wall held a radio phone setup and charger station for six walkie talkies assigned to a radio base unit, a CB, and shortwave radio, as well as two computer servers, two LED monitors, a power backup unit, a keyboard, and a mouse.

"This is your main radio room," Warren explained, "but another is below the cupola." He added, "The lamp room."

Jack nodded he understood.

"Pain in the ass to run down the stairs every time you have an emergency," Warren went on.

"Makes sense," Jack agreed.

"The servers run the automation for the lamp, and if all goes well, you shouldn't need to mess with them. One is the main, the other a backup. There's internet in the living quarters upstairs for your personal laptop and devices," Warren explained, pointing to a spiral staircase that wound up from the center of the room along the east wall. "The stairs go up to your living quarters and eventually the cupola. We'll check all that out in a bit."

Jack walked over to the base of the spiral and looked up. "Wow. It'll be fun moving all my stuff up that." His mind raced through potential scenarios as he worried for the first time if maybe some of his belongings would have to be abandoned, especially Abby's beloved piano.

"Most people don't bring a lot," Warren said. "We pretty much provide everything you need."

"Well, I was hoping to use some of my own things, if that's okay."

31

Warren shrugged. "It's not a problem, if that means you'll stick around a do the job for a while. Depends what it is, I suppose. We've got limited room. But…" Warren walked to the back of the room and opened a sliding door. Inside was a small elevator big enough to hold three people max while wide enough for a wheelchair. "It'll take several trips, of course, and you might have to assemble stuff once it arrives where you want it, but this makes things a lot simpler than carrying them up the stairs."

Jack let out a slight moan. "Great." He felt an unexpected release and lightness knowing it was workable.

"Anything you can't fit or decide against can go in our storage building to the north," Warren added. "We'll go there later."

Warren joined him at the staircase and offered Jack an official blue Coast Guard baseball cap. "It's both for sun protection and official identification," he explained. "The position doesn't require a uniform because you rarely deal with the public, but when you do encounter guests, it's helpful to look official."

"Makes sense." Jack accepted the hat and slipping it over his head.

"Isolation isn't the only benefit of the job," Warren joked.

"What else?"

"Lots and lots of exercise."

"Yeah, my mother will be pleased."

Warren laughed. "We've had more than one occupant try and talk us into installing a fire-pole. That'd be great for getting down but not back up." He shot Jack an amused look then started up the stairs and Jack followed.

The first room at the top of the stairs sat empty except for a cot and a lamp left on the floor, no table. Across the room in a corner, affixed to the wall, its pipes exposed, was a sink beside what Jack assumed was a closet door or small bathroom. "This is the guest room," said Warren, noticing Jack's stare. "Or at least, that's what we use it for."

"You have guests?" Jack asked, surprised.

"Well, it's expected the keeper's family or kids pay a visit." When Jack didn't respond, he added, "but it's mostly for the relief team. We cover the lighthouse Sundays during the day and then every third weekend of the month so you can have time off."

"Oh, okay." He'd already known there'd be days off. But his stomach rolled and a bitter taste filled his mouth at the thought there might be someone around asking a lot of personal questions and wanting to get to know him. He'd imagined one of the best parts of the job would be not having to talk about what he'd been through or where he'd come from every hour of the day. He hadn't planned on venturing out much. He didn't want to make friends or see other people regularly. He might have to leave on those days and avoid it all. He'd groaned inwardly. You'll figure it out.

Warren opened a small side door. Jack stepped forward and looked inside. A toilet was on one side, a shower on the other, with a curtain between. "It's pretty tight but gets the job done," Warren said.

"There's another bathroom on the floor below the master two flights up." Warren shut the washroom door and headed back to the stairs, climbing again.

The next floor was a kitchen with a square island containing a butcher's block that had four stools around it. Along the north wall a fridge and stove sat next to a double sink and small counter space with a microwave and toaster. Next to that was an oven with a pantry above it. Both the island and counter were covered in aged, faded laminate with a few stains and cracks. More cabinets filled the space above the sink and stove and a window looked out on across the island to the north with another facing south and the channel and a third facing the ocean to the east. The views were fantastic, and Jack noticed they all had shutters, no doubt for the hurricanes.

Unlike the other floors where the walls had been painted white, the same color as the outside of the lighthouse, this room had linoleum flooring and wallpaper on the walls—a dark blue with vertical brown lines on the bottom and a plain peach up top. It looked like a woman's touch to Jack, but he hesitated to ask, so instead, he said, "Looks like you could cook for quite a crew."

"Well, sometimes, when we're doing repairs or building maintenance, we may have four or five of us here, so yeah, it has come in handy," Warren said. "As I told you over the phone, you can order groceries online from one of the markets and either pay for ferry delivery or go over and get it yourself. Publix is the closest but there are other options all along the Pacific Coast Highway not too far from the jetty stop. Bert can give you directions. Pretty much anything you need can either be found or delivered. Bert does that a lot for us. Just ask him."

"I can leave my post unattended if I need?" Jack asked.

"Got no choice sometimes," Warren said. "A man needs supplies, but only when the weather's clear and the forecast too, and then for no more than two hours at a time. Anything else that needs doing you can do when relief is here."

"Gotcha," Jack said.

The next floor up was divided between a small sitting room/family room with a television, couch, and twin recliners and the master bath which had a full bathtub and shower combo along with the toilet and a double sink, medicine cabinet, and linen closet. Like the kitchen, it was wallpapered in an aquatic theme with blue waves and brown ships, the floor tiled in subway black and white. Jack noticed a hanging bag in the closet and a suitcase atop the dresser, signs he assumed meant Warren must be using the room during his visit. On the third floor, the master bedroom was smaller than the guest room in size because of the narrowing of the tower walls, but a walk-in closet and nice windows made up for smaller quarters. Warren offered little commentary beyond naming the rooms.

As Jack stopped to glance out the east window at the seashore, he heard the distant thump of waves lapping against the sand, sending crabs scattering. Birds dove and weaved in the distance, and his mind went back to the time he and Abby had attended a wedding in South Padre when Caroline was four years old. It had been the only time their daughter had seen the ocean, though she'd made them promise to take her back more than once over the last couple of years. Caroline had waddled across the beach giggling as she stopped at each new shell and bent to try and grasp them with her clumsy fingers. Sometimes she succeeded; more often than not she failed, though a few she'd managed to tip or turn over.

Abby and Jack had watched her play, ready to interfere if she found any occupied shells, but mostly allowing her to experience it on her own. They'd spent a glorious day from mid-morning to sunset on the beach the day after their friend's wedding. That night all three of them collapsed, exhausted but satisfied knowing they'd fly back the next day happy for the memory they'd created.

Only now Jack winced at the pain the memory evoked, wondering where he might go to escape the continual lapping of loss.

"Next," Warren said, shaking Jack out of his reverie as he turned and started up the stairs. Jack followed him up to the penultimate level, coming upon a smaller radio room and a large storage closet, a utilitarian use space Warren explained he could set up for supplies servicing the lamp room. "Beats the hell out of having to run all the way down to the storage shed or garage in an emergency." A toolbox and a few electric tools hanging on the wall and brooms, a mop, dustpan, and bucket with cleaning supplies completed the tools the keepers needed for upkeep. Jack admired the way space had been carefully considered and utilized. It was creative and imaginative, designed to maximize minimum space in a way he'd always tried to do with his designs.

A charger in the radio room had spaces three handhelds, one

of which was occupied, with another radio telephone and mini-radio base beside it on the desk. "You always leave an extra walkie to charge in each of the bases so one's ready if you need it," said Warren, stated in such a way he gave Jack the impression this might have been a problem in the past. "Keepers generally use the main room downstairs for every day communications and this for late nights or emergencies when they're required to be up in the cupola or awakened from sleep, but that's up to you. This base unit and phone reach all the same places and channels, so best judgment. Mostly to save you time and mileage running the stairs in a storm."

"Great," Jack said.

The cupola was round and contained a large set of Fresnel lenses, their tiered surfaces rotating around the lamp to shine the light out over the sea. The speed and direction of the setting on the lenses determined the pattern sent out—blinking slow or fast or steady. If needed, he could manually utilize a set of buttons to add filters of red, blue, or green on the control station along the east wall, designed as a windowed wall. Two long arced windows faced east and west, stretching around to provide the keeper good views of north and south, separated on each end by a foot of wall space. Those sported indoor shutters.

As Jack walked over to get a look out of one of the large, extra-long windows, a large, reddish brown cockroach skittered across the glass. Jack's hand shot up to swipe it down so he could step on it, and it suddenly sprayed him with a very foul smelling liquid. Jack pulled his hand away and jumped back as Warren laughed.

"Palmetto bugs. You see them everywhere," he explained. "They don't call them stinkroaches for nothing."

Jack scowled, wiping with a kleenex from his pocket at the secretion spotting his shirt. Abby would not be happy. She hated bugs.

"You can change your shirt when we go back downstairs," Warren said. "It washes out. You know about hurricanes?"

"Well, I've heard of them."

"But you've never experienced one?"

"Plenty of tornados, but not hurricanes."

"Okay, well, I'll prepare you—I'll give you a list, but first the basics of the lamp, after we finish the tour."

And those tasks took up the rest of the day until well after sunset. The job itself did seem better than he'd imagined and he'd greeted most of Warren's orientation with enthusiasm like one of the summer college kids his dad used to hire who was spending their first summer on a farm. He was so busy thinking about hurricane risks and preparation and other details, each of them pushing Kansas and his past further and further from the center of his thoughts that by the time they'd finished and headed back for a break, he realized he hadn't thought of Abby and Caroline in several hours.

His throat grew thick and his mind filled with self-loathing. How could he forget them? They were the reason he was here. He had to remember. He owed them that. He thought about rushing back to the hotel to call Josie and was so preoccupied with his thoughts that when Warren offered to cook them dinner, he just shook his head and bid him "good night," then hurried for the pier to catch the jetty. The stars sparkled above like specks on a charcoal canvas, yet Jack barely saw them as he padded across the sand. He didn't even realize until the next day that Warren must have radioed Bert to call the jetty. He could've waited out there for hours, but then he was so preoccupied at the time, he wondered if he'd have even noticed. He could have stood out there all night. None of this was on his mind as he rode silently back to town and caught another Uber to the Holiday Inn. In fact, he went through those steps by rote so much that he couldn't even remember doing them later. What he did remember was Bert making multiple attempts to strike up a conversation and being met with only silence. He swore he'd have to apologize and pay more attention. Mourning Abby and Caroline was no excuse to be inconsiderate, and certainly Abby wouldn't be happy about it if she were here.

The Lighthouse

That thought left him saddened all over again as he waited for his uber, then saw the flashing neon sign up the block just off the PCH reading, "Lou's" over a diner and realized he was famished. And he did have to eat. Sighing, he cancelled the Uber and started toward it, saying a silent prayer he could find a quiet corner table and be left alone with his food and his thoughts.

CHAPTER 4

THE ISLAMORADA DINER buzzed, an unusually busy shift for a Wednesday night in March Hannah Loaney hadn't anticipated. Her feet ached and the warm air and humidity drifting in from outside into the diner's already hot interior only worsened her sense of fatigue. She'd gone from one heat source to another with no relief. She wasn't even supposed to be here. She should have been on her way home, as her mother-in-law had called to remind her three times tonight already. She'd only taken the job because Ellen had urged her to find something to do besides sitting around the house feeling lonely and sorry for herself.

"I'm not feeling sorry for myself," Hannah had argued.

"You have responsibilities, Hannah," Ellen had scolded. "I'm not a free babysitter. And don't tell me you're not ready again."

"He's your grandson," Hannah countered. "And you're right, I need to do something. I'm just not sure where to start." She'd never finished college and with Rob, Ellen's son, who'd left her widow, she'd never had to think about it. He'd made great money as a marine engineer servicing the local shipping industry, so Hannah had stayed home to focus attention on their only son, Sam, whom they all adored to death.

"You couldn't have picked a job with more reasonable

39

hours," Ellen groused the third time she called that night. "Surely you're worth more than just being a waitress in some touriot dive Who's slacking this time?"

"Lou's great to us, and I'm just getting my feet wet until I find something better," Hannah said, not wanting have this argument yet again. "I'll be home as soon as I can." She hung up.

One of the other waitresses on duty, Janice, had wanted to leave early, an annoying habit, and begged Hannah and Denise to cover her tables, as usual depending on everyone else to cover her. Hannah had missed an appointment with her son's therapist the month before because Janice had called in sick. And the previous week her appointment to meet a realtor about a condo perfect for her and Sam at rent below market price had been lost when Janice showed up an hour late. Tonight, because the diner had been quiet from six on, Lou had let her go at eight leaving Hannah to take the shift, in part because she wasn't in the mood for another night alone at home with her mother-in-law.

Hannah paused to lean against the kitchen doorframe and rub her feet as she glanced at the clock on the kitchen wall, feeling like a sucker. Eight-fifteen p.m. Okay, the diner closed at nine in the off season, so she'd make it home soon anyhow. Lou's place, a throwback to the 1950s, its red faux leather booths and stools and faux chrome fittings a step back in time. A jukebox in the corner blasted out one oldie after another. Charge stations on the tables allowed credit-card-bearing diners to request songs without leaving their seats. The place even smelled retro, a mix of grease, bacon, frying foods, and eggs— all staples of the menu. Lou Richards himself mirrored the throwback vibe, due to his round belly and balding head and three-day stubble, his stained white apron flapping in the breeze from two fans hung high near the ceiling above the grill. Lou had become a close substitute for her own grandfathers who had both been gone over a decade. Her father and husband were gone too—her dad of cancer like his father and her husband Rob from a tragic boating accident she didn't like to think about. Before losing Rob, she hadn't worked since high school. He liked making her happy, supporting her as she stayed home to take care of the house and raise their son.

Now, she lived in her mother-in-law's house with her son Sam, accepting the only job a single mother with no experience could get around Islamorada—waitress. It wasn't awful, though she couldn't seem to convince her feet of that. It wasn't all that exciting, and the hours could be long, especially in the tourist season. Still, Lou was a kind man, a great boss, and always flexible when people needed time off for their kids' activities or doctor appointments and so on. Even if he had to spend an hour or two bussing tables himself, he always made it work. Hannah had heard enough from her friends to know that wasn't always the case with bosses, and she felt grateful for that.

"Just what we need, a latecomer," Denise groused. Denise, her best friend, worked alongside Hannah, chattering on and on about a hot date with someone new she had at nine-thirty. That was no surprise. Denise, ever the believer in finding true love, always had a new date, it seemed, but when the doorbell jangled and a stranger walked in at eight-twenty, Denise groaned. A latecomer, depending upon the order, might mean staying an extra half hour by the time he'd looked at the menu, ordered, then eaten his fill. If Denise took the table, she'd be late for her date.

"Hey, that's what pays the bills," Lou countered, all three watching as the stranger made his way to an isolated booth in a corner and slid onto the bench.

"Don't worry about it, I got it," said Hannah, immediately volunteering.

Denise broke into a big grin and gave Hannah one of those fingertips on shoulders hugs that girlfriends sometimes gave each other when in a hurry. "You're a lifesaver."

Hannah shrugged it off, squeezing her mouth into a grin to own it as Denise fetched her things and hurried out.

Hannah took in the stranger. He wore a brown polo and

Khaki pants with an official blue Coast Guard baseball cap. His brown disheveled hair and tired eyes gave him the look of one passing through town. That, besides how his skin was surprisingly lacking in sun burn or tan, meant it wasn't likely he worked outside. Though he avoided eye contact and she never got a good look at his face, she decided she'd never seen this guy before. So who was he? A substitute keeper? A transfer? Some supervisor come from somewhere else to train or hire or review? She'd heard the lighthouse at Cristof's Key needed a new keeper. Was this him?

Lights came on illuminating the Chesapeake Beach Resort sign near the road as daylight faded. She grabbed an iPad and headed for the table to take the stranger's drink order. His business was none of her business, of course. In Islamorada, any of them could assume these kinds of questions about an unknown stranger; discussing them had become a form of entertainment—a practice of occupying the time. She often found herself engaging in a private guessing game without thinking about it.

"Hi," she said with a smile as she stopped beside his table. He studied the classic-style laminated menus Lou had ordered in the shape of the jukebox. "Something to drink?"

The stranger stared at the menu a moment as if he hadn't heard, then just when she was about to ask again, replied, "Iced Tea, no sugar or lemon, please." He didn't look up or bother lowering the menu hiding his face.

"Okay, I'll bring it right over," Hannah said, still smiling, and when she got no further response, turned and headed back behind the counter again to prepare the tea. He hadn't looked up once or shown his face. Hiding in shadows. No concern for Southern politeness or was he simply distracted?

As she crossed behind the counter toward the drink station she glanced back at the stranger and froze, her breath caught. For a moment, she thought she was looking at Rob. She blinked, invisibly tracing the stranger's' profile. Did he really look like her lost husband or was her mind playing tricks? Was

42

she that tired? She took a deep breath, then shook it off. She revisited the drink station to grab a glass, fetching the tea.

Once she'd filled the glass with ice and tea, she grabbed a napkin-rolled set of silverware and walked back toward the corner booth again where the stranger's face was still buried behind the menu. "You memorizing it?" she teased, a skill she'd adopted to break the ice with the quiet ones as she set the silverware and glass on the table and readied her iPad. After a beat with no response, she asked, "You ready to order?"

"Yeah," he said, clearing his throat, then he lowered the menu and reached for the tea, taking a long sip. "That's good."

"Homemade fresh daily," she said, Lou's training. Around here, people placed real value on "homemade." It meant the good stuff.

"I'll have the country fried steak and potatoes with gravy, and the green beans, please," the stranger continued, folding the menu and sliding it across the table as he glanced out the window.

For a moment, as he ordered, he'd given Hannah the first good look at his face. Other than his haircut, he barely resembled Rob which made her feel relieved. Instead, he had haunting blue eyes and high cheekbones that tapered down around his mouth to a round chin—not too long, not too short. His skin was smooth and clean shaven, but he had age lines, perhaps from stress? She guessed his age to be around late thirties, a few years older than her. His accent was plain like the Midwest somewhere and he had large hands and muscles whose tone testified that he was no stranger to physical labor, though certainly not someone who spent all his time at it.

"Will do," she said after he finished his order, typing it into the iPad so it popped up on the screen for Lou in the kitchen. "You visiting for long? I see you're with the Park Service."

"Yeah," was all he answered as he looked out the window across Overseas Highway toward the Publix.

Taking his hint he wasn't up for conversation, she quietly

turned and made her way back to her station behind the counter. If he didn't want to talk, fine by her. Janice's exit left her tired and in a foul mood. She had to admit something about the man intrigued her. She wondered if he'd give her his name.

Almost immediately, she scolded herself. You don't like it when strangers get all up in your business, Hannah, so don't do it to him. But her curiosity seated, causing her to watch him from time to time as she went about cleaning the counter.

It wasn't like she didn't have plenty of her own business to think about anyway. Her boy Sam hadn't spoken since his father's accident. His next therapy appointment tomorrow meant she'd need to eat crow to borrow her mother-in-law's car. Her own Toyota Camry had dropped its transmission the week before and she didn't have the money to repair it.

Then there was Sam's grandma, Ellen, who worked thirty hours a week despite helping home school Sam and managing Hannah's life. Truth was, she'd be lost without her, but living with her mother-in-law meant surrendering to Ellen's constant need to get all up in her business expressing opinions on everything, the kind of oversight Hannah had longed to escape as a teenager. Though she tolerated it better out of necessity, found herself as eager to escape it now as an adult. Marrying Rob had taken her away from all that, earning her the freedom and right to decide for herself or with her husband. Her mother liked and respected Rob, avoiding interfering in their marriage because of bad experiences with her own in-laws in the past, but Rob's mother had no such compunctions. Hannah's parents now long gone, Ellen remained her sole support.

They shared Sam as a mutual worry. The aftermath of the accident had left him with two challenging problems. First he feared riding boats after dark. That one, Hannah figured would go away over time. Unfortunately the second worried her due to frustration to reverse it.

At first, the doctors wrote Sam's newfound silence off as a symptom of the trauma of his father's death. When it continued six months later, they suggested undiagnosed Asperger's and

44

ran some tests. When those came back negative, they tried testing him for various learning disabilities. All of them came back negative as well. In the end, the conclusion was PTSD with traumatic mutism, a form of selective mutism.

Hannah wasn't convinced. Sam's connectedness to his father meant a near-interdependence. Sam waited anxiously for his dad's arrival home daily from work, following him everywhere when he was home, even to the point of imitating him. If Rob was working with tools, Sam would use toy tools alongside him. When Rob mowed, Sam brought out a toy mower and walked alongside. She presumed Sam had closed himself off, self-protecting after the pain of losing Rob. He could speak but he chose not to. After all, he heard and acknowledged speech with body language. He simply didn't want to speak; she believed he wouldn't until the fear dissipated or he felt safe again. He needed time, something she continuously reminded his grandmother to remember. While her mother-in-law was anxious to "fix" the problem, Hannah advocated for the time needed to come around.

"He'll talk when he wants to, Ellen," she insisted. And that was that as far as she was concerned. If only Ellen would let it go. It wasn't that Hannah wasn't concerned about it. She used to regularly remember the conversations she and her son had used to have before the accident. Adorable things he'd said, favorite moments. But in the end, they'd just made her sad, and she knew she'd always have the memories. It was more important to focus on the present now and make new ones.

A bell dinged from the kitchen and Lou yelled, "Order up!"

Hannah spun. Whisking the plate off the chrome counter, she headed for the stranger's booth again. "Here ya go," she said as she set the plate on the table in front of him, noting his tea glass was half empty. "Can I get you more tea?"

"Yes, please," he said, still not looking up, as he unwrapped the silverware and looked over his food. Standing close to him now she caught a faint whiff of his cologne. Nice. Classy.

45

"That's not the usual uniform," she commented. It took a moment to register with him.

This time he looked right at her, and despite his profile, the resemblance to Rob was only fleeting, but he was quite handsome, his eyes piercing, and she liked the sense of strength that emanated from him. It made her feel warm in a way no one had in a long time. But as the seconds dragged on, the warmth faded as she recognized a deep underlying sadness there, almost hidden beneath the surface—the kind of sadness Hannah knew a little something about—and she wondered what had happened to make him feel that way.

"Oh yeah, well, I work on an island, not with the public mostly," he said, finally responding.

She smiled. "Ah ok, well, thank you for your service."

The customer looked surprised then recovered and grabbed the fork and knife, cutting his country fried steak into edible bites.

"Which island?" she asked, curious, then added, "There's lots of them around here."

He grunted. "Cristof's Key, it's private."

"The old lighthouse?" Hannah said, and again he looked surprised. "We used to fantasize about visiting it when we were kids. I didn't know anyone was keeping it these days."

"Mostly caretaker of the island," he replied.

"Ah ok," she said, then, "My name's Hannah." And offered her hand.

He chewed a bite of steak a moment, then hesitated a moment before setting down his fork and reaching over to shake her hand. "I'm Jack," he said.

The touch of his hand gave her a tingly feeling to her surprise. Probably starved for human touch. Sam's therapist had reminded her to use touch since Rob was... how did she put it? "... the affectionate parent." What did that say about her anyway? That she wasn't?

He withdrew fast when she lingered too long.

"Okay, Jack, well, I don't mean to disturb you, but if I can get you anything, just ask, okay?"

"Thank you," he replied and went back to his steak.

She stood there a moment, trying to think of something clever to say that would maybe lighten the mood, but he paid her no attention, so she turned and silently headed back to the counter. Something about Jack drew her—from his quiet demeanor to his seeming shyness at human contact. The perfect type for the isolated life at an old lighthouse, she supposed, yet he seemed nice enough, even if she had to coax it out of him. Her hand was still tingling from his touch. Not intentionally, her mind plowed into left field, wondering how a person might arrange a little side visit to Cristof's Key. Don't be crazy, Hannah, her inner voice chided, but whoever this Jack was she wanted to know more about him.

Though she checked on him from time to time, Jack said little to her for the next forty minutes while he ate. She offered him dessert. He declined. Asked for his bill.

Their last contact was at the register as he handed her cash. He made the first real eye contact of the evening, closing her fingers up over a few bills' tip.

"I hope you'll come see us again," she said, what remained of her humor draining from her expression. She handed him the receipt, and watched him turn and disappear out the door.

While the doorbell pinged the last time, Lou called, "Lock her up now, sweetie. Let's call it a night."

She reached behind the counter for the keys then headed to lock the door. It wasn't until she was turning the key that she realized she hadn't thought about Janice in almost an hour.

"So, what's his name?" Lou didn't even bother to hide his amusement.

"Who?" asked Hannah, manipulating the locks, her nervous hands flipping the sign in the window to "Closed." When she turned back toward the kitchen, Lou was grinning.

"The stranger you couldn't keep your eyes off," he teased.

"What? Don't be silly. I gave him the regular good service." She went to work cleaning the counter.

"Sure, sweetie, like you do everyone else." Lou set about his own clean up in the kitchen.

And Hannah found herself with more to be annoyed about than just her mother-in law, Ellen's, constant pestering and the nagging that always awaited her when she got home. The guy had been unfriendly. Unsmiling, and barely polite. A complete stranger acting as if she was bothering him just taking his order. She served fifty to a hundred strangers a day in the high season, not so many this time of year. But they meant nothing to her. Their lives intersected at the diner, and then they never saw each other again. Why shouldn't this guy be the same? And why did the thought of that cause a little pinching in her chest?

CHAPTER 5

J ACK LAY IN BED and thought about a conversation he'd had with Abby one night as they were lying down to sleep.

"What would you do if something happened to me?" she'd asked.

His phone pinged; a text from John at work troubled him. He was asking about Harry's cubicle across from his, and did he want it if it came open. "Was it yesterday you said you ran into John's wife at Trader Joe's. Did she act...different?"

She rolled onto her back and set the novel she was reading on her stomach. "Maybe we should talk more, you know, so we figure things out in advance, just in case something ever happened to one of us."

"I am up for a promotion," he continued, preoccupied, "but that's Barry's decision. Why would others know about it before I did?"

"We aren't promised another day, Jack. Have you ever thought about that, I mean, what if tomorrow didn't come? Shouldn't we plan for the future just in case? as if tomorrow doesn't come, given our insurance doesn't cover parallel universe abductions?"

"What are you talking about?" he'd said, suddenly realizing what she was talking about. He rolled onto his side and his eyes met hers as he reached out with a palm and gently caressed her forehead. "Nothing's going to happen to you, babe."

"How can you be sure? Accidents happen."

"I just do. I love you too much." The smell of her hair, the warmth of her body spooning with his—these were all too familiar sensations, yet they were always magical. He'd gotten so lucky that someone so terrific would choose him, love him. He could hardly remember a time without Abby, and in any future he imagined, she was always there.

She'd scolded him, and let him know she was serious, but Jack had never thought about it. He didn't want to think about it. The idea of waking up one day without Abby scared him to death. He just couldn't fathom it. He loved her too much. Then she'd said the something that scared him:

"Honey, I love you too, but if something happens, I want you to find happiness," she'd said, her voice rich with both love and concern. "I don't want you to think you can't still love me and find someone else."

She was making it too real. He wasn't ready for this. "Why are we talking about this?" he'd replied, annoyed.

Abby had continued but he'd refused to talk about it. Even when she brought it up again a few weeks later after they'd attended the funeral of her best friend Carol, whose husband had died in a hunting accident.

He'd blown Abby off, preferring to get lost in her kiss to plan for a raise. Maybe buy a house that would put Caroline in a better school. But now he wondered how many other times had ignored her when she was trying to say something that really mattered to her? His heart sank. Randomly, his thoughts skidded from his neglect of Abby to the waitress who'd kept trying to engage him in conversation at the diner. He supposed it was all part of the act necessary to squeeze good tips from customers. But he'd also caught the redhead watching him several times in a way he hadn't noticed since he was in his early twenties. Or maybe he didn't notice them because his practice of ignoring females mirrored how he'd treated Abby. Oh hell. He felt like an idiot, as if looking at that waitress was on par with cheating on Abby.

He cursed and rolled over groaning. What the hell was wrong with him? The last thing he needed was to invite more interaction. And yet here he lay at one a.m. reviewing her every word and picturing her face. Abby was the girl for him. She was irreplaceable. How could anyone else live up to that?

He managed to fall asleep sometime after two and woke again at five-thirty feeling like he'd barely slept. Great. Just what he needed on his first day as on a new job when he needed to be alert. After continental breakfast at the hotel again, he caught another uber to the dock and rode with Bert over to Cristof's Key where Warren was waiting, this time in keeper's gear— Dockers and a short-sleeved polo like Jack.

"Hope you slept well," Warren said. "Alertness counts, but just in case, I made a pot of coffee." He grinned. "We've got a lot to go over today."

"Not really, but a little coffee and I'll be fine," Jack said, climbing into Warren's cart. Seagulls' swooped down over the lapping waves and Jack felt as one dive bombed him and groaned, scooting to the side as Warren chuckled.

"On the job hazard," his supervisor joked.

"We get extra for that?" Jack replied as he tossed a piece of half-eaten toast toward the seagulls, hoping to distract them.

"Wait—" Warren called out, but it was too late. More seagulls swooped in and Jack felt more bombs strike his arm and then his shoe and he and Warren dodged and ran a few feet away as Jack cursed.

"Coffee we can do," Warren said, choking back amusement at the rookie mistake. "And some tissues and hand sanitizer too, if you'd like."

Jack sighed and smiled, chuckling at himself. He deserved that.

To his relief, Warren turned quickly serious again, "Today, I'm going to show you a bunch of maintenance tasks that will keep you busy all spring and summer. I hope you don't mind working with your hands."

"No problem," Jack said as they climbed into the cart and Warren drove along the vegetation line toward the lighthouse, a cool fresh morning breeze gently tickling his skin. "I wasn't always an architect. I actually worked construction two summers in college."

"Your resume said you have boating experience, too," Warren said. "That's essential living here."

"Yeah, I spent several summers as a kid with my uncle on a fishing boat in the Gulf," Jack replied.

"Good," Warren said. "By the way, there's a small motorboat in the shed you can use to go back and forth to town, if you prefer. Or we keep Bert on retainer."

"I'll think about it," Jack said, knowing it was a necessary evil. He hated the thought of depending on someone else like Bert, who'd barely spoken to him that morning and seemed very laid back. If you had to deal with people, he was far more desirable than someone like the waitress.

Once again her Hannah's red hair and green eyes came into his head and he winced, shaking it off. Stop doing that, dammit. It wasn't that she was some extraordinary beauty like a model, but she was pleasant enough to look at. It's just Jack didn't look at other women like that. Not since he'd met Abby. And especially since her death. He couldn't dishonor her memory like that. So what was it about this woman Hannah? He felt a tinge of guilt just recalling her name. And the conversation with Abby flashed into his mind all over again. "...if something happens, I want you to find happiness..." Abby had said. He looked around at the beautiful palm trees and shell-lined sand, the ocean waves lapping against the shore in perfect foamy rhythm. Happiness didn't mean he had to risk his heart being broken again, he decided. He could be happy here all alone.

Warren turned onto the small path that led to the lighthouse then and began laying out his plan for the day. After a quick break for coffee, to check the weather and maps on the communications room computers—and sanitizer and shoe cleaning for Jack—they set out again in the cart and worked all day together.

As they did, Warren took him around the island on a tour of all its features and the important things he'd be responsible for—like repairing fences or trimming weeds where they were starting to encroach onto the lighthouse property and might grow to hinder access and so forth. Warren was a hard worker and he treated Jack like an equal, working alongside him and sharing the tasks equally. Warren explained how Seagrass was vital to the local ecology, helping improve water quality by absorbing nutrients that runoff from the land and releasing them back into the water through their leaves, a bit like a nutrient pump. It also acted as a filter, collecting sediments and particles floating in the water and preventing erosion with its roots. Then he showed him how to monitor and measure erosion and Seagrass percentages so ecologists could be called in if it got sick or started to weaken from pollution or other causes.

"We don't maintain it ourselves?"

"No, for that we call the experts, but we look after it in case it needs help. That's one thing we can do very well."

Next, Warren talked about the importance of Conch and their shells to Keys culture; how native-born islanders are called Conchs and the Keys itself is nicknamed the Conch Republic. When they found an empty Conch shell, he demonstrated how blowing in it produced a unique sound. "They've been used as signaling devices for centuries here."

Whenever they saw wildlife, Warren also talked about that from Parrotfish and Damselfish and Yellowtail Snappers that Barracudas preyed on to Loggerhead Sea Turtles, Manatees, and Reef Sharks, the last three of which they never saw that day. "There's lots of books in the lighthouse about these things and what to watch out for. Might be a good way to while away the hours and improve your skills. You're the only one around here full time, so the more you can look out for things, the better preserved we can keep Cristot's Key for the future."

Jack's first thought was that he'd thought he'd left his animal husbandry days behind at the farm, and he'd never regretted it. Caroline had been asking for a dog for several years with Abby's full support when the accident stole them from him. Jack had always vetoed it, insisting a nine-year-old was too young to take on the responsibility, but if it meant he could have them back, he swore he'd adopt the first dog he saw. He realized this was the job he'd taken, and like it or not, he'd have to adjust. But maybe he could just keep an eye out and not have to do much actual husbandry. That would suit him just fine.

All throughout they stopped to clean up garbage or stray debris that had blown or floated ashore, while continuing to inventory the various fences and other infrastructure for what might need repairs.

"The biggest thing you have to look out for is mildew," Warren said. "There's some in the shed now that needs to be cleaned. I've got supplies coming in tomorrow to help with that when you get to it. It's important to keep it under control because we carry the spores on our clothes and spread them, and it becomes a serious problem for air quality.""I've dealt with mold back home," Jack said. "It's always a problem with old houses."

"Not like you do here," Warren said. "It's everywhere. On plants, outside, inside, vehicles. Trust me, most outsiders say they've never seen anything like it."

"Okay," Jack agreed as they continued worked. "Why is there a lighthouse here?" Jack wondered at one point.

"Rocks and a shipwreck," Warren said.

"A shipwreck?"

"It happened a long time ago," Warren explained. "Last century, and the wreckage is not that deep. Small recreational craft sail right over it, all clear, but larger ships might not, so the lighthouse was put here to mark it and warn them off."

"And the rocks?"

"The rocks caused the original shipwreck, and most of them have sunk a bit due to erosion of the seabed, so they aren't a problem anymore," Warren said.

Jack couldn't help but smile at the way Warren held back key details until the most dramatic moment. "You have a way with stories."

"My granddaughter says I'm all mysterious about it," Warren said with a grunt. "Calls me a drama king."

They both laughed.

"I read somewhere that most lighthouses are automated these days," Jack went on. "Why does this one need a keeper?"

"It was part of the contract with the Coast Guard when the original owner agreed to sell it," Warren said. "A legacy thing."

Jack shrugged. "Kinda seems unnecessary if the lighthouse is automated, doesn't it?" Warren's lips tightened and he dragged a hand through his hair. Jack realized he'd said something wrong and tried to backtrack. "I mean, I'd heard there weren't any lighthouse keepers in American anymore..."

"Well, Public Relations is part of public service, and so is giving back to the community," Warren said. "You serve the community, whether people come here or not, and Cristof's ancestors valued that. Some seasons are busier than others, and you may only see a few hundred visitors a year if that many, but the old man loved this place and he wanted it preserved, so with the state and local conservation and wildlife agencies understaffed, the Coast Guard doesn't mind pitching in where we can, so that's another big part of why you're here." He looked at Jack with eyebrows drawn together, his forehead wrinkled. "Okay?"

Jack nodded with understanding. "Okay."

Warren noticeably relaxed then, breathing deep as he admired the view. "Besides, my granddaughter finds them romantic."

"So did my wife," Jack replied, holding his breath as he waited for Warren to ask questions about Abby.

"What time's your truck arrive?" Warren asked, changing the subject to his relief.

"The moving company say tomorrow afternoon," Jack managed, feeling relieved.

"Okay, so Saturday is moving day," Warren said.

"Yeah, and I was wondering," Jack said, "how many trips do you think it'll take?"

"Well, that depends how much stuff you have," Warren said.

"Well, I got rid of a lot," Jack said.

Warren chuckled. "Now who's being mysterious? When they call, we'll go look and then make some calls. I'm sure we can get enough help to do it in one run. You can store boxes in the second bedroom and storage until you unpack. And I'll go through it with you and let you know anything that isn't going to fit."

Though Warren looked at him expectantly as if the plan was settled, Jack blanched at the thought of someone else determining what he could keep of his former life. He'd only kept the things with the most meaning for him, after all. He should be the one to decide, but as the silence stretched, he forced and smile and gave a slight nod. "Okay. It's a plan." Warren had already showed him a flatbed trailer, three wagons, and a rider mower in the garage.

"The mower can pull the wagons one after the other and the cart can pull the trailer. We'll make a real train out of it," he'd said.

Jack wondered how many Floridians moved that way. It certainly sounded like a uniquely Florida experience, and he looked forward to it.

When the call came the following afternoon around three from the movers, Jack arranged to meet them at the hotel. This time, Warren got the boat out of the garage and they pulled it down to the pier with the cart. "Might as well teach ya this, too," he explained.

Jack and Warren had made good progress on the task list, accomplishing things a lot more quickly as a team than Jack expected he'd be able to on his own, but then Jack couldn't deny the tasks would take him a lot longer to do on his own. He was out of practice working outdoors with his hands and relearning things would be challenging. Then again, it would also keep him preoccupied, and though he'd never forget what he'd been through, he certainly looked forward to spending hours not thinking about it.

As Warren taught him how to use the boat, it felt good to get away from the grueling handwork for a bit and shift gears. They took the boat across to Islamorada and docked at a marina closer to the hotel then met the movers. After Warren had assessed Jack's goods, he instructed them how to get to the pier and arranged to meet them early the next morning. Then turned to Jack. "You might want to gather your things and check out of the hotel. You should sleep at the lighthouse tonight. It'll be easier."

"Well, I don't want to disturb you," Jack said, still valuing his solitude after a day in someone's company. "I saw your luggage there—"

"There's two rooms for a reason," Warren said. "Besides, you'll be alone there soon enough, and this is part of your training—making sure you're prepared. The way he looked at Jack let him know there was no arguing, so Jack headed to his room to pack as Warren finished up with the movers and made some calls. Later, Warren helped him carry things to the boat. To Jack's surprise, a delivery boy holding a pizza warming bag that read "The Whistle Stop" was standing next to their boat waiting for them. The smell of warm pepperoni, sausage, and tomato sauce mixed with the salty scent of the sea and Jack's stomach rumbled.

"You Mister Gregg?" the delivery boy asked as they approached.

"Yep," Warren said and continued right onto the boat to settle Jack's things before turning back to accept the credit card slip and pen from the delivery boy.

After he'd signed and accepted the pizza and sent the boy on his way, he said, "Best pizza in Islamorada." And that was that. He took a seat in the back and motioned to Jack. "Take us home, Jack."

Jack concentrated and tried his best to remember the steps Warren had taken to prime the engine and so forth, before sliding behind the wheel and backing them away from the pier.

So far so good.

"Go west," Warren said when Jack hesitated before turning and checked the map.

"I knew that," Jack replied. He'd been searching for the route to Cristof's Key so he could spot the buoys and landmarks.

Warren patted the pizza in his lap. "At least if you get us lost, we won't starve."

"I won't get us lost," Jack said, accepting the challenge and turning the boat as he accelerated again and headed west.

"Heard that before," Warren teased but Jack ignored him, concentrating on the task at hand. The trip took ten minutes, despite Jack wandering off course a few times, and by seven-thirty they were down in the big radio room on the first floor, eating pizza and drinking beers because it was the only place with chairs. Jack had just finished his first slice and half a beer when Hannah's face popped in his head again.

"I hope you'll come see us again," she'd said as he left the diner. It was the first time Jack had thought of Hannah since the movers arrived, and he found himself momentarily wishing he'd grabbed dinner there.

"Want another?" Warren asked, interrupting his thoughts as he held out another slice of the delicious combo pizza.

"Thanks," Jack said and accepted it, even as he did his best to push all thoughts of Hannah and the diner back out of his head again and finish his beer.

"You okay? You're awful quiet," Warren wondered.

"Just tired," Jack said. There was no way he was going to discuss Hannah with Warren.

"Yeah, you earned your keep today, but you'll be even more tired tomorrow after the move," Warren said.

"Hopefully, I'll sleep well my first night here," Jack said.

"We'll take a cot and your things on up to the master bedroom," Warren said. "You'll be sleeping there anyway so you might as well get used to it. Besides, that way you don't have to listen to me snore."

Jack chuckled. "My wife used to complain about my snoring, too." Then he realized what he'd said and went silent. The last thing he wanted to talk about was his family.

"I saw an article about the funeral on the web," Warren said. "When we did a background check. I'm sorry."

So he knew. Jack hadn't considered that. Background checks were the norm for government service, of course, but he hadn't thought about what that might mean.

"It's a tough thing starting over after that," Warren went on. "If I can help or if you just need an ear, I'm here."

No, you can't help. No one can, Jack thought, then sighed. "Thanks. Maybe the move will help." The moment he said it he regretted it because it invited conversation and that was not what he wanted.

But as if sensing his mood, all Warren said was, "I hope so," and then finished his own beer in silence.

Jack ate the second slice Warren had handed him while his

mind raged silently. Here he was all angry and hurt and not wanting to talk about his family one minute while thinking about another women the next. What the hell was wrong with him? Guilt swelled as his body tensed and he grabbed another beer to wash the pizza down.

To his credit, Warren ate in silence, then went over to the computer and read through some notices that had come across the feed about weather and other Coast Guard matters. "You'll wanna check this often, just in case something urgent comes up," he told Jack. "It doesn't happen very often but when it does, it's important."

"Okay," Jack said, still brooding to himself.

The next morning they met the movers at the pier at seven a.m. and began transferring Jack's belongings onto a modified pontoon boat with a flat transom instead of the usual cabin. It was owned by a friend of Warren's named Henry who regularly moved people across water and from the looks of it, Jack figured it was all they'd need.

Between Warren, Jack, Henry, and three movers, it took an hour to unload the moving truck and pack everything safely on the pontoon boat. Then Henry set out for Cristof's Key with Warren and Jack riding along. By the time they left, they'd drawn a bit of crowd of looky loos who waved and cheered as they set out, mission accomplished. Instinctively, Jack had found himself scanning their faces for any sign of Hannah and was surprised to find he felt disappointed not seeing her.

He decided on the way back to the island it was a sign he should make whatever arrangements he could to avoid the mainland and keep to himself. That was the best way to honor the memory of his family and avoid entanglements and distractions that could only cause guilt or pain. By the time Henry pulled the pontoon boat to a stop at the island's pier, Jack had stiffened his jaw and his determination. He'd forget all about Hannah and hope he never saw her again.

CHAPTER 6

T HAT SATURDAY, THREE people told Hannah about the men loading a flat bottom boat with a flat transom at the pier before she finally took a break and went out to see for herself. She only had to go a block from the diner to catch a glimpse over the gathering crowd of Jack and five other men unloading a moving van. She stood under a Royal Palm with thick Spanish Moss winding halfway up its lower trunk to watch the men working. The gentle breeze felt good on her skin, drying away the sweat from her constant running in the hot diner. In the distance, dolphins frolicked in the waves as a sailboat cruised nearby, its mainsail and jib flapping in the wind.

Jack and three others were working shirtless, but Hannah saw only Jack, his skin and muscles growing shiny with sweat in the early morning sun. He was totally focused on the task at hand, working as fast as he could, while an older man supervised the loading. She could see the muscle striations in his arms and back as he lifted each box. Her heart fluttered a bit.

She'd been disappointed when Jack hadn't returned to the diner after their Tuesday night encounter and wondered what he'd been up to and where he'd been eating. Had he found another favorite spot or was he eating at the lighthouse? Maybe he hadn't liked the food. What if he hadn't liked her? Even worse, what if he'd met some other woman who turned him on, forgetting all about her?

After a moment, she chastised herself. He'd come in one night and barely made conversation only because she'd pushed him. For all she knew she'd never see him again. Why was she even thinking about this? Rob was the love of her life and always would be. They'd spent twelve glorious years together. She wasn't looking for anyone else. She'd never replace him, so why was she wasting time thinking about it? Still, why did her heart tumble awkwardly every time his muscles rippled as he moved those boxes? And she knew Rob wouldn't mind if she found someone who made her happy. He wouldn't want her to be alone any more than she wanted to spend the rest of her life that way. She was young. You could love more than one person, but this man had totally blown her off, and my God, what a terrible tipper! Did he even respect service workers? Yet she couldn't take her eyes off him, so she stood there, watching.

Her mind drifted back to when she and Rob moved to Florida. He'd handled the truck, while she'd dealt with toddler Sam and done some unpacking. Rob had looked good with his shirt off too—muscular, just the right amount of hair on his chest, skin glistening from a light sheen of sweat.

"You just gonna stare at me or you gonna help?" Rob teased when he caught her watching him.

"I've got Sam," she'd replied, motioning to the son who was making truck engine sounds at her feet as he rolled his Tonka up over her shoes and made her frown. "Ow, Sammy, be gentle. That hurts mama."

Rob had laughed. "Don't worry, I got it, babe. You just keep being you." And he went back to work without another word. That was one thing she'd always loved about Rob: he'd always encouraged her to be who she wanted to be and never felt threatened by it. She'd stayed home to raise Sam because she chose to. Several times he'd encouraged her to go back and fish her degree or take a job if she wanted to, but she'd always put him off, figuring there was plenty of time for that later. What she hadn't counted on was that later coming as a single mom.

In fairness, that day while he was unloading, she'd unpacked the kitchen and set up the bedroom and Sam's room—making beds, putting clothes in dressers, unwrapping plates and silverware so they'd have something to eat off of. The entire process had taken most of the day, and when he finally collapsed in a chair, she'd had dinner ready, and Rob had been grateful. But still, she knew she could have done more if she hadn't been so distracted watching him.

What was it about a sweaty, bare-chested man that set her heart aflame? She'd tried dating since the accident a half dozen times. None of those went beyond a date or two, and after they were over, none of those men entered her thoughts at all. So, what was it about this guy? She hadn't found herself this drawn to someone since Rob's death, and yet they'd only met once. *God, Hannah, you're losing your mind!* she scolded herself.

She took a breath as her focus came back to Jack and the team packing the pontoon boat. She only had only five or six minutes before time to return her attention to her duties with the morning rush but caught herself stepping outside a few more times to catch another look until the men finished before nine and sailed away.

As she stepped back inside the diner, humming to herself, Lou shot her a knowing look. "You know, those men'll be real hungry by the time they finish."

"Imagine so," she said nonchalantly, avoiding his eyes as she stopped humming and slid back behind the counter.

"So, if you want I could whip them up some dinner you could deliver," Lou suggested.

She frowned, shaking her head. "I'm not a delivery girl, Lou. I was just getting went out for some sun."

"Uh huh," Lou said with an amused look. "You and all the other ladies. Nothing to do with those shirtless men with rippling muscles." *Aim for some originality.*

She punched his arm far more gently than he deserved. "Shut up, Lou." Then went back to work, but the rest of the day, she couldn't get the idea he'd planted out of her head.

Finally, around three, she swallowed her pride and stepped into the kitchen where Lou was fixing steaks and potatoes on a sizzling grill. "Do you still want to make that dinner?" she asked as she savored the smell of grilling meat, while trying to remember if any of her customers had ordered steak.

Lou grinned and pointed to a box on the counter. "Already working on it."

Hannah scoffed and put her hands on her hips. "I thought told you 'no.'"

"Your eyes said, 'yes yes yes,'" Lou replied, laughing, and Hannah couldn't help but laugh too as she tsk-tsked him with her fingers and headed back out to the dining room to clean tables.

An hour later, he summoned her to the kitchen and pointed to the basket. "You're all set and Bert will meet you at the pier. I already called him."

"You know, Lou, I never knew you were such a matchmaker," Hannah chided as she walked over and inspected the box.

"Dinner for three," Lou said.

"Three?" Hannah's brow furrowed. "I think there are only two of them over there, Lou."

"Well, surely you're hungry too." He winked.

Hannah felt herself blushing, embarrassed that he'd read her mind so well as she reached inside the box and lifted out a bottle, turning with a surprised look to hold it up for Lou to see. "Zinfandel?"

"It's perfect with steaks," Lou insisted.

"We don't even sell wine," Hannah replied, shaking her head as she reached into the box again and pulled out three plastic wine glasses. She waved these at Lou, too.

He just shrugged and said, "I have lots of friends."

"Oh my God," she said, blushing again as she packed the

wine and glasses carefully back in the box. "How many people know about this?"

Lou crossed his index and middle fingers. "Two or three tops."

"Please tell me one of them is not my mother-in-law," Hannah said.

Lou made a face. "I forgot to call her."

Then he laughed and dodged as Hannah balled a fist and swiped at his arm again.

"Get going," Lou said. "Those men are hungry, and Bert's waiting."

Hannah surrendered, taking off her apron, which she promptly hung in its usual spot on a hook along the wall. "You are terrible." She straightened her dress then quickly grabbed a brush off the shelf above the hooks and ran it through her hair.

As she finished brushing, Lou handed her her purse from behind the counter and smiled. She quickly applied lipstick and a little perfume then put them back in the purse and slung it over her shoulder.

"I love you, too," Lou replied and grinned as he held out the box. Hannah grabbed the box and started for the door, sticking her tongue out tauntingly as she went. Lou raised his hands, fingers spread, shooting her a knowing grin, and his smug humming followed her out the door and up the street.

BERT WAITED for Hannah in his jetty boat at the pier, offering a wave when he saw her approaching, and stepping off the boat to help her with the box. "I'll hold that while you climb aboard," he said and she accepted.

Once she stood aboard the boat, she turned back and he handed her the box again, following her aboard and starting the engine but waiting until she'd settled into a seat before setting off for the island.

"No other passengers?" she asked as she noticed a few stars twinkling through the dark edges of the sunset overhead. Fall was approaching, and she loved the shorter hours so she could enjoy the night time sky earlier.

Bert shook his head. "We don't get many this late on weekdays. Lou said you're going to Cristof's Key, is that right?"

"Yes."

"To see Jack and Warren at the lighthouse, huh? They had quite a workday, moving Jack in," Bert added when Hannah offered no reply, he left her alone, stepping inside the enclosed cabin to pilot the boat in silence.

At the island, he took the box again, helping her onto the pier, then gently handed it over. "Smells great," he said, clasping his fingers together and raising them to his noise with a look of ecstasy. "Good luck."

"Thank you," Hannah said, balancing the box as she reached into her purse for her wallet.

Bert raised a palm. "Already paid for. Have a good night." Before she could react, he was already steering the boat back out across the water.

She watched crabs play on the sand as seagulls and herons fluttered about ahead, darting toward and around each other as if performing an intricate ballet to celebrate the sunset. The sky was already show shades of the purple hues that had led Spanish explorers to give the town its name, Islamorada, which meant "purple island." She loved the natural beauty of Florida and its native wildlife. With its position between the Atlantic Ocean and the Gulf of Mexico, it was on migration routes for so many varieties of birds and fish and other species, all so colorful and active and fun to behold. She never got tired of observing them, and on occasion, she reveled in discovering some new activity or quirk she'd never noticed before. Cristof Island was beautiful with it seemingly endless stretch of smooth, yellow, uncontaminated beach and the beautiful lighthouse which she'd never seen up close. It was hard to believe this was her first visit, and she made a mental note to bring Sam back to hunt shells. Maybe she'd even invite Ellen along as a goodwill gesture.

After a few minutes of enjoying the views, she remembered the box and the food getting colder by the minute. She turned and started along the beach toward the lighthouse a half a mile ahead. Two herons circled and dove down to surf the waves while nearby Cormorants dove under the water for food. The tide was halfway out, yet a few slow rollers lapped at the shore in an endless hum, breaking smoothly on the soft sand as they pushed ashore seaweed along with fish, crabs, and other objects. The sky was lit up with beautiful shades of yellow, orange, and purple hues as the sun slowly dropped toward the horizon. She stayed up by the vegetation line avoiding the water, although walking barefoot through the waves was one of her favorite things to do. Tonight, she was on a mission. No time for play.

As she walked, she noticed the sand contained many conch shells, a Florida staple, and an item Ellen used to make homemade jewelry and which Sam loved to hunt and collect for her. There were a lot of really good specimens here. She really had to bring Sam sometime soon to collect some. They made her think about the inmost life of the tiny creatures inhabiting conch shells, the only house around them shaped by outward forces. About twenty-five yards out, she passed an old, rundown white lifeguard stand that looked like it had been abandoned for years. Other than the lighthouse, it was the only sign of life on the island so far.

She fought the urge to stop and check her makeup and hair in the compact inside her purse as she drew closer to the lighthouse. He hadn't looked over once from loading the boat either, though he had scanned the crowd she noticed. But was he looking for her or someone else? And what did it matter? She'd drop the food and leave. That was the plan anyway as far as she was concerned. She just had to call Bert for a pickup.

Her feet scraped the sand as she walked, transitioning from the beach onto a dirt pathway that crossed the vegetation line and led past the lighthouse. A small hill of rolling sand and coastal herbage sloped gently down to the sea on her right. Ahead, she saw a path leading to the lighthouse and slowed her steps, debating. Was this a huge mistake? What if they already had food? What if he wasn't happy to see her? He hadn't even been polite at the diner. In fact, as she thought about it, he'd seemed distant, almost brooding. What if he was one of those crazies—the type you hear about who seem normal and can interact but when you get them alone they just snap? Only there was something gentle in his eyes. He just didn't strike her as the crazy type. But then how many neighbors did you see interviewed after a killer was caught talking about how ordinary and quiet they were... Ah to hell with it. She was bringing a gift, and surely they had a fridge out here if people stayed there over night. They could always reheat it later. She was being neighborly, and if they couldn't appreciate that, she'd just know better than to waste her time worrying about them in the future.

As she turned onto the lighthouse path, for a moment, she thought about turning back. As she neared the front door, someone stood looking out the window. Taking a deep breath, she continued on, straightening her shoulders to feign confidence and heading right for a door she saw on the southeast end of the building. Whatever happened, she was ready. After all, maybe the wine and glasses were a bit much but Lou meant well. She could explain it was a gift from her boss at the diner, not her idea. She was just the delivery girl. Stop overthinking, she scolded herself. You're nice, so what if he isn't? It just shows his true colors.

The night breeze was warm but pleasant as it caressed her skin, calming her as she continued toward the door. She resisted the urge to glance up at the window where she'd seen someone watching her and just focused on the door ahead, walking determinedly as the delicious smell of the warm steaks, potatoes, and corn Lou had prepared filled her nose and alerted her senses, reminding her of her own hunger. She flashed back to Jack's flexing muscles, slick with sweat as he loaded boxes onto the jetty that morning, and fantasized for a moment about sitting down with Jack and enjoying the meal like old friends, then laughed at the absurdity and shook it off. Dear God, Hannah, you need a date bad if you're so lonely you're fantasizing about a complete stranger! Really!

She shook her head as she reached the lighthouse door and stopped, gathering herself. You got this, Hannah. She crossed her fingers, hoping for the best, and knocked.

IT HAD BEEN Warren who first alerted Jack to Hannah, walking up the path carrying a large box. "Did you invite her? Odd for a man who fancies being alone."

"No," Jack said firmly as he came to the kitchen window and saw the cascading red hair. She'd had it up in a bun at the diner, but now even in the fading light of sunset, it seemed to frame her face and highlight its features in way that increased her natural beauty, and for a moment, he just stared. There was something wholesome and down-to-earth about her, the kind of girl who just put you immediately at ease. And then he remembered what a jerk he'd been. Avoiding conversation and even leaving a chintzy tip, and suddenly he felt embarrassed at seeing her again. Sure, he'd wanted to be alone. He'd been tired after his first day, but he could have had better manners. Should have.

That was when she looked up and saw him.

Jack stepped back quickly and nodded. "She's a waitress at a diner where I ate Tuesday night."

"Well, go see what she wants," Warren said.

"Me?" Jack asked. He didn't want to be the one to go. She had to be here because of him, right? Warren didn't know who she was. It was the only thing that she made sense. So whatever she wanted, if she saw Warren, maybe she'd leave quickly, and

Jack could avoid the feelings and thoughts he'd been having and get on with his new life.

"Yeah, I don't know her, so clearly she's not here to see me," said Warren noted, reading Jack's mind. "So, save us both time and go greet her, Jack. Let an old man rustle up dinner." With that he turned and started rummaging in the cupboards as if to say "conversation over."

Jack sighed, cursing to himself, and turned toward the spiral staircase as they heard the first knock at the door. By the time he made it down two flights of the spiral, he'd heard another knock and Hannah's voice calling, "Hello?"

When he opened the door, she'd balanced the box against the doorframe and was pushing stray strands of hair back behind her ear with a finger.

As soon as she saw him, she grabbed the box again and stepped back, smiling. "Hi. We thought you might be hungry after moving today."

"Sorry, I was two floors up," Jack said as he stepped forward to look in the box, the familiar aroma of warm meat and potatoes made his stomach rumble. She'd gone to the trouble of bringing plastic glasses and a bottle of wine. "Zinfandel?"

Hannah blushed and shifted the box in such a way the contents pinged like bells. "My boss may have been a little overzealous, but it goes great with steak." She added, "He also put some little containers with steak sauce and ketchup in there somewhere."

The food smelled glorious. His stomach rumbled again as she held out the box and he took it. "This smells fantastic. It's thoughtful of you. What do we owe you?"

She raised a palm, shaking her head. "No, it's on the house. Trust me, there's no use arguing with Lou."

"But I insist. I have cash," Jack said, reaching in his back pocket for his wallet. There was a sparkle in her bright green eyes as she stood under the overhead light above the door with the rainbow colors of a beautiful ocean sunset behind her. It struck him that he hadn't fully appreciated how pretty she was at the diner.

"Lou didn't include a check, so he won't accept it," she said, shaking her head again. "After your tip, he couldn't live with having disappointed a customer. Consider this his peace offering. A second chance of sorts."

Jack had found the food salty, but he hadn't said a word. He'd been irritable and regretted not tipping better. But he found himself struggling for words. The way her hair flopped up and down as she moved her head, made him grin, then feel guilty for different reasons. He'd stopped being attracted to other women the minute he first saw Abby. They were married and always would be. So, what was he doing ogling another woman?

He chided himself and shook it off. "Well, come in then," Jack said, hoping to God he didn't blush as he tried to keep his voice even and casual. He balanced the box in one hand and reached for the door, before realizing she hadn't made any effort to leave. She hadn't moved at all. They stood staring at each other a moment, until he finally said, "Do you have a boat waiting or do you want to come in and call one?"

She frowned and waved her cell phone at him, and he regretted the words immediately. Of course, she'd have a cell phone. No one would come to an isolated island alone, especially a woman, without a way to call for help in this day and age. But she didn't seem anxious to leave, and he wanted to be polite this time. Plus, despite his reservations, he found he didn't want her to leave. In fact, he felt a sudden urge to talk to her. Warren was here, too, so it wasn't disrespectful to Abby, right?

"I shouldn't stay long," she said as she stepped inside and he closed the door behind her. Jack caught a whiff of her jasmine perfume. He knew he must look exhausted and dirty himself, but if she'd worked all day, she hid it well. Her hair was slightly disturbed by the breeze but the slight hint of makeup accented her attractiveness and she seemed cheery and energetic.

Jack locked the door and motioned to the stairs. "The kitchen is two flights up," he said, then he realized they were alone and added, "Warren is waiting. Why don't you come up and make your call? There's better signal."

She smiled again and started for the stairs. "Okay, thank you. It'll be fun to see the lighthouse. I've been curious about it since I was a kid, but I've never seen it before."

Jack nodded. "Yes, they don't give tours. This is the main communications room, of course. Servers to run the lamp and communicate and radios as well." He repeated back what Warren had told him on the tour.

Hannah's eyes scanned the room. "Looks very official."

Jack grunted. "That it is. Coast Guard."

After a moment, she started up the stairs and he followed, catching the scent of jasmine again. They reached the second bedroom and Jack found himself suddenly self-conscious about the stacks of boxes. "Still a lot to do," he said. "This is the spare bedroom for relief workers who come to help from time to time."

She glanced back, her eyes meeting his as she started up the stairs again. "It's okay, I've moved myself too. Takes longer to unpack sometimes than it did to pack. I never would have imagined the inside of a lighthouse would look like this. It's interesting."

They reached the next level and found Warren tinkering in the kitchen.

"We have steaks and potatoes for dinner," Jack announced, a hint to Warren to stop preparing the alternative he'd concocted.

"Oh really? Wow," Warren said, turning and rubbing his hands together. He smiled when he saw Hannah and came over to check out the box Jack had gently set on the table. "This is very nice. To what do we owe the kindness?"

"Just being neighborly," said Hannah.

"Wow, wine even. Fancy," said Warren. Jack felt relieved Warren was taking over the conversation. He could just watch and stay out of it. Perfect.

"It goes great with steak," she repeated. He liked how the least thing made her blush. Kind of old fashioned. Abby would call him silly for his notions about women.

Warren gave a nod. "Yes, it does. Who knew they had such fancy offerings in a diner?"

"Well, actually we don't," Hannah explained, "but Lou, my boss, threw it in anyway. Housewarming kinda thing."

Warren chuckled. "Be sure and thank him for us. How much do we owe you?"

She shook her head. "Compliments of Lou's."

Warren pursed his lips, looking surprised. "I'll have to eat there more often."

"He's good people," Hannah said then began unpacking the box.

Warren shot a look at Jack then motioned to the kitchen. "Shall I get plates and silverware?"

"He threw in plastic," Hannah added.

"Ah, this is too fancy for that," Warren said as he spun and walked back to the kitchen to retrieve three plates and silverware from the cupboards. Then, as Jack and Hannah laid out the meal, he opened a third cupboard and pulled out three wine glasses and carried it all back toward the table.

What are you doing? Jack thought seeing the number of plates and silverware Warren had selected. Don't invite her to stay, Warren. No!

"He threw in enough for three it seems," said Warren said, eyeing the three steaks she unwrapped. "Surely you're hungry after a long day at work."

Hannah shook her head. "It's for you. I have to get back."

73

Warren put on his most charming smile. "Please join us."

Jack fought the urge to argue, trying to signal Warren with his eyes—No! Don't do this! Stop! —but Warren was focused on Hannah, who replied, "Well, I am hungry."

"Good," Warren said with a pleased look and began distributing the plates and silverware around the table, and Jack knew he'd lost. To hide his discomfort he went over to the fridge and grabbed three bottles of water, carrying them back to the table.

As he finished with the place settings, Warren yawned. "Actually, if you don't mind, I think I'll take mine downstairs to the radio room. I hit the road early tomorrow and I have to check on some arrangements. You two can talk and enjoy."

Hannah finished uncovering the dishes. She arranged the food onto plates.

"Don't go," Jack said, breaking his silence. "Really, we'd love the company."

"Absolutely," she said. Hannah agreed.

Warren shook his head as he poured himself a glass of wine. "The wine will make me even sleepier anyway, and as soon as I'm done, I'm heading to bed. Don't worry about me. Enjoy it." He grabbed the glass, plate, and a set of silverware and started for the stairs then turned back. "Nice to meet you, Hannah."

Jack winced, realizing he hadn't introduced them or spoken her name, so there was only one way Warren could know it. But Hannah didn't seem to notice. She smiled and walked over to shake his hand. "You too."

"Warren," he offered.

"Warren," she repeated, effusive. "Nice to meet you, too, Warren."

Warren disappeared down the stairs without a further word, leaving Jack and Hannah alone. When he didn't return, Jack set the empty box on the floor, trying to come up with conversation starters as he did.

74

Hannah slid into a chair and looked at him. "As long as you don't mind?"

Jack took a deep breath and forced a smile to hide the war going on inside him. *You can't do this! It's the last thing you need. Warren trapped you, but you can still get out of this. Think of an excuse.* But he wracked his brain for one and nothing came. Finally, when the silence had stretched to an unbearable length, he said, "Of course not. It's the least we can do after you came all this way with free dinner."

Hannah watched him a moment as if waiting for him to change his mind, and finally he added, "Welcome to Cristof's Lighthouse."

At that, she finally relaxed. Jack resigned himself. Tonight, he was having dinner with an attractive woman. *This is happening.* Whatever his reservations, she was here and she was staying.

CHAPTER 7

THE BACK OF Jack's neck prickled as Hannah settled into chair at the table. Why did he suddenly feel like a teenager? *Act natural!* Jack chided himself as sat on the opposite side.

Hannah filled their glasses, waiting while he picked a place to land. She raised a glass. "Well, here's to new neighbors and new adventures."

Jack took the glass she'd poured for him and raised it as she drank from hers. "Cheers." Then he took a sip as well. The wine was fruity and sweet, a pleasant change. Abby had always preferred them dry and bitter. He grabbed the knife and fork and set to work cutting his steak as Hannah did the same.

"There's more space in here than I expected," she said.

"It'll be enough," Jack said as he finished cutting his steak and eyed the two small containers of steak sauce sitting in the middle of the table.

Noting his interest, Hannah picked up the bottles, one with each hand, and held them out. "Help yourself. There's A-1 and Heinz both. What's your poison?"

Jack selected the container with the darker sauce. "A-1. Thanks."

"I'm a Heinz girl," she said and grabbed the Heinz bottle

from the center of the table as Jack used his clean spoon to scoop a little bit of A-1 onto his plate.

"It's a bit dated," Jack said, motioning to the kitchen, "but they give us everything we need."

Hannah shrugged. "I guess if you can have supplies and food delivered, you're all set."

"I guess so," Jack agreed.

She chuckled as if it was a joke then seeing his expression, put her smile away.

Jack grabbed a bite of steak with his fork and dipped it in A-1 before lifting it to his mouth. He savored it. It was really good for diner food. "Mmmmmm."

"Any more tips for the chef?" Hannah teased, looking somewhere between relieved and happy.

"Not at all," Jack agreed as he washed the bite down with another sip of wine and reached for another. "In fact, I wanted to apologize about that. I was tired. But that was no excuse to be rude. I'm sorry. And for the lousy tip, too."

Her eyes met his as the tension left her shoulders, then she offered a slight nod. For the next few minutes, they both concentrated on their food, Hannah cutting up her steak as Jack supplemented his with a bite each of baked potato and corn. The vegetables were as delicious as the steak with just the right amount of salt and butter added. And Hannah seemed to be enjoying them as much as Jack was, content to eat in silence for the moment and savor a fine meal.

"I think I ordered the wrong thing the other night," Jack observed after another sip of wine.

Hannah swallowed a bite of steak and laughed. "Yeah, it's one of his better creations for sure," she replied, her voice cracking slightly. She grabbed the glass of wine quickly and took another sip to moisten her palate. "Are you a decent cook?"

Jack shrugged. "I'm all right. My wife used to be the real chef in the family."

Her face showed no reaction at the mention of Abby. Instead, she said, "Well, I hope this isn't setting an impossible standard. That can only lead to disappointment."

Jack chuckled, raising his glass in toast again. "It's certainly great starting on such a high note."

Hannah grabbed hers and toasted back then they both drank again.

"It's been a while since I've done this," Hannah said then grabbed another bite of steak with her fork and slid it into her mouth.

"Done what?" Jack asked, taking another bite of corn.

"Eaten alone with man," Hannah said matter-of-factly and Jack felt himself stiffen, grabbing his glass to try and cover it. "Did I say something wrong?"

Jack took a long sip of wine and shook his head. "No. Me too."

"You too?"

"I haven't had dinner alone with a woman since my wife died," Jack confessed.

"Oh, I'm sorry for your loss," Hannah said, her eyes brimming with sympathy. For a moment, they looked at each other and it almost seemed to Jack like she knew exactly how he felt. But how could she? The thought made him angry. No one understood his pain and loss. He had lost everything. She couldn't possibly understand.

"I lost my husband, too," she said.

Jack was overcome by a sudden urge to leave the table and run. This is too much. She lost her husband, too? He couldn't bear to think about it. I don't want to know her that well. Why is she telling me this? Why did I tell her? The whole thing made him feel things he didn't want to feel. It was bad enough his thoughts had dwelled on her—another woman—when he should have been thinking of his beloved Abby and dear sweet

79

Caroline, but this! No. It wasn't right. He had to end this now. Send her away.

She frowned, watching him. "What's the matter? You look upset."

"I'm fine," he snapped, regretting it immediately. Taking out his anger on her wasn't the solution. He had to remain calm, keep his cool. "Just thinking about my wife. It's still hard."

"I'm sorry," she said. "I understand."

God damn it! Don't say that! This was going all wrong. He didn't want sympathy and understanding. He didn't want to let her in. Why in the hell was this happening? He had been fine, all set to start over—a life alone in mourning for his loss—but she was messing up everything.

"I didn't mean to upset you," she added now, the concern on her face deepening. She wiped her mouth with a napkin and scooted back her chair, the legs scraping on the linoleum. "Maybe I should go now."

"No... I..." The words wouldn't come. Emotions whirled like a hurricane in his head. Instead, he shook his head but she was already standing, heading for the stairs.

"Thanks for sharing it with me," Hannah said in a rush. "I really am sorry. And I hope you have a better night."

She disappeared down the stairs before he could say a word. Jack heard her talking briefly with Warren, and considered going after her, but he couldn't move. Instead, his stomach hardened and a lump formed in this throat. What the hell was wrong with him? She had been kind and the dinner perfectly lovely until he got all bent out of shape. It wasn't her fault. He wasn't even sure why he was acting this way. He hadn't had any physical contact with her. Nothing romantic in intentions or outcome. It's not like he'd cheated on Abby. He knew he should rush after her and apologize right now, but instead his feet were frozen. Moments later, he heard the door open and close downstairs followed by footsteps on the porch. He put his face in his hands, fighting back tears. This was why he wanted to avoid people, dammit! This was why he was better off alone.

Warren climbed the stairs with a puzzled look. He stared wordlessly at him.

Jack took a deep breath, wiping at his eyes. "She had to leave," he said.

Warren eyed Hannah's half-full plate.

"She had to get home," Jack repeated.

"What did you say to her?" Warren asked.

Jack couldn't bear his kind eyes. He would have rather Warren scolded him; lectured him about how he represented the Coast Guard now and had an obligation to be polite and kind at all times or something similar. Even kicked him in the nuts. Anything, but being nice which was the last thing he deserved. When Warren said nothing, awaiting Jack's answer, Jack stood and hurried to the stairs, climbing up toward the master bedroom and leaving Warren alone, his question unanswered.

AS SOON AS she left the lighthouse, Hannah called Bert, asking him to come back and pick her up. He was five minutes out, he said. She promised him she'd be waiting as she hurried up the path away from the lighthouse and headed for the pier. Ellen would be fit to be tied, of course, as she always was when Hannah was late, but tonight, Hannah hardly cared. Her mind was on Jack and what had happened between them at the lighthouse.

She wasn't certain what had gone wrong, but she recognized the signs: the pulsing vein in Jack's forehead, the coldness in his eyes, the change in his voice. He'd been angry with her. Only she had no idea why. What had she said to deserve his anger? They were getting to know each other. It was only the second time they'd ever met. Was he one of those men who just went off with the flip of a switch? Her stomach rumbled and she felt a tension headache coming on. If that was the case, she'd steer far clear of him. She had no need for that nonsense. He'd seemed so quiet and nice. But then what did that mean? Again, the neighbors of killers interviewed on the news came to mind. Was his quietness hiding a deep-seated rage?

She doubted it. Maybe he'd discovered something about her he just didn't like.

She suddenly felt hot and her mind raced back over the entire evening. There had been something about the way he'd looked at her when he'd opened the door at the lighthouse. He seemed to be admiring her, she'd thought, and though he had seemed reluctant when Warren had invited her to join them for dinner, he'd been polite and friendly, keeping up good conversation as they sat down for the meal. He'd even apologized for the way he'd treated her at the diner. She didn't know what to think. It was like a light switch suddenly flipped.

She did know it had been time for her to leave. She heard the splashing of fish jumping out in the sea nearby and the calls of gulls mixed with the chirping of crickets and tree frogs split the night air as she marched determinedly toward the pier. These were the sounds of home she'd grown used to hearing every day. Most of the time, she paid no attention to them, but being out here on this island in a strange place, they seemed to punctuate the oddness of what she'd experienced with Jack. It was too bad. Lou had outdone himself with the meal, and even now she wished she could have finished it.

She reached the pier and waited, hearing a motor in the distance and hoping it was Bert. Two minutes later, she caught sight of the jetty boat's lamp and felt herself relax a bit. Whatever had happened back at the lighthouse was over. In less than half an hour, she'd be home with Sam and her Ellen again—no doubt facing interrogation, of course—best to think about other things and put the dinner behind her.

It had been crazy and impulsive to think she could just show up like that with a meal uninvited, and Lou's wine probably hadn't helped. Sure, Lou had pushed her to do it, but she could have refused if she'd wanted. She should have seen Jack's behavior when they met as a clear sign to steer clear. Lou meant well, of course, and she couldn't be mad at him for it. But she definitely would have to reconsider such impulses in the future where men were concerned.

The jetty boat appeared in the waves less than two yards out and motored toward the peer, slowing and turning as it came alongside and stopped.

"Good evening, Hannah," Bert called as he held out a hand to help her aboard. "How was dinner?"

"Fine," she said as she settled into a seat. Bert motored off again headed back to Islamorada. The trip back took ten minutes and the entire time, Hannah found herself reviewing the dinner with Jack in her head—every word they said, his every expression, every feeling—wondering if she could have done something differently to change how it ended. Despite Jack's anger, she couldn't shake the feeling that it came from a place of deep pain related to his wife. He'd said he hadn't had dinner alone with a woman in a while. She wondered how long it had been since the wife's death? Could it be he felt guilt about it? Or was there something more complex?

By the time they pulled into the pier, Hannah found herself only wanting to know more about Jack, not less, despite the angry outburst. But it seemed unwise to initiate contact with him without an invitation. She might have to wait until she ran into him around town, however long that might be.

Bert pulled the jetty boat alongside the resort's pier and again held out a hand to help her onto the pier. She thanked him and headed off into the night along the street past the diner toward home, still deep in argument between her head and her heart. Damn it, how could a stranger be having such a strong effect on her so soon? Especially one who'd been such a jerk more than once. The last thing she needed was to date a jerk. That's why she'd felt so lucky with Rob. Sam was enough of a challenge. Nope. She didn't need another. Yeah, Hannah. Listen to your head, she chided herself. But her heart just wouldn't listen, thump after thump.

IT WAS SEVERAL blocks' walk from the resort to the house where Hannah lived with Ellen and Sam. Fortunately, she lived near the diner, because Islamorada stretched for nineteen miles across four islands, making being without a car a real disadvantage. Both were located on Upper Matecumbe Key, the house in a residential enclave on South Hammock Road while the diner was in a business strip along the Overseas Highway just across from the Publix. Most of the city was focused on the lower island so getting around on foot or bicycle was feasible enough for Hannah to get things done. Her mother-in-law had a car, too, of course, but she drove down to Key West four days a week for work, so borrowing that was rarely an option.

The night air was crisp and cool and traffic was light, even on the Overseas Highway, which was good, since Hannah had to cross it to get home. The highway stretched 113 miles along the Florida Keys from Key Largo to Key West, and as such, was the main thoroughfare of most of its cities and the only highway. Lou's Diner, like a lot of businesses, had a parking lot facing the highway, which ran north to south, and South Hammock road split off across the street a block north headed west.

Rob's parents had purchased the home in the 1980s and he'd grown up there, once telling her its bright blue doors filled his head with warm thoughts every time he saw them. There were three bedrooms, a large kitchen, a combined family and living room, and an indoor pool with beautiful lush landscaping and plants surrounding the pool and house.

Hannah entered through the enclosed front patio where the bikes were parked. Since she'd only been going to the diner, she hadn't taken hers today. She opened the door with a key and let herself in to find Ellen waiting for her in the long foyer, arms crossed. Her blonde hair was streaked with gray and her tan skin had its share of wrinkles, but Ellen Clark had the figure of a woman twenty years younger. She was wearing jeans and t-shirt that declared her "World's Best Grandma." But at the moment, she looked more like "World's Angriest Grandma." Yet another reminder why Hannah was anxious for her and Sam to have a place of their own.

"You're late," Ellen scolded, her words short and succinct as she offered her daughter-in-law the same cutting look she'd been giving for lateness since she and Sam moved in.

"I had to visit friends after work," Hannah said.

"You couldn't have called?" Ellen asked.

"I texted," Hannah said, and she had.

Ellen held up her phone. "'Be home a little late. Pit stop. See you soon.' You got off at five. You call nine soon?"

The last thing she needed was Ellen interrogating her about Jack when Hannah didn't even know yet what the answers were. He was just a guy she met and liked but barely knew. There was nothing definite to say yet so better her mother-in-law didn't even know enough to ask questions. "Sorry," Hannah answered. "I'm fine. Your grown adult daughter-in-law is fine. Where's Sam?"

"He was tired. He's in bed."

Hannah sighed. "Is he waiting on me?"

"Supposedly. Like the rest of us." With that Ellen turned dramatically and marched off into the kitchen. Hannah headed the other way toward her son's bedroom.

Like every other room in the house, the hallway walls were decorated with pieces from her mother-in-law's precious art collection, items purchased on various trips and at art shows over several decades. A few were known across the country, but most were by unknown artists few outside of the Keys would ever hear of. She passed her own bedroom and Ellen's and came to a stop at the third door where Sam had hung his name, spelled out in bright red wooden letters. Her heart fluttered seeing his name. Her baby boy, the light of her world.

The door was cracked open but dark inside, so she carefully pushed on it, opening it slowly and peeked in. Even in the dim light, she could see the whales and sea creatures decorating the walls in semi-phosphorescent paint. A few toys and discarded pieces of clothing cluttered the floor. One side of the closet was open as always but the other had been closed, no doubt to hide whatever mess he'd cheated on cleaning up by shoving in there. She'd address that next time she asked him to clean his room.

Her eyes went to the twin bed in the corner across the way where a lump wrinkled the covers. Sam rarely went to sleep until she came home, because he worried about her. Yet another consequence of losing his father. He couldn't sleep unless he knew his mama had come home safe too. But tonight, for some reason, he was dozing. As she stepped inside, light from the hall stretched across to the bed and spotlighted his face—eyes closed, mouth open a crack—and she caught a glimpse of reddish blonde hair on his forehead. He must have worn himself out, making her wonder what Ellen had done on her day off to occupy them both.

She went over and bent down to straighten the covers over him quickly. Had started for the door when she heard a cough. She turned again to see Sam staring up at her. He didn't speak, not that she expected him to, but his eyes said it all—I missed you. I love you. I'm glad you're home.

She smiled and bent to kiss his forehead. "Good night, darling. Sleep well."

Since a botched dinner had left her famished, it made sense to look for leftovers from whatever dinner Rob's mother might have made. Ellen was sitting at the table reading a Craig Johnson novel and didn't even look up when Hannah walked over and opened the fridge.

"What did you have for dinner?" Hannah asked.

"You'd know if you'd bothered to show up," said Ellen,

perturbed in such a way.

"Ellen, I already apologized. Cut me a break, will you?"

"Not until you tell me where you were."

Hannah found Tupperware containers with a couple cooked burger patties and baked beans and deduced Grandma had gone for the win with her grandson. "What did you all do today?" she asked, changing the subject.

"I spent the day with a grandson who hasn't said a word to me in two years," Ellen said with a sour expression. "Grocery shopping, collecting shells on the beach, showing some jewelry, and watching the dolphins feed. I had fun. Someday maybe he'll tell us he did, too."

"He tells me in other ways, Ellen," Hannah said, irritation rising. This was an old argument—how to "fix" Sam. And Hannah had tried several methods, but she was concerned that might be making it worse by causing her son stress. She set the Tupperware on the counter and pulled a plate from the cupboard.

"He needs help," Ellen said. "And the school offered, too."

"We've tried so many things," Hannah said. "I've told you before he'll speak when he's ready." She opened the bread box beside the fridge and pulled out a bag of hamburger buns.

Ellen sighed, angrily flipping a page in her book. "You might as well not speak to me either. All you ever say is the same nonsense. You're not even grateful. If only you'd gotten that condo."

Ellen had been making snide remarks ever since learning Hannah had lost the condo to the couple who had an appointment right after the one she'd missed. As much as Ellen complained about having them live with her being a burden, inside Hannah knew her mother-in-law took secret pleasure in having it to lord over her. The irony was they'd actually gotten along when she was married to Rob. This treatment hadn't started until after the accident when Hannah had needed Ellen's help to survive.

"As always, I so appreciate your loving support," Hannah said, warming her hamburger and beans. "I'm eating in my room. Night." Unfortunately, losing the condo meant she'd have to wait months to find another affordable option, especially one with such a good deal. She could dig into the remainder of Rob's life insurance, she supposed, but she'd been saving that for Sam's medical bills. Considered using part of it to buy a new car. Truth was, Hannah felt trapped. She needed a fresh start. Having her mother-in-law support them after Rob's death had been a blessing, but she'd always known the situation could only be temporary.

"What you need is a good man to take care of you," Janice often told her. A good man. God, Ellen would hate that, too. Though Hannah's mother-in-law planted thoughts about a white knight sort to carry her away to a happier life, in the end, what she needed was to get her own place. Hannah could take care of herself, no matter what her Ellen thought. She didn't need a man, and Rob had never treated her like she did. Being together was a gift from each to the other, and they'd always cherished it as a privilege, not an obligation.

She pictured Jack's face, and her thoughts went back to the lighthouse. In many ways, he reminded her of her husband. Rob had been quiet too and hard working. And when he was mad, everybody knew it. He didn't hide emotions well. But on the other hand, he didn't show them often. Only at the extremes— when he was really feeling—would he let it out. With love and joy, this was a great blessing. With anger and sadness, not so much. She wondered if Jack was the same way. Obviously he'd also lost a spouse and she knew how that felt. Grief cycled in and out. In some ways, you never get over it. In others, you heal and learn to go on. She had lived it. If anything, knowing they had that in common drew her toward Jack when she should've known better.

After finishing her dinner, she decided if she saw Jack again, she'd treat him just as she had before, respectfully. Like any other diner customer. So, she found him attractive? Attractive men weren't hard to find in the Keys. It was the available part that could sometimes be tricky. And Jack was the first man she'd felt drawn to like this since Rob, but then maybe that was their common grief rather than physical attraction or some other connection.

Unlike Ellen, Hannah didn't believe she needed a man to be of worth or even get along in life. She'd make it, or die trying. Whichever, she'd put up a hell of fight for sure. Thinking about it now, her teeth gritted at remembering how Jack treated her. Twice now. What was wrong with him? Being aggrieved didn't give him the right to be rude or take out his anger on her. God, Hannah, get a grip. You can find someone who treats you the way you deserve, so stop wasting time on him, her inner voice chided.

No, Hannah Loaney didn't need a man. And besides, she was damned attractive if she said so herself. She still had her figure, the constant standing and running at the diner plus her commute by bicycle no doubt helping keep the pounds off. And for a woman in her thirties, her legs were toned and nice, too. Yeah, Jack Pace would be lucky to have her. He was the one missing out, not her. Except why couldn't she stop thinking about him?

CHAPTER 8

"WAIT! LET ME get this straight," Josie said the next morning, after Jack called to tell her about Hannah's visit to the lighthouse. "A beautiful neighbor brings you a meal after seeing you move and you assume it's a date, freak out, and run her off basically?"

"She was dressed up and wore makeup," Jack said, already regretting he'd called his sister for advice.

"Maybe she just wanted to look nice," Josie snapped. "It's what women do. You know, we have this thing called 'welcoming the new neighbors' around here. Mom used to do it."

Jack was embarrassed. Josie was right. He'd lost it. Caught up in his own feelings and totally disregarding Hannah's. He'd treated her terribly again, and it wasn't her fault. All she'd done was be kind, giving charitably to a stranger. It wasn't her fault she found him in a foul mood. Why was he punishing her for that? Abby would have been ashamed of him. And he was ashamed of himself, too.

"Jack Allen Pace!" she'd scold him, sounding way too much like his mother.

"What?" he'd reply, feigning innocence, all the while shrinking inside with embarrassment and shame.

Abby would shoot him that mother's look—the one equivalent to "you weren't raised in a barn" or "what's wrong with you" or some such, and he'd quickly apologize or make a joke to cover. Abby had always been better at dealing with people than Jack ever had. For that reason, he'd come to rely on her in most social situations they faced together. It was the times when she wasn't there to rescue him that he usually messed up.

Like with Hannah. "Are you listening to me?!" asked Josie.

"Yes, I hear you."

"Look, you may live on an island now, but you still have to deal with people. Sure, you're sad, you're forever broken, you're going to live out life as a hermit in black. We all get it, but that's no excuse for being a jackass to people who show you kindness." Josie had a way of cutting to the quick that Jack had never particularly liked, especially when it was aimed directly at him.

"I owe her an apology," he said, hoping she'd back off.

"An apology ain't gonna cut it, bro. A grand gesture, that's what this calls for."

Jack sighed. "I'll think about it."

"Don't call me again until you do it, jerkface."

"Okay," said Jack, acquiescing as the typical rump-end of how things had finished between them since third grade, when he'd tried to help her learn to ride a bike and instead sent her flying downhill into a ditch. Maybe that's who he was—the undependable man who always let women down.

"Hey," she said. "I love you."

"Yeah, yeah," he said, hanging up.

Josie was right. He had to learn how to deal with people no matter how much he hurt or how emotional he got. Hannah was the first to try and reach out to him, but he doubted she'd be the last. Warren had tried though he'd been more subtle about it. It could just as easily have been him who bore the brunt. And the last thing he needed was conflict with his supervisor or co-workers.

After Hannah ran off and he'd dodged Warren's question, Jack had headed upstairs to his bedroom and stayed there the rest of the night. It was rather adolescent, he realized, but he was afraid if he tried to talk about it, he'd just take it out on Warren. Now, lying in his bed for the first time in the lighthouse, his brain worked overdrive. If he hadn't felt sure Warren had long since gone to bed, he'd have gone down to talk with him. But instead, that conversation would wait until morning.

Ultimately, he knew he needed to apologize to Hannah, as Josie had yammered at him to do. He'd wait a few days to let her feelings recover and then go find her at the diner. He probably couldn't bring himself to explain, so that would have to be enough. Maybe it would be. Maybe after suffering her own loss she'd understand moodiness. Ah! A ray of light. This would blow over. For now, he needed to fall asleep. Exhausted from the physical demands of a long day of moving, he knew fatigue had only aggravated his behavior. What he wanted most was a good night's rest—not only to reenergize his body but to bring clarity to his spinning mind.

Abby had always complained about his lack of self-awareness. He was thirty-eight-years old, probably about time to come to terms with that, and learn to do better, right? But sitting across from Hannah had felt like cheating on his wife, and he wasn't sure how to deal with that, let alone what it meant. Part of him felt guilty, of course, but another part dismissed that as silly. His wife was gone. He was single again, and human. He'd had dinner with a kind neighbor, that's all. So how should he deal with the pain lingering in the back of his throat ever since?

The dueling melodies of tree frogs and crickets competed as he lay there waiting for sleep to overtake him, reviewing the dinner conversation in his mind. He'd done his best despite his discomfort but then Hannah mentioned losing her own husband. Combined with his attraction to her, a simple revelation, one person relating to another—oh hell. Why did it feel so complicated? Complications he didn't need. Wait. A simple girl was only responding to his own revelation about losing Abby. A human thing to do. That's it. Still, something about the intimacy of it, the implied empathy, as if they shared a common connection outside loss that might help them understand each other... His teeth clenched at the thought of it. Touchy feely hogwash, Jack. Get a grip!

My pain is my own. No one else's, he'd long believed. But other people had lost spouses or daughters. That gave them something in common, right? Could Hannah really understand how he'd been feeling? Abby had always been the empathetic one, the more compassionate. She made time to comfort and listen to friends with problems, whether on the phone or in person. She'd hug them, encourage them, and she'd pray for them. Jack loved this about her and had always wished he was better at it, but Abby seemed to have room in her heart to love everyone. Jack had always loved only a select few. Not that he didn't care about people. He just didn't emotionally invest in a lot of people. His circle was small, a few people, and he'd always been comfortable with that.

Once he'd calmed down, it occurred to him how irrational his reaction had been. No one had the same experience exactly, of course, but similar experiences certainly were possible, and perhaps there were things they had in common. He didn't want to know. His pain defined him—it was who he was now. He couldn't share his that way. Because that identity drove him to get up mornings and focus on figuring out why he was here—and why they weren't.

BREATHE! NEED AIR! Jack awoke in his bed to find Caroline sitting on his chest, grinning down at him. "Hi Daddy!"

His lungs sucked in air as he realized she'd jumped on him while he was asleep, causing his momentary distress. Once he caught his breath he yawned and smiled up at her. "Morning, baby girl. Daddy was asleep."

Caroline shot him one of those chastising female that made her resemble her mother. "It's time to get up. Mommy sent me."

Jack surrendered, transported by her Fruit Loop scented breath.

"Breakfast is waiting, come on!" said Caroline, sliding off him to stand on the floor, before she grabbed his hand and pulled as if she had the power of the gods.

Jack groaned, his breathing normalized again. "Coming, baby. Give daddy a second."

"It'll get cold."

"All right," he said, sitting up and throwing his legs over the side of the bed. "What's mommy making?"

"Pancakes."

"Mmm, Mommy's pancakes are the best," Jack said, licking his lips as the smell hit his nose. He could almost taste them. Caroline continued dragging him out the door, down the hall, where the house vanished. The shoreline oddly stretched a mile into the sea.

He awoke in the lighthouse to the thumping of waves on the shore while the songs of seabirds hunting for breakfast startled him awake. His mind tried to sort out which was reality. Rolling over, he felt robbed of sleep. He thought of sleeping longer, but then saw the clock on the bedside stand pointing straight down to six. He got up, scrambling to see Warren off.

Warren mastered breakfast like a firehouse chief. He'd fired up the griddle, mixing batter in a large yellow bowl. As Jack crossed the room from the stairs, Warren looked up and asked, "In the mood for pancakes?"

"No thanks."

"Don't tell me you're one of those food intolerants, all due respect? I have two speeds for breakfast—carbs and fats," Warren said.

"Sorry, just not in the mood, I guess," Jack said, opening the fridge to pull out a carton of eggs.

Warren shrugged. "Okay, I can freeze any leftovers in case you're in the mood later."

Warren was a generous host, and Jack didn't mean to be rude, but pancakes were a family thing, and escaping the overreaching attentiveness back home was part of why he'd moved here. Normalcy. He looked out the window to the east and saw waves rolling in under a train of clouds interposed against a blue sky. It looked like something right off a postcard or painting. "Do you ever get bored with the view?"

"No. That's one of the best things about living down here. That, and sunsets."

Jack wished he'd paid more attention the night before. "I'll have to start watching them better."

"Sure you don't want some?" Warren asked as he finished stirring and picked up a small cup, scooping several blobs of batter onto the griddle with a quarter inch separating them. "You sleep well?"

"Not long enough," Jack said, yawning.

"I hope you're feeling better," said Warren said.

Jack leaned against the kitchen island and sighed. "I'm sorry about the pancakes, and about last night. I really overreacted."

"Overreacted to what?" Warren asked.

"Hannah," Jack said. "She reminded me of something that has nothing to do with her."

"Something to do with your family?"

"Yeah," Jack admitted, not meeting his gaze.

Warren used a spatula to check the edges of the pancakes, then turned and put a hand on Jack's shoulder. "Cut yourself a break. I'm sure if you apologize, she'll be fine."

No "tell me more," or endless questions or anything. Warren just accepted it and turned back to tending the pancakes. Jack realized he could learn a lot from his new supervisor about more than just being a lighthouse keeper.

Jack cracked two eggs on the side of a skillet and watched the whites and yolk drop onto the surface. "Another advantage of working here is I can avoid those situations."

"And avoid people." Warren plated up the pancakes. "If you like your syrup warmed, you might get some out of the fridge. There's a small pitcher up in the cupboard Two minutes on high in the microwave should do it."

Jack puzzled a bit at the assumption he still wanted pancakes, but Warren flipped the pancakes and didn't look. As Jack went to the fridge to find the syrup, Warren continued, saying, "No one can avoid people altogether."

Jack pulled a bottle of Log Cabin syrup from the fridge and closed the door again.

"Yesterday was a long day," said Warren as he scooped the ready pancakes off the griddle and reached for more batter. "Makes a man hungry."

Jack located the syrup dispenser. "It's been a long time since anyone cooked for me."

"If you cook, we can take turns."

"My sister taught me some," Jack replied.

"Good. Except Sundays, of course, since you'll be out." Jack remembered Sunday was his day off. He'd expected another keeper, but it sounded like Warren would be filling in for him, and he liked it. Warren seemed like a pleasant person to have around if he had to deal with someone. He sniffed. His pancakes smelled delicious, too. Jack walked over and opened the fridge, sliding the skillet onto the top shelf.

"We're almost ready," Warren said. "Grab yourself something to drink and I'll meet you at the table."

THE DAY DIDN'T start well for Hannah. Almost as soon as she woke Sam up and stepped into the kitchen, Ellen started in on her again—about Sam's not talking and about Hannah's neglecting her responsibility, exemplified by her careless attitude about coming home several hours late from work. Hannah loved her mother-in-law. She'd done a lot for her. But sometimes she really wanted to strangle her.

Ignoring Ellen, who was busy pouring cereal into a bowl, Hannah prepared eggs and bacon for herself and Sam. To divert them off Ellen's morning path, she led him out to the patio table beside the pool to eat. Out here he might be open to working on his speech. Although it hadn't worked before, Hannah exercised diligent daily effort to induce him to speak. Her mother-in-law's method of threats and commands, never produced anything but tears from Sam. Hannah preferred a gentler approach.

She started by reading from one of Sam's favorite story books, The Little Prince, and asked questions in an attempt to illicit responses, sometimes pointing to illustrations, and so forth. He responded, smiling, when she used a small, hand-held dry erase board to use for writing answers, although no verbals. This morning, though, no luck. Sam spoke and interacted eagerly with school peers before Rob died, though, so she knew he was capable. And he'd suffered minimal injuries during the accident, the doctors said, so it wasn't brain damage or some physiological thing either.

Knowing him better than the doctors convinced her it was the trauma of watching his father die. Sam didn't speak because he was afraid, and when that feeling started to go away or healed, he'd speak again. She believed it with all her heart. And with a mother's dedication, she spent at least an hour every day working with him to encourage it.

Sam also saw a speech-language pathologist once a week, who coordinated with his pediatrician. Hannah had taken to repeating the SLP's treatment methods at home for the Selective Mutism—his diagnosis. The positive reinforcement goal associated non-stressful and rewarding experiences with the act of speech, slowly moving the child away from the association he or she had created with anxiety-inducing events and speech. To begin, specialists had taught Sam a series of gestures and hand signals as a substitute for basic speech, then worked with him on using the dry erase board and a mini-chalk board he carried with him in his backpack.

As Sam became more comfortable with communicating again, the SLP, pediatrician, and Hannah used whispering to encourage Sam to make soft sounds, making sure that any speaking to him they did was always calm and stress free. Both doctors also encouraged Hannah and Ellen to show Sam old home movies of him when he was speaking, revisiting pleasant, fun memories that reminded him of the association between speaking and those events.

They also employed role-play activities to aid in building his confidence, and Hannah had been given specific training in using these tools so that she could continue working with him at home. She'd tried to get Ellen involved, too, but her mother-in-law was impatient and felt Hannah and the doctors were coddling Sam, instead of pushing him to behave appropriately for a child his age. So the resulting frustration and conflict between Ellen and Hannah caused Hannah to mostly leave Ellen out of it. Thankfully, she cooperate enough to avoid yelling or loud speech in his presence, especially any directed at Sam himself.

When they finished The Little Prince, Hannah used gestures and hand signals to discuss the plan for their day—everything from reviewing her grocery list and asking if he wanted her to add anything to it to discussing his school schedule or other plans. Involving Sam in regular conversation, even if it wasn't verbal, was a key step to helping him overcome his anxiety and resume regular speech. Another big step would be getting him to engage in short conversations with strangers, but Sam was nowhere near ready for that yet, with the exception of his teachers and a few close school friend, who talked while he mostly listened.

As usual, Sam had a few requests for the grocery list. Some, typical of most seven-year-olds, Hannah shot down quickly but gently. Others she agreed to as possible rewards or special treats, and he even reminded her of a few items she'd forgotten on her last trip for which she praised him profusely, "This is why mommy wants to talk to you, because you're so helpful." This elicited a smile and a hug from Sam before they continued on with other matters.

"Captain Crunch!" Sam called again.

"You get enough sugar in other places," Hannah chided. "We don't need it in cereal too."

"But Luke's mom buys it, it's delicious," Sam whined.

"See? You get it at their house. You don't need it at home," Hannah said and added cereal to her shopping list.

"Oreos?" Sam asked plaintively, and she turned to find him leaning against the doorframe now, his eyes pleading up at her.

"As a special treat, maybe," she said with a sigh. "If you behave at the store and don't make yourself a pest."

God, how she missed such conversations with her son, Hannah thought, as she snapped back to Ellen's living room where Sam made a sign for "please," the word on the flash card she was holding up for him. She'd made a few of them for key words and phrases, so they could practice—anything to maintain some sort of communication. She regularly drilled him, just to make sure they both kept them in their minds. As always, when Ellen came in and saw this, she accused Hannah of coddling him.

"How can you expect him to speak if you let him off the

hook with sign language?"

"I want to talk to my son, Ellen," Hannah snapped. "Whatever form it has to take."

"You're just giving him an excuse!" Ellen replied, glaring. But Hannah had heard it so many times, her mother-in-law's attempts at guilting her were becoming ineffective.

After finishing the flash cards before noon, Hannah praised Sam for his hard work and sent him off to play, heading into the kitchen to double check her grocery coupons and fix lunch. Ellen came in the door ten minutes later.

"You're just now fixing lunch?" Ellen scolded. "The Harris' will be here in twenty minutes for Sam's playdate."

"What playdate?" Hannah asked, hoping she'd heard wrong. Tim Harris was one of Sam's best friends, besides being one of the few who remained willing to regularly tolerate playing with a mute companion. His mother, Judy, also fantastic with Sam, was one of Hannah's favorite people. Unfortunately, she had to work at five, planning to hit the grocery store right after lunch.

"Judy called yesterday," Ellen said. "I told her to drop Tim by. She has a women's group until three. You're not doing anything, right?"

Hannah tensed. Ellen habitually did this to her—springing appointments on her without asking first. "Actually, I have to be at work at five so I'm stopping by Publix ahead of work, which means I have to drop off my shopping first here. So can you take Sam shopping later? I have a list." She managed to keep her voice calm and sweet, hiding her inner turmoil.

Ellen shook her head. "I have to go deliver some orders in Key West. I'll be gone 'til six."

"But my schedule's on the fridge," Hannah said, her voice rising, no longer hiding her anger.

"Don't yell at me, young lady," Ellen said, using her jewelry business as leverage. "I forgot to check. I'm sorry, but Mrs. Watkins has to leave tomorrow to see her grandkids; that's why

101

she wants some of my jewelry as gifts. I'll try and postpone my last two deliveries and come back by five, but I won't be able to grocery shop for you."

Hannah bit off another smart retort, keeping her voice even. Ellen could certainly find time to help out more. She just didn't want to. "What about tonight? They're open 'til nine." Her mother-in-law going along in the car would actually help a lot. Hannah could only carry so many bags on a bike, even with the baskets she'd added to the back.

"You know how I feel about driving at night." Ellen had been scared to death of night driving ever since her childhood best friend Grace had a near fatal accident on the Overseas Highway, especially since she, like Grace, now had to wear bifocals. "I don't trust my eyes," she repeated for the umpteenth time. Personally, Hannah thought she was fine, but it was not worth an argument. They had plenty already.

Hannah growled. "Fine. I'll figure it out."

Ellen scowled and threw up her hands. "Call Judy. She's your friend. Me doing you a favor and this is the thanks I get." And with that she disappeared down the hall toward her room.

So Hannah went into triage mode, calling for Sam to come eat, even as she scrambled to change her menu plans, popping two pepperoni Hot Pockets in the microwave for a quick lunch. Judy dropped Tim off just as the finished and the boys immediately hurried into the living room to play, while Hannah explained her dilemma. Judy promised to leave her group a bit early and be back just after three, leaving Hannah forty-five minutes to run to Publix with Sam before heading for the diner. Tim and Sam had a great time together as usual, playing almost the entire two hours nonstop, despite the fact Sam had missed his usual nap.

They rode their bikes together the few blocks down to the supermarket, parking and locking them in the coin racks out front. She handed Sam a list and headed with a cart for the aisles.

CHAPTER 9

AFTER BREAKFAST, JACK and Warren went down to the radio room to check the computer for messages. The day organized for Jack, Warren said his goodbyes and headed for the pier, leaving Jack to begin his first day of duties alone at the lighthouse. Ironically, it was Sunday, which would typically be his day off, but because Warren had spent almost a week training him, he was on his own for a whole week before he'd have a day off. No problem. He'd treat the day like any other workday.

First, he climbed up to the cupola. Best to check the lamp to make sure everything was operating properly and the settings correct. After, a second wind motivated him to change into work clothes and gloves, dropping by the shed to retrieve the cart. Before leaving the lighthouse yard, he loaded the cart with tools, nails, and several stacks of replacement wood. Warren had taken the initiative to order them in advance of his arrival from a nearby lumber mill. The fence line project had the most appeal and urgent need—he'd been designing and building things for fifteen years as an architect and as a kid on the farm he'd worked on plenty of fences—so it seemed the logical place to start. It demanded a tedious list of tasks Warren had shown him during their tour.

He spent four hours repairing a section of fence along the beach on the far side of the island before taking a break and heading back to the lighthouse for lunch. He parked the cart in the shed for safekeeping, his stomach growling like a beast. Returning back to the mess quarters, the fridge was still mostly bare, except for Warren's leftover pancakes in the freezer. They warmed up fine for a quick lunch. And he also cooked the eggs he'd left in the skillet. A full lunch would give him the energy needed for a busy afternoon.

Sitting alone at the table, he watched birds foraging in the sand and brush and crabs frolicking on the beach and thought about a trip to town. The truth was, as much as he'd enjoyed the morning's isolation, he needed supplies. Food, especially. Of course, the diner loomed across from the supermarket. He needed time to prepare what to say to Hannah. No point rushing into it.

He deliberated on it for a bit, then decided on a plan. He'd arrange a way to get his groceries back to the jetty boat. Maybe take an Uber or ask Bert to drive him, planning to shop and return right away to the island. He went down to the radio room to check the computer for any Coast Guard messages about the weather or other issues. Found the phone book. He had to call Bert to summon him anyway. He flipped through the phone book, found the number, then dialed him up.

Bert met him at the pier around three-thirty, saying he had an hour free. Having also suggested that the Publix would be less crowded between mid-day and evening rush, they headed off. Jack rode beside Bert in the enclosed cabin's spare seat. The pier was empty, so they parked the jetty boat after the ten minute ride and tied it to the dock, then headed for the parking lot together. Five minutes later, they headed into the Publix where Jack grabbed a cart and set about navigating the aisles while Bert headed to the sandwich shop to pick up early dinner.

The supermarket was mildly busy with customers spread out throughout the aisles. Bert had been right about the timing. Jack could get what he needed and avoid chit-chat, like back home where everyone knew him.. He immediately relaxed and grabbed a cart, making his way through the bakery and produce sections, picking out items as he went. Through overhead speakers, Heart's "Alone" came on, and his mind flashed back to his younger days. It would always remind him of meeting Abby. Even though their tastes had become more sophisticated over time, the ballad of yearning for that special someone and not knowing how to tell them had been something they both related to—young, attracted to each other, but nervous and not sure how to make the first move. Plus it was catchy and had great crunch guitars. Jack fought the urge to sing and do air guitar as he rolled his cart on through the aisles.

The faint smell of coffee and baked goods teased his nose as he glanced around. He grabbed a couple handfuls of Twinkies and Hostess Cupcakes from a sale rack, realizing after how Caroline had loved them. He'd loved them himself as a kid. A grown man could enjoy Twinkies and cupcakes, especially on an isolated island where no one was there to see it. He moved on to the frozen meats, deciding on the ground turkey, boneless chicken breast, some bacon, remembering he needed canned goods and pasta. He found those aisles before heading for the eggs.

As he rounded the corner, a young boy a few years younger than Caroline, similar reddish blonde hair, stood in front of an open egg carton, picking up the eggs carefully one at a time and examining them before putting them back. It evoked a memory.

"This one's good, daddy," Caroline would say in her best adult voice as she did the same thing at the store sometimes, imitating her mother. She'd check each one delicately, then purse her lips and nod at him as if signing off in approval while playing adult.

Jack knew to take that carton and put it in the basket, even though he double checked it later to make sure she hadn't missed anything. "Thank you, baby," he'd say. "You're so good at this, like your mom."

Caroline always lit up when he acknowledged her. She melted his heart.

Overhead, an announcement about free samples at the deli

came over the intercom. A few shoppers hurried past with carts, clearly headed for the samples. Then the boy glanced up and saw Jack watching and set the last egg back, quickly closing the egg carton but struggling with the foam latch.

"Looks like you picked a good one, buddy," Jack said and smiled, hoping to put the boy at ease. "Your mom will be pleased."

The boy finally got the latch closed, double checking to make sure the carton was sealed, then picked it up and glanced at Jack.

"My wife never trusted me with eggs," Jack said, remembering. "I was always in too much of a hurry to check them carefully. Your mom's lucky to have you." All it took was one carton with two broken eggs for Abby to make sure she was the one buying the eggs from then on. Thankfully, Caroline had always been better at it—one reason Jack tried to always take his daughter along when he did the shopping.

The boy watched Jack, perhaps assessing if he was friendly, then smiled and nodded.

"You wanna pick some for me?" Jack asked the boy.

The boy stood silent a moment, their eyes meeting then held out the eggs he'd already picked.

"Those are for your mom. I wouldn't want to take those," Jack said.

The boy shrugged, walked over, and held them out to Jack.

"Are you sure?"

The boy nodded.

Jack accepted them. "Thank you."

Without a word, the boy turned back, selected another carton, and started inspecting the eggs again.

Jack put the eggs in his cart and watched him. "My name's Jack. What's yours?"

The boy didn't answer, and Jack wrote it off as shyness, but then the boy started scanning the shelves until he saw something that caught his attention. He set the egg he'd been inspecting back in its slot, walked over, and pointed at a container of cottage cheese that read: "Sam's Best."

Jack shook his head. "Thanks, but I don't like cottage cheese."

The boy smiled and shook his head, then reached out and ran his finger along the word Sam, underlining it.

"Oh, is Sam your name?"

The boy nodded.

"But you don't talk to strangers, right?"

Another nod.

"Well, you're pretty good at getting your point across anyway, bud."

The boy spotted something in Jack's cart and walked closer pointing.

"Twinkies? Yeah. You like those?"

The boy wasn't giving him more than a nod.

"Well, I'd give you one but maybe you should ask your mom first."

Then he heard a female voice. "Sam? Where are you?"

Sam glanced in the direction of the voice and went back to inspecting the second carton of eggs.

"Sounds like your mom's looking for you."

Sam hurriedly finished his task.

When a cart appeared rounding the corner, Jack recognized the redhead pushing it. Hannah! For a moment, he considered turning to make his escape. Then he felt the warm surge inside, same as before. Despite what happened, she still had the same effect on him.

"Sam?" she said looking at Jack and her son with a stunned look. She looked as pretty as she had the night before at the lighthouse, only there was a coldness in her eyes as she looked at him almost as if she wasn't seeing him at all, as if they were strangers. He could only guess why.

"He was helping me pick out eggs," said Jack, hoping some humor would ease the tension.

Hannah looked at him then shot a questioning look at her son. "Is that right?" Sam nodded and she looked surprised. "I was wondering what was taking so long."

"He's very meticulous," Jack added, then to Sam, "Thanks, pal. I appreciate the expertise. It's my first time shopping alone in a while." It wasn't far from the truth. Abby had always done the shopping, and since the accident, both Josie and his mother had been making sure his fridge was kept full, so he'd rarely had to go alone.

Sam smiled and looked at his mom before he closed the second carton to set it gently in the cart before walking toward Jack's cart. That's when he pointed at the Twinkies.

"Sam, we have to get going or mama will be late for work," said Hannah said, still standing on the opposite end of the egg case, a safe distance. As if she didn't want to come any closer.

Sam shook his and kept pointing at the Twinkies.

Jack ran interference for Sam. "This is on me. He told me he liked Twinkies and I told him he could have one if his mother said it was okay."

Hannah frowned, softening a bit as she looked at Jack again. "Did he really pick out eggs for you?"

"He sure did," Jack said, lifting the eggs Sam had given him. Thankfully, Sam backed him up with a nod. Actually, the boy was picking them for her but he spared her the details, still expecting her to cut him off any second, recognizing him.

Hannah grunted. "Wow! Well, I guess that much effort deserves a reward."

Sam smiled, pleased. Jack bent over to open the Twinkies, pulling one carefully from the carton; he handed it to Sam, who grabbed it and unwrapped it lightning fast before, unceremoniously popping it into his mouth.

"Sam!" Hannah was too late to stop Sam's runaway Twinkie grab. "He always eats so fast, no matter how many times I tell him to slow down."

"Busy guy, lots to get done," Jack joked.

Sam's wide eyes and big smile denoted great pleasure, enjoying his snack. Jack was pretty sure that if the boy were left unattended there wouldn't be enough of it left for anyone to notice.

Hannah glanced at a camera overhead, part of the store's anti-shoplifting system. "I hope they don't give you any trouble at checkout."

"I'll be fine, I promise," Jack said, then added, "I can always show my Coast Guard ID, right? 'Official business.'"

He could tell she tried to resist but that brought a chuckle. "You government guys and your secret tools. Okay, thanks," she said then looked at Sam. "We gotta go."

Jack felt an urge to apologize right then but he probably shouldn't say anything in front of her son. And he didn't want to risk ruining their nice moment. Finally, he managed, "Good luck with your shopping," while waving at Sam. "Thanks, buddy. Nice to meet you."

Sam handed his mother the empty wrapper and smiled at him. He took his mother's hand the same way Caroline would take his, following her out. The pair left the store.

As he passed the spot where Hannah had manned her cart, his nose caught a familiar trace of jasmine. Her face stayed with him longer than the cologne, causing his skin to prickle. He'd go and look for her at the diner later. If nothing else, he had to make it right... if he could.

HANNAH COULDN'T BELIEVE it. It was something that hadn't happened since his father died. Something she'd never expected to see for a while to come. Yet there they were, right in the aisle of Publix.

At first, she'd just been amazed to see them interacting comfortably, but then Jack revealed Sam had actually chosen eggs for him, leaving Hannah so overcome, she hadn't known what to say. It lasted just a moment but the emotions strobed through her heart like crashing waves. She was so happy, she almost wished she could see it again, but it was Jack, and she couldn't afford to start a discussion she couldn't finish it in front of her son. Besides, she was too overjoyed by her son behaving almost normally with someone he'd never met.

When Jack offered Sam a reward, she gladly agreed, even though he'd already had snacks earlier with Tim, and then he joined her and she turned and finished her shopping without any attempt to talk further with Jack.

She caught another glimpse of him in line at the checkout stand ten minutes later when she and Sam were unloading the items from her cart and carefully packing them in the large baskets she'd had installed on the back of her bike. But though he glanced their way, he didn't wave or make any attempt to approach, and as soon as they'd finished, she hurried home.

She and Sam unloaded and put away the groceries just in time for her to hand him off to a just arriving Ellen and head back to the diner for her shift. The whole ride she kept playing over and over Sam's encounter with Jack at the store. She really wished she'd seen more of it, but what little she had seen blew her mind. Somehow Jack had connected with her son in a way no stranger had since his father died.

It might not be that big deal to most people but to Hannah it was the first spark of life that gave her hope there really was light at the end of the tunnel with her baby. That all her hard work and stress and prayers and dedication to breaking through her son's mutism wasn't in vain. That it could really pay off some day. In fact, it already was. For her, it was the first indication that she might get the life back she'd lost on that terrible day—the accident.

And for the first time, in a long while, she realized how much she wanted her life back.

CHAPTER 10

O N THE TRIP back to Cristof's Key, Jack joined Bert in the cabin. He kept thinking about seeing Hannah leaving the grocery store on her bike. "Is it common in the Keys for people to ride their bikes around to grocery shop and other errands?" he asked.

"Depends on the person," Bert said. "Lots of outdoor lovers drawn here, for obvious reasons." He looked out to sea, and Jack did the same. Around them, fishing vessels, large and small, worked the waters, gathering the day's catch, while a few teenagers surfed the late afternoon waves along the nearby shore. In the distance, a pod of porpoises played beneath the horizon.

Jack took in Hannah's biking transportation before adding, "It seems like the highway has a lot of traffic, beings how everything is so spread out. I mean, that it wouldn't it be time consuming and dangerous?"

Bert chuckled. "Going out anywhere these days is dangerous. Anyway, Hannah lives a few blocks from the store, and since her car's in the shop, she has no choice these days."

"Her car's in the shop?"

"Yeah, dropped its tranny," Bert said. "Real bad luck, too. On her salary, may take a while to replace it." Bert turned the boat along an arc as he guided her along the route to the island.

"Did you find someone to look after your car yet?"

"No, but I'm paid up to park at the hotel through the weekend," Jack said, "so I've got a little time left."

"Offers still good at my place." Bert had offered to park it on the street outside his house but his drive was full of vehicles between himself, his wife, and two teenagers. Jack's 2012 Jeep Cherokee was hardly brand new, but he'd kept it in tip-top shape. He hated to chance having it hit while parked out on the street for long periods.

"I appreciated that. I may still take you up on it," Jack said.

"What do you think of giving the station wagon to the church?" Abby had asked one Saturday after they'd visited a car dealer looking for an upgrade.

Jack's brow had furrowed as he considered it. "Rather than trading it in?"

"The IRS will give you a tax write-off, won't they?"

"I think the trade in value might be higher than that," Jack had said.

Abby had smiled and tousled his hair. "Remember that new family, the Johnsons, who joined the church last month? Pastor Jim told me the father hasn't worked in six months," Abby went on as he pulled a Coors from the fridge and popped the tab. "They moved here for a fresh start. They lost their house, their car, and they're in an apartment."

Salina wasn't huge but there was no such thing as public transportation and unless you had funds for Ubers or one of the few taxis, a car was a necessity. The Johnsons certainly sounded like they didn't have money for that. "What does this have to do with giving the station wagon to the church?" Jack asked as he finished another long drag from his beer.

Abby sighed. "The church can give them the car." She nudged his arm. "Bob is too proud for charity. Pastor Jim already tried, but if the car was donated and the church didn't need it..."

That was vintage Abby. She had a heart of gold, and never missed a chance to help others in need, no matter what the sacrifice entailed. Jack felt humbled just knowing her. It wasn't that Jack wasn't generous or caring. Abby just had different instincts and spent more time focused on serving others. She'd been a good influence on him, for sure. Even though Jack hadn't donated the car at the time, he'd never forgotten the look of disappointment on Abby's face—almost like the looks Caroline gave him when he missed one of her recitals or a school play.

As the jetty boat slowed and pulled up alongside the island pier with a thump, Jack remembered what Josie had said, "A grand gesture, that's what this calls for." Hannah needed a car. He needed somewhere to store his car and someone to look after it. He'd only need it from time to time, maybe once a month at most, to run errands or for an emergency with family, and he didn't expect any of those. So most of the time he knew it would just sit. He wanted someone to not only watch over it, but wash and drive it from time to time, just to keep it in decent condition. He'd keep up the insurance and offer them money for any maintenance, even an occasional tank of gas in return.

"An apology ain't gonna cut it, bro," Josie had said. After seeing Hannah and meeting her son at the Publix, Jack wanted to more to make up for his bad behavior than a simple apology. She had a great kid who apparently had some sort of issue, probably a cause of stress and concern, so he wanted to do something to help make life easier. It wasn't like he needed the car right now. And he could always call her and arrange to use it when he did.

"Jack?" Bert said, "This is your stop."

"Sorry." He followed the captain out of the cabin to the boarding gate, which Bert swung open. Jack stepped over the side onto the pier as Bert began handing him grocery bags, which Jack promptly loaded into the waiting lighthouse cart parked nearby.

As they did, Jack considered another dilemma. Would she

even accept it? Jack's parents had been raised in a community where people helped each other when someone had a need. His grandparents had served as missionaries in Africa, in fact, and his mother had been born in Ghana. Service to others was a family way of life, and so was sharing good fortune. So coming up with the idea didn't feel odd to his mind. But Hannah might feel differently, and so he began pondering how he might convince her.

She knew he was new to the area and knew almost no one, and anyone he did know he knew as well or less as he knew her, in fact. So whoever he left his car with, unless he spent the extra and rented a locked garage at a storage place and left the car there, he'd be trusting a stranger. He'd considered the locked garage. He'd also considered selling the car. Both ideas assumed he'd never need it, and he wasn't so sure about that. Putting it in storage also would demand he regularly visit and check on the car, run the engine, do maintenance when necessary, and so forth. You couldn't just let a car sit unused for months or years without serious problems. The fact was it was better for the car to be driven regularly, and that scenario was what Jack preferred.

Why not trust Hannah? She was the kind of person who'd go to the trouble to pack a meal and take it to some remote island to show kindness to strangers, after all. Plus, she was a single mom with a disabled child. Surely that made it more likely she was more responsible than most. If nothing else, she had no choice. And a car was made to be used, after all. So who better to keep it than someone who really needed one and can use it, rather than some strangers who had plenty of cars and would have to go out of their way to drive and care for it?

They finished unloading the groceries in a few minutes and Bert bid him goodbye as he set to work pulling the jetty boat back out onto the water and retracing his route to the main island again.

The more Jack thought about it, the more Hannah seemed like the perfect recipient for loaning his car. At least, he was convinced of it. But how would he convince her? Good. For the rest of the night, as he returned to the lighthouse and ate and went about his evening routine, that question consumed his thoughts.

HANNAH WAS OUT mowing the backyard in late morning, while Sam played happily alone in the sandbox at the back of the yard. The cool sky overhead was dotted with wispy clouds. Robins and starlings sang from the bright green trees. They'd spent a couple hours after breakfast working on Sam's therapy exercises. Her phone reminder pinged, prompting Sam's appointment with his Speech Language Pathologist. Hannah was excited to tell her about Sam's encounter with Jack.

She couldn't get it out of her mind. Most of all, she craved a few more details about all that went on between her son and Jack. She didn't suspect anything wrong; on the contrary, everything was so right. That had nothing to do with Jack really. Sam interacting with anyone he didn't know was huge progress, but what made it most exciting was that instead of being nervous and reticent, Sam had seemed totally relaxed, as if he actually enjoyed Jack's company.

It still amazed her just thinking about it. Was it the familiarity of the supermarket and the task that made it so easy for Sam? After all, he had gone there with her for years and been picking out the eggs for her for almost two. Or was it something Jack had said or done that made Sam so comfortable? Jack certainly hadn't put her immediately at ease when she met him at the diner, and the dinner had been pleasant but awkward until he snapped.

For a moment, she had a horrible thought as images from news stories and television flashed through her mind. Was Jack some kind of pedophile? They supposedly had special talents at putting children at ease. No! The thought was absurd, and she dismissed it almost as quickly as it came. Jack had been almost four feet away from Sam the entire time she watched them

117

interact. He'd made zero move to approach her son. Obviously, if Sam had picked out the eggs for him there had been some contact, but it must have been innocent. Otherwise, Sam would never have been so at ease with him.

So what was it about Jack? He'd mentioned his wife had died. Did he have kids or was he just good with them? There were people like that she knew. Kid-charisma, her friend Judy called it. Literally people kids were just drawn to. She'd had a friend like in high school. He worked at the supermarket bagging and had told her of times when stranger's kids would just walk up and take his hand or hug him. The mother had come and saw them and thought it was cute. Back then was a different time though. Now, if that happened, the parent would be far more suspicious, of course. Maybe Jack was one of those types of people kids liked.

What did it matter? Sam had made a big step of progress. That was what counted. And none of the questions flashing through her head lessened her excitement and enthusiasm about it.

So caught up was she in her joy in pondering Sam's progress, it was several minutes before she realized Sam was gone. The last time she'd noticed, he'd been quietly driving his trucks through the sandbox but now she looked up and he'd disappeared.

"Sam?" she called, stopping the mower and glancing around her. The smell of fresh cut grass, oil and gasoline, pollen and sea air filled her nose as she did. There was no sign of Sam in the yard. Had she been so distracted she hadn't seen him run inside to use the bathroom perhaps?

"Sam?" she called his name again, letting the mower's engine die as she released the handlebars and walked the sandbox nested in the corner of the fence opposite the shed. Not too fast but not too slow. Breathe. She squeezed her eyes shut, clenching and unclenching her fists. She wasn't panicking yet, but she was definitely concerned.

As she reached the sandbox, she noticed the back gate

cracked open more than usual. It shouldn't be. The latch had been broken for over a year and she hadn't gotten around to hiring some to fix it; why it always hung slightly open. Now that she thought of it, it hadn't been open this far when she'd taken the mower out of the shed an hour before. She hurried toward the fence and glanced out in the alley. Sam knew he wasn't supposed to leave the yard alone, especially not into the street or alley.

She pulled the gate wider and stepped out to the edge of the alley and there he sat—across the alley atop a pile of bricks, beams, and lumber scraps from the neighbor's construction, still driving his trucks as if nothing had changed.

"Sam," she scolded gently. "You need to get down from there. It could be dangerous. You know you're not supposed to leave the yard."

Sam looked up at the sound of her voice and smiled, waving happily.

She shook her head. "Come on. And be careful climbing down, okay? There could be nails and who knows what." She hadn't seen any as she scanned the pile but that didn't mean they weren't there. The childhood experience of seeing a friend who'd run a nail through her foot once on a similar pile flashed through her mind and made her shudder.

Sam made a disappointed face then turned and gathered his trucks before starting to climb down. He wobbled as he went, worrying. How on earth had he gotten up there? The pile was uneven with lots of holes and tilted sections.

"Do you want me to help you?" she asked, starting forward with a worried look.

Sam waved a hand dismissively, like his Grandma did, but as he did, he took a big step, trying to semi-leap over a particularly deep hole in the pile. For a moment, she thought he'd make it. His foot touched the tip at the other side, but then it slipped, and he was falling. Hannah ran fast to try and catch him.

She got there as his foot sank down into the pile, making

119

him cry out in pain, wincing, scattering his toys in every direction. and dropping his toys. "Oh my God, honey, are you okay? Don't move!"

He wiggled a little before wincing, looking up at her as tears poured down his cheeks.

As Hannah closed in, he stood with his right foot angled on its side slightly in the hole, his other foot still stretched out onto the pile above, his knee bent as his hands tried frantically to pull himself off the injured limb.

"Hang on, I'll help you, honey," she said, climbing carefully toward him, watching her every step.

As she reached him, she looked him over quickly with a mother's eye, seeing no immediate signs of any other injuries, not even cuts or bruises. "Okay," she said. "I think you're okay. Mommy's gonna lift you."

Sam nodded then pointed to his trucks.

"I'll get those in a minute. You first," she replied.

He gave another nod and stayed still as she bent and reached down, grabbing him by the waist, and pulled him up toward her. She lifted him out of the hole and swung him around beside her to a safe spot before gently setting him down, but the moment his right foot made contact, he cried out again and grabbed her, leaning in and lifting the foot off the ground.

"Oh no, does your foot hurt?" she asked, worried again.

He nodded.

"Okay, let me help you down, hang on." She carefully repositioned herself and then lifted him again, swinging him down, repeating it a couple times before they were both in the alley. Sam leaned against her and pointed toward his trucks.

"I know, honey, but let mama see that foot first," she said as she knelt beside him and reached for his right leg.

Gingerly, he raised it and let her examine it, wincing when she lifted his pant leg and pulled at his sock.

"Sorry, baby, I just want to see your ankle a bit," she said, trying to sooth him.

The ankle was swollen, the skin was bruised. It didn't show a puncture or any damage otherwise. It definitely didn't look right, though. She slowly put the sock back and let her eyes meet his again. Stay calm. Don't make him panic.

"We need to get you to the doctor," she said, realizing doctors brought up other issues. "Grandma's got the car so we have to figure out what to do. I'm going to carry you inside."

His eyes widened in panic as he motioned toward his trucks again.

"Sam, you first, then the trucks," Hannah said with gentle reproach. "Mama needs to know you're safe."

Sam sighed and nodded as tears streamed down his cheeks, more from the pain in his ankle than worry over his toys, Hannah felt certain.

Bending her knees, she swept him up gently into her arms with one arm across his back and the other across his thighs and said, "Hold on to me, baby." Then carried him through the open gate, across the yard, and into the house where she gently set him on a sofa. "Just keep weight off that leg. I'll be right back."

Pulling out her cell and hurriedly dialing her mother, she headed back out to the neighbor's construction pile to retrieve his toy trucks. As she made her way toward the gate, Ellen answered.

"Where are you?" Hannah demanded.

"That's how you talk to me? Where are your manners?" Her mother-in-law scolded immediately.

"I have to take Sam to the hospital, mother!" Hannah said, raising her voice to be heard over her mother's whining.

Ellen stopped talking in stunned silence. "What happened?"

"It's his ankle," Hannah said, "I think it's broken?"

121

"How did that happen?" Ellen demanded in a tone that was filled with blame.

"He was playing somewhere he shouldn't," Hannah explained. "I was mowing the lawn. Where are you?"

"I'm..." Ellen paused before continuing, "I'm in Plantation on my way back from a delivery."

"Well, we'll be waiting," Hannah said as she slipped through the gate and approached the construction pile, looking for the trucks.

"Maybe you should call an ambulance," Ellen suggested.

Hannah had briefly considered it, but she had good reasons for wanting to avoid it. "It will use up my deductible for the year," she said. "How will I pay for his therapy?" With the Affordable Care Act, her deductible was still $3000 a year even on a subsidized plan. But she'd already used several hundred on doctor bills for Sam. And what she had left from life insurance and death benefits could help a little, but that was also her escape plan. God, Hannah, it's your son having a medical crisis. Why are you making worried about money at a time like this?

"All right, I'm coming," Ellen said with urgency and hung up.

To quiet and calm her son, Hannah spotted the trucks and carefully climbed the pile to retrieve them.

"Hurry!" she whispered.

CHAPTER 11

ELLEN DROVE THEM to the Emergency Room at Mariners Hospital in Tavernier. Altogether, they'd been there for three hours, not including the thirty minute drive each way. Once the nurse had removed his shoe and sock, Hannah noticed several scratches on the surface of his skin in several areas, and after examining him and taking an x-ray, the doctor confirmed Sam had fractured his tibia.

"You're lucky he didn't break the fibula as well or even puncture the artery in his foot," the doctor, whose name was Blake Warner, explained. "We see that kind of thing happen. But this is minor as such injuries go." He patted Sam on the head and smiled. "Congratulations, kiddo. Your first broken bone. It's a rite of passage, but you'll be fine, I promise."

Hannah saw no reason to smile, and the mention of the artery in particular had alarmed Hannah. What if it had been worse? How long might an ambulance have taken to get there? Could he have bled to death? Been permanently disabled with a limp? All the worst case scenarios she could imagine filled her head, and she realized that from now on, until she got the car fixed, she would worry about such possibilities. The thought disturbed her.

As it was, Doctor Warner reset the bone and put Sam in a temporary splint for two days until he examined him again. He explained to Hannah and Ellen that Sam would have to use crutches or stay off his foot for at least a week, until he was ready for a walking boot. Hannah knew this would cause problems. Despite his mutism, Sam was an active child, not prone to lying around all day, and either she or Ellen would have to watch him carefully to ensure he obeyed the doctor and didn't injure it further. Not that the pain wouldn't serve as a good deterrent, of course, but she wasn't taking any chances.

Lou, as always, was great about rearranging her schedule. She and Ellen had been trading off watching Sam anyway ever since she'd started waitressing, but Hannah wanted to be home the first couple days until Sam called the doctor again. Call it an abundance of caution or an overprotective mother. She was probably being both, but this was her baby, and he'd broken a bone. It was something she'd always prayed would never happen to Sam, and that it had happened while she was supposed to be watching him was something she'd never forgive herself for.

Doctor Warner explained the healing process and applied a new splint and a full cast, urging Hannah to help Sam learn to walk on crutches.

"Some people take to it right away, others struggle," Doctor Warner said. "Depends how determined he is." He smiled and eyed Sam who was lying on the table looking up at them both. "This guy strikes me as the determined type." He patted Sam on the shoulder. "But you listen to your mom and grandma and let it heal, okay, pal?"

Sam nodded.

"In another week or so, we can get you into a walking boot," the doctor continued and added, "that'll make things easier." Sam nodded again and the doctor lifted him down off the table as Hannah held the crutches ready to go under each arm.

"Give 'em a try, okay?" Doctor Warner said. The first two days, Sam had only used the crutches a couple times when he needed to use the bathroom and struggled, becoming easily frustrated. Hannah had decided to forgo them and carried him at least twice. The doctor looked at her. "No more carrying him. He needs to do this."

"Okay," she agreed, hoping she had the strength. She was so wracked with guilt over what had happened that she found it hard to let him suffer or struggle with any of it.

"He'll be fine," the doctor assured her and sent them on their way.

Ellen, on the other hand, was determined to get him up and about as quickly as possible and, despite Hannah's warnings to "take it easy with him," spent time working with him on the crutches the next day when Hannah was at work. In her heart, she just wanted to stay home and nurse her son but extra days off just meant that much longer before her car could be repaired and the whole incident had given that need a whole new urgency. By the time she came home, Sam was getting around pretty well and proudly demonstrated.

"He's fine, Hannah," Ellen said. "This is better for him. Good exercise."

Ellen and Sam hunted shells outside on the beach, despite Hannah's worries about the sand and his crutches. When they walked in, Ellen carried a pail of shells for Sam.

"He did fine," Ellen insisted. "Moving slow. Stopping and sitting down to pick out shells when he found a good spot. I made sure to watch and help."

Sam gave her two big thumbs up, marshaling the crutches. His face showed his pride in the baskets Ellen brought inside, setting them on the table where she picked out their booth.

"That's great," Hannah said, glad to see Sam so happy again.

Lou interrupted. "Wow, look at that cast, big guy! Bet that has quite a story behind it," her boss said, smiling as he came over to join them.

Sam grinned and nodded as Lou examined his cast.

Lou made a face. "Darn. Thought I could trick him into

telling me."

Hannah laughed. "He's too smart for that one, Lou."

"Maybe I should just sign his cast, then," Lou said and looked at Sam again. "Want me to sign it?" He was the first one who'd asked, and from Sam's response, it was obvious the idea had never occurred to him. His whole body showed his excitement.

Lou motioned. "Okay, you sit down on that bench there while I go get a pen." And he disappeared into the kitchen. Soon, Denise and Janice and several regulars were all waiting their turn, and Sam was reveling in their attention. Seeing her son was well attended, Hannah went back to work delivering orders to her tables, so it wasn't until Jack spoke that Hannah even noticed him.

JACK HADN'T MEANT to wait four days to talk with Hannah, but he'd been caught up with cleaning mildew out of the lighthouse shed—a task which seemed to become more and more endless, the longer he spent on it. Then the lighthouse radio went down, so that became a priority. Thankfully, Warren had gone over basic radio repair. It was Saturday night before he felt he could afford the time to take a quick trip over to Islamorada. He not only needed a break from the lighthouse but a break from his own cooking.

He spent the day finishing work across the island cutting down branches off some large trees that had been damaged in storms, then called and arranged for Bert to pick him up about six.

He arrived at the diner twenty minutes later. Steaks, burgers and fried pies danced in grease vats, hidden from the counter back in Lou's kitchen. The potent smells tickled his appetite; even the fact he and Abby had avoided greasy food in the past didn't prevent him from craving it. A waitress not Hannah pointed him to a booth that he took, although keeping an eye out for her. Instead, the boy, Sam, held court. Hannah's son sat with some kind of cast on his leg propped up on a booth bench. Locals crowded around him, pens up. It was a cast-signing party, of all things. Sam seemed to be loving it, and other than the cast, showed no evidence of other injuries. But what had happened in the week since he'd run into them at the grocers, he had no idea.

Then he saw her. Hannah carried an order to a table across the way. Though she was smiling, it looked forced, her eyes worried and tired. There was an older woman sitting in the booth next to Sam who kept staring at him with narrowed eyes. Maybe his grandmother or Hannah's aunt? She watched Hannah appear for a second, but turned her eyes back on Sam.

Jack took a leap of chance and got up. He moved to the counter, closer to where she refilled customers' drinks.

Hannah crossed the room to acknowledge her seated customers; she returned toward the counter again, but still hadn't seen him, so he stepped forward. As she crossed in front of him, he asked, "What happened to the boy?"

Hannah turned, startled to see him.

"Hi," he said, smiling.

"Please seat yourself," she said avoiding his eyes, her voice as tired as she looked, "I'll bring you a menu."

Jack stayed where he was, taking a wobbly stool. He asked, "What happened to Sam?" He hoped beyond hope he showed concern instead of sounding nosey.

Hannah went to work behind the counter, pouring some drinks as Jack found a seat on one of the round stools lining the other side.

"He was playing where he shouldn't have and he broke his leg," she said.

"Ouch," said Jack said. He'd done the same once or twice as a boy. "I'm sorry." He meant it, but she didn't seem to notice.

"It happens," she said as she put several glasses she'd filled with water and soda on a tray and reached for some napkins and bundles of silverware.

Jack watched her silently for a moment, her coldness stinging more than he expected. He glanced over to see the older woman still staring and looking downright pissed at him. Since they'd never met, Jack assumed Hannah must have told her about him. Well, then he'd come just in time. Turning back to Hannah, he said, "I owe you an apology. I'm sorry it took so long to get here and deliver it."

"For what?" she asked as she picked up the tray and headed out from behind the counter to deliver the drinks.

He'd crossed a sound to get here. He couldn't let it go. A few minutes later, when she came back, he said, "For how I behaved at dinner. It had nothing to do with you. I treated you very unfairly and rudely, and I'm sorry. I've been ashamed of myself ever since."

"I shouldn't have stayed," Hannah said as she went to work wiping the counter. "I mean, I wasn't invited, right?"

"You were invited," said Jack said. "You brought us plenty of food." He waited a moment until she raised the rag and looked up, then his eyes held hers. It was the first time he realized the amount she brought might have been intentional. "I'm sorry. I mean it. I haven't done that since my wife died."

"Done what? Been rude to a woman?" asked Hannah asked.

"No. Had dinner alone with a beautiful woman," said Jack replied.

Hannah softened a bit, then looked away. "It wasn't a date or anything."

"I know, but I—" Jack hesitated, choosing his words, "I wasn't ready."

"Well, sorry if I pushed you." She slid a menu in front of him before she started wiping another area of the counter.

Lou centered himself in the cook's window looking at her.

Jack picked up the menu to appease him if he were getting ideas. "You didn't," he said. "None of it was your fault. You did a really nice thing, and I'm sorry that I took my guilt out on you."

At that, Hannah looked at him again, her eyes narrowed, searching his. "Guilt for what?"

"Never mind," he said, looking quickly away.

Her eyes stayed on him as she abandoned the rag and moved along the counter, closer to him, and Jack caught the scent of jasmine. "You know, I lost someone too," she said. "I know about guilt."

Jack swallowed then nodded. "I'm sure you do."

"I'm a good listener," she said, facing him across the counter.

Jack grunted. "I'm sure you are, but that isn't why I'm here."

She looked away, head down as she went back to work. "Why are you here then? You apologized already."

Jack pulled out his car keys and set them on the counter. "I was wondering if you might do me a favor."

Hannah froze. "Really? You came to apologize for being rude and chasing me off the island, and now you want me to do you a favor?"

"Yeah, it's very forward of me, but I think it'll help us both," Jack said, agreeing with her assumptions about him.

"Ease your guilt and add to mine?"

"Not that at all," Jack said. "Believe me, I debated this for several days. I think you're the right person. I hardly know anyone in town."

Hannah left the rag on the counter and came closer, grabbing a glass and filling it with ice and water, then setting it in front of him. "This I want to hear. What's the favor that'll help us both?"

"Well, I live on an island with no road access," Jack continued. "I need someone to look after my car."

HANNAH WAS SHOCKED seeing him there, though she immediately realized she shouldn't have been. Islamorada was a small town really. There were only so many places to eat, and Lou's was closest to the pier where Jack generally arrived from Cristof's Key. When he saw Sam, his concern was immediate and obvious, but that was being a good person. Offering her his car though? Her smile faded, replaced with a wary look. Her? A stranger? Had someone told him to do this? Told him about her problems? "You want me to watch your car? Why me?"

Jack nodded again. "I need someone I can trust, and when I saw you riding bikes from the Publix..."

Sure, part of her wanted to jump at the offer after what happened to Sam, but she'd met him twice. Who offers to trust a stranger with their car like that, especially someone who lives across a body of water? "Cars are expensive. Why would you trust a stranger?"

Jack watched her a moment, perhaps sensing her doubts or considering his words again, then said, "Someone who came all the way to an island to bring strangers a meal out of sheer kindness doesn't strike me as a car thief."

No. He felt sorry for her. That was the last thing she needed. She sighed. "I don't need charity."

"I'm not giving you the car," Jack said. "But I can't leave it at the hotel forever. And I'd rather not have it parked on the street unused either—you know if you don't turn them on occasionally, the batteries die. I already had someone offer to garage it for me. What I want is someone who will drive it, you know, make sure it isn't stolen or vandalized."

There had to be a catch. He didn't know anything about her driving history, did he? Or her own car? "They have storage places for that."

"Yes, but then I'd have to come drive it regularly to keep it in working condition, and what if I don't have time?"

"What if you need it?"

"I can call and give notice and we can make arrangements," he said. "But being on the island, I shouldn't need it often."

She was running out of excuses. "I can't afford extra insurance or a mechanic."

"I'll keep my insurance, pay for repairs."

He'd been so mad at the lighthouse, switching moods like the flip of a switch. She'd questioned his mental stability. Only he wasn't sounding crazy now. He sounded kind, generous. The whole thing sounded too good to be true. She ran a hand through her hair, her head tilting slightly. "Even if I got in an accident?"

"As long as it's not on purpose," he said and smiled.

This time she laughed. That's when Lou crossed in front of them, shooting her that look of his that said she should notice when the fates were smiling on her. The man could not mind his own business. Tonight, it was a good thing.

"I'm serious," he said. "I need someone to help me. You look like you need a car."

She gave a half-hearted shrug. "Well, mine needs repair and I can't afford it. But I will get it back at some point."

"When you do, I can find someone else if you want," said Jack said. "By then, maybe I'll know a few more friends here."

Friends? "Is that what we are?"

Jack shrugged, making a sincere effort to win her trust. He took her hand in both of his, a platonic gesture, saying, "I'd like to be. Promise I'll treat you better." He nodded toward the booth where the woman with Sam continued staring daggers. "I have a feeling your watchdog friend over there might have it in

131

for me."

Hannah glanced over toward the booth and snorted when she saw the all too familiar look Ellen was giving Jack. Then she blushed, embarrassed because she hadn't meant to. "You better," she said, attempting to recover and motioned to his car fob on the counter between them. "Tonight?"

"I can bring it over tomorrow," Jack said. "I have tomorrow off and can bring it to you. If you'll trust me with your address. Or I can meet you here."

Hannah thought a moment, considering. She really did need a car. He was being neighborly and kind, genuinely. She could see that now. His voice was soft and caring, his eyes too. And he looked nice and cleaned up. She even thought she'd caught a whiff of cologne as she'd passed him.

She glanced at Sam again, and the cast. What if something else happened and Ellen was gone? The thought of that still scared her more than anything. It had haunted her, making sleep difficult for the past week. She needed a car. And he didn't imply she'd keep it forever. If things didn't work out, she'd just tell him to find someone else. That was fair and reasonable, wasn't it?

Jack waited patiently, watching her for a bit, then flipping half-heartedly through the menu, giving her space and time to think.

After a moment, she grabbed a pad and wrote down her address and phone number before she tore off the page and slid it across the counter to him. "Call me before you come, please." She nodded toward Ellen. "So I can lock my mother-in-law up for your protection."

Jack laughed out loud and they shared a moment, then Hannah turned serious again. "And this is a trial only. If I change my mind—"

"Of course," he said, before she could finish. "You're doing me a big favor, and I appreciate it."

"Sir?" Lou's voice carried across the room. He seemed to be calling on Jack. Ellen, Lou, and Sam all three looked cued in, as if watching them. Sam held a pen out in Jack's direction, a small gesture, but he caught Jack's eye. "I think he wants you to sign his cast," said Hannah.

Jack smiled, then looked at Hannah, who shrugged. "You have to give me your phone number anyway in case of emergencies."

Jack laughed as he stood from the stool. "I'll write that down separately." Then he walked over and accepted the pen, ignoring the daggers coming from Ellen's eyes at him. Bending down beside Sam, he looked for a spot on the cast before writing a message and signing his name.

Sam beamed at him.

"Thank you," said Hannah said as she came over to join them.

Jack finished and offered Sam back the pen. Sam took it, smiling ear-to-ear as Jack stood and turned to Hannah. "I'll call you tomorrow."

Ellen's and Lou's eyes widened, distracting Hannah as she nodded. "Okay."

Jack left with a piece of Lou's pie, two roast beef sandwiches, a bag of chips. Loaning her a car. It was like God was looking out for her, even if He had chosen an odd man for an angel.

"You have a date!" Ellen exclaimed from behind her, sounding less than delighted, and despite herself, Hannah felt herself blushing.

"He's loaning me his car," Hannah said. "Now shut up. I have customers." And she hurried back to work on her tables, wishing to God Jack had picked any day to come in but the one when her mother-in-law visited. And wondering if she wanted to risk getting involved with a man whose moods seemed to switch on a dime.

CHAPTER 12

JACK AWOKE TO a sky that was robin egg blue, the early morning breeze cool and soft on his skin as he unlocked the downstairs door for Warren and stepped outside for a quick walk around the property. Once Warren arrived, it was his first day off in almost two weeks and he planned to run a few errands ahead of delivering his car to Hannah's. Afterward, he'd come back to the island to relax on the beach.

Warren arrived at seven, a half hour after the usual start time, apologetic. "Traffic on the Overseas Highway was jammed out of Miami," he explained. "It happens sometimes. How was your first week on your own?"

They sipped coffee in the kitchen as Jack recapped his first week alone, Warren mostly listening though offering suggestions and praise from time to time. But Jack found himself anxious to start his day off. His mind returned to his meeting with Hannah last night,. Even if he said so himself, he'd handled the matter like an expert with women. Maybe, after all his years bungling things up with Abby, he finally had them figured out. An hour later, after a quick change into a t-shirt and shorts, Jack met Bert at the dock and headed for Islamorada.

His first stop was the Holiday Inn, where he picked up his Jeep Cherokee. The drive to Tavernier north of Islamorada proved as backed up as Warren had told him. No matter. No reason to hurry; rolling down the windows to let in the breeze set the trip into town on a pleasant course. Realizing he was dropping off his car meant he needed one last replenishments trip; he dropped by the Ace Hardware store for paint and supplies for the lighthouse. Next, he found a second hand store on Google Maps and parted with the furniture filling the back, which turned out to be a lot easier than he'd expected. It's just furniture. Not heirlooms or handmade, his inner voice chide. He had ready-made replacements at the lighthouse, and he'd decided if he planned to live out his days there, he might as well let them go. He certainly couldn't drive around with them or give Hannah a car filled with furniture. After that, he headed south to a bookstore to pick up some novels. A sale display on the sidewalk gave him a plentiful stockpile of some he'd missed. Finally, he visited the Post Office to check his designated post office box.

Islamorada was laid back with a very small town feel. In some ways, even more small townish than Salina had been, but in part, he guessed that came from its being so spread out. Much of the way you could glimpse the ocean on either side because the buildings were spread out and only a row or two, but others, there were whole neighborhoods or long streets of houses. People were friendly, and so many shops and restaurants still used hand written signs hung in windows to promote specials or sales. Still, from the bright pastels and fluorescent colors to the neon lights, hurricane shutters, and palm trees everywhere, it was obvious he wasn't in Kansas anymore. By arrangement, Bert delivered the important official mail to the island. But it was up to him as the keeper to check for personal mail. Josie had stuffed his mailbox with vacation postcards from her family trip to Cancun. The images of the Mexican resort resembled those on the island around him in many ways. His final stop was a gas station where he filled up the gas tank for Hannah and called her number, getting voicemail. He left a message he'd be on his way soon.

By the time he headed for Hannah's, the sky turned a shade of light azure. He took the busy Overseas Highway north, noting the landmarks as he passed, attempting to familiarize himself with his new home. He passed another supermarket called the Trading Post he hadn't noticed before while keeping his eye out for the Publix; after all, the GPS indicated Hannah's street was just north of it on the left.

He spotted the Publix up ahead, signaling as he moved into the left lane, preparing for the turn. South Hammock was a street of typical upper class Florida houses, which Jack took to mean Hannah had either inherited a house or lived with her parents. There was a good mix of luxury and mid class cars in the driveways. Good landscaping finished the oversized homes; the outside elevations demonstrated a typical mix of Florida colors and styles. Kids played in some of the yards while in the distance toward the end of the street a group of youths kicked a soccer ball around the asphalt. It looked like a safe, quiet, comfortable place to raise a family, making Jack wonder how long Hannah had lived here.

Two minutes later, he pulled up in front of 121 S. Hammock Road, a white house with blue doors and white shutters over the windows. A quick glance up the driveway revealed windows looking into an enclosed patio surrounding a large indoor pool. There were lots of palm trees, thatch palms, sea oats, dwarf lantana, blue porterweed, and other foliage decorating the well-landscaped lot lining the path leading to the front door. Jack could see the edges of a white, wooden privacy fence stretching from the sides toward the back. 'He'd been making use of the library at the lighthouse to fill himself in on the flora of the region and its importance and role in the ecosystem down here. Since sea oats created the necessary barriers for his island post, he made it his business to know these things.

Parking the Jeep in an open spot on the drive behind the garage, Jack climbed out and followed the path to the front door. The air had a pleasant odor from the combination of pollens where pretty butterflies fluttered from plant to plant around him as he walked. Reaching the door, he pushed the doorbell and waited. From inside, he heard voices calling back and forth before the door opened to Hannah's smiling face.

"Hope you didn't have any trouble finding us," she said, biting her lip as she smoothed the right leg of her jeans down with her hand. .

"Not at all," he said. "First left after the Publix. Simple enough." Her hair was pulled back in a ponytail and she wore little makeup. She wore it well. Jack found her natural beauty striking. She wasn't plain but she was an everyday woman, the kind he'd always felt comfortable with. Hannah wore denim jeans with those little ripped tears in them, not because she couldn't afford them. Abby had assured him that was a fashion statement, meaning the tears had probably cost extra. But it also showed she wasn't caught up in looks or appearances, but comfortable being herself, and that made her far more attractive him.

Then he realized something—he didn't know her last name and she didn't know his. "You know," he said, extending his hand, "we were never really properly introduced. I'm Jack Pace."

She hesitated a moment, then reached out and shook his hand. "Hannah Loaney."

He smiled. "Nice to meet you, Hannah. Officially."

Theeir eyes met and he noticed hers were deep, filled with strength and passion, despite her subdued manner, but alongside the strength, there was a sadness, a history, and his throat thickened at the memory of how he'd dismissed her feelings, her empathy at the lighthouse. He wanted to know more about her.

After a moment, she nodded and glanced over his shoulder toward the drive. "A Jeep, nice."

"Well, she's a few years old, but she's in great condition and runs great," said Jack, pointing outside to where he'd parked it. "Want me to show her to you?"

"Sure," Hannah said, stepping outside.

While they walked along, a motorist not two blocks up

stalled out, smoke pouring out of his engine. Jack was glad, for once, it wasn't him in car trouble.

"How's Sam?" Jack asked as they walked back along the path toward the drive together.

"Fine," Hannah said. "The crutches sure haven't tampered any of his energy."

As she moved ahead of him, he caught himself glancing at her firm behind and liking it, then looked away quickly, hoping he wasn't blushing. Jack laughed. "Boys are boys."

"Yeah."

They reached the Jeep and Jack led her around to the driver's side, pulling open the door. "What kind of car do you drive?"

"A Camry hybrid," she replied.

He nodded, pursing his lips. "Nice cars. My next one will be a hybrid for sure." He hurried around to the passenger side as Hannah climbed in and situated herself behind the wheel, taking in the dash.

Jack climbed in beside her and ran through a few of the car's features that might be different from her Toyota. He showed her the hands-free Bluetooth, the features on the multi-disc CD player-radio combo and media console.

"Seems simple enough," she said.

"It should be, but Jeeps handle a bit differently, so you might wanna take it easy and get used to it."

"You sure you trust me with this?" she asked, frowning as her eyes met his.

"It's a car," Jack said. "Anything that happens can usually be fixed. Trust me, you're doing me a huge favor watching her for me and keeping her active."

"Her?" she giggled. "You men and your cars."

Jack smiled. "Well, that's how my dad always referred to them."

"Mine too," she admitted.

Jack pulled out the keys and pointed to the clicker. "Alarm. Trunk. Panic. I filled her up on my way over."

"Got it," she said, accepting the keys. "I promise to treat her like my own. And I'll only drive her when I need to."

"Drive her as often as you want," Jack said. "That's what she's for."

Hannah looked at him a moment, as if reading his face, then said, "Thank you." Her tone sincere. "You really are rescuing me."

"I'm glad."

They sat there looking at each other in silence for a moment, but then, breaking the awkwardness, Hannah said, "Do you want to come in and say 'Hi' to Sam? I know he'd like to see you."

"Sure," Jack said.

They climbed out of the Jeep, closing the doors. Hannah used the remote on the key chain to lock the doors, then led him back along the path toward the house again.

Hannah opened the door and waved him inside. They entered a long, high-ceilinged entryway with tan spotted tile flooring and white slate base walls with wood grain highlights leading up toward the ceiling above. Large cylindrical lamps hung centered above them. To the left, a glass wall looked out on the enclosed patio and pool area; the right side opened to the kitchen and family room leading to the rest of the house.

"Wow," Jack said. "Tips must be terrific." He cringed as fast as he said it. Instead of rolling her eyes at him, Hannah smiled in a way that said she was learning to overlook his gaffs.

"My husband's parents own it," Hannah explained. "It's just, Sam, me, and my mother-in-law now."

He found her explanation generous. "I was kidding. It's very nice."

Hannah glanced at the family room, and Jack headed toward the open doorway leading into it from the entryway. Sam was sitting on a couch engrossed in Bugs Bunny cartoons on the television, propping his cast on a coffee table. Two recliners and a love seat formed an arc with the sofa aimed at the large screen LED TV. Beachy art decorated the walls lit by track lighting overhead. It was a homey place that looked both stylish and lived-in.

"Hey, buddy," Jack said as he approached and came alongside the boy, looking down at him and smiling. Spread out on the table in front of him were varied sized rows of seashells of similar shapes. "What ya got there? Conch shells?"

Sam grinned up at him, looking please Jack recognized the shells, and moved to get up, but Jack raised a palm to stop him then went over and tousled his hair. "It's okay. You stay where you are. You look comfortable."

"They're a dime a dozen down here," Hannah explained. "Anyway, my mom uses them for handmade crafts like jewelry and so on. Sam helps her collect them."

Jack nodded as if it were the most fascinating thing in the world then he thought back to his interaction with Sam in the Publix. He'd never said a word. Was that a choice born of fear or some other challenge? Sam had seemed totally comfortable with Jack at the store. He remembered when he and Abby hired a speech therapist to work with Caroline as she started kindergarten, because their daughter slurred and jumbled words a bit, and they wanted her to be able to fit in and socialize. "Some children's heads get ahead of their mouths," the therapist had said, encouraging them. "They just need a little help to catch up with others." Sam was so charming. He hoped he would catch up without too much pain or difficulty.

. "I see." He winked at Sam. "Cool. Want to show me?"

Sam nodded as if energized by his suggestion and scooted over slightly so Jack could sit beside him on the couch. Then Sam pulled his cast off the table and sat up, leaning forward so he could point at or hold up various shells and show them to Jack.

THEY STAYED that way for the next several minutes—Jack and Sam—as Sam singled out various shells and pointed to their features. He still didn't talk but Jack acted as if he had, behaving as if it were the most fascinating conversation he'd had all week.

Hannah watched them together with interest. Jack was so good with Sam, and Sam was responding so warmly to him. She suddenly felt more nervous than she should with him in the house. It wasn't like he might lose it and go off on her for no reason, right? Okay, it had happened at the lighthouse kind of that way, but this was a much more laid back, comfortable Jack she hadn't seen before. He talked to both her and Sam with real respect and genuine interest, and in Sam's case, he was the first man Hannah had ever seen do that. In truth, having him here and watching him with her son touched her heart in a way she hadn't been prepared for or experienced in a long time.

Without meaning to, her mind flashed back to Rob and Sam on the same couch, examining toy cars or baseball cards or more shells, and all at once she felt a warm comfortable feeling swelling through her. She remembered how Jack stared into her eyes after they shook hands on her front walk. For just a moment, she'd wondered if he would kiss her. And for just a moment, she'd actually wanted him to.

"You know, I've seen a lot of these on the island around the lighthouse," Jack observed as he finished examining a particular conch shell and set it back on the table. "Maybe your mom or grandma could bring you over sometime to hunt for them."

Sam stood and limped over to where a plastic beach pail and small shovel sat beside the door to the hallway as Hannah warned, "Be careful, honey."

Ignoring her, he scooped them up quickly as both he and

Jack looked at Hannah. She felt their eyes boring into her and raised her hands in surrender. "We'll talk about it."

Sam grinned wider and gave her a thumbs up, as he set the pail and shovel on a recliner and went back to his shells.

Jack chuckled. "I really like the house. I don't suppose you'd like to give me the tour while I'm here?"

Hannah looked at him a moment as if gauging his sincerity. "Sure. Follow me."

Suddenly, she was self-conscious about her mother-in-law being in the kitchen and surprised Ellen hadn't already made herself known. She decided to skip the kitchen and lead him through the rest of the house, narrating as she went. There were four bedrooms—one for each occupant and a guest room—a nice full kitchen, a play room for Sam, the family room, a laundry room, and a small office Ellen used for her side business. Then they headed out to the backyard.

"Did you grow up here?" Jack asked.

"A few miles from here near Tavernier," Hannah said. "Since I was about ten, at least. Before that we were in a smaller home in Key Largo."

"It's beautiful here," Jack said, but his eyes stayed on her in a way that made her think he was talking less about the house and more about her.

She turned away, absent mindedly fiddling with a strand of loose hair dangling against her forehead and continued her narration. "The gate leads to the alley and we have the gardening shed and you see the rest."

"Is that the gate Sam slipped out of?" Jack asked.

"Yes, it is."

"Is it always open like that?"

"It's broken," she said. "I need to get someone over here to fix it."

"You know, most of my job at the lighthouse is maintenance and I grew up on a farm. Why don't I take a look?" he asked.

She hesitated a moment, trying to think of a good excuse to stop him, except he full on plowed ahead, crossing the yard, headed for the gate. All she could think to say was, "It's your day off. I don't want to bother you. We can call someone—"

"It's no bother," Jack said in a way more gentle than her first encounter with him. "I want to help. Keep Sam safe." He examined the gate with particular focus on the latch before inspecting the shed. "Do you have tools somewhere?"

She shrugged. "Yes." Her mind still searched for an excuse, but he was determined.

"I'll need a Phillips head screwdriver and extra screws if you have them, oh, and a pair of pliers should do it," Jack said. "If you want, show me where you keep your tools, and I'll get what I need."

Hannah led him to the shed, sliding open the door and pointing to a toolbox on a bench in one corner. Jack stepped inside and crossed to the toolbox, unlatching and opening the lid, then removing the top tray and clanging around inside for what he needed. Moments later, he had shut it and crossed back toward her with a pair of pliers, a small box, and a screwdriver.

"Should only take ten or fifteen minutes, unless I have to redrill," he said.

Moving past her, he headed straight for the gate and set to work as Hannah watched. His muscled arms and the determined set of his jaw reminded her of Rob. Both moved with such deliberation and confidence when it came to doing simple at home repair. And it occurred to her that the way Jack showed concern and interest in Sam was similar to that of a father with his own son. She had to admit the way he'd noticed the shells and Sam's fascination and taken an immediate interest had impressed her. She hadn't been able to take her eyes off them as they interacted, just like at the Publix. But God, she was staring again! She'd already decided she didn't want the drama he seemed to bring, even if he was having a good moment. She had enough of that already with Sam and Ellen, thank you. But he did look good in those blue shorts. Stop it! The last thing she needed was for him to see her staring and get the wrong idea. Go do something, Hannah! Her inner voice scolded, so she turned and headed for the house to get him a beverage, mostly just to have an excuse to leave him alone with the task.

As she passed the family room, she saw Sam still frozen in front of the TV and called over her shoulder, "Honey, would you like some lemonade? I'm making some for Jack."

Stepping into the kitchen she glanced back through the opening to the family room at Sam who nodded, then she turned to the cupboards and pulled out two glasses, then went to the fridge and pulled out a pitcher of homemade lemonade.

"You were staring at his butt," Ellen said, appearing in the doorway with a frown.

"Ellen, stop." My God, how did she know.

"Well, you were," Ellen said, then shot her a scolding look. "I noticed how you didn't introduce us."

"I figured you were busy," Hannah said as she put several ice cubes in each glass.

"No, I was waiting."

"Or spying on us." Hannah poured the lemonade and returned the pitcher to the fridge.

"You call it spying, I call it looking after my daughter-in-law. Sue me," Ellen said.

Hannah could tell Ellen didn't like seeing her showing interest in a man other than Rob, so she held her tongue and shot her a look instead, then grabbed the glasses and carried one into the family room where she set it on a side table within reach of Sam.

"Here you go, sweetie," she said. Sam nodded his thanks.

On her way out to the backyard, she stopped to observe how

Jack looked bent over handling the electric drill once held by Rob. She had no right to compare; Jack's not him, and vice-versa. Yet how she felt watching Jack handle the tools like they were sacred, wiping them off, holding drill bits up to the light to inspect the sizes, she had this strange free-floating sensation. Rob had always had the same reverence for tools.

As she stood in the open door, looking out across the yard, she stayed back, watching Jack work. There was something really thrilling to her about seeing a man doing repair work again. It was something she hadn't seen at this house since Rob died and her father before, realizing she hadn't had that reaction to anyone in a very long time. What was it about Jack? Okay, flattering blue shorts, glutes of a gym rat. He'd cut the sleeves out of his northerly plaid shirt to make it a southerly work shirt. It suited him. Made her want to touch the fabric. She wondered who had sewn the sleeves up properly—did he know how to do that, too? Oh my God, Hannah, cut it out! She took a deep breath and started to sip from the glass of lemonade she was holding, then remembered it was for Jack and quickly stopped. Looking across to where she could see over the back fence to the neighbor's yard she scrunched her face at seeing their dog was getting way too friendly with a tree. Reason number 101 way she'd never let Sam have a pet.

Jack stopped and used the back of his hand to wipe the sweat from his brow and as he did, his pants bunched up in his crotch. Without thinking, he reached around a tugged them out, not even noticing her. Okay, that brought her down to Earth real quick as she snickered. That reminded her way more of Sam than Rob. Good. Now that she had that out of her system, she could be around him, maybe like he said. Like they're friends. Platonic and all.

By the time she'd crossed the yard, he was firing up the drill to make two new holes, then reset the latch mechanism in place and screwed in the screws. His sinewy arm muscles flexed with each turn of the screwdriver; she hoped he wouldn't look up and notice. Thank goodness he didn't, finishing after only a couple minutes. He tested the lock mechanism by opening and closing the gate.

"That was fast," she said.

"Yeah, it turned out it just needed new screws, two holes, and a couple adjustments," Jack said. "Simple." He looked up and saw the lemonade. "Is that for me?"

"If you want it."

He grinned. "Yes, I was just thinking how thirsty I am. Thank you."

She held out the glass ignoring the slight jolt she felt when their fingers touched, her pinky lingering against his. Jack accepted the drink as he had promised, like a friend might. He brought it to his lips for a long sip. Those lips. She looked away.

He sighed and wiped his mouth on the back of his arm. "That's good stuff. Hits the spot. Thanks again."

"Thanks for fixing the gate," Hannah said.

"If it goes out again, we might need to replace the mechanism," Jack said. "I think the holes are getting worn. It was built a while ago."

Now she couldn't help noticing how he was looking ahead, as if inserting himself back into her life—"If it goes out again," he'd said. Maybe he didn't mean it that way. Or else it means more. "Yeah, Rob's dad put it in when I was pregnant with Sam."

"Well, the weather here is probably hard on this stuff," Jack said. "They're cheap to replace really, so if we have to go that route, it won't be a big deal."

"Thanks again for doing that," she said as he took another long sip of lemonade. "I know who to call next time."

He finished and swallowed before replying, "My pleasure." He didn't take off, instead making a turn around the yard. "Got anything else I can fix for you while I'm here?"

She laughed, far more relaxed than before. "You know, if

147

you'd been this nice at the lighthouse the other night, I might have asked for your help."

He shot her a mischievous look. "But then I wouldn't have had the pleasure of returning your random act of kindness, right? Would you really deprive me of that?"

"Yes, of course." she said, eyes narrowing as she creased her eyebrows somberly. "I want that pleasure all to myself."

He raised both hands in mock surrender. "Oh, I see how it is. Well, then, I'll stop while I'm ahead and thank you for your mercy."

She laughed again and he reciprocated before taking a final sip from his lemonade.

"You know," he said, "this is damn good lemonade."

"My mother has made it since I was a child," Hannah said. "Ellen has two lemon trees on the side of the house."

"Oh, home grown's even better. Be right back." He walked back over to the shed and disappeared inside, she assumed, to clean up from the project. The clanging of metal indicated he returned the tools to the toolbox. Moments later, he reappeared, and they walked back toward the house together.

"Where is your mother-in-law?" he asked. "Working?"

"She was in the kitchen earlier," she said. "And trust me, we're better off ignoring her."

"That bad, huh?"

"She has a special way of showing her love," Hannah said.

He grunted and something about the empathetic look he gave her told her he knew a lot about mother-in-laws himself. "I know the type," he said as they walked up the stairs, and into the house.

As they headed along the wide entry corridor that ran from the back of the house to the front and separated the living areas from the patio and pool, Ellen appeared, smiling—the kind of smile Hannah expected of barracudas not people. Ellen held out her hand and hurried toward them as Hannah tensed. "This must be Jack. I'm Ellen. Hannah's mother-in-law."

"Nice to meet you," Jack said as they shook. Hannah appreciated how he took no notice of Ellen's subtle implication. "Hannah showed me your lovely home." This time Ellen's smile seemed so kind and friendly that for a moment Hannah wondered if body snatchers had taken over her mother-in-law. Then, as Jack smiled at Hannah, Ellen shot her a hideous scowl, and everything was back to normal. Yet another thing she'd missed out on when she lost that condo—no awkward moments like this with her mother-in-law and men.

"Thank you," said Ellen said, ignoring Hannah. "We've been very happy here."

Hannah released the breath she'd been holding waiting for her mother-in-law to say something embarrassing. Except for the hidden glances, Ellen had stayed on shockingly best behavior so far. Still, Hannah figured she should take charge of their conversation before it came to that. "Jack fixed the gate for us," she interjected.

"Oh, wonderful," said Ellen said. "It's good to have a man around to help. We'll feel much safer after Sam's accident knowing that's been done."

"We should have gotten around to it ages ago," Hannah said, still feeling guilty. It had been so easy for Jack to fix that she blamed herself for not looking into it sooner. Time had just slipped away.

"Well, it's fixed now, and we're grateful," Ellen said, looking at Jack with a semblance of sincerity. Jack looked fooled but Hannah knew better.

Jack nodded and handed Hannah the glass. "I should be getting on my way, I suppose. Thanks for the wonderful lemonade."

"Oh, did you like it? It's a family recipe," Ellen said, pressing together her palms as her eyes gleamed a bit.

149

Jack popped his head into the family room and said a quick "goodbye" to Sam before following Hannah toward the door. Ellen stayed put, for once, her reticence to interfere shocking Hannah.

"I hope the Jeep is helpful," said Jack said.

"It will be. Thank you," Hannah said.

They reached the front door and stopped, looking at each other a moment, before Hannah opened the door and stepped out onto the walk with Jack following.

"I promise to take good care of it," she added as she closed the door behind them, cutting off her nosey mother-in-law's view.

"I never doubted that," he said.

Hannah suddenly realized he had no transportation. "Oh, how will you get back?"

"Well, I have to stop at the Publix for a few things and then I'll meet Bert at the pier."

"Let me drive you to Publix," she said.

He shook his head. "The walk will do me good. But thank you. See you soon."

With that, he turned and lumbered off down the drive, heading away from her down the street. Hannah watched him leave until he was out of sight. The whole time she imagined what it would be like if he stayed longer. If he'd have let her take him to the grocers. Unfortunately, this was one of those moments she couldn't reconcile with her prior goals for protecting herself and Sam and keeping Jack at bay, however good he looked in plaid. On the one hand, every date she'd had in three years had been a nightmare more or less, with men who excited her about as much as a lump of moldy cheese. Either they had the personality of a fallen leaf pile or they were macho and braggy—two big turn offs. None of them were Rob, but then again, part of why she'd fallen in love with Rob was because it had seemed so natural. She couldn't help herself.

None of those men she could picture a future with though. And a man with a future together was what she'd secretly dreamed of once she started trying to put the pieces back together.

With Jack, she found herself picturing moments that hadn't happened together but might. A future of sorts, she realized. And it scared her. The last thing she needed was to get hurt again or let Sam get hurt. Get out of my head, Jack! she chided herself, and then she remembered his smile and felt her heart skip a beat all over again.

CHAPTER 13

JACK WALKED AWAY from Hannah's house picturing her lips and imagining what it would be like to kiss her. As lips go, hers had a plumpness, and none of those hard makeup lines. Natural like the curves of a sofa. Two: Okay, so he'd not been physical for a long time, so maybe Josie got it partly right. Hannah's pretty so what if picturing kissing her is a natural chemical response? Why the hell make the leap beyond what nature intended? Three: Although he'd struggled with guilt over that... urge while at her place, it subsided some, not as heavy and overpowering as the night she brought dinner to the lighthouse. Maybe he isn't sure what means, but he also doesn't regret it either. So—number one—he'd wanted to kiss her? Momentary impulse. Ultimately he wanted to be her friend, and though he'd come to Florida expecting to live like a hermit, he'd come to realize he couldn't fight nature.

The truth was he liked spending time with her and Sam, and he got the sense they liked spending time with him, too. What he liked about Hannah had little to do with kissing or romantic overtures. He liked talking and laughing with her, learning about her life, her hopes and dreams. He liked watching her chew her bottom lip when thinking deeply about something; plus in the way she absent-mindedly tucked loose hairs back behind her ear with the swipe of a finger without a conscious thought. He'd found that each time he spent with her he came away with a stronger sense he couldn't wait to spend time with her again.

153

And he liked that he could help her and Sam making life a little bit easier for them.

Oh my God, he had to stop! He was looking for friendship only, so why was he even going there? Hannah was becoming a good friend, nothing more. No matter how he felt about Abby, he knew she would never have wanted him to live the rest of his life without friends. Hannah was merely the first person he'd felt had friend potential since Abby's death. No need to feel guilty. Everyone needs friends. Humans thrive in communities, and having a few carefully chosen friends wouldn't be all bad. Besides, being with Hannah and Sam felt good—and that was the first time since the accident, he'd felt happy being with other people.

It wasn't until Jack got back to Cristof's Key that he realized he hadn't thought about Caroline and Abby for several hours. Immediately, his inner voice chided him: How could you? You came here to honor them and you get so busy you forget them? And with another woman and child, too?! He felt sick to his stomach as fatigue overcame him, and he barely managed to unload all the groceries and carry them inside before collapsing into a chair at the kitchen table. He'd let them down—the most important people in his life. So he did the only thing he could think of and called his sister.

"Now that's a grand gesture!" said Josie said after Jack told her the whole story and about loaning Hannah his Jeep. "I'm proud of you, big brother."

"But I forgot Abby and Caroline. How could I do that?" He put his head in his hands, elbows propped on the table as he kept his cell phone against his ear with a shoulder.

"Oh God forbid you should stop grieving for a couple of hours and live," Josie replied, and could almost see her rolling her eyes. "Jack, everyone knows how much you loved them. Including Abby and Caroline. And you always will. That doesn't mean you have to spend the rest of your life thinking about them every moment and being said."

Jack bristled, stiffening in the chair. "I have happy memories, too."

"Of course, but that's not my point and you know it. We're Kansans, Jack. Abby was too. You both grew up learning to help your neighbors. So you got preoccupied for bit. Do you really think either your wife or daughter would be ashamed or angry for you finding time to be kind to others?"

"Okay. I was raised right, Jos," Jack said. "No need to pile it on so thick."

"Why not? Me piling on you is fun."

He'd spent the past two hours mentally revisiting his visit to Hannah's—until he'd realized he'd forgotten his family. He'd enjoyed seeing her in a different environment from the diner more than he'd imagined he would. He took great pleasure in doing things for her making her life easier and better. He admitted how good it felt to have someone to take care of again, She seemed a bit reluctant to see him at first, of course, but relaxed as time went on. By the end, he felt she was enjoying his company.

"So you like this chick, huh?" Josie probed. "Gets your panties in a twist? Makes you hot under the collar?"

Of course not. He pulled the phone away from his ear a moment as bile rose in this throat. Then he realized she was just trying to get a reaction as usual. "Do you have any original jabs or are you all about cliches?"

Josie chuckled. "Hey, if the classics work, stick with 'em." She laughed, underscoring how much Jack's new chapter entertained her. "So you gonna ask her out or what?"

Jack coughed. "What? Of course not. I'm not looking to date, you know that. You know why I'm here. But you were right about being a good neighbor."

"And that's all there is to it?"

"Yes. I'm sure romance the last thing she needs right now." And it was the last thing he needed too, especially if it made him forget his family. Wasn't it? "Why?"

"This girl is available, right?"

"I told you already she's a widow," Jack said as he rose from the chair and went over to the counter to start a pot of coffee.

"Okay, then she of all people would understand what you're going through. Have you talked with her about it?"

Jack poured grounds into a filter and swapped it with the old one still sitting in the top of the pot. He tossed the old filter a garbage can next to the counter and grabbed the glass pot, carrying it over the sink for some water. "Of course not. We just met," he finally said.

"So, you enjoy her company, right? And her son, too. What's wrong with spending time together? You can't live out the rest of your life with no friends, right?"

Jack scoffed as he poured the water over the filter, filling the reservoir. "I suppose not. But I'm just a burden to them."

"Did she say that?" Josie said quickly, almost like a cop drilling a suspect.

"Not exactly."

"Don't assume, Jack. It's the biggest mistake men make in relationships."

Jack shook his head vigorously before realizing Josie couldn't see it anyway. "Who said we're in a relationship?"

"Friendship is a relationship, calm down," Josie said. Eye roll number two, he suspected. "You've been in love, Jack. There's no point denying yourself or this girl what comes naturally. Love isn't a choice. It's chemical."

Josie was a hopeless romantic.

"I didn't say I was attracted to her. I'm mourning my wife and child, a loss I don't think I'll ever get over. You know that!"

"Sure, I believe you," she said, taking digs via her typical sarcastic snark, while inside Jack, a little voice asked the same things. Jack couldn't say if he'd answered her truthfully. "When she talks to you, how do you feel?"

Oh Christ almighty! "Like a normal person feels talking to, you know, a friend."

"This is bull and you know it, Jack." Her voice faded. She must have turned from the phone to yell at the kids.

"I'm at work, Josie."

"Call me later. Ask her out, Jack." She hung up.

He drank his coffee in silence, then put away the groceries he'd forgotten sitting on the counter, and went back down to the cart and headed out to clear weeds on a beach south of the lighthouse.

As he parked the cart, hiking over the dunes while he followed a path through a cove of palm trees, he saw crocodiles sunning themselves on the sand. He was surprised to see them so far from the swamps, but Warren had told him they preferred the coastal regions, even recalling sightings of crocodiles walking down sidewalks in the middle of town. Most looked fairly small, maybe juveniles. But one was quite large. He hoped he never ran into them by accident on foot.

As he set down his tools and prepared to start weeding, he heard voices in the near distance, just across the dunes. As he passed beyond the palm cove and topped another dune, some voices grew louder, laughter too. The sky overhead was clear blue with cotton ball clouds, the temperature a perfect seventy-five.

At the top of the dune, he found himself looking down on a group of teenagers—three boys and two girls—frolicking on the beach without a care, a small motorboat resting partially on the sand nearby. Their campfire roared, battered by winds as foamy waves rolled in to crash against the shore. Two of them set out the fixings, prepared for a wiener roast. He frowned, though. Garbage was scattered about—empty soda cans, candy wrappers, and so forth, littered the beach. Since he'd walked the same beach two days before on a garbage sweep, he knew it was fresh. The chance these kids weren't responsible overshadowed his first reaction, of course, until the open Igloo cooler near the

157

campfire held cans of the same soda cooling on ice.

The island was private. "No Trespassing" signs stood only yards from them, posted at regular intervals. Warren had told him the Coast Guard were tolerant about it and to use his own discretion. If the kids cleaned up after themselves, he wouldn't bother them. Still, seeing the garbage irritated him to the point he decided he'd rather not deal with the consequences, so he put on a stern face and marched toward them.

"Hey there!" he called, glad he'd worn his official uniform shirt.

The laughter faded as one of the boys noticed him and quieted the group, who turned to watch him approach.

"This is private property of the U.S. Coast Guard," he went on. "You're not supposed to be here."

"Awwww come on, we're just having a nice picnic," a blond boy said. He looked like a typical California surfer-type, tall and thin with a dark tan.

"Well, you can't do it here, I'm sorry," Jack said. "Please pack it up and move along."

"You suck," said the boy.

"We're not hurting anyone," said a brunette girl, frowning.

Jack bent and retrieved an empty soda can from the sand. "Is this your litter?" From the looks in their eyes, he knew immediately it was.

"We would have picked that up," said the brunette.

"I don't see any trash bags or containers," said Jack said. "In any case, there are 'No Trespassing' signs for a reason." He motioned to signs equidistance apart to either side of them. "You can read, right?" He finally reached them, standing on the dune above their fire.

"Yeah, we can read," said the blond kid, coming to his feet. His fists clenched.

Jack remembered acting like that as a kid to impress his

friends. He chose a less threatening tone, saying, "Okay, then, let's get loaded up and find another picnic spot, please," He reached to toss the empty can to the brunette who caught it, although staring at him, sullen. "And please take what you brought here out with you."

The kids moaned and mumbled complaints but gathered up their things, carrying them toward the motorboat while Jack stood watch. He wondered if these kids' parents knew what they were up to; he still imagined an older Caroline. How might he have imparted values to help her choose wise behavior in similar circumstances. Was any parent immune from the what-ifs? A memory of her came flooding back:

"Daddy," she'd once asked him at the zoo as they watched a boy in a wheelchair navigating the ramps of the insect exhibit. "Why can't that boy walk?"

"I don't know, baby," he had said. "Something must have happened."

"What, daddy?"

"He got sick or had an accident. I don't know, babe."

Caroline had frowned. "Does it hurt?"

"Maybe, but the wheelchair helps," Jack assured her. "It allows him to get places without his legs."

"Will it happen to me, daddy?" she'd asked.

Jack had felt a clamp on his heart so tight it hurt just imagining Caroline in a wheelchair, but managed to keep it off his face as his eyes met hers with reassurance. "No, baby. You're going to be fine." Of course, he had no way of knowing. So much for never lying to his daughter. That had been one of the few times he'd broken that promise.

"It makes me sad, daddy," Caroline replied.

"Me, too," Jack said.

Jack thought of Hannah and Sam. Sam had been on his mind a lot the previous afternoon as he pondered how he might have felt if he'd been faced with a daughter who had traumatic mutism. He imagined he would have struggled with it. To him, Hannah seemed incredibly supportive and patient, so much so he wondered where she drew the strength. Sure, she'd blamed herself for Sam's injury like any parent would, but those things happened to every kid, especially teenagers, who tend to be active and adventurous. It could have just as easily have happened to Jack if he were in her shoes. That had nothing to do with her incredible attitude toward Sam. He was a lucky boy, and he hoped Sam would grow up always appreciating that.

After a few minutes, the group of kids had loaded their stuff in the motorboat and extinguished the fire. To his surprise, the blond boy put out the fire like a scout. A couple of the girls had even gathered up the scattered litter and taken that, too. As one final kiss off, the girls glared at Jack from inside the craft as their two friends pushed the boat off the sand. The third boy steered them away from Cristof's Key.

Jack smiled and offered a friendly wave. Sorry, guys, maybe some other time, he thought. Then he turned and walked back up the dunes toward the palm trees to return to his work.

As he did, he decided he ought to scout out the best location for Sam to collect conch shells, maybe choose an ideal picnic spot for them while making a mental note to put that on his agenda for later in the afternoon. It didn't matter that Sam wouldn't be ready to make such a trip until he got his walking boot at the end of the week. Jack liked planning ahead. It inspired him, and it was what architects did, after all. He realized to save time by driving the cart along the beach and circling the island, he could decide the details. But first he had to finish his weeding.

As he set back to work, Hannah stayed in his thoughts, including their foiled dinner at the lighthouse.

No use beating himself up for it all the time. Or was he copping out?

By the time he'd finished weeding the target portion of beach an hour later, he'd come up with a great idea he thought might help him see Hannah sooner rather than later. He pulled out his phone to make a call.

HANNAH SIGHED, RELIEVED, as she headed to the diner for a week of morning shifts. Normally, she rotated between mornings and evenings. Lou relied on her, given how Janice's vacation rolled around this week. He needed Hannah's steady attention to customers and since Denise didn't know mornings, Hannah took her shifts five days in a row. But at least it kept her away from Ellen more often. Ellen had torn into her the minute Jack left.

"How dare you betray my son like that!" her mother-in-law had scolded. "It's practically adultery."

"Rob is dead," Hannah said. "Last I checked that doesn't constitute adultery. And we weren't doing anything but talking."

"I saw how you looked at him!"

Hannah fought the urge to roll her eyes. "Oh, heaven forbid I would ever find another man attractive again."

Ellen's harassment had been relentless ever since Jack visited the house the previous Sunday. She seemed to want to know everything about Jack from who he was, his background, and what they'd said to each other, to every other detail she could think of. The diner was an escape and she relished it.

It wasn't like Hannah hadn't been thinking about Jack already. He'd been on her mind almost constantly since Sunday, but with her mother-in-law constantly interrupting her thoughts, it had been a challenge to reach any conclusions about what she wanted next. Yet another reminder why she needed to move into her own place again soon. And inside she cursed Janice again for making her miss her appointment with that realtor. She'd even driven the Jeep a few times if for no other reason than to get a chance to breathe. The car was nice and drove fairly smoothly, though Jack had been right to warn her. It was a different feeling sitting so high off the road from what she was used to, and certainly the maneuverability took some getting used to.

Sam would get his walking boot Friday if all went well, and ever since Jack had mentioned it, he'd been bugging his mother to take him shell hunting on the island. As soon as Jack had left, she'd sworn Sam to secrecy about that. "Do not tell grandma under any circumstances. We're going to surprise her, okay?" she'd said. Sam loved surprising people with gifts, so he enthusiastically agreed.

Part of her held out hopes he'd show up at the diner sometime, but she knew with her working days the chances were slim he'd be available when she was working. Instead, she tried to think of reasons she might use to justify a visit herself. Sam couldn't go yet but maybe she could. But everything she came up with seemed so lame and obvious that she dismissed it immediately. She wasn't about to embarrass herself. Besides, after the reaction she got surprising him the first time, she did wonder if surprising him might be a bad idea.

By Wednesday, the diner stayed fairly busy, the early Spring Break crowd having arrived in the Keys over the weekend. But around four, as her shift drew to a close, she came in the kitchen to find Lou fixing steaks and potatoes again, a bottle of wine sitting in a box on the counter.

"What is all this, Lou?" she said hands on her hips.

"Special delivery order," Lou said.

"Since when do we deliver?" she asked, knowing he was up to something because they didn't.

"Only for special customers," Lou said. "I need you to deliver this on your way home."

"Where to?"

"Cristof's Key," Lou said.

"The lighthouse?" She shook her head, scoffing. "Lou, no.

162

What are you thinking?"

Lou shrugged. "The customer called to request it. Apparently his first order got ruined by some rude stranger. He wanted to try again. He's paying this time."

Hannah tipped her head, shooting him an accusatory look. "He called and requested it?"

Lou nodded and raised his hand, index and middle fingers crossed. "Scout's honor. I have his credit card number right here." He lowered his hand and raised it again with a piece of paper from the counter. "Want to see it?"

She waved dismissively and narrowed her eyes in warning. "Lou, you know I love you, but I don't need you to play matchmaker."

"He called last night," Lou said. "I swear it. Asked for you personally. Who am I to say no? He's adding an extra tip."

Hannah sighed. "I have to get home—"

"I called Ellen and she said it's fine."

"Lou!" Hannah frowned at him.

He giggled. "The guy called. The customer is always right. You know our philosophy."

"I swear to God, Lou, this is not a game," she said.

Lou glanced at the clock on the wall. "You're right. And I'm running late. Get out of here and leave me alone. He expects you by five-thirty."

Lou turned back to his cooking, ignoring her as Hannah's mind raced. Had Jack really called? He wanted to recreate their earlier dinner? Because? Okay, she had to admit, it was either a romantic gesture or yet another apology. But was she ready for romance? He was the one who freaked out last time. What if it happened again?

Had Lou said he was paying for it? Was that true? What had changed in Jack's mind? If she were smart, she'd refuse to

163

participate and go straight home. Let Lou deal with it. She was too old for silly games. Or for getting hurt again. God, that was the last thing she needed with all she had already—especially Sam, and worse, Sam liked Jack. They'd met long before she'd ever have let a date meet her son. So Sam's heart was at risk, too. Risking her own heart was one thing. She'd been there before and knew she'd survive, but losing Rob had left Sam traumatized and mutism was one of the symptoms. No way would she risk causing him serious damage again.

Only this was a chance to see Jack again. The guy she hadn't stopped thinking about almost since they'd met. And maybe a chance to get right the romantic meal that had gone wrong before. And God, she really wanted to see what that was like with him. Oh my God, you're so weak, Hannah! What are you—a teenager? Jack's face came to mind with his high cheekbones and haunting blue eyes, the dimples on his cheeks when he smiled. She thought of Rob. When she'd first met Jack, the resemblance had been striking but now that she'd spent more time with him up close in daylight, she realized it was mostly a few little things—the delight he took in tools, his handiness around the house, kindness to Sam. Okay, the last one was big. Real big. And Jack and Rob did share the same kind determination and generosity. The way he'd been with Sam, loaned her his car, and taken care of the gate. Those were things that reminded her of Rob. And Jack was handsome. And he'd been so kind the other day, nothing like the night at the lighthouse or even the first time at the diner. So maybe she'd caught him on a bad day. It happened, right?

"Hannah, table six is waiting," Denise said as she slid around Hannah behind the counter and butt bumped her in the process.

Hannah blinked, looking at her fellow waitress. "What?"

"Order's up," Denise reminded her. "You okay?"

Hannah turned toward the counter between the kitchen and the front to retrieve her order and set it on a tray. "Yeah, fine. Just thinking."

Denise grinned. "Oh that's right! I heard you got another hot date tonight. Lucky girl."

"It's not a date," Hannah whispered, looking over her shoulder suspiciously at Lou, back in the kitchen.

Denise grinned. "I know, hon. Lou's just teasing you. You know we love you. He said he only told Jack he'd ask you to deliver food. Whatever happens after that is up to you."

"I don't know if I should," Hannah said, chewing her lip as she poured some soft drinks for one of her tables from the fountain.

"Honey, it's just a delivery," Denise said, brushing Hannah's arm lightly with her hand. "Relax. If you want to come right back, no one will be upset. It's your life."

Hannah leaned against the counter, the tension in her body lessening a bit. "Still, I'm going to tell Lou to stop meddling."

"You got it, girl." They exchanged a quick high five. "We can run our own lives thank you very much."

They both laughed and then Denise moved off, busy with her own tables. And that's when it occurred to Hannah: Sam wasn't here. It was just here. So she'd only be risking herself. They could always slow things down with Sam, but shouldn't she see if this was more than just some out of control fantasy her subconscious had contrived out of boredom or sheer loneliness? Sure, Lou was going a bit overboard, and she'd talk with him about that. But just because he was ahead of her didn't mean she couldn't spend more time with Jack. They were friends, right? It felt like it after the visit at the house.

Yep. She was going to see Jack tonight.

A dinner date. Oh my God! I must look awful! She wished she had time to run home and change, do her makeup.

"Hannah!" Lou called from the kitchen.

"I wanna talk to you, Lou!" she said as she turned and hurried back behind the counter again.

165

Later, she stopped home for twenty minutes to freshen up. It might not be a date, but she was damn well going to look good. She still had her pride, after all. As she emerged from her bedroom and headed for the Jeep, she glanced through the adjoining door to see Ellen and Sam watching her. Sam was grinning. Ellen shot her a suspicious look as she held out a duffel bag.

"Makeup and a clean dress," Ellen said. "Where are we off to?"

"Out with a friend," Hannah replied. "I decided I deserve a night off. I won't be late, I promise."

Hannah rushed over and leaned down to kiss Sam on the cheek, tousling his hair, then shooed them both. "You two have fun tonight, okay?"

Ellen shot her a cross-eyed look. She was clearly suspicious. "Which friend?"

"Denise, okay?" She hated lying, especially in front of Sam, but involving Ellen... Oh my God! She of all people needed to stay out of her love life. As she hurried back out and through the front door, her mind couldn't escape images of the lighthouse and Jack and her heart beat a little faster with anticipation.

CHAPTER 14

JACK CALLED LOU around seven the previous evening and explained his idea. Being an old romantic, the diner owner had loved it and promised he'd make arrangements for getting Hannah to come. Jack had offered to call Hannah himself, but Lou wouldn't hear of it. "I got this, trust me," he'd said, and so Jack had thanked him for his help and only felt a little guilty for plotting with Hannah's friends.

It was clear Lou commented that he was supportive of her dating and it was clear he considered Jack a good potential match. Jack hadn't really thought of it as an official date, but he understood how it might appear that way to others. For his part, Jack insisted it was just friendship and he only wanted a chance to make up for his rudeness to her in the past. He enjoyed her company, but he still wasn't over Abby and doubted he ever would be. He wasn't ready for anything too serious, but he was ready for a new friend.

As he hung up the phone, he asked questioned himself again. Enjoying the company of a friend was no crime, right? It seemed like Hannah could use the same thing. Okay, yes, he'd thought about what it would be like to kiss her, but he'd been caught up in the moment. Since then, he'd had time to clarify his thoughts. His intentions were pure and honorable—to have a really good, fun dinner with great conversation and great companionship. Beyond that he had no aspirations. If he could erase the memory of the spoiled dinner his first night at the lighthouse and solidify a new friendship, it would be more than enough.

As he debated this, he spent time trying to select an outfit. He'd never been big on that, Abby had always done it for him. He'd kept a couple of suits just in case, though he'd wondered if he'd ever have occasion to wear them. He pulled out the jacket and pants and laid them on the bed, then thought about the casual dress of people he'd seen around Islamorada and put them back. Florida was a different vibe for sure. He'd seen Miami Vice. Did he need to buy a tux? Oh my God, Jack. Chill. It's dinner with a friend, remember? Instead he chose a pair of Dockers that he hadn't worn in a while, which were neatly pressed and hung, and then set about trying to decide between his one nice Hawaiian shirt and a couple looser fitting button downs. Sleeves or no sleeves? Oh my God, where's Abby when I need her? And then he started wondering all over again why he was even doing this. It wasn't cheating, right?

He glanced at his watch and cursed. The dinner would be hours from now and he had work to do. He hurried down to the cart, grabbing his coffee thermos as he went and set out to do some fence work, but instead he drove the cart around the island scouting out shells and picnic spots. There were two or three that showed promise but he finally decided on three spots with hundreds of conch shells ready for Sam to collect to his heart's content. Then he proceeded to the spot where he'd planned to start repairing a fence damaged by storms, but after half an hour of fumbling around, unable to concentrate, he gave up and went back to the lighthouse.

Sitting at the kitchen table, sipping coffee, he pulled out the iPad and began making two lists. One for Hannah that would fulfill his promise to Sam. The other for himself, so he'd not screw this up again. On the "Jack-Let's- Not-Screw-this-Up" list, he notated the three prime picnic spots he and Hannah could explore, if they ever got that far. Then he also wrote down: "It's okay to make friends, relax and enjoy yourself" three times and then "Don't overreact," which he underlined too.

He checked his watch. He was running out of time. He looked around and crinkled his nose. The lighthouse looked like a bachelor's paid—dishes stacked in the sink, scattered soda and water battles on the counter and table, a couple shipping boxes emptied but thrown in the corner. He had to get the lighthouse ready!

He spent the afternoon cleaning the place, something he hadn't really attended to since Warren left. He swept and mopped the floors, put away dishes from a strainer, checked the bathrooms and gave them the once-over, dusted the surfaces, and so on. Then he set about transforming the kitchen into a dining fit spot. He set out cinnamon scented candles he'd picked up on his day off along with a red tablecloth and matching napkins. He straightened the chairs and then put the flowers he'd gathered on his circle of the island in vases and set them strategically around.

He wasn't going for frou-frou romantic, instead more lived in, comfortable touches—the kind of place to put a girl like Hannah at ease. When he was done, the kitchen smelled as good as it looked. Not bad if he said so himself. He might not have his mother's touch, but he thought he'd done good. Nonetheless, when he'd finished and went back up to the kitchen for a drink, he panned the room, taking in the results and Hannah's plump, perfect lips and found himself imagining where they might kiss.

Stop it! His inner voice chided and as he shook it off, he checked the clock and saw it was four-thirty. He had an hour until time to meet her at the pier on his cart. Had he cleaned it? Too late, time was up. He hurried upstairs to the master bedroom and decided on a change of clothes—slacks, a navy button down shirt, and a whimsical tie dotted by seashells. A birthday gift from Caroline. Then he hopped in the shower.

Thirty minutes later, he finished dressing by sliding into his leather dress shoes and slapping on a little cologne, then headed for the shed to pull out the cart.

The sky overhead was fading from blue to shades of violets, oranges, and yellows—all the makings of another amazing Florida sunset, the temperature dropping into the mid-60s; he must remember to take along a blanket in case Hannah got cold or some such, like women sometimes do. He selected one from the closet that smelled less like Warren and brought it with. Before climbing into the cart, he hosed off the sand and debris until his ride was shiny and clean, better suited for the effect he wanted. Unfortunately the hose sprayed his shoes. He pulled a rag from his cart, got them shined up again. Noticed sand on his trousers. Brushed them clean. Good as new. Bert was set to arrive right around five-thirty, so he checked his watch and headed for the pier at five-fifteen.

He suddenly had an empty feeling in the pit of his stomach. His mouth was dry and his heart racing. "Relax and enjoy yourself. It's okay to make friends," he repeated to himself over and over, and then tried to remember what Josie had told him about meditation techniques but couldn't remember an ounce of it. He really wished he had a shot of bourbon at that moment, then groaned at himself. "Yeah, great idea to show up for this with alcohol on your breath, Jack." So, he began mentally running over his lists again. "Just be yourself... Casual, keep it casual..." Then he slipped into dude mode with "You got this, bro... Who could resist this?..." and a couple "She'd be lucky to score yous."

He reached the beach and felt thankful no one was around to read his thoughts. What a moron. You sound like such a loser. Oh my God, Jack, what would Abby say?

As he drove along the edge of the beach, pelicans dove for their evening catch while crabs frolicked in the sand. Further out, dolphins leapt amongst the breakers and a few sailboats and fishing boats cruised the waves. The carefree, joyful ambience was the opposite of his inner turmoil as he stopped beside the pier and climbed out, standing to wait for the jetty boat's arrival. Within five minutes, he spotted Bert with Hannah seated behind him, turning and slowing the boat as he maneuvered in an arc to land beside the pier.

He suddenly panicked. Had he overdressed? Maybe she wasn't even planning to stay. This was just friendship, remember? But then the jetty boat pulled to a stop, the engine still humming, and Bert helped Hannah to her feet and off onto the pier. Jack came over to greet her.

Against the dying sun, the shape of her in a fitted red dress disintegrated all he had planned to say, his list he'd made for her boy—what was his name? The other list he'd created to keep from screwing up—gone. The wind carried her perfume straight to his olfactory glands, whipping from his lips any hope for intelligent thought. The scent was fruity but light, very pleasant—a stark contrast from onion rings and bicycle chain oil.

"I made it," said Hannah, stepping onto the sand. She wore a stunning form fitting red dress with heels and makeup that perfectly highlighted her features, her long red hair hanging loose down her back. Despite the windy boat road, it looked surprisingly undisturbed. As she smiled in the fading light of dusk, Jack's heart skipped a beat. She was stunning.

Jack found himself at a loss for words as they stood their staring at each other, Bert waiting patiently beside the pier, he supposed, for Hannah to decide if she was staying.

As Bert waited on the boat, the ocean breeze carried the scent of her perfume.

Finally, he took a deep breath and managed, "You look amazing."

"THANK YOU," HANNAH replied as Jack greeted her, looking handsome in his navy button down shirt and black slacks with dress shoes. He smiled and motioned to the cart.

"I hope you'll stay and join me."

It's just dinner, she reminded herself and then turned to Bert

171

and said, "I'll call you later, okay? Thanks."

Jack stepped forward and accepted the delivery box from Bert, slipping him his fee and tip, then followed Hannah to the cart.

She slid into the passenger seat in front as he set the box on the back seat and used bungee straps to secure it before taking his own seat beside her in the driver's spot. She caught a pleasant hint of amber and citrus in the air from his cologne as he settled in. Behind them she head the hum of the jetty's motor as Bert set out back to town from the pier.

As he reached for the ignition, she twisted her seat and he stopped, their eyes meeting.

"If you want to spend time with me, I'm fine with that," she said, her face somber—somewhere between anger and determination. It reminded her of the look Abby had given him when she'd been frustrated or disappointed. "But no involving my friends. I can make up my own mind. And who I spend time with is none of their business. Okay?"

Jack's shoulders sank, his chin lowering as his eyes found the ground at his feet.. "I'm sorry. I was trying for charming surprise, but I shouldn't have assumed."

"No, you shouldn't have," she agreed, but gently so he knew she wasn't angry. At least not now. She let the moment pass a beat, then trying to change the mood, said, "Thank you. I appreciate it." When Jack merely nodded, she went on, "So do you have anything you need to get off your chest before we eat? Anything upsetting? Stressing you out?" She'd meant it to come out as teasing, but Jack looked more like a deer in the headlights as he froze, his face somewhere between a scowl and a blush.

Finally, he laughed, and Hannah joined him.

"Well, that was sufficiently awkward," he replied. I'm fine. I promise. No drama tonight. Just two friends enjoying a beautiful Florida sunset and some fine coastal diner food." He glanced back at the delivery box and seemed to sniff the air, smiling. "It sure smells fantastic." Then he reached down again and started the ignition, shifting the cart into gear as he slowly accelerated away from the peer, following the path to the lighthouse.

"I can't believe we're doing this," Hannah confessed nervously, feeling awkward with the quiet.

"Having dinner?"

"Well that and…" she trailed off. It was just friendship, should she really be being so honest?

"It's not a date," he said, almost reading her mind. "Just two friends. And I promise you will only be seeing the best Jack tonight," Jack said.

"No angry Jack?"

He frowned, looking at her. "Only if you don't finish your veggies, young lady."

She laughed. "I'll try and remember that." She looked back at the box. "Lou even sent the same wine."

"Good, I liked it," Jack said.

"You finished the other bottle?"

"Oh yes, and your half full glass, too," Jack said.

"Wow, you may have a drinking problem," she teased.

"Oh, it took me several days, but it was delightful," Jack replied. Then his face formed a slight cringe and she thought she caught a flush of red creeping into his cheeks. "I was tempted to have a shot before I came tonight."

"You definitely have a problem."

They both laughed again. Hannah found herself really enjoying this playful side of him. She'd thought they had established a new level of comfort after his visit to her home, and she was glad it had carried over to tonight.

They casually and comfortably chatted the rest of the way to the lighthouse, where Jack parked the cart outside the front door then came around and helped her to her feet before retrieving Lou's box and leading her to the lighthouse, stopping to unlock the door, before politely inviting her inside.

They made their way up two floors to the kitchen where Hannah was amazed. Scented candles, flower bouquets, the table beautifully set with a fancy tablecloth and matching napkins. Jack took the box to the kitchen island and immediately began unpacking its contents, transferring some to serving dishes, which he arranged attractively on the table. When he'd finished that, he returned to the counter area and carried the wine and glasses over to the table where a corkscrew was waiting along with silverware. Hannah was very impressed. And momentarily speechless.

"Shouldn't Warren be here?" she joked, adding, "for accuracy?"

And Jack chuckled. "This is not a do over. We're starting fresh," he said as he strode over to the table and swung a hand invitingly. "Please, have a seat. We're almost ready."

She managed a "Thank you" as he pulled out a chair and waited for her to sit before gently pushing it back in.

"I'll be with you in just a bit," he promised and went back to work carrying the serving plates over along with serving spoons and other implements—everything necessary for a fancy dinner. After a few minutes, he joined her at the table, stopping to uncork the wine and pour each of them a glass before taking his own seat across the table.

"This may be the best fresh start I've ever seen," Hannah said, still amazed by what she was seeing.

"You thought the apology at the diner was the entire apology?" Jack shrugged. "True gentlemen never stop saying 'I'm sorry.'"

She laughed. "Is that from a movie?"

Jack mock recoiled in horror. "No, that was all me."

Their eyes met and Hannah realized he was sincere, feeling a sense of guilt. "I'm sorry."

He raised a palm to stop her. "Please, this is my apology."

She couldn't help it, with the sincerity in his eyes and those dimples on his cheeks—the kind little kids just wanted to stick their fingers into—he was adorable. She laughed. "Okay, don't let me get in the way then."

He pushed a platter of steaks toward her. "Please, help yourself."

For the next hour, they took their time and enjoyed one of the finest meals Lou had ever prepared in Hannah's experience, chatting like two old friends all the while. They fell quickly into an easy banter that was playful yet sincere, starting out with nothing of consequence but gradually moving into deeper, more personal subjects, and Hannah found herself learning a lot more about her companion than she'd expected. He told her about his family and growing up in Kansas, his childhood antics on the farm and in school, and boating with his uncle and cousins in the summers. He talked about his job as an architect and some of the jobs he'd done and various incidents. Finally, he got around to meeting Abby, how they had been childhood sweethearts from middle school on, and about the ups and downs of that and how they'd fallen in love.

To Hannah it sounded like they had come from similar families, and had similarly loving marriages, although Hannah and Rob had met late in college. Jack's parents had been hardworking but supportive, despite not being outgoing with their emotions. He certainly sounded like his relationship with his mother had been far better than hers, or at least less filled with conflict. And when he spoke about Caroline, it reminded Hannah of how she often spoke about Sam. He was so filled with pride and love that at times he struggled for words, and at the end, he grew more silent because of tears forming in his eyes at the memories, not shyness.

When that happened, Hannah simply reached over and put her hand atop his across the table, waiting in silent support until he recovered. And then it was her turn.

For her part, Hannah filled Jack in on her own life as well: childhood in the Keys, her closeness with her father, her own schooling, childhood friends, and then marriage, including meeting Rob, and then Sam's birth. She too teared up a little in the telling, despite steering away from Rob's death as Jack had done, and in the end, they ended up staring across the table at each other's tears until they both broke into laughter, which served to break the melancholy mood and cheer them both.

"We're both a couple of sentimental saps, aren't we?" Jack teased.

Hannah laughed and nodded. "Yep, that's me."

"We have a lot more in common than I'd realized," he said as he leaned back in his chair, the meal finished.

"Yes, we do, and I appreciate your opening up to me," Hannah said. "It's nice." Jack seemed like a completely different person from the one she'd met at the diner originally and then tried to have dinner with at the lighthouse. Though the underlying sadness she'd seen then was still present, it didn't dominate everything. He seemed less dark and troubled, more carefree and relaxed with her, and she was enjoying every minute.

"It is," Jack agreed.

When Hannah excused herself to use the rest room, Jack got up to prepare the dessert—a banana cream pie, another of Lou's specialties.

AS HE SLICED the pie, Jack glanced out the window at the purple night with its twinkling stars, reminded of many nights like this he'd spent with Abby, gazing up at the endless heavens in awe. It was beautiful and peaceful and he suddenly realized he wanted to share it with someone for the first time in a long while, When Hannah returned from the bathroom, he made a suggestion, "How about dessert under the stars?"

"Sure," she said, smiling.

Jack packed the pie and a serving spatula in a box along with two plates and forks, grabbed and recorked the wine, and put it along with two glasses in the box as well and then motioned to the spiral staircase. "After madam."

"Thank you, sir," Hannah said and led the way.

They wound up sitting on the east side of the lighthouse overlooking the beach on patio chairs Jack retrieved from the shed and set out for them, with a small patio table in between to hold the pie, the wine, and their plates and glasses.

The pie was delicious and Jack savored each bite as they looked at the stars to a symphony of crickets, tree frogs, and birds. Hannah pointed out some favorite constellations. In particular, she talked about Cancer, the crab. "As the Greeks told it, Hera sent the crab to distract Heracles while he was fighting the Hydra serpent beast with many heads," she explained. "When the crab tried to kill Heracles, he kicked it all the way to the stars."

Jack chuckled. "That's a hell of a kick. He should have played for the Dolphins."

Hannah nodded. "The other version is that the crab was crushed and Hera placed it in the sky to honor its efforts, only in a region of the sky with no bright stars to signify its failure."

"Poor crab," Jack said. "Forever marked a failure."

"The Greek gods were not exactly the forgiving sort," Hannah reminded him.

"Yeah, as I recall they were pretty harsh."

"Cronus castrated his father and ate his kids to prevent them from turning on him. But Zeus' mother hid him and when he grew up, he forced Cronus to vomit up all the kids so they could launch a war of vengeance against him," Hannah cited, recalling the story from her college reading.

"That's pretty harsh all right."

She pointed. "The mass in the center is called the Beehive or Praesepe, which is Latin for 'the manger.' It's one of the nearest and most populated clusters to our solar system with at least a thousand stars supposedly."

"That's amazing, isn't it?" Jack said taking it in with true admiration. Her face lit up with delight as she talked about it, an almost childlike wonder and enthusiasm that was inspiring to behold.

"Anyway, growing up in Florida, with crabs so common, I always liked that story," Hannah said, looking at him.

He stared at the stars a moment, lost in thought, before their eyes met. "I like it too. Thanks for sharing it with me."

She nodded, satisfied, and reached for another bite of pie with her fork. "Lou really does make fantastic banana cream," she said.

"The entire meal was amazing," Jack said. "Just as good as the first time." He looked at her again and added, "The companionship was even better."

"Yes, it was," she agreed as their eyes met again. "I'm so glad you decided on a fresh start."

"That was one of Caroline's favorite phrases when she made a mistake or had a problem. 'Can we have a fresh start, daddy?'" He said it then looked away, in thought, growing somber again.

"There's something to that idea I've always liked," Hannah said. "Kids and their eternal hope and faith things can get better. Second chances are rare sometimes, but sure great when you get them."

Jack looked back at her then, her smile warm and genuine, and he couldn't help returning it. "Yes, they are." They watched each other a moment, saying nothing, and then Jack said, "So is Cristof's Key all that you imagined?"

Hannah grunted. "Well, you haven't shown me the island yet. But the lighthouse is certainly terrific and fascinating. It's really beautiful out here."

"Yes it is," Jack agreed. "You know, I need to give you the tour," he added, after finishing his last bite of pie.

"Yes, you do, but what about waiting until Sam can come along?" Hannah asked. "I know he'll be excited to see it, and I wouldn't want to make you repeat yourself."

Jack's heart leaped and did a little dance as he fought to keep the pleasure hidden from his expression. She was planning to come back, and bring Sam. This had clearly gone better than he'd hoped. He stood then and offered her his hand, helping her from her chair before bending to repack the box. "Well, to be honest, I could probably use the practice. You'd be my first tour subjects. But sure, we can wait...for now."

Hannah glanced at her watch.

"Do you need to get back?" Jack asked.

"Not just yet but soon," Hannah said. "I have another morning shift at the diner tomorrow. We go in at five and open at six."

"Early bird. Fortunately, I can sleep in a little later if I want to."

"It is nice when it's hot, to beat the heat," Hannah said. "It's the humidity that kills you. Thick as butter."

"Well, Kansas gets pretty hot and humid in the summers." He grabbed the box and carried it toward the lighthouse. Hannah started to fold the patio furniture but he waved her off. "I'll come back and get that after I walk you to the pier. No one around to steal it."

"Oh, right," Hannah said. "I'm so used to crowded beaches."

"Cristof's Key has its advantages," Jack said. He carried the box into the first floor communications room and set it on a desk, then came back out and joined her under the stars, shutting the door behind him.

They started off together, walking down the path from the lighthouse, then turning just above the vegetation line and heading slowly toward the pier.

"I scouted out some great shelling spots and a couple picnic points as well," Jack said. "Whenever Sam gets his walking boot, feel free to come back."

"Oh, he's ready," Hannah said. "He's written a note about it every morning since you mentioned it. He can't wait."

Jack chuckled, feeling good as he imagined Sam's smile. "That's great."

"Honestly, I think he's just as excited about seeing the lighthouse and the island, though," Hannah said.

"Maybe I should set up a treasure hunt and hint at lost pirate treasure," Jack said.

"That sounds like a lot of work."

"The cart makes it easier. Besides, I think it would be fun."

"Me too. You're so good with him. It amazes me sometimes."

"Really?"

Hannah nodded then stopped walking, choking up. Jack put a hand on her arm, just a light touch, gentle, and their eyes met. "He doesn't do well with strangers. Ever since the accident." She swiped at her tears with the back of her hand. "You're the first one."

"Wow. I'm honored," Jack said, meaning it. He'd had no idea. He felt a sudden urge to ask about it. What had happened exactly? When? But then he thought of Caroline and Abby. He wasn't sure he was ready to talk about that either, so he bit back the urge and simply waited for her to continue.

"He responds to you in some ways like he did with Rob," Hannah said. "It's bringing out a side of him I haven't seen

180

since the accident."

Tears were pouring now and Jack reached out and gently pulled her to him in an embrace. "I don't know what I did," he said, "but if I'm helping, I'm glad."

Hannah sniffled. "Me too."

He held her a minute as she cried and then sniffled again, wiping the tears with her fingers before gently pulling away. "Sorry."

"Don't be," Jack said. "Having a child is..." He looked away as his own emotions swelled. "...special." He felt his own tears forming and quickly pinched his face to hold them back. "There's really nothing like it, is there? The whole idea that you created this whole other person...out of love. A person that looks like both of you in certain ways and yet is completely unique, alive, breathing—the best part of who you are." Then to lighten the mood, he added, "Well, you hope and pray at least."

"Yeah," Hannah agreed, sniffling turning to a slight chuckle.

Jack was truly touched at the realization he'd had such an impact on Sam. He hadn't realized the significance until Hannah explained, and he understood why she was so emotional about it. He hadn't made any special effort, but he and Sam had connected naturally. Jack liked kids, and they liked him. And something about the boy standing there in the egg aisle had drawn him in. Now, he was glad. And he hoped he could somehow help Sam come further out of his shell again, not for himself, but for Sam and his mother.

They looked at each other for a moment, just breathing, letting the moment pass, then started walking together again toward the pier as if in some unspoken agreement.

"He's a great kid," Jack said. "You're very lucky."

"Yes, I am," she said. Soft moonlight drifted in on the waves and illuminated her face, lending it a slight glow just for a moment. It was almost like she was glowing. And once again,

Jack was taken with her natural beauty. More than ever, he wanted to pull her to him and kiss her right then.

Hannah pulled a cell phone from her pocket as they came in sight of the pier. "I guess I should call Bert, and see how soon he can pick me up."

Jack gave an amused grunt. "Good idea."

He waited as she made the call, then hung up. "He's on his way."

"Thanks for bringing me dinner tonight," Jack said then as they stopped beside the pier and turned to face each other.

Her eyes met his. "Thanks for giving me the royal treatment."

"It was the least I could do after..." Jack's voice faded off but from the look in her eyes he realized immediately she knew he meant their previous attempt.

"You know, we don't usually deliver," Hannah said.

"I feel special," Jack replied as she reached up and brushed back some hair that had blown across her forehead. For a moment, as they looked in each other's eyes, Jack thought she wanted him to kiss her. He pondered it, then stepped forward and quickly bent toward her.

"No," Hannah said, pressing him away with a palm against the chest.

Jack stopped, feeling the blood rush to his cheeks. "I'm sorry." What had he done wrong? Had he completely misread her?

"We're just friends, right?" she said.

And even though he'd planned it that way himself, his heart sank a little bit as he mumbled, "Yes. Absolutely." He swallowed, trying to recover, then added, "I'm sorry. I just thought—"

"I know. It's okay," Hannah said. "I've had a lovely evening, really. And you kept your promise."

He frowned a moment, not sure what she meant.

"No angry outbursts," she explained.

"Oh yeah. Sorry again about that."

She shook her head. "It's okay to grieve. It's a roller coaster ride. I get it. But I'm just not sure I'm ready to rush into anything, and I'm pretty sure you're not either."

Jack saw the spotlight from the jetty boat as it approached and nodded. "You're right." He said it as much to convince himself as her, because inside he felt conflict. What did he really want? What was right? He sighed and offered a soft smile. "I hope we can do it again." And he meant it.

Hannah nodded. "Only if you ask me yourself. Okay?"

Jack raised a palm like a Boy Scout then crossed his middle and index finger. "Scout's honor."

Bert appeared and turned the boat, slowly pulling up alongside the pier.

Jack motioned. "Your chariot awaits."

She nodded and reached out to squeeze his hand. "Good night."

"Good night," he said, then walked forward with her hand in his and leaned over to quickly kiss her on the cheek before helping her onto the boat and stepping back.

Bert called a greeting then shifted the engine back into gear and pulled away again.

Jack watched them disappear into the night, then turned and slowly walked back to the lighthouse along the beach.

CHAPTER 15

HANNAH ARRIVED HOME to find Ellen waiting at the kitchen table with a cup of decaf coffee. "So?"

"So what? How's Sam?" Hannah countered.

"Sam's fine," Ellen said. "He went right to sleep. Denise says 'hi.' I stopped by the diner."

Hannah sighed. "I just needed a night to myself. I'm allowed. You don't need to treat me like a child."

"Okay." Ellen said, eyes locked on Hannah's. "How's the man with the great butt?" She looked smug.

Hannah stared at her mother-in-law a moment, not wanting to get into it. But Ellen's eyes said it all. She already knew. Hannah didn't have to say a thing.

"He was fine," Hannah said, finally surrendering to the inevitable.

"See? You knew who I meant," Ellen said, furrowing her brow, eyes narrowing—a sure sign she was displeased, even angry, so Hannah added, "We had a nice time."

"He's handsome," Ellen said, "but he's certainly no Rob."

Hannah rolled her eyes and set her purse in its usual spot on the corner of the counter, calling over her shoulder as she went to check on Sam, "That's all I'm going to say." Ellen had been letting her know for a while that she believed the best way to honor Rob was for Hannah to live like a nun, but Hannah had no intention of giving up another chance at happiness. It wasn't worth bothering to explain that she and Jack were just "friends," though. Once Ellen had made up her mind, it was like arguing with a brick wall. No, instead, she walked away, knowing that seeing her sweet baby boy would be just the thing to cheer her up after her mother-in-law's drilling.

Sam was in his room, tucked under the covers, lying asleep on his right side—his favorite position. She pushed the door open a crack wider and slipped inside, moving silently over to adjust the covers and then gently rub his hair as she kissed him on the cheek. As always, her heart swelled at the smell of her little boy. Tonight it was somewhere between chlorine from the pool and peanut butter—not doubt from a before bed snack. No sand, so they hadn't gone shell hunting, which was fine with her. Maybe she'd surrender soon and take Sam to Cristof's Key. It had been her idea, after all, and when she'd told Jack he had looked pleased about it.

Sam mumbled something but didn't awaken, so she watched him for a bit, then quietly slipped back out and returned the cracked door to its previous position.

The dinner had gone better than Hannah could have ever expected and she found herself still feeling both relief and excitement in the aftermath. Jack had taken her scolding with genuine remorse, and they'd still been able to recover and enjoy the night. He'd been nothing less than a charming, funny, personable gentleman, and Lou, of course, had given them his best, which made it all easy. The ambience of the lighthouse and the island had also been terrific. And though Hannah found herself unsure if Jack had actually considered it a date or just friends having dinner, to her it felt like a bit of both and she didn't mind one bit. It had the makings of a date for sure. But because they hadn't defined specifically, they'd been able to relax and get to know each other better while erasing and replacing the memory of the earlier failed dinner with a brand new, happy one. A spectacular one, in fact.

It was the best time she'd had since Rob died, and certainly the first night alone with a man she'd had in ages. All things considered, she'd actually arrived looking pretty, even if the boat ride over had played havoc with her hair. Jack hadn't seemed to notice, and before she left he'd even complimented her.

Jack had done a remarkable job with the lighthouse, too, and she was flattered that he'd gone to so much effort just for her. He'd also put on dress clothes that were quite flattering. And the slacks he'd chosen had indeed flattered his sexy ass quite well, giving her a chance to sneak a couple nice peeks once or twice.

Altogether, she'd almost forgotten all about Ellen's anger and how Lou had schemed with Jack to get her there. They meant well, but she'd put them both on notice how she should be treated, and she expected them both to respect that from now on.

After she'd showered, as she was getting ready for bed and contemplating the dreadful conversation she'd be having with Ellen in the morning, the phone rang. It was Jack.

"I just wanted to thank you for a lovely evening and make sure you got home safe," he said.

Hannah sighed. Such a gentleman. "I did, thank you," she said. "It was delightful."

"Okay, well, sweet dreams," Jack said. "I'll look forward to talking again soon."

She thought about him all the next day, even as Ellen decried her displeasure and Lou and Denise grilled and teased her about the date, the Diner slower than usual for a Thursday. That night, he called again a little earlier and they wound up chatting on the phone for over an hour, the same kind of light, enjoyable banter they'd carried on throughout the dinner.

On Friday, she had the morning off to take Sam up to the hospital to get his cast off and a walking cast put on. She and Sam were both excited, and afterward, he was hobbling around so fast she took him to a park to burn off energy before heading for the Diner.

That night after dinner, Sam drew a picture of her and Jack following him around a beach as he gathered shells, a lighthouse in the background. In his image, the figures representing she and Jack were holding hands. She considered warning him against expecting too much, but her hand grew warm from just imagining it. Sam liked Jack, after all, and Jack had gotten him communicating on a level she wanted to encourage. So if they went, it would be as much for Sam as for her. In the end, she let it go. For now. And when Jack called later that night, he asked about the walking cast.

"He got it on this morning," Hannah told him.

"Great," Jack said. "So you guys can come shell hunting tomorrow, and we'll have a picnic."

"Don't you have to work?" Hannah asked.

"I can monitor the feed remotely for a few hours," Jack said. "That's the most important part. The rest I can do after you go and before you arrive."

"Are you sure it's okay?" Hannah said, not wanting to seem eager, even though her heart had already leapt at the idea. Ellen would just have to get over it. It was time for Hannah to get on with her life, and do what she wanted, and she knew Rob would support her in that, wherever it led. If he were here, he'd be the first one to tell his mother that to her face, too.

"Absolutely," Jack assured her, and so they made plans. The trick with getting Sam on a boat after his dad's accident was to do it during daylight. Sam would absolutely refuse to go near a boat at night, because that was when his father had died before his eyes. So Hannah made sure to plan a trip with plenty of time to get back before dark, agreeing to leave her shift early at two and come over, heading back by five. That left plenty of time for a good shell hunt and a picnic.

That night, she dreamed of walking on the beach with Jack. It was the first time she'd dreamed of being with a man since

Rob, and though she awoke feeling all warm and cuddly, she also felt a little tinge of guilt and concern. She realized she hadn't dreamed about Rob in quite a while either, and that was notable. For several years since the accident, she'd dreamed of Rob almost every night and it was only recently that had changed. The fact that it had changed to another man was significant. She enjoyed Jack's company more than any man she'd met since Rob, she had to admit. And though she was certain he had the makings of a really good friend, she also found him good looking and romantic in a way that made her imagine more than that, too. But she'd seen him struggling with his emotions, especially his grief. She didn't want to be the rebound girl, and besides, she was old enough to know it took much more than physical attraction to make a long term meaningful relationship work.

Thankfully, she knew with Sam there, nothing would happen. She just had to be wary and not let her heart get ahead of her head. That was the last thing she needed.

She took the dream as another sign she was ready to move on, but the question remained: was Jack the right one? And who occupied Jack's dreams at night?

She got up for a glass of milk and had a few apple slices before going back to bed, restless and stirring for what seemed like forever until finally falling into dreamless slumber.

THE NEXT MORNING once she'd told Lou her afternoon plans, he insisted on letting her off around one, just after the lunch rush, and though usually no amount of arguing from her would change his mind, Hannah stayed anyway, working until almost two-thirty before taking the Jeep home for Sam—her point made. She changed into beach wear and packed his shell collection backpack and supplies, sunscreen, two water bottles, and some snacks. Then they headed down to the pier to meet Bert, who ran a regular schedule most days, leaving Jack's Jeep parked in the diner lot where Lou could keep an eye on it.

They arrived at the base of the lighthouse around two and Jack was there waiting for them. "Welcome to Cristof's Lighthouse," he said as Sam stood in awe, looking up at the lighthouse, the first of any size he'd ever seen up close.

"We're here," Hannah said, her eyes meeting Jack's.

"I'm glad," he said, then focusing on Sam, added, "Would you like a tour, young man?"

Sam nodded, dancing about a bit despite the walking cast, and Jack led them inside.

For the next thirty minutes, Jack took them on a tour of the lighthouse. Once again, Hannah found herself amazed at how good he was with her son. Though he directed his anecdotes at Sam, he did it without ever talking down to him. Instead, he phrased things in simpler words and just the right details that Sam could both understand as well as making it all sound so important and exciting. Sam was thoroughly rapt, interrupting again and again to pester Jack with questions. Though Hannah expected him to get annoyed, Jack surprised her by making a game out of it, and one that Hannah enjoyed as well. She found herself making up questions just to join in. She hadn't toured a lighthouse since she was a child herself, and the uniqueness of this one—with its larger than common quarters—fascinated her. She particularly admired the way the planners and keepers made great use of every available space. She wished she was so good at that and decided when she finally got a condo or her own home, she'd make more effort. Maybe if she and Jack were still in touch, she'd ask his advice.

As they finished the tour up in the light tour, Hannah's eyes panned the incredible view, Sam bouncing around awkwardly at her feet. The walking cast wasn't for jumping, so he kind of just leaned back and forth, putting a bit more pressure on his healthy foot in a way that made the rhythm a bit more abrupt every time he leaned back off the cast.

"If you come back another time, I can show you how

everything works," Jack said. "If you want."

"Oh, we don't want to be a bother when you're working," Hannah immediately said, but then she looked down. Sam looked up at her, his eyes glistening as a wide grin consumed his face. He was clearly asking her to say it was okay. She didn't want to commit to anything just yet, even though this adventure was going well, but it was hard to say at seeing Sam so happy and excited. "Absolutely," she said. "Thank you."

"Now let's go find some shells," Jack said.

They both had to scold Sam for rushing on the spiral stairs in spite of his walking cast as they headed down. Then they loaded in the cart and drove along the beach.

"I can't believe you live here alone," Hannah said as they circled the island. It was a stunning landscape, appearing almost virgin and undisturbed compared to that of the main Keys islands. The flowers, trees, and plants, of course, were all familiar, some from Ellen's own landscaped yard, others from those of the neighbors—poisonwoods with their green and yellow flowers, sea grapes with their clusters of budding fruit, cocoplums, palmettos, and various palms. On the mainland, they were usually tended to and landscaped, whereas these were totally natural with Spanish Moss draping from trees unchecked. Sargasso Weed and other seaweeds littered the sand, sometimes in large clumps that buried it. And though it was as tropical as anywhere in the Keys, the seventy degree weather and cool breeze lent it an otherworldly quality that added to the ambience. The idea of Jack living here alone amazed her. It seemed so isolated.

"It's beautiful," Jack said as the sun cast prisms of light across the emerald-green water and waves. The foliage was light in some places and dense in others, but there were a few clear paths that obviously had been driven on or walked through often, Hannah assumed, by Coast Guard personnel.

As they rounded the island, she also saw the remains of a few old foundations in amongst the trees. It was beautiful here no doubt, but she wasn't sure she saw the appeal of living here alone. "Don't you get lonely?"

"Well, when I came here, I wanted to be alone," Jack said.

She hesitated a moment as she thought of her dream the night before and the questions she'd asked herself after, then it just came out, "Because of Abby?"

Jack was silent a moment then he nodded, his eyes meeting hers. "I don't think I'll ever be over it."

"I don't think anyone ever is," Hannah said, feeling as if she understood completely. "It just becomes easier to live with it." It had taken her a while to find that solution herself. She'd always love Rob; always cherish the time they'd had together, the greatest legacy of which, of course, was Sam. But she no longer felt the need to honor the memory by putting life on hold, and she wondered again where Jack was in that journey. "At first, every little moment, every little thing reminds you of them. But as time goes on, you have to get on with life. You stop forcing yourself to just get up and breath and you get out there again—go back to work, church, life, whatever. Eventually you start accepting invitations from friends again for simple gatherings, even small parties, until little by little, it becomes more comfortable to move on. You never forget them, and you never will, but you learn to manage the pain and still carry on." She reached over and put a hand on his forearm, with gentle soothing strokes. "It just takes time."

Jack nodded, saying nothing, and Hannah decided to change the subject for the moment.

"Are you sure they'll be any shells left at this time of day? Most of the barrier islands get picked clean every morning by visitors," she said, and then stopped as they topped a hill overlooking a small fenced in cove. The sand was almost white here and she saw shells poking out and lying about all over. She looked at Sam and smiled. "Look at all the shells, Sam. I guess our host here has been keeping people away."

Sam bounced in his seat as they both took it in.

"Well, this is the north end, the opposite corner from the mainland," Jack explained, "so people don't get out this far as often. This one is marked 'No Tresspassing' and fenced because of the tidepools. It's not safe for swimmers. Besides, I think most casual visitors have no idea it's here."

Sam shot him a thumbs up then glanced at her and she tousled his hair. This was usually a grandma-Sam thing, so she was pleased to see the enthusiasm carrying over to an Ellen-free excursion.

It took five minutes to work their way down a winding path to their destination, and Jack had to stop and unlock two padlocked gates along the way. As soon as they arrived, Sam sprang from the cart and hobbled excited around the beach, pointing. There were conch shells everywhere of all shapes and sizes. Hannah grabbed his backpack and held it out.

"Well, go get busy," she urged. "Grandma's gonna be so happy. But don't go in the water, okay?" Sam snapped the backpack from her hands and nodded then rushed off as quickly as the walking cast allowed. She had plenty of time to convince Sam of a story they could tell Ellen to explain where they'd gone to get the shells...and why.

"Should we help him?" Jack asked.

"Oh, he'd be offended," Hannah said, looking at Jack with admiration. The time and care he'd put in to find just the right spot for them touched her. He looked so satisfied as he watched Sam bouncing across the sand to pick just the right starting spot. "I tried once. It's his and Ellen's thing. In fact, we're lucky she didn't know about it or she'd have insisted on joining us."

"Would that be so bad?" She wasn't used to a stranger, especially a man, taking such interest and care with her son, and at the moment, she felt a strong urge to kiss Jack.

"Not if you think inviting a barracuda into a gold fish pond is a good time."

Jack snorted. "Point taken. So we should wait here?"

She laughed. "Oh we can do whatever we want. He won't care. But I do want to keep him in sight." Besides Sam's safety, she didn't want to risk being alone with Jack while her feelings were so raw.

"Of course," Jack said. "I just thought maybe we could walk around the beach a bit before we pull out the picnic stuff."

"Great," she said.

Together, they walked down toward the waves, stopping just short of the waterline. Hannah stopped and took off her sandals, letting her feet touch the cool, off-white sand. This time of year it was such a nice feeling—the sand between your toes. In the summer it got so hot, it could burn your feet, but not in early Spring. She loved it. She tucked her sandals under her arm and started walking, Jack keeping pace alongside.

"You know, it's very peaceful," Hannah said. "A nice change from the beaches in the Keys. Even this time of year, there are always people about. Do people ever visit uninvited?"

"I chased some teenagers off the other day," Jack said. "But so far, uninvited visitors are rare."

Hannah watched two crabs darting back and forth in the sand as the tide came in and knocked them off their feet. She laughed. "They're such silly little creatures sometimes. Fun to watch."

"So many of the animals and plants here are new to me," Jack said. "I'm making discoveries every day." He pointed to a school of fish circling near their feet. "Like those damselfish. Sergeant majors there. I love how some have a deep blue-black color that changes as they move, while others have yellow, black, and silver stripes."

"They're actually two varieties," Hannah gently corrected. The striped ones are the Sergeant Majors, and the blue ones are blue tang."

"Well I… that's interesting…" Jack stumbled for the right words. "I probably should've known that, but they both have those diamond-shaped bodies and small tails."

"Yeah, and they like bid class sizes in their schools," she joked.

"I did notice that," Jack admitted. "You're good. Did your dad teach you this or did you learn about it in school?

"I know a lot about them from growing up here, but it didn't hurt Rob was a marine engineer. When we first got married, he took me out to explore sites with him before finalizing the plans, and I got to see a lot of variety. He started telling me about them. Then I learned more stuff on my own or from friends or TV. So if you want me to point anything out, just let me know."

Jack motioned. "Everything really."

She laughed. "That might take more than a couple hours."

"I guess I'll have to keep inviting you, then."

They looked at each other, their eyes meeting, and for a moment, and Jack's eyes were so gentle and soft. She saw great compassion there amidst the sadness and a little fear. But at the moment he was smiling as if there were nowhere else he'd rather be, and she realized she felt the same.

"I enjoy your company, too," Hannah finally said. "What made you change your mind?"

"About what?" Jack frowned, puzzled.

"You said when you came here you wanted to be alone."

"I thought I did," he said with a nod.

She shot him a questioning look. "You changed your mind?"

He sighed. "Well, to be honest, you did."

Hannah's heart fluttered.

"And Sam."

It had been so long since a man had said anything so sweet and romantic to her, and the warmth rushing through her reminded her how much she'd missed it. "How?" she asked.

"Well, he's an expert at eggs, for one," Jack teased, and she laughed. "And he was so good at getting his point across, I didn't even find it odd that he didn't speak. I figured he was taught 'don't talk to strangers,' like most kids."

"And me?"

Jack hmmmed, his eyebrows creasing and hand going to his chin as he thought about it. "You kind of wore me down, I guess."

She laughed again and he joined her.

"Seriously," she said as she reached up to push back some loose strands of hair the breeze had blown in her face.

He shrugged, but in his eyes she caught a hint of the struggle he'd been going through. He'd been conflicted. She remembered that stage of grief—the wanting to just revel in your anger and sadness and be left alone. But somehow he'd overcome it and decided to let her and Sam in. It touched her more than she expected it to and they walked on in silence for a bit. "I just decided it would be good to have a friend," he said finally.

"I'm glad," she said, unable to resist the urge to put a hand on his arm. They walked on without speaking for a bit, until she glanced back. Sam was behind them, out of sight. She stopped and turned, walking back up a rise to check on him. He was happily gathering shells as if oblivious to their presence. She turned back to Jack and smiled. "Thank you. He's in heaven."

"I'm glad I could help," Jack said, automatically turning and leading her back toward the sand and Sam. "I don't think anyone's gathered shells here much in years."

Hannah nodded. "Ellen is going to be thrilled. She uses them to make jewelry, and I've never seen so many sizes to choose from in one place."

"Will I have to chase her off like those kids?" Jack teased.

Hannah giggled. "Probably."

Jack pointed to a "No Trespassing" sign nearby. "She can read, right?"

"Yes, but the real problem is she won't care."

Jack chortled, and at first, Hannah thought it was just at her comment. Then she noticed where he was looking and turned to see Sam with his arms out wide, circling in the air as he hopped on one foot, struggling to keep his balance. "Is he pretending to be a stork?" Jack wondered.

"Probably."

In a few seconds, Sam fell over, landing in the sand on his butt. That's when he looked over and saw them watching...and grinned. It was adorable. She couldn't help but laugh, too.

"I guess we should go help him," Jack said.

"Oh, no, he'll be fine," Hannah said, "but I wouldn't mind something to drink. Can we set up the picnic stuff?"

"Sure," Jack said and they started back together.

CHAPTER 16

F OR THE NEXT hour, Jack and Hannah leaned back on a blanket, chatting, as they watched Sam's endless shell hunt. Every once in a while he'd carry a bucketful over and dump it in the backpack before going back to search for more.

Watching Sam on the beach took Jack back to the time Abby and he had taken Caroline to South Padre Island and how she'd toddled around, exploring, with seemingly unending energy, laughing and giggling as she played in and explored the sand. Both Jack and Abby had delighted in watching their daughter—the way her face lit up when she picked up a handful of sand and let it slide through her fingers. The fascination mixed with delight she showed as she discovered seashells or watched crabs scurrying about and chased them. The way she delighted in waves sweeping over her bare feet and danced about in the wet sand. Something about beaches and nature were so intriguing to children—so many things to see and discover—and Jack smiled at the memory, wishing Caroline could be here now to play with Sam. She had always wanted a brother.

And then his chest tightened and he felt a pain rise at the back of his throat. Caroline and Abby weren't here. They never would be. And god he longed to hold them just one more time—run his hair through Abby's hair and smell that sexy perfume with its hints of apple and soft, silky cream. He missed the musty smell of Caroline's hair and that fruity princess perfume she insisted on wearing despite his protests that she was growing up too fast; the smoothness of her young skin, and the way she threw herself against him and held onto him like her very breathing depended on it. He'd never smell those smells again or feel their hugs—so precious. They were what had made life worthwhile for so long for him, and now they were gone. He swallowed hard before realizing where he was again. Sam was filling his bucket rapidly with some decent sized shells.

"That backpack's going to be heavy when he's done," Jack said as Sam continued filling his bucket.

"Yeah, I think he's blissfully unaware of that fact," Hannah said, oblivious to what he'd been thinking. "One of us will have to rescue him." As she said it, he looked up at the sky where cotton-ball cumulus clouds floated slowly across a peaceful sea of blue. It was perfect weather on a perfect day. It startled him to realize he felt that way. The first perfect day he'd had in ages. His chest tightened all over again and he wondered how he could ever think a day was perfect without Abby and Caroline?

"Have you ever had sea grapes?" Hannah asked.

Jack shook his head. "No. Are they safe?"

Hannah laughed. "Usually. You might want to skip the rotten-looking ones."

"Sounds like a good general rule," Jack said. "I'll have to try them."

"If you're really nice, maybe I'll help you pick some later. They seem to be all over the place." She motioned.

Jack grunted. "Well, at least I know I won't go hungry out here if I get behind on groceries."

They both laughed.

Jack's stomach rumbled. "I'm hungry. Want to break out the food?"

"Sure," she said as he stood and held out a hand to help her up. She took it, and he felt a euphoria, his heart racing, as their hands touched. Her skin was gentle and clean, as if the sand wouldn't dare stick to it and mar it, and the trust he felt from her surprised him as she allowed him to pull her to her feet, then walked with him to the cart.

"You think Sam's hungry?" Jack asked, glancing down the beach toward her son.

"Oh yeah, but he's probably too busy to notice," Hannah said. "We'll get everything ready then drag him over."

Jack suddenly couldn't take his eyes off her. The way she seemed so relaxed and at ease wth him, unselfconscious about the sand stick to her legs and shorts or even the way the wind tousled her hair. "Okay," Jack agreed and they set to work. As they did, his thoughts went back to the last picnic he'd had with Abby and Caroline, a few weeks before the accident. They'd gone down to Oakdale Park beside the Smoky Hill River in Salina to listen to a local country band at the gazebo, taking dinner along. Caroline had played with other children on the playground as Jack and Abby visited with friends and neighbors who'd also come out for the show. The weather had been perfect that day, too—a gentle wind whispering through the oaks and pines, accompanying the energetic music of the band and the laughter of children. It was one of his favorite memories, and he suddenly felt itchy, his stomach queasy at the realization that he was enjoying his time with Hannah and Sam so much. He had to guard his heart; keep his feelings and memories for Abby and Caroline close and safe.

After a minute, Hannah tapped him on the arm. "Can I have that?" She tugged on the basket he was holding. He'd carried it over from the cart and just frozen, lost in his thoughts.

He released it. "Yeah, sorry."

"What are you thinking about?" she asked. "You seemed somewhere else for a moment."

"Just enjoying the perfect weather and good company," Jack said quickly.

Hannah raised an eyebrow as if wondering if there was something more, but instead of questioning, she took a slow breath and cocked her head to one side with a peaceful smile. "Me too." Then she swung the basket slightly as they walked down the beach. "But wait 'til you taste this food."

"Really?" He smiled back. "Lou cooked again, huh?"

"Hey!" She punched his arm as he laughed and dodged. "I made this."

"Oh, sorry," he said, not really meaning it.

Hannah frowned, making a sad face, then sighed. "Lou taught me everything I know."

Jack both laughed loudly and then went back for the second basket as Hannah knelt and began unpacking the one he'd given her.

When they had everything ready, Hannah called for Sam, who stayed focused on his shells and didn't respond.

Hannah tried again, then put her hands on her hips when he still didn't answer. "We may have to get his attention."

"Allow me," Jack volunteered. He handed her the beer he'd opened and scuttled down the sand in a silly zigzag, then scooped Sam up, surprising him, and lifted him up in the air as he carried him back. "I got 'im! I got the shell pirate, Captain!" he called in his best pirate voice and Sam started giggling. Soon Hannah was, too.

"Where do ya want 'im, matey?" Jack asked as he lowered Sam toward the ground. "The brig?" As he said it, he twisted his face with silly menace and began tickling Sam.

"On the blanket will be fine, matey," Hannah said, shaking her head.

Jack growled. "Arrrggg-Kay." And then swung Sam down and set him on the blanket on his rear.

"Are you having fun, honey?" Hannah asked.

Sam closed one eye and shot her a mischievous look like a

pirate right out of a tv show or movie, twisting his mouth. She couldn't help but laugh.

"Okay, well, let's eat something, okay? We have to get going soon," Hannah said. "We'll have to collect more shells another day."

"You can come back tomorrow if you want," Jack offered. "I've got the whole day off."

Sam looked at his mother like he loved the idea, and she hesitated, thinking, then said, "We'll see, okay? First, eat." She handed Sam a turkey and cheese sandwich and then a juice box and then made a face, "Or we'll make ye walk the plank."

Sam giggled as he took a bite of the sandwich and Hannah handed Jack back his beer. "You want this or a juice box?"

"Beer, arrrgh," Jack said, accepting it. He took a long slug, savoring the cold bitter taste as it rolled down his throat.

Hannah laughed. "Okay, Captain Cristof," she said, dubbing him with a pirate-like name, "sit down and let's eat."

Hannah had prepared quite a picnic. As she laid it out in front of him on paper plates, she said, "I hope you're hungry. It's all homemade. Family recipes." She laid out homemade potato salad and coleslaw, sliced carrots and celery, apples and oranges, soda, potato chips, and homemade cookies and brownies.

"When did you have time to make all this?" Jack wondered, truly impressed.

"Well, Ellen made some of it," Hannah admitted with a sheepish look. "I co-opted a few portions."

Jack's tongue and stomach hummed with every bite he took. Everything was among the best he'd ever tasted. In the tradition of good moms, too, she offered him more every time he finished a few bites. "Don't want you to go hungry."

"No, I'm fine. Really getting full," he replied.

"You sure. It's homemade—family recipe?" she reminded

him, and then he relented.

"All right, yes, just a little more. It's all so delicious."

Jack ate until he was ready to explode, then fell over on his back moaning as Sam giggled and did the same.

"You okay?" Hannah asked, looking down at them.

"I may explode," Jack confessed.

"That's how you're supposed to feel after a good Southern meal," Hannah said.

"You sound like my grandmother," Jack said.

"She sounds like a smart lady," Hannah replied. "Smarter than her grandson. Grandma, huh?"

Jack chuckled. "She used to say that." And so had Abby when she was teasing him. He winced a bit as he remembered. How could someone so perfect and lovely have ever put up with him?

"Sam, go finish your shelling," she said, glancing at her watch. "You've got forty-five minutes until we have to head back, okay?"

Sam nodded and shot to his feet, hurrying off as Jack closed his eyes and moaned again.

"You gonna be okay?"

He grunted. "Yeah, just give me a minute. That was delicious. I'm savoring."

"Savoring, huh?" Hannah said, crossing her arms over her chest. "Well, don't savor yourself to sleep. We have to pack all this up."

"Should I join Sam?" Jack asked with a yawn.

"I don't think he'll let us," Hannah replied. In truth, "join" was a misnomer. Sam didn't want her help. If asked, he'd reject it. Every once in a while, Sam would come over to show her his latest finds, delighting in sharing them with her. She hated that she was so ignorant about his hobby because Sam seemed to take pleasure in the most subtle of differences. Unfortunately, it was something he'd started with Ellen and she'd nurtured it. It hadn't bothered Hannah until Rob was gone and she realized she was missing out on something important to Sam when she so badly wanted to connect with him. While she treasured the joy he found in such a mundane pleasure, it felt like just one more barrier to their communication now. One more thing separating the person she loved most in the world from her when they were both grieving their loss.

Soft snoring interrupted her thoughts and she looked over to see Jack stretched out on the blanket fast asleep, his Gilligan hat over his face. Oh well. Guess you're cleaning up alone, she thought, and she did. Half an hour later, she shook him awake. He looked around to see the picnic had all been put away and repacked in baskets on the cart. "Five minutes, huh?"

"You shouldn't have let me sleep," he said.

She shrugged. "Well, the drooling was so adorable."

He wiped self-consciously at his mouth with the back of an arm. "I drooled?"

"Yeah, made a big ole pool there on the sand, too," she said, shaking her head.

He rolled over to look and she laughed.

"That's not nice," he said, frowning and trying to hide the amusement from her eyes. God, she was fun. And he'd missed having fun like this with a woman.

"Neither was letting me pack up the picnic alone, buster," she said.

"I forgive you," he said immediately, as he looked around for something to do. "Uh...how can I help?"

She rolled her eyes. "Typical man." She turned and called, "Gather it up, Sam, We've got to head back."

Jack got to his feet. "I better get that backpack for him."

"Okay, I'll let you," she said as he hurried off to help Sam.

205

Sam was struggling to lift the backpack as Jack approached and picked it up by the straps. As they reached the cart, he saw Hannah was holding a bunch of sea grapes.

"I thought maybe you'd like to take some sea grapes home for dessert," Hannah said, holding them out.

"Not going to feed them to me?" he asked as he helped Sam into the cart and set the backpack gently down beside him on the back seat.

Hannah looked at her watch. "Bert's on his way. I'll hold them while you drive."

"Thanks," he said, amused as they slid into their seats and he started the cart, driving back around the island along the beach toward the pier.

Five minutes later, they were waiting beside the pier. A sailboat glided slowly across the horizon, its sails flapping in the wind as, closer-in, several dolphins dove and spun among the breakers. Overhead increasing clouds moved in to blot out the blue sky, matching the mood in Jack's heart as the jetty boat appeared just offshore, making its arc toward the pier. He noticed a few other passengers seated on board.

"We had a wonderful time," Hannah said as she handed him the sea grapes and gave him a quick hug. "You're a great host. Thank you."

"I did, too," Jack agreed. "Come back any time."

Sam nodded and rushed over to hug Jack around the waist. Jack felt a surge of emotion he hadn't felt since Caroline died as he reached down to pat the boy's back. It surprised him, and for the rest of the day, he debated how he felt about it. Despite his guilt, he was sorry to see them go and felt a sudden impulse. "You're an amazing cook. I have tomorrow off. You know, if you need some work done around the house or something."

Hannah chuckled. "I think we're good at the moment. How would you like to see more of the Keys? I assume you haven't toured it yet."

He shook his head. "No."

"Okay," she said as she began unpacking the cart and carrying baskets toward the edge of the pier. "So tomorrow, come to my house around noon, and we'll start with Key West and make an afternoon of it."

"You don't have to work?," Jack said, liking the idea, as he joined her.

The hum of jetty boat's motor increased as it came alongside the pier and stopped.

"Morning shift, five to eleven," she said.

"Ready?" Bert called.

"Sounds good," Jack said quickly.

"Yep," Hannah said looking at Jack then Bert and clearly meaning both. Jack set down two baskets and stopped to help Sam aboard then hurried to retrieve the backpack from the cart.

Hannah climbed aboard the boat and Jack handed it to her. "Good night," he said.

"Good night," she said, taking a seat beside Sam, who had found two seats together. Sam smiled at Jack as the boat pulled away again, and they sailed off into the evening light.

All the way back to the lighthouse and throughout the evening, Jack thought about Hannah with mixed feelings. There was no doubt he'd had a great time with her. It truly had been the best day he'd spent with a woman since Abby died, but then again it was also the only day he'd spent with a woman, other than his sister, since then. He really liked Sam, too. And it was fun having a kid to interact with again.

But there still wasn't an hour that went by that he didn't think of Abby and Caroline or what he'd lost. And part of him felt guilty moving on with someone else, even if it had been two years, even if he felt in his heart they would approve. He felt like he was betraying them in some way by opening his heart to other people. And that worried him. Because he never wanted to lose his love for them or his memories. He wanted to be loved and to love and to have companions. He'd been wrong about that for a while now, and coming to Islamorada had opened the door for him to see that he had to admit. But he had to be sure that connecting with someone new wasn't the same as erasing them, and until he was confident and comfortable with that, he could never truly be open and give his all to anyone new.

Was it fair to ask Hannah to live with that? That was the question that preoccupied his dreams and haunted him until he fell asleep.

That night he had another nightmare, reliving the scenes he'd remembered at the beach only with tragic twists like Caroline sinking into quick sand and crying out as he rushed to save her, then heard Abby screaming for help, caught in a tide pool. Then watching horrified as she drowned because he couldn't save Caroline and free himself from the quick sand in time.

He awoke the next morning soaked in sweat, the nightmare still haunting him. He took a quick shower and then grabbed a thermos of coffee and some toast as the headed for the cart, wanting to busy himself in work as fast as possible to forget. It was almost one when he remembered he was supposed to meet Hannah and Sam. He checked his cell immediately, but there was no signal where he was on the island. It took thirty minutes to pack up his tools and navigate the cart back into range near the lighthouse. He continued on as he dialed her number.

The moment she answered, he knew she was pissed. It was all in her voice. "Where are you?"

He winced. "I'm so sorry. I got caught up in work."

"I thought today is your day off."

"It is," he said as he pulled the cart to a stop in front of the lighthouse.

"So how were you caught up in work?" She spoke with the same irritated tone Abby had used when he'd missed obligations with her or Caroline due to obligations at the firm. He could almost imagine Hannah scowling—brow creased, lips pursed and turned slightly downward, eyes narrowed. The problem was, he didn't know what to say. He really didn't want to lie, but telling her he'd nightmares after spending time with her and Sam wasn't exactly ideal either. Come on, Jack, have a back bone.

"I didn't sleep well," he finally said, climbing out of the cart and moving toward the locked door of the shed. "I went out to do one thing just to clear my head, got caught up in it, and lost track of time. I'm really sorry. Can I still come?" His voice was sincere, and what he'd said may have excluded details but it was basically the truth. Now, if she'd only forgive him somehow.

He heard her sigh over the phone. "How soon can you get here?"

"I'll be there by two, on my way," Jack said. Even as they said goodbye, he was already scrambling to open the shed and put away the tools. He'd have to hurry, but with a quick shower and a change of clothes he could make. I swear I'll make it up to you, he promised, then parked the cart inside, locked the shed, and raced inside.

HANNAH WAS HOME by eleven-thirty a.m., after a busy lunch rush and waited with Sam until one p.m., when she gave up and fed him lunch. Where was Jack? She'd thought about calling his cell, but figured he got tied up in traffic or errands or something. Surely he'd call soon. About one-thirty, she was picking up the phone to dial him when it rang. Jack's name popped up on the callerID.

Forty-five minutes later, Jack arrived by uber, wearing a Hawaiian shirt, beach shorts, and a Gilligan hat. As she opened the door, prepared to give him another chewing out, he lowered his head, his eyes resembling some sort of sad puppy and said,

"I really screwed up. I hope you can forgive me."

She couldn't help melting. He reminded her of Sam and Rob when they apologized. They'd had such a great day yesterday, and it wasn't like she wasn't late herself from time to time. So she waved him inside and said, "We're almost ready. Just let me get our things."

As she turned, Sam raced to the door as fast as the cast would allow and hugged Jack, looking up at him with such fondness her heart melted all over again.

"Hey there, bud," Jack said, smiling and smooshing Sam's hair with his hand. "I'm sorry I'm late. I was a jerk. Hope we can still have some fun."

Sam nodded, clearly not minding at all now that Jack was here.

Hannah grabbed Sam's backpack, a purse, and a beach bag she'd packed with snacks and drinks and five minutes later they were headed south on Overseas Highway in his Cherokee toward Key West, Hannah at the wheel.

Jack commented that most of the surrounding area they were passing through resembled most small towns in the Midwest, with the exception of the palm trees, Spanish moss, and nautical color schemes. The buildings were mostly one story, with a few exceptions, and the storefronts were the usual with houses looking like most of them would be at home anywhere in the Midwest. Sam tapped them on the shoulder from the backseat excitedly at one point, and Hannah pointed out a local beach not far from home where he loved to go shelling. Jack noted an ice cream shop and a donut vendor's trailer, both with colorful logos similar to those he'd seen at many zoos and children's areas. Even the lifeguard stand was painted rainbow colors.

"So what was so important you had to work on it during your day off?" Hannah asked, after checking the mirror to see that Sam was raptly looking out the window silently counting cars or trees or something he found fascinating.

Jack let out a breath before answering, "I had a nightmare last night, maybe more than one."

Hannah immediately switched from teasing mode to serious, her lips pursed as she glanced over at him. "About Abby and Caroline?"

"Yeah."

She noticed Jack smelled different today—a combination of musk and plum. Maybe a new cologne or aftershave. "I'm sorry. We don't have to talk about it if you're uncomfortable."

"Just another exciting night as a widower," Jack joked, then his smile faded as he took a deep breath.

"So you set to work to get your mind off it?"

"Yes, and I'm so sorry." He leaned back against the passenger seat and made eye contact before continuing, "I did that so many times to Abby and Caroline and now I can't get the time back. I never intended to do it to you and Sam." He absentmindedly rubbed his belly as if it ached and winced as he finished, his voice a monotone. God men were cute when they sincerely apologized!

"It's not like you missed something important," she said, deciding to let him off the hook and move on. "It's just casual plans as friends. It's okay. We can still see a lot. Don't worry."

"I hope so," he said, lowering his head as his eyes darted away. "Thank you for understanding. I feel terrible."

Hannah chuckled. "Did that puppy dog look work on Abby? I mean have you worked on that or something?"

"Me?" Jack's brow furrowed as he tried to assess if she was serious. "No, I mean it."

"I know you do," she said with a grin, then immediately changed the subject. "Seriously. What's it like being a lighthouse keeper? I really am curious."

"Fairly simple so far," Jack said, admiring the reflection of several buildings off the water in the distance. "It's mainly a

211

maintenance job. Warren said they only have a keeper because the original owner required it in the contract in order to sell it to the Coast Guard."

"Really? So why have a keeper there?" Hannah said.

Jack shrugged. "Well, if anything goes wrong with the lighthouse, someone has to fix it, so I guess it will be more prompt with a keeper than it might be without."

"But most of them are unmanned these days—computers and automation, right?"

He grunted. "You've done your research. Cristof's will required it to be manned so the surrounding environment would be carefully maintained and protected."

"Makes sense." Hannah nodded as she slowed the Jeep to wait at a stoplight.

Jack continued, "From the Coast Guard's perspective, Warren said they went along with it because it allows them to have a place to train keepers, so they have qualified personnel available if they ever need them. You know, if automation actually failed or some other unexpected crisis occurred. And there's plenty of repairs needing done on the island anyway, plus, since the owner left a subsidy to partially fund the cost of the keeper, it also is cheaper having a keeper train there than other places."

"So what does a keeper do?" Hannah asked as she started forward again, following traffic. "I guess you're the expert since there's almost none in the United States these days."

"Yeah, but they have them in Canada and other places. Other than maintenance of the lighthouse works and grounds," Jack said, "I monitor the radio and messages in case any emergencies are coming. There are settings and things I do in various circumstances mostly related to weather conditions and such. And then I make sure the lamp is regularly tested and working properly, and I look for unsuspecting waitresses to lure there for shells with their sons...you know, the usual stuff."

Hannah made a mock shocked face then they both laughed. "You know, you shouldn't joke about that."

Jack grunted, looking relieved she'd understood it as the joke he'd intended. "Probably not. I'll show the basics sometime if you want."

"I don't know," Hannah said. "We got so many shells yesterday, it won't be so easy to lure me again. You'll have to up your song."

"My song?"

"Your siren's song," she said with a wink. "How you lure me and all."

"Ah," Jack said, smiling. "Yes, believe me, if I sang, you'd run the opposite direction. No one wants to hear that."

"That bad?"

"People have tipped me to not sing."

She laughed then motioned, "This is the very south end of Upper Matecumbe Key, these resorts. We'll be at the bridge shortly."

"Then what next?"

"Lower Matecumbe Key."

"What city?"

"Still Islamorada."

"Wow, this city stretches quite a ways," Jack said, surprised.

"It does," Hannah said. "Welcome to the Keys." She paused a moment, concentrating on waiting to pass a slow truck on the road ahead, then continued once she'd made it past, "Lower Matecumbe Key is next. Fairly similar to Upper Matecumbe, except much smaller. Then there's Long Key and Walker's Island, basically blips—all connected with long bridges—and then we hit the lower keys: Fat Deer Key, Boot Key, and Knight Key which almost seem like they're one but they're not."

"Wow," Jack said, looking impressed. "How many islands are there?" "Forty-five over one hundred and thirteen miles, in case you wondered," she replied quickly.

"You really have that down. Were you ever a tour guide?"

Hannah smirked. "No. Locals have to do this a lot whenever we get visitors, plus I always took an interest in it because I grew up here."

"Sure, I can understand that," he said. "So when's this long bridge—several miles right?—I keep hearing about?"

"Seven mile bridge is after Knight Key. It's a very long stretch of roadway, basically a a two lane highway with ocean on either side as far as the eye can see and only a guard rail to protect cars from going over the edge."

"Well, that sounds scary."

"It kind of is and it isn't," she agreed. "You'll see when we get there. I'm used to it by now, so it doesn't worry me."

JACK FOUND HIMSELF impressed with her knowledge. She'd filled him in as she drove like a real pro, and she was really good at summing up and not getting long winded or boring. He couldn't help but wonder how often there were accidents and how many people had drowned going over the side of one of the bridges, especially the seven mile one. That, of course, made him think of Abby and Caroline. They'd both been killed almost instantly. At least that was a comfort compared to the concept of death by drowning stuck inside a submerged car. He shuddered just imagining such horror.

As they passed through the Keys she'd mentioned, Hannah continued her narration, pointing out a few interesting landmarks mixed with just the right amount of history and local legend. Since Jack had never been south of Islamorada in the Keys, he found it quite fascinating seeing a whole part of the

United States he knew very little about. The entire trip took about two hours, but it passed like a flash, thanks to Hannah's interesting commentary. Thirty minutes after they left the seven mile bridge, they were passing the Naval Air Station on Boca Chica Key then passing signs that read: "Welcome to Key West."

Although Hannah graciously asked if there was anything he wanted to see, Jack was content to let her take the lead. "Just show me whatever you think I should see, okay?" he suggested. And so she did. Their first stop was the large painted cement cylinder marking the Southernmost Point of the Continental United States. Located at the corner of Whitehead Street and South Street and painted with alternating grey, red, and yellow stripes and a crest that read "Conch Republic," the marker hailed 90 miles to Cuba.

"On a clear day, they say you can see all the way to Cuba," Hannah stated, the ocean breeze gently tousling her hair.

"Have you ever done it?" Jack asked as he stared across water so pristine it reflected the clouds and sky like a mirror, the fresh air a delight to his lungs.

"Well, no."

"I doubt anyone has," he added. "Not even 'they.'"

Hannah frowned. "Hey, it's still a fun idea."

Jack cocked his head and locked eyes with Sam, giving his best mischievous look. "Shall we swim it?"

Sam's eyes widened as he shook his head vigorously, then Hannah shook her head and said, "Don't worry, he's teasing, honey," and they headed back to the car.

The next stop was the Key West Lighthouse Museum across the street from Ernest Hemingway's house on Whitehead.

"Now, this is more like it," Jack said.

"I thought it might be a fun basis of comparison," Hannah said, taking Sam's hand, as they walked together toward the black topped, white tower.

As they climbed the stairs and toured the lighthouse, and later, the keeper's home, Jack added comments about the equipment on display as compared to that at Cristof's Lighthouse, and they wondered together both at how much technology had evolved and how much it hadn't. Sam seemed enthralled by everything about it, content to follow along with them in happy, wide-eyed silence, leaving any discussion to the adults. Jack noticed immediately the air was more humid down there, and the way the trees and houses were positioned, unless you were elevated or in the open, the ocean breeze didn't seem to mitigate much. Since Spring was supposed to be the less humid season, he had to wonder what it would be like in the Fall and Summer. In his mind, he pictured something like the humid misery of the Ozarks in summertime, a heat he could barely tolerate.

After the lighthouse museum, they went across the street to Hemingway's house, a must see extravagance, and took an official tour there. Then they headed down Whitehead and took Fleming one block north to Duval where they ate lunch at Jimmy Buffet's Margaritaville. Buffet being a big figure in Key West itself, and the margarita being Hannah's favorite drink, which she said she wanted to share that with Jack. He enjoyed it thoroughly, finding it as good or better than any he'd had at Mexican restaurants back in the Midwest. The food was good and the margaritas were terrific. Jack found he was enjoying himself as much or more as he had the day before, and he felt relieved that despite his rudeness and lack of consideration, they'd been able to move past it and still enjoy each other's company. For his part, Sam didn't seemed rattled by it at all. Several times, Jack caught him looking wide-eyed at one thing or another, giving Jack a chance to appreciate it through the eyes of a child, even if Sam wasn't making comments to explain how he was feeling.

Afterward, they went to the Key West Aquarium for the early afternoon tour and then spent some time wandering around the downtown area looking at sights and shops and watching the activity on the ocean off the pier.

"Sometime we'll have to come down here for a sunset," Hannah said. "They're really amazing."

"They're amazing everywhere in the Keys from what I've seen," Jack said.

Hannah nodded. "It's true."

"Kansas also has spectacular sunsets," Jack added.

Hannah raised an eyebrow, looking ready to challenge him out of local pride. "Really? As good as these?"

"Yes, but different," Jack said. Kansans were proud of their sunsets too, and both his parents and grandparents had taught the children to appreciate them as they grew up. His grandfather used to refer to it as "watching God paint." Sunsets had had a special kind of ethereal, magical quality for Jack ever since, though he certainly wouldn't argue that Florida's weren't just as stunning. So far they seemed to change second-by-second. People gathered and walked until the edge of the sun met the western horizon and then froze, not breathing as they took it in with silent appreciation. Then they'd gasp as the sky was lit by jewels from the heavens. Kansas pride aside, he would never argue Florida could give his home state fierce competition.

As they drove home later, Jack at the wheel, he noticed a number of banners decorating poles that advertised something called Island Fest in Islamorada, scheduled for the following weekend, and he asked Hannah about it.

"It's the Islamorada Chamber's annual fundraiser," Hannah explained. "They hold it every year in Founder's Park on Plantation Key. It's like a giant street fair meets Carnival kind of thing with lots of food and crafts booths, souvenirs, clowns, face painting, kite flying, games, concerts, and so on. It's a lot of fun."

"Are you going?"

"Probably. You?"

"I didn't even know about it until now, but it sounds fun."

"You should go with us," Hannah said. "If you can tolerate my mother-in-law, it'll be a great chance to sample a lot of local specialties from various restaurants and so on, plus, you might enjoy getting your face painted, too." She laughed.

Jack made a face. "I think my face is funny looking enough already."

Sam joined his mother in laughing as Jack screwed his face up further and then they were crossing the seven mile bridge and every one's eyes went back to checking out the water surrounding them for miles in every direction.

They stopped by the diner and had dinner, Sam drawing a quick picture of Key West for Lou with crayons on the back of a paper placemat, while Hannah and Jack told him about their trip.

It was close to eight before they dropped Jack at the pier and said their good nights, Sam giving him a big hug as usual, while Hannah and he looked into each other's eyes searching for words for a moment before he finally said, "That was a great day. Thanks so much for showing me around."

"I had fun, too," Hannah said. "We barely scratched the surface, though. There's so much more to see."

"Well, I'm sure we'll get to it," Jack said. "I'm free every Sunday." He smiled then noticed Sam had wandered back toward the Jeep and was walking around it, rubbing the sides with an open palm as he hummed to himself.

"Okay, well, thanks for sharing the driving, too, and buying the meals," Hannah added.

"It was the least I could do after you took care of the gas," Jack replied.

"Actually, the whole way there was the tank you left me with so you bought that too," said Hannah.

"Damn, you took me for a ride," Jack said with a mock frown. "I'm gonna have to watch you like a hawk."

They stared at each other a moment, Jack debating whether to kiss her or not. Part of him really wanted to, but another part wondered if it was the right thing. He liked spending time with Hannah and Sam a lot. It reminded him of what he was missing. They question was—was that a good thing or a bad thing? He couldn't decide yet.

They stared at each other for what seemed like forever, neither seeming to want to move. Then, finally, to ease the tension, Jack spread his arms and pulled Hannah into a hug, kissing her on the cheek.

"I'm glad I made a good new friend," he said.

"Me too," she replied as they finished the hug and their eyes met again.

"Call me soon," Jack said, and then he turned and headed down the pier toward where Bert was waiting with the jetty boat.

As he climbed aboard, he looked back and saw Hannah watching from beside the Jeep. He offered a quick final wave, then grabbed a seat, his eyes never leaving her face, until Bert turned at an angle that he couldn't see her anymore as the boat left the shore.

CHAPTER 17

THE NEXT DAY a floral delivery man surprised Hannah at the door delivering a lovely Spring arrangement with roses, carnations, peonies, tulips, and hydrangeas in a colorful mix of oranges, reds, and yellows. After she'd tipped the driver and watch him pull away, she checked the card. They were from Jack. He'd called her "a new good friend" yet he'd sent her flowers.

Opening the small envelope, she scanned the typed message inside: "To Hannah, a beauty to rival a sunset, a warm heart to rival the sun—thanks for a great weekend. Jack." Romantic. But then again, she'd thought he was going to kiss her, and she'd wanted him to. But after a long moment of staring into each other's eyes, he'd simply hugged her. God, he was so confusing.

The next week didn't clear anything up either. As had become their routine, he called her every night for a chat—sometimes short, sometimes stretching for hours. And he even invited them over to shell hunt and tour the lighthouse or both any time she wanted. Wanting time to think, she'd managed to put him off until Thursday when he showed up at the diner mid-day during her shift.

"Hi," he said, smiling.

"What are you doing here?" she asked, trying to hide her wary surprise.

221

"Hungry," Jack said. "Something to go. Is that all right?" He looked everywhere but at her. Said hello to Lou, spent a lot of time fidgeting with a button.

She hesitated a moment, recovering, saying, "Of course. Do you want to sit at the counter while you wait?" but stopping short of calling him "sir," for the simple reason he seemed standoffish. She would have meant it as sarcasm.

"Sure, thanks," he said, but stood there facing her.

She motioned, aloof herself, saying, "Pick any open stool."

"I will," he said, his eyes finally locked on hers. "It's good to see you." But he said it so matter-of-fact with no emotion, she wondered if he meant. He must have left Charming Jack beached in a school of dead blowfish.

She busied herself, shuffling scattered menus into an organized stack.

He turned and made his way to a stool at the center of the counter, where he sat, then spun, watching her.

She caught sight of herself in a mirror behind the counter. Lou put it up years ago with a sign saying, "Remind your face it's happy." So what if her frazzled hair might not look as good as it did last week in the red dress. Maybe he was one of those guys who acted differently in public around girls deemed undesirable by their Joe College friends. If that's true, best she find it out now. She took her time walking over to hand him a menu. "Just wave ... or whatever, when you're ready to order," saying it like she didn't care.

"I don't suppose I could have more of that steak?" he asked.

She shook her head. "Not if you want it quickly to go."

He grunted. "Worth a shot, okay, I'll see what sounds good." He began reading the menu as she stepped behind the counter and grabbed two plates from under the heat lamps separating the kitchen from the front, then hurried off to deliver them to a waiting table.

Afterward, she made her rounds to refill glasses and check

on her other tables, and when she returned to behind the counter, he nodded and closed the menu. "I'll have two BLTs and slaw on the side, please."

"Anything to drink?"

He shook his head. "I'll grab something back at the lighthouse."

"You sure?"

He paused to think. "Well, okay, how about some tea?"

"Sweet or straight?"

"Lemon twist," he said, except now he said it as if he thought he was being cute. Today it wasn't landing.

"I'm sorry, we don't do that," she said.

He raised his hand in the air and snapped his fingers, his face taking on a sad look. "Darn it."

What was he about? First cool and irritatingly off-putting. Now cutesy? What is he thirteen? "I'll get that right away." Maybe those flowers were a good-bye bouquet. She dated a guy like that once. Whatever Jack was doing, it wasn't dating. It was ... friending. Like on social media.

Later, she brought out his bag of food, motioning for him to follow her to the register to pay. He said, "I've missed seeing you the past few days. Guess you're having a busy week."

Not knowing what to say she said, "Yeah," then stepped behind the register and punched in his order. "Twelve seventy-two."

He handed her cash. "Well, maybe this weekend?"

She looked up as she handed him change and their eyes met again. Now he looked eager, like Sam on Christmas morning. She couldn't help herself. "How about tomorrow afternoon?" she blurted out before she could stop the moving train that was her mouth. "Sam has a half day off school."

"Great," said Jack as she stapled up his order and handed

him the plastic bag by the handles. Hey, Hannah, wake up. "Parasailing? Jet Skiing?" he said, casually but without the usual enthusiasm she'd expect. "I'd love to go snorkeling, but not sure he's ready for that with the cast still on."

She chuckled and said she'd call about the time, then watched him walk away, his thighs looking great in those shorts.

She didn't know why she was being so wishy washy. She was enabling him, making him comfortable with doing nothing. Like the guy who strings the girl along, no commitments, no strings. Calling it a friendship. That's how she talked to nerdy boys in high school who she had no intention of dating. Things were clearer back then. Defined. She'd been a cheerleader, one of those girls high on the dating food chain. When she dropped to the level of bottom feeder, she didn't know because as an adult keeping tabs didn't matter. She had Rob and a baby who needed her. Marriage hides a woman's desirability behind a confidence that stretch marks and crow's feet no longer matter.

Back to Jack: There was that hug, the hesitation— remembering it through circumspect made her wonder about his motives. The last thing she wanted was to push him into something and then wind up hurt, the rebound girl. Even worse, she didn't want Sam hurt. She'd lost her husband to the sea and her son to mutism in one summer night two years ago. She couldn't bear another swipe at her heart, beings as how hers now suffered from chronic dread. It happened in a second, starting with a doorbell ring.

"Mrs. Loaney?" the sheriff's officer had asked when she'd opened the door at ten that night, already beside herself because her husband and son hadn't come back from fishing amidst a now raging storm.

"Yes," she'd said quickly.

"There's been an accident, ma'am," the officer said, looking like policemen do when they'd rather be anywhere but here. He'd looked down at a small notebook, double checking the address on the door, and then asked her name. "Your husband's Robert James Loaney?" he asked, and when she confirmed, said, "Could you come with me?"

Hannah didn't know why he'd come here. Was someone in trouble with the law? Why wasn't he telling her anything? Her heartbeat exploded and her legs wobbled, as she grabbed her coat and purse, asking, "I think you should tell me what's going on."

"Your husband's been in an accident. You need to come to the Mariner's," said the officer replied. "I'll take you there."

Hannah had forced herself to gulp down breaths the whole way in the back of squad car, her stomach rock hard. She felt guilty later remembering how it took time for the tears to come. Therapists called it shock.

A kind nurse met her at the E.R., and that's when her world fell apart. Rob was dead, Sam had had his stomach pumped of water. Had nearly drowned. She wondered now if she didn't fight hard enough to stay strong for Sam. He's an intuitive kid. She clearly remembered the urge to run away from the things being said to her. She took off running at one point, causing the nursing staff to run to her aid. She couldn't recall what they gave her. Something strong. One minute, she wanted to scream and pound her fists, the next her mind was blank, like she was a walking zombie.

People had expected her to go on. It was like waking up every morning to her unfinished chapter with Rob. Open-ended, like a silent slow leak of all she holds dear.

She knew what Jack must be feeling, after all, she'd been there. Having a sudden lost thrust upon you brought a mix of emotions. They could change moment to moment. She'd experienced the gauntlet. But two years later, she was better, healing. Jack was not. And as many good qualities as he had, as attractive as he was, she wanted more than someone who kept falling apart at moment's notice over the past, while she was standing there ready and working hard every day to move toward the future and let go. She and Sam had been through enough pain and suffering to fill volumes. Still, what if this was the universe's way of throwing her a rope? Maybe spending time with Jack as a friend was the way to go. He was the one who'd said "good friend" after all. Here was her out clause. She would treat him like a friend. Because she had and deserved better than another vacuum in her life. One thing was certain, Jack wasn't boyfriend material.

Later, when the diner slowed a bit, she discussed her feelings with Denise.

"You're right, you don't need it. You do deserve better," her best friend said as they sat on a bench in the alley just off the kitchen. Her eyebrows drew together as she chose the right words. "But I'm not sure I'd let the friendship go much farther either, knowing how you feel. Maybe some distance is what you need. For him as well as for yourself. I just don't know."

"I don't know either, Denise," Hannah answered. "Come on. You're my best friend. Tell me what to do."

Denise snickered. "Life should be so easy. Besides, I don't want that responsibility for someone else's life. I can barely handle my own."

Hannah laughed out loud. "I love you so much. Even when I'm frustrated and confused and all serious, you find a way to make me laugh."

Denise shrugged. "Just telling the truth."

They sat in silence a moment as they watched a mama robin swoop down to land on a nest in the gutter of a small abandoned warehouse that was almost falling apart across the alley. Robins were usually gone this time of year, but this one had obviously hung around longer until her young could leave with her. And that made Hannah think of Sam. That's what life had been all about for her since he was born—every day lived to support him and his every need. It hadn't changed much after Rob died either, except that she'd gone to work for some extra income, and sold the house and some belongings to downsize the budget after moving in with Ellen. That was a decision she often wondered if she'd do over given a chance.

Surely there would have been another way than having to be tortured by a mother-in-law who never let anything go. If anything, what she wanted, no needed, most from a man was to take her away from this. Not to hold her back until he was ready. And that was Jack, unfortunately. She wished for a moment she'd met him a few years more after he'd lost his family. Maybe by then he'd be perfect, but right now…

"It is the truth," she finally admitted aloud. "You're right. I don't need to handle someone else's life. I need someone who wants to build our life and handle it together. I just don't think he's up for that."

"I'm sorry, hun," Denise said, leaning over so the sides of their heads touched. "On the other hand, I think you kinda like the challenge."

"The challenge?" Hannah chortled. "I have enough challenges already. I don't need any more."

"I hear you, honey," Denise said.

Hannah closed her eyes, breathing slowly as Denise sighed beside her.

"Life's a bastard and then you keep on living," Denise said.

"Amen," Hannah agreed.

And then they both heard Lou calling their names and hurried back inside for another round of customers.

JACK CALLED HER again that night and asked if she and Sam could meet him at the lighthouse for lunch on Friday. Hannah considered just flat out refusing, but then she thought of Sam. He'd really taken a liking to Jack, and she didn't like the idea of just cutting him off from someone he was responding so well to. Besides, she wasn't the type to just walk away from someone, especially a friend, without explanation. What she needed to do was talk to Jack and set some clear boundaries.

She knew Sam would enjoy visiting the lighthouse again. He'd been drawing pictures of lighthouse almost daily since their last visit. She could easily let him wander the beach or explore the cupola while she chatted with Jack. That seemed safe enough as long as they were nearby.

When they arrived, just before one p.m., the place was filled with the smell of bolognese sauce—onions, garlic, ground beef, tomato sauce, and spices. He greeted them right off as they took off their windbreakers.

"Sam, you came," Jack said, while training his eyes on Hannah. "I figured we could eat together, then I'll show you how the lighthouse works. Would you like that?"

Sam offered a thumbs up as Hannah said, "Sam would love that. Something smells wonderful." She sniffed the air again, savoring the spicy goodness.

"Secret family recipe," Jack said, flicking his eyebrows. He quickly showed Sam around the communications room, promising a more detailed tour later, then led them up the spiral staircase toward the kitchen two levels up.

"Make yourselves at home," he said as he quickly returned to the stove and began stirring two pots on the stove. The smell was even stronger here and accompanied by warmth radiating from the stove. Stepping closer, Hannah determined that one contained steaming spaghetti noodles, while the other was the sauce. "Hope you both like spaghetti. I should have asked," Jack added.

It smells like heaven. "We do. Thanks, friend," Hannah said instead, her voice even.

Beside her, Sam rubbed his stomach and smiled.

Jack glanced up a moment then went back to stirring as she walked over to the windows.

"Bet the views from these windows are amazing," Hannah said as she stood beside the windows looking north, then glanced back to the south windows, admiring both views.

"Words can't describe it." Jack said, and Hannah had to agree.

"It's been a while since a friend cooked me dinner," Hannah said. "You're very kind."

A few minutes later, he tasted the sauce and emitted a pleasurable moan. "Perfect." Reaching across the stove, he flipped off the burners then opened a cupboard and withdrew two serving bowls. "I hope you're ready for a great meal!" He motioned as he dumped the spaghetti into a strainer propped on one corner of the sink, letting it drain. "Please. Sit."

Moments later, he carried two serving bowls—one with spaghetti, the other with sauce—over to set on the table in front of them. "One second," he said, raising a finger, then spun and hurried back to the fridge where he pulled out a chilled bottle of wine and two glasses and carried them back to the table. Then he made one last trip to the fridge for a grape juice box which he brought back and set in front of Sam. Looking at Hannah and Sam, he smiled. "Dinner is served."

The first bite of spaghetti and sauce exploded on Hannah's tongue. It was amazing, some of the best she'd ever had. She realized Jack was watching her with real interest and her eyes met his. "Mmmmmmm. Amazing. So delicious."

Sam nodded his head beside her as he shoved another spoonful in his mouth.

"Good," Jack said, looking a little relieved. "That means I did it right."

"You had doubts?"

He shrugged. "Well, I am a bit out of practice, even following fancy recipes."

Hannah chuckled and they began chatting about their week so far, including Sam's school, the diner, Jack's work at the lighthouse, and so forth. It was comfortable and relaxed, even though Hannah knew she might ruin it later when she told Jack what she'd decided. Oddly, it was still enjoyable and Hannah realized it was the first time she'd felt like a family since Rob's death. What was it about Jack that put her so at ease, especially after their rough start and the knowledge she had of the pain he was carrying? When she was with him, it wasn't work, that was a big part of it, plus he was so good with Sam. He made it look easy, and Sam had been anything but easy since the accident. If only he were in a different place.

The spaghetti was so good, she surprised herself and had a second portion, but not a second glass of wine, even though Jack had chosen the perfect classic Chianti that added just the right accent to the food. Altogether, the meal took just over an hour, and then Jack scooted back his chair and waved an arm. "Who wants to go check the lamp?"

He looked at Sam and his eyes widened with a kind of excitement as he raised his hand and bounced on his feet, smiling ear-to-ear.

"Sam, you run on ahead, while I help Jack clean up, okay?" Hannah said as she stood beside him.

He shook his head. "I'll get it later. Don't worry."

Sam was already running up the stairs, but Hannah put a hand on Jack's arm before he could follow, then hollered, "Slow down so you don't slip and fall, honey!"

Jack's forehead crinkled as he shot her a questioning look, as Hannah gathered plates and silverware to carry to the sink. "Is something wrong?" he asked.

"I appreciate you doing this," Hannah said. "And taking good care of me and Sam."

"Of course, it's my pleasure," he said as he retrieved the serving bowls, then went back for the wine glasses.

Hannah plugged the sink and turned on the water, searching for the dish soap.

"In the cabinet underneath," Jack said as he set the wine glasses on the counter.

She opened the cabinet and retrieved the soap, squeezing

some into the water, before returning it. "I'll wash, you dry."

"We have a dishwasher."

"It's not enough for a full load," she countered.

"Okay, will Sam be all right alone up there?"

"It's safe enough, you said, right?"

He grunted. "Sure. But I really can do this later."

Typical clueless man. God she hated being the bad guy, but she launched in anyway. "Jack, you're very sweet, and you've been really good to us, but I think we should set some clear boundaries for this before we go any further." She started rinsing plates and handed them to him for drying.

"Boundaries for our friendship?"

"Exactly. That's all I want right now. I needed to make sure you understood that," she went on.

Jack offered a smile, but she caught hurt in his eyes, despite his attempts to hide it. "Sure. Fine with me." He set the first plate in the strainer and accepted another.

"I don't mean to hurt you."

He brushed it off with a wave of his right hand as he put the second plate in the strainer with his left. "I'm not ready for anything more, I told you."

You've made that obvious, especially when you came to the diner again the other day, she thought. But then why did he look like she'd just shattered his world? Damn those puppy dog eyes of his. "Okay, I'm glad you understand. I have to think of Sam."

"He seems to like me," he said with a short laugh as she handed him the third plate.

"We both do, and we're grateful," she said. "Thanks for understanding."

"Do you still want the tour?" Jack asked as the third plate

went in the strainer and she handed him a serving bowl.

"I think Sam would refuse to go home without it," she said, chuckling.

He gave a forced grin and they finished the dishes in silence. Afterward, they went upstairs to join Sam. Jack showed them the lamp and all the controls, then opened up the light housing and showed him some of the parts, explaining it all simply and knowledgeably so even Sam could understand. Hannah was once again impressed as well as fascinated.

After that, they worked their way down each floor with Jack talking about the various jobs and duties related to various stations as well as sharing a few personal reflections as items of his own sparked memories. His sadness seemed to fade as he spoke with eloquence about the purpose and history of lighthouses, about how they came to be, the purpose they served, and how they'd evolved to become mostly automated as technology caught up with them. He explained the origins of Cristof's Key and its lighthouse as well and the purpose it served as one of the few remaining manned lighthouses and so forth. Along the way, Sam started referring to Jack as "Keeper Jack," and Jack to Sam as "Lieutenant Sam," while Warren was "Commander Gregg" as they pretended Sam was a keeper, too. It was a very personalized, unique tour and that made it all the more meaningful. Altogether, it took another hour from the time they finished dinner, and by the time they emerged to head for the beach, Hannah was surprised to find the sky had turned overcast with grey clouds moving in.

She frowned as she looked at Jack. "I forgot to check the forecast. Is it going to rain?"

"The weather report this morning gave a forty percent chance of light showers," Jack said.

Thunder rumbled overhead and Sam was starting to look concerned.

Hannah fumbled in her purse for her cell. "Sounds to me like a lot more than light showers." She quickly dialed Bert to see if he was in the area.

"I'm sorry," Jack said. He looked at Sam and saw him shivering and frowning. "I didn't expect this. Do you need to get back?"

"Sam doesn't like storms," she snapped. She hadn't meant to. It's not like it was Jack's fault, but why wasn't Bert answering? If they tried to take the jetty in a full blown storm, Sam would throw a fit. He'd been scared of going on boats at night ever since the accident, and it was only his love of Jack that had gotten him here the first time. That wouldn't be enough to calm the storm brewing in her sun if they didn't get out of here before the showers and thunder started in at full tilt, a deep echo rippling across the sky. She noticed Sam and reached down to gently caress his arms as she leaned in to press her cheek to his. "It'll be fine. We're leaving, honey."

"We can wait it out inside, it's fine," Jack assured her.

"We can't wait," she said, trying Bert again. The phone rang and rang. "Damn it, Bert." She glanced up a moment later and bile rose in her chest, her heart thudding. The sky had grown ever darker, the blue skies now foggy white, the clouds increasing. And the calmness that had once been the waves was showing more foam and disturbance. She had to get back to Isla with Sam before they were stuck.

"You can come back inside," Jack said. "There's plenty of shelter. We've got board games, books, my laptop has WiFi. He can even take a na--"

"But what if it lasts all night?" Hannah cut him off, her voice shaking as heat flushed her body.

Noting her anger, Jack raised his hands in the air. "I'm an honorable man. Scouts honor."

"That not what I'm was concerned about."

"We'll just call Lou and explain," Jack said, misunderstanding. "He seems accommodating. How can he be mad about a last minute storm? I'll talk to him."

Hannah grabbed Sam by the hand. He looked closed to tears now, so she pressed him to her side and led him back inside. "Maybe it will be over quickly," she said, wanting to reassure her baby, but not really believing it. Sam would feel safe enough as long as they were inside the lighthouse. She could already see the tension leaving his body and the bounce returning to his steps as Jack led them toward the stairs.

"You're welcome as long as you need," Jack said to her, then looked at Sam, "Let's find a book or a game, okay?"

Sam brightened at the thought at least, following Jack eagerly now, but Hannah stalled at the stairs, debating the wisdom of even coming here. She could have waited to talk to Jack. It was obvious from the way he phrased it he'd intended a kind of date, and it had sure looked like one when they arrived. Now there was a real possibility they could be stuck all night. Was she ready for the rumors that would incite amongst her coworkers and Ellen? Even Denise would have questions after what Hannah had told her. And how would Jack feel about it? She knew there was a guest room with two beds that she and Sam could use if they wound up staying, but still, he'd looked so hurt when she'd told him they could just be friends. Was he really ready accept that? Certainly wasn't what anyone else would think if she spent the night here. Was she really prepared for this?

Then she took a deep breath. Slow down, Hannah, maybe the rain won't last. Nightfall was several hours away. She just had to wait and see.

Then the rain started pouring and thunder pounded overhead. Moments later a bolt of lightning crackled through the window on her way up the stairs. And she knew then the storm was going to last a while.

"Welcome back," Jack said as he stood at the kitchen counter stirring a mug of cocoa, while Sam waited anxiously seated at the table. "Make yourselves at home," Jack added.

Sam was clearly excited by the prospect. Hannah forced a smile and said, "Thank you."

CHAPTER 18

THUNDER RUMBLED OVERHEAD as Jack stood in the lighthouse kitchen and looked out the window at the foaming sea. The dinner had gone well, his spaghetti turning out better than he'd hoped. And Hannah and Sam seemed to have enjoyed seeing how the lighthouse worked as well, until the storm, that is.

Hannah had been in a serious mood when she arrived—insisting they could only just be friends and the getting so angry over the storm. Now, he'd realized it was because of Sam and the accident. His father has died in a storm at sea, and Sam had almost died as well. He couldn't believe he'd been so insensitive to that, but he'd been thrown off by what had transpired between him and Hannah. It had stung, he had to admit, more than he would've imagined. It wasn't that he was ready to rush into anything serious either, but he'd been more enamored with the possibility than he realized. And her words stung.

Was it because he'd been late? Abby always hated that, too, and he wanted to kick himself for ever treating Hannah and Sam that way. He should have learned from his past. It also hurt that Hannah got so angry about the storm. Sure, he'd been oblivious, and he shouldn't have, but it wasn't like the storm was his fault either. And she'd kind of acted like it was. Abby had never been one of those women who insisted the man was always wrong. He'd been lucky that way. If Hannah was one of those, he wasn't sure he could take it. Not after all the mistakes he'd made before. He wasn't perfect, he didn't need to be reminded, but he would damn well do his best not to repeat old mistakes. If he ever found love again.

Earlier, Hannah had called Ellen and Lou to inform them of the situation, and from what he'd overheard, the conversation with Ellen had not gone well, so at three-thirty, Sam was sitting at the table sipping cocoa as Hannah and Jack shared a fresh pot of Brazilian coffee he'd bought at the store for a special treat.

"Wow," Hannah said from a seat at the table beside Sam, "this is delicious coffee but very strong." It was the first nice thing she'd said to him all afternoon.

Jack chuckled. "Yeah, Brazilian coffee tends to be that way. I use a third of the grounds I'd use for Folgers or some American equivalent."

"A third? Wow." Hannah looked surprised. "How'd you figure that out?"

"Trial and error," Jack said. "Actually, it was Abby who figured it out after a couple nights we spent sleepless and bouncing off the walls." He laughed and Hannah smiled. He took that as a victory. And then she sipped silently, so Jack took the hint and turned to look at Sam.

"How's the cocoa, buddy? Did I get enough marshmallows in there?"

Sam gave a thumbs up then took another sip. Jack had bought the hot chocolate mix and marshmallows on a whim as he prepared for their visit. Though he had to admit, he did enjoy a cup of cocoa every once in a while himself.

"So, I don't have a lot around," Jack said, "but there are a few board games down in the guest quarters other staff put there, and a few novels and other books, though not sure what we might have that's age appropriate for Sam." Then Jack remembered he'd forgotten his duties. "Actually, I forgot to change the lamp, which I'm supposed to do in a storm. When it's automated, they have settings, but those are off while I train. Let me just run up and do that."

He turned for the stairs and heard a chair scrape the floor, turning back as Sam hurried toward him.

"I think Sam wants to go with you," Hannah said with an amused look.

"You wanna help me, bud?" Jack asked and Sam nodded with great enthusiasm.

"Okay, lead the way," Jack said and motioned Sam toward the stairs.

Together they climbed to the top of the lighthouse where Jack explained the lamp's settings to Sam in simple terms then demonstrated each one. Afterward, he let Sam try them before putting the lamp in the appropriate setting for the rainstorm. Sam looked thrilled the entire time. Next, they checked the radio, with Jack sending a test call out just to double check it was functioning as required, and a friendly ship captain answering back, chatting for a moment as he rode out a swell. He was cheerful with a seaman's vocabulary and a cadence that made him fun to listen to. When they'd finished the conversation, they headed back down to join Hannah in the kitchen.

Jack left Sam with Hannah while running down to the first floor communication room to check for any Coast Guard bulletins or messages, then returned with the all clear and joined them for a game of Life Hannah and Sam had set out on the table in the meantime.

Caroline had adored board games, regularly engaging one or both of her parents in playing them, sometimes even two nights in a row. At times they'd had to insist she take a break, despite her protestations. Abby and Jack enjoyed games, too, and especially anything that gave them extra time with their daughter but two nights in a row was a good fix for at least a week for them. Tonight, the mere act of playing with her son seemed to but Hannah in a better mood. She shared laughs with them more than once and even did a mini-dance in her chair when her family jumped ahead.

Afterward, Jack offered to retrieve a few books that looked kid friendly from the guest room shelves for Sam or loan him the iPad. Sam, unsurprisingly, chose the iPad and set to work downloading his favorite game. Once Jack helped him get that set up, he made a fresh pot of coffee and joined Hannah in chairs by the window to watch the storm. By this time, it was almost seven and the sky was growing dark. The clouds were thick and grey and the sunset was in its final stages. A few seabirds soared in the remaining light, diving toward the waves for fish, and Jack caught a glimpse of a boat bobbing further out. The muffled squawking of seagulls drifted across the water.

"I'm sorry I didn't check the weather reports more frequently, but it really wasn't predicted this morning," Jack said as he handed her a mug then sipped from his own.

"It looks like we're in trouble," Hannah said after she swallowed her first sip, chewing her lip as she took in the stormy seascape.

"Why? You guys can have the guest quarters to yourselves, or if you don't like it, take my room. I can sleep anywhere," Jack said. This was his first full weekend off since he'd arrived, and Warren would be arriving early the next morning to relieve him, so having guests overnight wouldn't inconvenience him in the least. In fact, if Hannah hadn't had to work, he'd have invited them to stay for the following day, too. He could always crash on a couch downstairs in the office.

"I don't want to put you out," Hannah said, shaking her head.

"Is this about Sam or about what you said earlier?" Jack asked. "

Hannah took another long sip of the coffee and swallowed before answering, "Both."

Jack said nothing, waiting for her to elaborate.

"I just don't want him getting confused," she said.

"About getting to spend the night in an awesome lighthouse helping the keeper?" Jack joked. "I think a lot of kids would find that very exciting."

Hannah narrowed her eyes, her forehead furrowed, clearly not in a joking mood. "No about us."

"We're friends, I respect that. I'll even leave you alone if that's what you want."

Hannah scoffed, looking around. "This lighthouse may be bigger than a lot of them but it's not that big."

"Look," Jack said, feeling he owed her an apology. "I'm sorry about being late the other day. And being moody. I'm still trying to adjust to being here and what it means to be without my family, but I shouldn't take that out on you."

Hannah sighed. "I appreciate you saying all that. Really. But I don't think you're ready for more, and I don't need more drama in my life. You're a great guy, but—"

Jack finished for her, "Just friends."

"I think it's best."

Jack shrugged. "I can be a great friend. Like right now. If you want to relax, I can just take care of you two for the evening, like a concierge."

"I don't think that's necessary."

"I'll lock the doors so Sam won't wander out, and I'll get you some more wine or soda. And what do you want for dinner?" Jack smiled.

"Sam won't go back in a storm or after dark," she said, still somber, then seemed to brighten a bit. "How about you let me cook?"

"I'm here offering you a night off being spoiled and you want to cook?"

"I want to stay busy," Hannah said. "It'll help me relax."

Jack shrugged. "Okay, let's go see what's in the fridge." She shot him a look that said I can do this. "I just want to make sure you find everything you need. The lighthouse was organized by men. We think differently."

At that, Hannah laughed and then finished a sip of coffee before standing. "Okay, show me what you got."

Jack led her to the fridge and opened the door, letting her take inventory, then she did the same with the freezer compartment and the cupboards.

"You are well stocked," she said.

"Well, I like to be prepared...and save trips." He grins.

"A real hermit in the making."

Jack sighed. "Yeah, when I came here I thought that was what I wanted."

"What about now?" she asked, her eyes meeting his.

"Well, I needed to be sure I wasn't loaning my Jeep to a crazy woman," he teased.

She nodded. "You definitely are. You have no idea."

Jack laughed, then turned serious again. "I decided having a friend or two was probably a good idea."

They stared at each other a moment longer and then Hannah sprang into action, breaking the spell. Pulling lettuce, carrots, two tomatoes, and bell peppers from the fridge she motioned. "Why don't you start a salad. I'll get to work on some chili. It just feels like a chili night."

"Sounds great," Jack said, pulling a knife from a nearby knife rack and holding it up with a gleam in his eye. "Chop chop!"

For the next half hour, they worked side by side—Hannah retrieving a soup pot from under the oven and setting it on the stove then digging into the cupboards for ingredients while Jack chopped and tossed beside her. Jack watched out of the corner of his eye as she found and pulled out chili powder, cumin, sugar, tomato paste, garlic powder, salt, pepper, and cayenne.

"You know, for a new bachelor, your spice rack is impressive," she said.

"I think Warren supplied most of what's here, but I bought a few things," Jack said, then added, "Variety is the spice of life, they say."

"Or the key to a good spice rack," she amended.

Standing beside the soup pot, she poured in olive oil, then minced two small onions and added that as well. This she set to cook and left for five minutes while she dug a pound of ground beef from the freezer and ran it under warm water in the sink to thaw it a bit. When the five minutes was up, she added the ground beef to the soup pot, breaking it into smaller pieces with her hands. She set the temp again and said, "Six minutes," then went to work dicing two tomatoes as Jack finished his salad.

"If you'd told me you needed those, I could have diced them with mine," he teased.

"You focus on salad, I've got this," she said with mock sternness.

From behind them at the table, they heard the beeps, whistles, and mini explosions of whatever video game Sam had immersed himself in. Looking back Jack saw he was totally focused and oblivious to the world around him. As he turned back to making salad, he noticed Hannah was smiling. They were actually having fun together again and she looked much more relaxed.

As the meat sizzled and Hannah gently stirred the pot, Jack carried his salad over and set it on the table, adding two large salad tongs and then pulling out three varieties of dressing from the fridge and setting them out as well.

Grabbing another pot, Hannah drained kidney beans in a strainer then tossed them in along with her diced tomatoes before adding tomato paste and a can of beef broth. A few minutes later, she poured this mixture in over the ground beef, olive oil, and onions with a spatula then adjusted the temperature and turned around, sighing. "Twenty minutes to glory."

Jack's mouth watered at the wonderful smells filling the kitchen as he wondered what to do to kill the time. He grabbed saltines and Wheat Thins from a cupboard and set the boxes on the table beside his salad, then Googled what wine might go best with Chili. Checking the wine rack, he pulled a Cabernet Sauvignon. "Well, Shiraz or Malbec were what Abby always served, but we don't have those. Hopefully this Sauvignon blends all right."

"I'm sure it will be fine," Hannah said.

Grabbing two wine glasses from the cupboard, he carried the wine and the glasses over and set them on the table, then went back for silverware and plates and set those out as well. Sam's books and tablet were spread over most of one end, but Hannah motioned, "Just tell him to move."

Jack shook his head. "I will when we're ready. In the meantime, why don't I take you down to the guest room to make sure you have what you need?"

"Great," she said and they headed for the spiral stairs.

From his own furniture, Jack had added twin beds and a bedside table for the lamp to the guest room as well as a small bookshelf and filled a cupboard with linens, including sheets, comforters, and towels. He pointed to the cupboard where the guest workers had left games and books then opened the bathroom door. "It's small, but there's a couple new toothbrushes, toothpaste, and hotel shampoo and soap I inherited in there that should do the trick."

Hannah smiled. "Are you going to tuck us in, read us a story, and leave chocolates on our pillows, too?"

"What kind of host would I be if I didn't?" he joked then turned serious again. "Just want to make sure you two will be comfortable."

"I think we're fine."

"Well, that's my cue then." He started back toward the stairs.

"A perfect host knows when to leave," Hannah teased.

"Well, Abby was a great hostess and she trained me—or 'pounded it into me' might be a better phrase." He wondered if he should warn her about Warren's pending arrival the next morning.

"She made you a better man?" Hannah suggested.

"Yeah, that sounds better," Jack agreed.

Hannah smiled, eyeing the bathroom again. "Man, this is one small bathroom. It's almost like being on Amtrak."

"Right?" Jack agreed. "They could have used more room, but it's functional."

"We'll manage," Hannah agreed.

"By the way, I have this whole weekend off, so Warren arrives early tomorrow," Jack said.

"Okay," Hannah accepted it without any noticeable reaction, and

together they turned and headed back up to the kitchen.

Hannah went straight to the stove and checked her chili as Jack noted the chili smell had filled the room, making his mouth water.

"Smells fantastic," he said.

"Don't try this at home, I'm a professional," she joked. "About three more minutes or so."

"Okay, I'll set the table," Jack said. Walking over, he gently tapped Sam on the shoulder. "I need to clear some room, buddy."

Sam planted both feet and scooted his foot back with one move, not missing a beat on his game as he did.

Jack chuckled and then set out plates, silverware, and napkins. "What do you want to drink, bud?" he asked Sam.

Sam made a drinking motion with one hand and grinned.

"Liquid," Jack surmised. "So helpful and specific."

Hannah laughed. "Just give him some juice or milk and he'll be fine."

"Coming up," Jack said and went to the fridge to retrieve it. For a moment, he felt like he had a family again and he was surprised how much he liked it, a small tinge of guilt the only sign of his grief for the moment.

When Hannah finished the chili, she used a ladle to make three bowls, then carried them over to the table and went back for a bag of shredded cheese, Parmesan, and sour cream from the fridge.

"Ready," she announced as she set everything on the table.

It took another few minutes for Hannah to coax the iPad out of Sam's hands but once she did, Sam grabbed their hands again and they bowed their heads in prayer. Then they ate what Jack decided was some of the best chili he'd ever tasted, and the wine complimented it perfectly. The salad wasn't half-bad either, but he was biased.

Afterward, Hannah and Sam helped clear the table and pile dirty dishes in the sink. Jack insisted on washing them himself while Hannah took Sam down to the guest room to start getting him settled. In their absence, while he worked, Jack turned on the radio to an oldies station that seemed to be having 80s night. All the songs he was hearing were songs from his parents' high school days, much to his amusement. Since he'd been raised on them, though, he could appreciate some and even knew the lyrics to sing along.

He found himself involuntarily moving to the beat—a little at first: a toe tap, maybe a leg jiggle or two, and eventually more hip action and even some movement. He was so caught up in it, twirling and dancing as he finished drying a dish with the towel and setting it on a rack on the counter—that he didn't even notice Hannah returning.

"Wow, nice moves," she teased.

Jack turned, surprised, then grinned. "I got rhythm. It's in my soul."

"Yeah, the future's so bright you gotta wear shades, right?" she countered with a laugh.

"Don't knock it 'til you try it," he said, swinging and dancing across the room to her, then offering his hand.

"Sam's supposed to be having quiet time, you know?" she said, perhaps as an excuse not to accept it.

He grabbed her hand anyway as the song changed from a rocker to a slow ballad and pulled her toward him, then swung her around as she cried out with surprise, and began slow dancing with her, cheek to cheek.

She giggled. "You're not a very good hermit."

"Not when it comes to you, for sure," he agreed and they danced that way a bit, slowly turning and circling. She smelled of jasmine and fruity soap and he loved the way her hand fit into his. Jack's other hand found its way to her waist and curved perfectly around the side. He felt a jolt of electricity at her touch then a pleasant warmth as they moved together like a team.

"Rob used to love taking me dancing."

"Abby too."

"She trained you well."

"This? Oh, this is all natural, baby. I'm gifted."

"Yeah, right."

They both laughed, dancing cheek to cheek and then each leaned back as their eyes met and Jack felt a sudden urge to kiss her. They stared at each other a moment, then their faces were moving toward each other, when Sam appeared on the stairs, watching with curiosity. Just as their lips were about to meet, they both felt it and turned, Hannah gasping.

She pulled away from him and hurried over. "Sam, I thought you were reading 'til I came back."

He shrugged.

"Sorry, pal," Jack said. "It was my fault. I was being silly."

Sam nodded, offering a slight cockeyed smile.

"Go brush your teeth, okay?" Hannah said, taking him by the hand and leading him back down the stairs as Jack turned and lowered the volume on the radio, feeling a sudden need to catch his breath. They'd almost kissed in front of Sam. He hoped Hannah wasn't upset or Sam either. His only choice was to wait until Hannah came back.

And for the next half hour, he did exactly that, sipping from a fresh glass of wine as he looked out the window at the stormy night sky over the sea.

THEY'D ALMOST kissed. *And in front of Sam, too!* If he hadn't walked in, they would have. Hannah wasn't exactly sure how it had happened. They'd been having fun, she had to admit. Jack had been relaxed and Sam too. Somehow they wound up dancing, being silly together, and it just sort of happened. But then Sam was there, and she did what anyone would do—turned away and focused on her child.

Sam had given no indication he'd known what was going on as she took him back down to the guest quarters and tucked him into bed. He'd asked no questions as she'd knelt beside him and prayed with him—a ritual Ellen usually handled but which she knew Sam treasured and she wasn't sure how well he'd get to sleep without.

And speaking of Ellen—she'd all but forgotten her mother-in-law, caught up in the moment, but when she'd called to tell her they'd be staying overnight at the lighthouse, Ellen had been angry. The conversation was short but heated. Thinking of her now as she watched her son praying, Hannah felt no guilt. It was the storm that forced them to make the choice, She certainly hadn't planned it—an accusation Ellen would likely make as soon as they got home. Another part of her felt excited—we almost kissed! Which brought back her confusion—was Jack just being impulsive or had he planned this? He'd had no way of knowing they'd get stuck there overnight, of course, but everything seemed to have led up to it perfectly. She shook off any thought of Jack manipulating things. They'd been caught up in the moment—a feeling inspired by working together like a couple on dinner and caring for Sam and perhaps aided by wine and maybe a little exhaustion. That was all.

It took almost a half hour, including prayers and two stories, before Sam settled down enough to fall asleep. Hannah watched him for a few minutes before quietly making her way back up to the kitchen to find Jack reading Time magazine at the table, a cup of coffee resting on a coaster in easy reach. The music from the radio was still playing, but he'd changed from the oldies station to one playing blues and jazz, perfect music for a stormy night to Hannah's thinking.

Jack looked up from his magazine as she stepped off the spiral staircase and crossed toward him. "Did he get to sleep okay?"

"Well, it took all this time, so I'd say he was a little wired."

"Sorry about that."

She shook her head. "I don't think it was because of..." She couldn't say it but from the look he gave her, she knew Jack understood.

As she turned to go back to the table, she found herself face to face with Jack, who had stood, their faces inches apart as their eyes met. The smell of his cologne—lavender, amber, a hint of Brazilian rosewood—tantalized her nose, and then suddenly, they were leaning in again, like magnets drawn together, and their lips met—soft, moist, warm. It was the first kiss for Hannah in two years and she savored it, managing to avoid spilling her coffee in the process.

When they parted, they stared into each other's eyes a few

seconds more before she pulled away. "That was..."

"I've been wanting to do that all day," said Jack admitted, then she saw a tinge of guilt in his eyes as he turned away.

"Perhaps I should head to bed, too," she said. "We may want to get an early start tomorrow once the storm clears."

Jack smiled. "Good night. Let me know if you need anything."

She headed for the stairs, stopping to glance back and find he was sipping his own coffee and watching her go.

"Good night," she called back and then forced herself down the stairs, trying to catch the breath she'd somehow been holding since the kiss. It had been wonderful, but what did it mean? She fought the temptation to call Denise for advice, fearing Jack might overhear. Besides, she didn't want to wake Sam and have him hear all about it either.

She set the coffee on the bedside table and went to brush her teeth and hair, a nightly ritual. Then she sprawled out on the bed, lost in thought, as she slowly sipped her coffee, her mind going over and over the kiss and everything leading up to it. She didn't feel bad about it.. Ellen would just have to accept Hannah was moving on. She knew Jack was the type of man Rob would approve of her finding to share her life and help raise Sam. Her only concern was—were they moving too fast for Jack? Was she ready? What about Sam?

She wrestled over those thoughts for quite a while as she finished her coffee. Then, she set the empty mug on the bedside stand and slipped under the covers. A half hour later, she drifted off to sleep.

CHAPTER 19

HANNAH AWOKE TO a blinding ray of bright sunlight beaming across the room onto her face and groaned, rolling over to cover her eyes as they tried to focus. The clock on the nightstand read 9 a.m. She'd overslept.

She sat up and looked around. Sam wasn't in the other bed, and the lighthouse was quiet.

"Sam? Jack?" she called.

Sitting up and climbing to her feet, she took the stairs up to the kitchen to find it empty, then hurried toward the windows checking the beach outside. The sun was shining and the sky was clear and blue. Except for debris scattered around the beach, it was almost as if the storm hadn't happened. There was no sign of Sam or Jack.

Where could they be?

It wasn't that she didn't trust Jack with Sam. That part she felt perfectly comfortable with, but she had missed Friday, and Sunday they had plans for Island Fest, so she really needed to work her Saturday shift. Since she had to be there at noon, they needed to be on their way home. Crossing to the windows on the opposite side, her eyes scanned the horizon. Nothing. Then she heard the rattling of a lock as a door opened below and Sam giggled—something he did nowhere near as often as he once had.

Just as she turned back toward the stairs, she heard Jack's voice. "Let's go wake your mother, okay? She's a real sleepyhead this morning."

And then she heard footsteps climbing the stairs and called, "I'm in the kitchen."

Moments later, they appeared, Sam with a very satisfied grin and Jack lugging a seemingly heavy backpack. "Morning," he said with a smile. "We went shelling while you slept."

"You did?"

Sam nodded enthusiastically as he rushed over to hug her around the waist. She reached down to hug him back.

"That's really great, Sam, but mommy has to be at the diner at noon, so we need to gather our things and call Bert, okay?"

Sam lifted both arms, elbows out and two-handedly blew a kiss out the window as if he were sending a message out to the island. She interpreted it as his way of loving their time there. He hurried down the stairs to the guest room.

"Shouldn't take long considering how much you packed," Jack joked. "Do you want breakfast?" He opened the fridge to reveal a plate of scrambled eggs and bacon and biscuits. "We cooked. I can reheat it all in the microwave, just like new, promise."

"Wow," Hannah said, suitably impressed. "We cooked?"

Jack said, "Sam was up early so he helped me, and Warren pitched in too. Sam did the scrambling while Warren flipped the bacon. I supervised and set the table." He grinned.

"Sam's a good scrambler," Hannah admitted, then looked around. "Where is Warren?"

"He's making morning rounds to check on everything. He'll be a while," Jack said, grabbing the plate and heading toward the microwave on the counter. "Just two minutes."

"Sure thing, thanks," Hannah said. "Let me go help Sam."

"Be ready when you get back," Jack said.

Was it weird they'd kissed and Jack didn't seem to be acting any different? Did that mean he wasn't feeling guilty or nervous? Or did he hide it well? She watched him a moment as he closed the microwave and expertly set the timer, then headed for the stairs.

She wasn't sure what to think, except that she'd enjoyed every minute of it, and she hoped whatever his worries, they could continue seeing where it led as they spent more time together the following day at Island Fest.

She found Sam making his bed, with the toothbrushes they'd opened sitting out on the bedside stand.

"Wow, such a good guest, Sam," she said, impressed and proud. "I'm so glad you remembered to make your bed."

He winked, the little parrot picking that up from Lou. He and kept on tucking and primping then looked over at her own bed which was a mess.

"Yeah, I'll make mine too," she said and did so.

In five minutes, they were back up in the kitchen where Sam joined her at the table as she ate her breakfast. As she picked up the fork, Jack returned from a fridge run, each hand full, carrying a glass of orange juice and mug of coffee.

"Wasn't sure what you wanted so brought both," he said.

Hannah took him up on it, needing an eye-opener. Sam took his while she downed the coffee.

"Are these scrambled ?" Hannah said after taking another bite of eggs.

"You-you can't tell?" Jack frowned. "How's the bacon?"

"A little overcooked," Hannah said, fighting the urge to laugh as he stared down at his hands.

"I guess I need some practice," he confessed.

"That'll teach ya to fish for compliments, huh?" she joked.

Jack grinned. "You're mean."

Sam smiled and winked as Hannah shrugged. Actually, everything was perfect and he'd added some spices and cheese that made the eggs delectable on the tongue. An architect who could cook? How had she gotten so lucky? And then she thought about the kiss again—he was good at that too. In so many ways, he was the perfect man. Now, if she could just be sure the timing was right.

"We're lucky you took us in for a night," she said.

"You want me to call Bert?" Jack asked.

She checked and still had no signal. "That would be great. Half an hour tops, though, tell him," said Hannah. Lou's testiness would be at an all-time high.

After he hung up, he asked, "We're still doing the festival tomorrow, right?"

She'd forgotten she'd invited him. It was an annual tradition with Ellen and Sam. Did she want him there? Was she ready for him to deal with Ellen yet? Was he ready for that?

"Shall we meet for breakfast at Lou's and go from there?" Jack asked, not picking up on her hesitation.

Sam made a happy face, his lips moving almost forming a word. Or else she dreamed it.

Why not? If he proved he could handle Ellen, they could get through anything, right? No trial like a trial by fire. "I guess that's two votes for that plan, eight-thirty," Hannah said.

"Sounds good," Jack said as he let Hannah finish her breakfast and went back to the sink to wash a few dishes he and Sam had left there earlier. Moments later, they heard footsteps climbing the staircase. Warren appeared carrying a coffee mug, his eyes having formed pouches underneath as if he didn't sleep through the storm either.

"Good morning," he said and looked at Hannah. "I see you got breakfast."

"Yes, you didn't see Bert did you?" She checked her watch.

Warren shrugged, stopping to refill his mug from the coffee pot. "I may have noticed him trolling on in. Yes, I'm almost certain it was him," he said before disappearing upstairs.

"Off to his rounds." Jack filled in, overly friendly, as he often was when she was the one being off-putting.

"Rain's moved on," she said, checking outside again.

"Need a ride to the pier?" he asked.

"Can we leave now?"

So they headed down the stairs together and climbed in the cart. They arrived just as Bert was pulling up.

Bert looked at Jack and back at Hannah. Neither of them spoke.

"You're in good hands," he told her, before gunning the cart and leaving.

Hannah's last image of him that morning was the back of his head. Maybe she had perturbed him with her teasing about his food. But she'd let him know she was joking. Why was he acting like nothing happened? Had he actually taken the "we're just friends" comment seriously? They'd gotten carried away. Swept up in the moment. The stormy weather. Stuck in close quarters. The family moments. What if that was all he thought, and he'd immediately course corrected to "friends only" because he thought she expected it? She had said it... Did she need to clarify that?

Only she'd rounded a bend last night, starting to think of him against as something more. It was the way he'd handled the situation, calm and collected, reassuring. He'd taken charge when she was angry and panicking, and found a way to make both her and Sam comfortable. Then they'd cooked together, played games. It was a fun night.

And that cologne. Friends or not, he'd clearly put on the good stuff. It had done something to her being close to him for

253

sure. Only now he wanted to act like nothing had happened? Okay, she'd broken her rules, her fault. But then her kiss wasn't friendly at all. She'd wanted the kiss, kissing him back. A real kiss. Why was it suddenly so hard to think of him as a just a friend? And what happened now?

HE'D KISSED HER. Jack replayed the moment, over and over, in his mind. And he liked it. Liked it way more than he'd imagined. He wanted to do it again. What's more, he was pretty sure she'd kissed him back. If only he hadn't screwed it up. Left her standing alone in the kitchen, lightning and thunder rattling the windows.

The morning had gone okay, but he hadn't been sure what to say to her. Especially with Sam there. Despite her teasing, Hannah seemed impressed with his cooking skills. No one had liked his cooking that he could recall. His mother had taught him along with basic sewing and laundry and several other key life skills, saying, "You're not getting sent back someday by your wife because you're not done." Abby had done most of the cooking—mostly because she loved it. Now that he thought about it, she'd never said so. He chalked it off to another unspoken between them. Besides how he worked long hours— he'd kept it up when he could—it was easier to let Abby man the kitchen stuff.

As he drove alone back to the lighthouse from the pier, the memory kept him smiling, but then he got back and returned to the kitchen to finish dishes. Memories of Abby flooded his mind. He scrolled to a normal day in his phone's video log.

Caroline swung and wove and hummed loudly as she danced around the kitchen while Jack stood at the sink helping Abby with the dishes. She washed, he dried, standing shoulders touching—an intimacy that sent chills through him every time they touched.

Caroline had a habit, like kids do, of turning on his phone

recorder. He hadn't discovered the video until a few weeks later, after the accident.

"That was a great meal, honey," he told her for the fifth time since they'd finished the sumptuous feast. For their tenth anniversary, Abby had made steak, mashed potatoes, gravy, buttered corn, and cheesy broccoli, and served it all up like something out of Better Homes and Gardens or a fancy restaurant. She was great at presentation. It came naturally to her, and consequently the anniversary had looked like a photograph. Picture perfect in appearance, and picture perfect in taste. He'd gone in early that day, so he had no idea how many hours she'd put into it but the effort showed. And it made his own card, chocolates, and flowers seem woefully inadequate. Of course, he'd gotten her the new microwave and bread maker she'd been coveting. To him, it was barely adequate for what he got in return, but she'd kissed him and said, "It's perfect. Thank you."

Perfect. Just like Abby. As they worked together side by side, her brunette ponytail bobbed back and forth while she regaled him with how she'd tried his grandmother's bread recipe. Had to throw it out. She was confessional like that. No subterfuge with Abby. With one short experimental exception with curls and a perm, for as long as he'd known her, she'd kept her hair long. Jack loved when she let it down. He didn't care if she pulled it back into a ponytail. That was sexy too. He loved running his hands through it down, though, liking how it drifted down over them as they made love.

"Thanks, honey," Abby replied, shaking her head to brush stray hairs from her nose as she did. She saw him watching her and smiled, handing him another dish. "Keeping going, we're almost done."

"Yes, ma'am," he said and smiled back. He didn't know what he'd done to deserve her, but as his grandfather would put it, he knew he'd caught way above his limit when he met Abby.

He finished the lighthouse dishes and set them on the rack to dry before he wiped his hands on the dishtowel and walked over to the window to look out at the beautiful mid-morning sea. Peaceful, calm—the waves perfect as they slowly flowed and crested and flowed again. He'd had his chance at near perfection. Why was he so greedy as to think he could find it again? Was it fair to Hannah to even try when he knew he'd always be comparing her to Abby? Surely she knew that, too. How did that make her feel?

The image of her kiss stayed with him, like her scent, and he could almost feel what she'd have felt like in his arms; he'd hardly given her soft lips a fighting chance. Kissing her was magic, he had to admit, and he hadn't thought anyone could make him tingle the way Abby did. Until Hannah. None of it was exactly the same as Abby, of course, but different in its own pleasant way, and why not? Before Abby he'd only dated a few girls once or twice, and since Abby, he'd only met one, Hannah. So he didn't have much basis for comparison, and he wondered if doing so was even a reasonable thing to do. Abby had often scolded him when he'd compared Caroline to other children, but it was hard not to compare. What did he have to go on but what he'd experienced? Anyway, why did it matter whether they kissed the same? He liked it. What bothered him were the pangs of guilt that arose after every time he got caught in a moment with Hannah when he thought of Abby.

His mind flashed back again to a moment he'd replayed a lot recently. "Honey, I love you too, but if something happens, I want you to find happiness," she'd told him, her voice rich with both love and concern. "I don't want you to think you can't still love me and find someone else."

At the time, he'd been somewhat annoyed with her, puzzled as to why she'd brought such a thing up. It was sad and morbid and he hadn't wanted to think about it, but that was Abby—always pondering the future, planning ahead to take care of the people she loved.

Both Abby and Hannah were beautiful and smart and wonderful mothers. And he knew Abby would like her. Their personalities were similar and they had a lot in common. They'd probably even be friends, as weird as that was to think about.

No, the issue wasn't what Abby would think, he decided. The issue was with Jack. What did he think? Was he okay with it? Was he ready?

Wanting to escape the torture of such thoughts, he headed down to the shed and loaded a shovel and toolbox into the cart, then drove off on his daily chores, hoping work would distract him.

After a day spent repairing fences and digging up weeds, he returned to the lighthouse exhausted. But only as he warmed up leftover spaghetti did it occur to him that despite his busyness, it seemed to him that he'd spent way more time thinking about Hannah and picturing his time with her than he had Abby. He wondered what that meant.

Josie called around seven. "Are you actually comparing Hannah with Abby? Really?" Josie chastised when he told her about the night at the lighthouse and what he was thinking. "Oh my God, you are so clueless, Jack."

"What do you mean?"

"It's not a contest. They're two different people. What are you—in seventh grade? Stop being a jackass, and appreciate her for who she is." He hated when Josie sounded just like their mother, May.

"I mentioned her good qualities. I thought I was doing that." His mind raced as he tried to figure out what he was doing wrong. "It's been a long time…" he mumbled, trailing off.

"Obviously," Josie said and chortled. "Look, I'm so happy you've found someone to spend time with, someone who enjoys you. That's great. So enjoy it. But stop trying to finish the race so fast."

"Race? What race?" He could practically hear her rolling her eyes.

"Slow down. Relationships take time," she said. "Give Hannah time to see your better qualities while you learn about hers. Then see what happens. It doesn't all have to happen in a few dates. Relax."

Jack sighed. "I thought I was relaxed."

This time she laughed loudly. "Bro, you're the least relaxed man I know these days, and you know how uptight dad can be. Seriously. Stop it. The falling in love and dating are some of the best parts. Enjoy it. It doesn't last forever."

After that, she changed subjects, and they spent an hour in catching up and general chitchat about lighthouse and the Keys. After he hung up, he spent the rest of the evening reading Outside Magazine though the words and stories didn't seem to stick. Only temptations to buy camping gear. Instead, he thought again about Hannah and Sam. Being with them the past few days had been like having a family again, and it was the happiest he'd felt in two years, since the accident. He needed a reason to see her again. He'd confused her, not calling his invitations dates. Not protesting when she'd tried to rule them just friends.

Better qualities.

At any rate, Island Fest was tomorrow, and it was a big deal, an annual family tradition. He Googled the website, reading up on the activities and schedules and making mental notes of what might interest Sam. Around nine, instead of calling Hannah, like before, he changed his mind since they'd spent time together yesterday, even though it had been ... what to call it? Edgy? Yes, that's it. Josie said it sounded awkward, but edgy wasn't so bad. It gave him something to work from.

Next he made his nightly rounds—climbing all the way up to check the lamp, shinnying back down to check for messages at the comm center before returning to bed. Nothing from anyone in particular. No flashing light in the message feed.

Brushing his teeth and washing his face, he settled back into the bed and turned off the lamp. It wasn't long before he relaxed so he could drift off to sleep, his last thought one of contentment knowing that even if Sam had pushed her, she'd still invited him. He'd been told at work he was a fixer. By sundown tomorrow, he'd fix what he'd screwed up with Hannah.

CHAPTER 20

DENISE AND JANICE were already hustling when Hannah and Sam arrived at the diner. Dishes clanked, meat and eggs sizzled on the grill, machines hummed, and people were chatting all around. The whole place smelled of grease and fat and delicious breakfast. Hannah was so used to it she almost didn't notice anymore, but Sam's face formed its usual smile as he sniffed the air. He loved eating at mommy's work.

"Hey, girl, thought you had the day off," said Denise "What brings you in?"

"Quick breakfast before we head to the Island Fest," said Hannah, leading Sam to a booth.

"It's terrific. We had a blast," said Denise over her shoulder, setting out plates for one of her tables.

"Milking the employee discount, eh, Hannah?" said Janice, racing past delivering orders to Lou's packed house. He'd be in a stew. Festival traffic set him on edge, especially Island Fest. He much preferred local patrons. Hannah felt an ease watching Janice working for once while she took a booth as a customer.

Sam picked up a menu and opened it, his eyes carefully scanning each item to Hannah's amusement. As many times as they'd been there, he should have the whole thing memorized. Besides, he always ordered from the Kid's Menu on the back, so why was he bothering with the rest? But one by one, Sam read each item, from the top of the first column, working his way down.

The door jangled and she glanced up. A couple piled in, dragging two small kids and a bouquet of festival balloons. Not that she was looking for Jack. She looked around, checking the clock on the wall. He'd been at least five minutes early in the past. It was annoying she was keeping tabs. He'd not given her a reason to. Lou waved back at Sam from behind the grill in the kitchen while he muttered under his breath. Denise walked past, prompting Hannah to touch her arm. "Coffee please."

"Sure, babe," Denise said and hurried on. Hannah knew her friends would take good care of them like always.

A moment later, the door jangled again, and Hannah looked up to see the narrow, furious blue eyes of her mother-in-law locked right on her.

Hannah's heart sank. Please, not here. Not now. Ellen had been gone when they'd arrived home the day before from the lighthouse—off delivering items to various vendors who'd show off her wares in their booths at the Island Fest the next few days. She'd been gone all day, and tired from their adventure at the lighthouse, Hannah and Sam had gone to bed early. They had yet to speak.

Ellen came charging over.

Sam brightened, beaming at his grandma who managed a forced smile then pointed. "Sam, go wash your hands."

Sam frowned, shooting Hannah a confused look.

"He already did that before we came," Hannah said.

"Well, these places are filthy," said Ellen, acting as if she'd hadn't eaten there for years. "Imagine how many germs he picked up just walking through the door or in this booth." She raised her arm and pointed toward the restroom then stared at Sam, who shot his mother another glance.

Hannah sighed and gently stroked his hair. "It can't hurt to wash them again, honey. Why don't you let Grandma and I talk for a minute."

Sam sighed then shrugged and slid from the booth, heading for the bathroom. Hannah watched him a moment, forcing a smile when he glanced back to be sure she was okay, and didn't relax until he'd disappeared inside. Then she whirled to Ellen and glared. "What the hell's the matter with you?" She whispered it, although those seated front and back turned to look.

"Where were you?"

Hannah sighed. Ellen's capacity for confronting never ceased to amaze. Now, here she sat, her mother-in-law embarrassing her at a place where everyone knew them. the diner. "Could you please sit down? You're making a scene."

Ellen's brow wrinkled and her eyes looked about ready to pop out of her head as she reluctantly slid into the booth across from Hannah. "You slept with him!" It was a whisper but loud enough people at the next booth glanced over with curiosity.

Hannah's face dropped into her hands.

"You slept with him with your son right there," Ellen accused again.

"I think you should leave," Hannah said.

"What were you even doing out there?" Ellen replied, without even acknowledging the call. It was another accusation.

"Sam wanted to see how the lighthouse worked," Hannah said. "Beyond that, it's none of your business what I do."

Ellen scowled. "Do not use Sam as an excuse. You spent the night with another man. My God, have you lost all love and respect for my son?"

"You can't be serious." Rob stood at the foot of her bed smiling as she slept. He knelt beside her at the beach when Sam played. She could still smell him on his favorite T-shirt stuffed in her underwear drawer. Hannah said nothing.

"Didn't you check the weather before you went out?" Ellen countered.

"You know how storms can just spring up out here sometimes." Like the one Ellen sprung on her here at Lou's.

Ellen sighed as Sam appeared, returning from the bathroom.

"I'm a grown woman, and I still have life," Hannah whispered back through gritted teeth. "I'll decide what's right."

Sam smiled as he neared the table, bouncing across the floor with excitement as he hurried past them and slid into a booth across the aisle. It was his favorite booth—the one he'd sat at with his dad after T-ball games.

"Oh, honey, do you want to sit there?" Hannah said as she ignored Ellen and went over to join Sam.

Ellen sat there a moment, her face reddening as her nostrils flared, while Sam and Hannah just went back to looking at menus. Finally, she stood and marched past them, glaring at Hannah. "You should be ashamed," she mouthed, then continued for the door.

As she did, the bell jangled again and Hannah looked up. This time Jack was standing in the doorway. Seeing her, he smiled and seeing Ellen approach, nodded to her. "Hello again."

Ellen whizzed past him without a word, shooting him dead with a look.

Jack raised an eyebrow as he slipped past a few people waiting and joined Hannah and Sam at the booth.

"Good morning," he said with a smile as he slipped onto the bench opposite them. "Was it something I said?"

Hannah offered a half-hearted excuse for her mother-in-law's bad behavior. "No, she's just mad about something stupid as always."

"Stupid."

"My mother-in-law has the wrong idea about things she

creates in her head."

Jack frowned as he appeared to decide where to sit. Hannah didn't budge, but that didn't stop Sam from sliding over. He had a habit of making room for strays. "Sorry, I feel like I'm intruding." He turned to greet Sam, but Sam had gone back immediately to studiously reading the menu. "He's focused."

"He's silly," Hannah said. "He knows it by heart."

Jack laughed.

Denise arrived with a mug of coffee and handed it to Hannah. Hannah introduced Denise to Jack, something she regretted the instant Denise reacted with only slightly hidden disdain.

For his part, Jack seemed confused by the not-so-hidden hostility, looking at Hannah as if to ask, 'What am I missing?'

"You all know what you want?" Denise asked, glancing from Hannah to Jack in her weighted way when she wasn't saying what she was thinking.

Hannah just smiled and gave her order, then Jack followed, Denise recording it all on her iPad and then they all looked at Sam because the air had gotten thin between the adults.

"Sam," said Hannah, elbowing her son. "Order please."

Sam shot her a look that said "Duh!" And raised a palm in the air like a TV evangelist.

"He'll have his usual—the kids two by," said Hannah said. Two by two by two, a diner staple—two eggs, two bacon, two pancakes, sides of hash browns and toast.

"You got it," Denise said then held out her hand for the menus. Jack and Hannah gave her theirs but Sam kept reading. Hannah tried shooting him a motherly look, while inside she was fuming. She'd been embarrassed enough already this morning at the diner. Come on!

"I really don't know what his deal is today," Hannah said. "Sam!" She grabbed for the menu, grabbing air. He held it out of reach.

"I'll come back for it when I bring the food, it's fine," said Denise said, hurrying off, one thing giving Hannah a modicum of relief.

"Sam, I know you're excited about Island Fest," said Hannah said, looking at her son, "but if you're not going to be on best behavior, we might as well not go."

Sam, a full-fledged art of the mime expert, made a sad face, closing the menu and pushing it across the table toward her.

"Honey, it's okay if you read it until Denise comes back, but please don't ignore mom."

Sam appeared satisfied, snapping the menu back up, returning to his reading.

Hannah shook her head as her eyes met Jack's. "It's gonna be a weird day, I suspect. I wasn't sure you were coming today." Most of what had transpired between them added up to not a lot of interest from him. She'd seen him treat Sam and Warren with more interest than her. Denise had called it from the beginning. She needed some of Denise's moxie about men.

Jack frowned then swallowed, his brow creasing. "Why wouldn't I? I thought we made plans. We'll have fun. I checked the website last night. So much to do."

"Yeah, it's a big deal," Hannah said, running out of what to say, wanting him to leave them. She said, "and despite being Sunday, it'll be crowded, though not as bad in the morning because people are at church." She was sure she sounded lame, stating the obvious.

"No church for you?" Jack asked.

Was he judging her? "We go usually," Hannah said. "But this is the only day we can do the Festival and we always look forward to it, so we're playing hooky."

But his face showed no judgment as he took a breath and unwrapped the napkin from around his silverware. "Understood. I haven't really been since the accident."

Their food came in less than ten minutes and they all went to work eating, and, thankfully, conversation taking less priority. By eight-forty-five, they were in the Jeep headed north on the Overseas Highway for Founder's Park, with Hannah driving and the whole time wondering if Jack could possibly feel as awkward about spending the day together as she did. He certainly didn't show it. The road was crowded, with lots of people headed north for the festivities. Jack commented it was the most crowded he'd seen it, and Hannah admitted it was heavy traffic but nothing compared to hurricane evacuations, for example.

The parking lots at the park were usually packed, but there were other lawn areas roped off for extra parking and shuttles bussing people in from nearby lots. Hannah drove to the park first and lucked into a spot on one of the lots, one of the last two available. So they parked the car, cracked the windows, and headed for the festival.

The air smelled of carnival delights—funnel cakes, hot dogs, baked treats, and everything you could think of—and the crowd was dispersed for the moment in small clumps, but Hannah knew it would only get denser and denser as the day went on.

"This festival is one of the first things Rob and I did together when we moved to the Keys," Hannah said, taking deep breaths to relax. Might as well try and make the most of it. They did agree to be friends.

"I thought you grew up down here," Jack said.

"I did, but we were in Orlando for college and he worked up there for a couple years before we were able to find better opportunities here," she explained.

"So Island Fest wasn't around when you were a kid?"

"Well, it's been around thirty years, so yeah, but it's changed a lot since it started. Becoming much bigger and way more popular."

The first area they came to were tents and booths with food vendors galore—everything, from the aforementioned delights, to burgers, fries, steaks, giant turkey legs, soup, popcorn, and more. Of course, there were plenty of beverage options as well from water to soda to beer, lemonade, and shakes. As Sam's eyes took it all in with his usual wide excitement, Jack was right there asking him questions about the various options in a way that made Sam feel important and telling him, "You can have whatever you want." The hair stiffened on Hannah's nape. Not that she wouldn't have said the same thing, but why did Jack have to be so damn charming? Couldn't he sense her discomfort? Did he even care? Besides, they'd just gotten here. The time to eat was around noon when the Taste of Islamorada brought out all the local restaurants offering samples of their best delectables, something Hannah wouldn't miss. Finally, Jack bought Sam a lemonade.

Postponing the inevitable lull in chit-chat that allowed her no sense of relief in expressing herself to Jack, she hurried them on through into an area with tents, stages, and various arts and craft displays. There were items for sale like CDs of the entertainers featured on the stages, t-shirts, bumper stickers, and the usual frippery. Local crafts and artists drew her attention the most—many featuring images of the Keys or the ocean and related themes, but others more of a departure. Some of the artists were famous around the country or even the world, while others were little known locals awaiting discovery.

As expected, as soon as the carnival rides and play areas came into view, Sam was off to the races, and it was all Hannah and Jack could do to keep up with him, or even keep him in sight. For the rest of the day, Hannah insisted he hold her hand, although Jack stepped up to pinch-hit, taking his hand when it slipped from her reach. She blanched, resisting the way her heart wanted to soften. It was things like that that made her think more than she should about him. Jack was acting like they were a couple here with their son, not a couple adult friends, damn it. And she hated that deep inside, she liked it.

When they got to the Ferris wheel, Jack took charge of buying the tickets, and then he offered his hand to help her and Sam aboard like a true gentleman. Sam, of course, accepted the help, but Hannah refused the hand. "I've got it."

Jack smiled and stepped to the side, allowing her to slide in with Sam in between them before he settled onto the seat himself. Damn it, why was he acting like there was no tension between them? He looked totally at ease, and it was driving her crazy.

Next to the Ferris Wheel was a spinning centrifugal disk-type of ride called the Comet—or according to local teens she overheard "the vomit comet." Then they slowed Sam down, signing him into the bounce house. That was followed by a giant ball vat which Sam enjoyed even more when Jack invited himself in and continually dove under then erupted from random places around the vat, shouting "Bazinga!" like Sheldon from the Big Bang sitcom. Sam erupted giggling fits time and again, and Hannah couldn't help laughing and enjoying how much fun he had with her son.

After that, Sam got his face painted before they headed down to the beach to look at sand art—which included everything from large, intricate sand castles, including one so big you could walk beneath its arches, to geographic maps, recreated art masterpieces, and original drawings that were so realistic it blew the mind.

Sam grabbed their hands and led them over to one that featured a lighthouse, looking eagerly at Jack. "Hey, that's pretty good, isn't it?" he said, grinning. "Not quite as big as ours, but I love the detail." He thought a moment, reflecting on it. "I like how the curved edges lend it a kind of peacefulness, you know? It's a happy place. Joyful. Always a good day when a lighthouse can just exist without storms or other dangers for ships they signify. Abby always found that romantic." He looked at Hannah. "I'm starting to see her point."

Sam nodded as if he agreed, making Hannah giggle.

"I'm just amazed what they can do with sand," she said, but his observations were perfect, and she couldn't help flashing back over their time at the lighthouse now as she looked down on the sand sculpture. To her relief, Sam grew bored quickly and pulled them away moments later, breaking the moment.

At that point, it was lunch time, and Sam's declarations of hunger—through signals—had grown more adamant and frequent, so they headed for the Taste of Islamorada and began sampling the goods. Jack started with a beer from the Islamorada Brewery and Distillery, while Hannah and Sam opted for lemonade and iced tea from the Baby's Coffee stand. Next, Sam wanted pepperoni pizza from Tower of Pizza while Jack and Hannah selected items from Puerto Vallarta Mexican Grill and several seafood places like Islamorada Fish Company, Hungry Tarpon, and Captain Craig's. Hannah spotted Ellen's wares on display at several booths and on tables but saw no sign of her mother-in-law, so she relaxed again as she settled in across from Jack at a table.

"You think we have room for all this after that big breakfast?" Jack joked.

"I'm being selective for a reason," Hannah said.

"You've picked enough for two people," Jack teased.

"Well, it's all about sampling a wide variety here," she explained, remembering it was his first time at Island Fest. "We take a lot, eat what we can, and throw the rest—which usually is commandeered by birds and other creatures."

"Well, so Island Fest is for the whole community then?" he joked.

Hannah couldn't resist a laugh.

Once they'd filled bags with their selections, they carried them south to one of the stages where a comedic bluegrass trio was just starting their show and took seats at a nearby table to eat and enjoy the show. The crowd was definitely denser now with people constantly moving back and forth and jostling around each other, Hannah hoped Sam was getting tired. Her feet were killing her, and she was fatigued juggling what to say to Jack without understanding his unspoken motives. She was glad they'd gotten an early start.

The bluegrass trio turned out to be kid friendly and quite good at comedy. Sam laughed more than Hannah and Jack, but they all enjoyed it and stayed for the entire hour performance, allowing time to not only stuff themselves but recover their bearings some afterward.

Opting for a slower paced afternoon, they went down to view the entrants of the annual What Floats Your Boat?, an annual wacky homemade "boat" race. The challenge was to create a floatable "boat" using non-maritime materials. They were all quite entertained by the varied results from the welded 1970s VW bug hoods hull to the all-milk-carton pontoon to even wackier entries. Hannah most enjoyed watching the unusual makeshift boats through Sam's eyes. Sam even pantomimed that he wished he could go out on a couple of them, but that was not an option due to festival safety and legal regulations, so instead they went down to the beach to "swim with the mermaids," in which women and men dressed up in mer costumes and swam and posed for photos with attendees. Sam was all caught up in the fantasy, of course, and Hannah and Jack enjoyed watching him play and frolic in the water.

"You know, some of these people give new meaning to the term 'mer people,'" Jack said, "and it's not always an appealing one."

Hannah chuckled then fired back, "Well, I'm sure you'd be welcome to bring your own costume next year and show them how it's done."

Jack scoffed. "Yeah, that would be dignified."

Hannah made a pondering face. "I don't know. I think you'd look kinda sexy in that one," she said, motioning to man wearing a merman tale with a pink tutu and a gorilla suit chest, the weirdest combination yet.

Jack made a face. "Don't they have guidelines or something?"

Hannah raised her palms in surrender as they both said together, "They probably should" then laughed. Somehow

269

they'd been getting along so well, she'd relaxed her resistance and started enjoying how their interactions felt like two good friends spending the day together. To her surprise, Jack had never shown any frustration with her mood. For a guy who'd been an emotional hurricane when they first met, he was the calm in the storm, and that just made her like him more.

"You know, we have a festival like this in Salina called the Smoky Hill River Festival," Jack said. "It takes place at Oakdale Park every year and has some pretty big music acts and artists from all over the world come in."

"Really? But do they have mer people," Hannah teased.

"No, dueling banjos, which can bring its own brand of weird," Jack responded.

When Sam tired of the mermaids, they took a two hour dolphin watching cruise, then meandered through the car show display checking out the various vehicles, with Sam and Jack making a sport of posing for silly photos in their favorites. At five-thirty, they headed for the annual awards ceremony for the Taste of Islamorada. Leftovers were set out free for the crowd while the various restaurant winners received their accolades to the friendly heckles of their many competitors. Hannah tensed as they wound their way amongst the gathering crowd. It had been a surprisingly good time so far, but this was the one event at the Festival Ellen adored and would never miss, and Hannah dreaded what would happen if they ran into her here.

"Ouch," Jack said, wiggling his hand in hers, and she let go.

"What happened?" she asked.

"You," he replied, his brow furrowing as he looked at her. "What's wrong? You tensed up as soon as we entered the crowd."

Hannah shrugged. "Sorry. Just a mother's usual wariness with having her son in crowded places, especially one with special needs like Sam."

Jack glanced to where Sam was on the other side of her,

taking in all the colorful displays and enticing smells of the food with renewed excitement. "He looks fine to me." He let go of her hand and wrapped a gentle arm around her shoulder for a quick hug. "Don't worry, we'll keep him close." Then he took her hand again and they started back into the crowd as Hannah did her best to relax.

An hour into it, Hannah spotted Ellen. In fact, she ran right into her as both converged on the same kabobs booth.

"Sorry—," Ellen started saying until she realized who it was and clamped her mouth shut, glaring, then glanced around for signs of Jack and Sam. "Where's Sam?"

Hannah glanced over to the table Jack was holding for them where Sam sat tearing into some fried chicken. "I didn't know you were coming."

Ellen stiffened, but held her tongue, then whirled and marched off past the other end of the kabob booth as Hannah stepped into the line. Too bad, Ellen, guess you'll have to come back later.

It was about twenty minutes before Hannah rejoined Jack and Sam at the table with the kabobs, just as Sam was finishing off the last bits of chicken.

"Mom's Famous Kabobs," Jack read off the sign of the booth where she'd been. "So these are the legendary kabobs I keep hearing about, huh?" He looked over the two plates she'd returned with.

"Yes, dig in," Hannah said. "There's barbecue and middle eastern, and several varieties. I got a couple of each so we can both share."

As Jack started examining the kabobs more closely, considering his first choice, Ellen appeared, marching toward them and Hannah tensed, bracing herself for another confrontation, but to her surprise, Ellen put on a hug smile and marched right to Sam. "Hey, sweetie!"

Sam finished wiping his hands, piling up an impressive stack of napkins.

Ellen took Sam's hand and mumbled something about "Grandma and Sam time," then took him off with her, leaving Hannah and Jack alone.

"Wow. Alone time. What shall we do with ourselves?" Jack joked as Hannah considered running after Ellen to retrieve her son. Strange move for a woman who didn't want her daughter-in-law spending time along with other men.

"Are you okay?" Jack asked, his eyes softening as they met hers. Damn it, he was being so fantastic, and Ellen had left them alone so far, which was unusual. Clearly she had gotten the message from Hannah earlier at the diner. She and Sam did always enjoy the festival together. Maybe she should just let it go and deal with it later?

"Want me to go get Sam?" Jack asked, his eyebrows raised with concern.

Hannah shook her head. "No. They'll have together. I'm thinking we should enjoy these kabobs." She took a slow breath then allowed herself to smile. She was having a nice time, and no way Ellen would win by destroying it. "Then I thought we'd take a cruise under the stars. They're romantic and fun." It was also a great way to end the festival and avoid Ellen, a fact she kept to herself.

"Sounds great." Jack relaxed, taking another bite of kabob, and Hannah reached for her beer.

THE STARLIGHT YACHT cruise left the dock just after six-thirty, and with early sunset, the sky overhead was already dark and starry. Jack and Hannah lucked into a seat on a bench on the rear deck and sat with his arm around her as they sipped strawberry daiquiris and took in the view. The ocean breeze was light and gentle, cool but not cold. The boat was moderately full—the crowd light enough most people spread out in small

272

groups all around.

"This has been a great day," Hannah said, and she meant it. Since Ellen had taken Sam off their hands, she'd all but forgotten the earlier tension and let herself enjoy spending time with a handsome gentleman.

"Amazing," Jack agreed. "It was really nice of your mother-in-law to take Sam off our hands like that." Hannah felt a momentary flash of anger at Ellen, but bit back a comment, forcing a smile, as Jack went on, "Nice gesture and no embarrassing comments," Jack teased. "Who is that woman with your son?"

Hannah chuckled. "Stop reading my mind."

"I get the feeling she doesn't like me much."

"She'd be happy if I spent the rest of my life a spinster. It's not you."

Jack chuckled turning his eyes to the horizon. "It's beautiful out here. I'm glad you suggested this."

"It's a great way to appreciate the Keys," she said watching him as he just stood there, slowly breathing, taking in the beauty.

After a moment, he turned, catching her looking as she quickly turned away. "Oh..." Jack put his hand to his temple. "Wow. Are thinking some dirty thoughts?"

Hannah elbowed him. "No, I was appreciating the view just like you."

"Really? Is that all?" He shot her a mischievous look.

"Actually, I'm really grateful to have found someone I can do this with again. You spend your whole life here and sometimes you forget how amazing the Keys are."

"They're amazing but so are you," Jack said, his eyes locked on her.

It wasn't a lustful look. Instead it was the same look of peace and wonder he'd had when he admired the horizon. He respected her—flaws and all. It was far from the seeming disinterest he'd shown the next morning after her night at the lighthouse. She fumbled for words, "I have my moments." This was the Jack she'd been attracted to—playful, relaxed, attentive, and fun. The Jack who had won her over time after time and had done it yet again tonight. The way he was looking at her made her feel like the only woman in the world, and God, it had been a long time since she'd felt anything like that. Not since Rob.

"Yes, you do," Jack said, leaning over to let his lips gently brush her cheek. The stars above were crystal clear, the storm clouds from two nights before having totally cleared out. Right away he could pick out the Big Dipper, Cassiopeia, the Little Dipper, and Draco, along with Venus low off the horizon to the northwest. Jack pointed them out to her, reminding her they were looking into the past at stars that were born aeons ago.

"I used to love looking up at the stars as a kid," Hannah said, then the words seemed to catch in her throat.

"I still do," Jack said.

Hannah turned sad. "I did, but it's tainted."

Jack looked at her, trying to discern what was wrong. "Why?"

She sighed. "The night Rob died was a night like this."

"He was on a boat or at sea, right?"

She nodded, taking a deep breath. She hadn't told the story in a long time. "He'd taken Sam out fishing. It was only the third time they'd gone deep sea fishing, in fact. They went out with a friend of his in a small boat. A storm had been predicted but it wasn't expected until the wee hours, so they went, but then the storm came early."

She closed her eyes a moment, recalling the memory, before going on. "It was one of those storms that just comes up on you all of a sudden. First, there were winds, and then rain that got harder and harder. Visibility was terrible. They'd started back as soon as the winds hit, but when the rain came down in sheets and they couldn't see..."

She looked at him. "The other boat came out of nowhere. Some kids racing around. And like idiots, they were racing to get back from the storm. Not hurrying, racing."

Jack winced at the realization of what she was about to tell him, but he didn't turn away. Instead, he leaned in, his hand gently rubbing her shoulder.

"The speed boat hit theirs at top speed and cut it in half," Hannah went on. "They had life jackets on, but they were all in the water. Rob's friend, Ted, was killed instantly. Rob was there floating, trying to stay above water, keep Sam calm, who was scared to death, of course."

She choked up a moment, and he squeezed her shoulder. She took a deep breath before going on. "With Rob's encouragement, Sam managed to climb atop some debris. A piece of the boat. And Rob was trying to get to him when a wave came. It swept over the top of him. Sam floated up, Rob went down. And when Sam saw him again..."

She cried, not something she'd planned. But retelling it always took her there because recalling what happened had been the last time Sam spoke any words after the accident. She accepted a tissue from Jack. "Sam watched his father die. He was stuck out there with Rob for an hour or two before the rescue boats came. The kids didn't bother to call it in until they were at the dock and one of them felt guilty. The Coast Guard found Sam clinging to his father with all he had, and he hasn't spoken a word since."

She sobbed then, and the sound was so full of pain and loss and despair that tears filled Jack's eyes too as he wrapped his arms around her and pulled her close. It was like something pent up that had needed to be released in them was coming out right there in that moment, so they held each other for a moment, there on the yacht, wrapped in each other on a bench,

275

until the sobbing had passed.

"They prosecuted them, right?" Jack asked as they caught their breaths again and she pulled away, trying to catch her breath.

She nodded. "The driver, yes. Reckless endangerment, involuntary homicide, various maritime charges. But Sam never spoke again, and God knows what horrible image of Rob he carries around with him." When she'd identified the body, his tongue was out, his eyes were wide and he was bloated. It was awful for her, let alone for a little boy to see for hours.

Jack's face went through a surge of emotions—concern, sadness, anger, and compassion, all combined, her own loss and pain clearly making his own fresh again. He took her in his arms once more and whispered, "I'm so sorry."

"Rob had this waterproof camera and he was videoing some stuff," Hannah said. "One of the last things Rob had done was point out constellations, narrating a panoramic of the stars right before the winds hit."

Jack exhaled. "Wow. If Sam was the only witness, how do you know?" Jack asked.

Pulling away gently, Hannah wiped at her tears and sniffled. "I'm so sorry I'm ruining this night."

"No, you're not," Jack said. "I understand grief. I live with it every day."

"The thing was," Hannah said as she tried to gather herself again, "Sam loved fishing with his dad. It was their thing. He was always begging Rob to take him, and Rob loved it, too. So many afternoons out on the water. Rob and Ted were expert boatmen. But those stupid kids..."

"The guy who hit Abby was texting," Jack said. "Ordering food for lunch from his office. Can you believe that?"

"You two look like you need more wine," a voice said and they turned to see one of the yacht crew, a young woman in her early twenties, standing there with wine glasses and two bottles.

"Red or white?"

Hannah tensed. She'd wanted to hear Jack's story, but when Jack chuckled and wiped at his eyes, she knew it would have to wait.

"White," he said.

Hannah nodded beside him. "Definitely white."

The crew member poured them each a glass and handed them over one at a time, then smiled and went on her way.

Jack raised his glass. "To Rob and Abby."

"And the sad souls they left behind," Hannah joked.

They clinked their glasses then drank, slowly savoring the wine. It was a really good vintage. "I like how they went all out," said Hannah, as she finished and took another sip.

"So Sam's afraid to go out on the water at night, I get why now," Jack said. "But I'm glad you're not."

"Oh yeah, I'm loads of fun getting all melancholy and sad on you," Hannah said.

"I'm having the time of my life," Jack said. "I mean... not about your story. But just being with you, it's so nice. The nicest I've felt in so long."

She liked how vulnerable he was when he struggled to say the right things.

"Me too," she said, smiling, and another tear formed in the corner of her eye.

"Don't get sad on me again, you silly thing," he teased. "Maybe we need a lot more wine."

She laughed. "Or some dancing?"

Jack laughed too. "Right here? With this music?" The light jazz playing through the upper deck speakers wasn't causing others to get up and dance.

"We danced to it in high school why not?" Hannah said, like

277

it was a challenge.

Jack took another long sip of wine, then set down his glass on the bench and stood. "All right, lady, may I have this dance?" He offered his hand.

Hannah joined him, downing her last sip of cab and leaving her wine glass on the table. Although she hadn't heard his story yet, it was clear something had changed between them as he listened to hers. The wall she'd kept up insisting they were friends had given way inside her, and as they started to move, she felt his heartbeat jump unexpectedly at the touch of her soft breasts against his chest. The manly musk of his cologne drifted on the air past her nose as they moved in unison, bodies gyrating slightly, feet shuffling in perfect time with the beat, just two people alone under the stars.

For the next few minutes, she was oblivious to the world around them—the yacht, the passengers, the crew—it was just her and Jack, dancing in the night. When the song changed, they shifted seamlessly, transitioning to the new beat and continuing on as if nothing was different. Their bodies worked in unison like they'd danced together all their lives, and when the explosion of fireworks followed by colorful bursts lit the night, it seemed the perfect exclamation to their pirouette.

As the music changed now to something more celebratory that matched the fireworks show, they parted, catching their breath, but continued holding hands as they stood there, faces pointed toward the heavens, and took in the view.

"It's spectacular," Hannah said.

"It really was," Jack replied, then realized he didn't mean the dance. Their eyes met. Or had he?

Their lips came together again then like magnets drawn together with an irresistible pull, and they kissed as the fireworks continued.

Afterward, as the yacht cruised back to the dock, the pure night air now filled with the smell of sulfur, charcoal, and a hint of rotten eggs, they munched on hors d'oeuvres and sipped champagne in silence, just enjoying being together as they rested and recharged from the emotion and physical drain.

As they disembarked, they saw Bert standing beside the peer, and approached him hand in hand.

"Need a ride?" he asked cheerfully.

"To the lighthouse?" Jack asked.

"I'm running a modified route, but of course," Bert said.

Jack looked at Hannah, but before he could ask what she wanted to do, she burst out, "Yes, please. We do."

As Bert led them down the docks to another pier, Hannah leaned over and whispered, "I don't want this night to end." And Jack took her hand in his.

THIRTY MINUTES LATER, Bert let them off on Cristof's Key, where they took the cart back to the lighthouse, heading upstairs. Hannah led. She didn't stop until she reached the master bedroom, where she turned and faced him as they pressed against each other again, their lips meeting with explosive energy.

Jack sat on the edge of his bed, studying her lithe frame as she cupped her left hand to light a candle on his desk. His grand scheme to live out his life alone in the dead center of a tourist haunt was a dismal failure. And then came Hannah, a woman self-possessed of a keen sense of her own worth validated by the friends she'd surrounded herself with. That awful lonely night when he ruined hope by treating her like a one-night stand spoke to the temporary insanity of a misguided lunatic. Hannah was more than the girl he judged at a small town diner. What he felt most was grateful. Grateful Hannah had forgiven his missteps. Had trusted him again with Sam's tender heart.

He turned on a song for them. It was the first song they danced to that night at the lighthouse, their last good hour together up until now—"When You Say Nothing at All" by Ronan Keating. Too bad he sang like a rat with laryngitis. Ignoring his nerves as his heart swelled to the guitar arpeggios and flute, he sang the lyrics aloud: "It's amazing how you can speak right to my heart…"

Just as he decided the upbeat song might not be the right mood, Hannah unbuttoned her blouse, stepping out of her trousers. While Jack lip-synched the lyrics, the light returned to her entire face. The first time she looked at him this way was over dinner, before he blew his chances with her—and with Sam. Tonight, the light was back.

Hannah ran toward him, jumping into his lap, wrapping her bare legs around his waist. "Thank you for bringing him back."

"Who, my darling?"

"The Jack who wants to live."

Jack didn't hesitate like a dolt, like before. He kissed Hannah long, moistening her lips and mouth with his tongue.

Hannah pulled up his shirt, running her palm slowly across his belly before lifting his arms and pulling it over his head. The brush of her fingers on his skin opened him up, like a sensei of vulnerability. He let her teach him from her masterful soul. "I'll do anything you say," he said. He turned to lay her naked across his bed.

They came together then—caressing, kissing, short of breath—the warmth of their skin touching sending chills through him. It had been ages since he'd made love, and it felt like the first time all over again. He fumbled at first, nervous, hesitant, but the way she touched and kissed him made it clear, she had no hesitation at all. His lips brushed the tops of her breasts as her hands caressed his arms and chest and then moved lower toward his stomach. They teased each other with foreplay and whispered words of love as they did, and when their bodies finally joined, they moved with the same unified rhythm they'd found on the dance floor.

She moaned against his ear, and he quickened his pace until

they reached that moment together where her back arched above him as they both exploded from within and cried out in surprised wonder and joy. After, they cuddled, then fell asleep in each other's arms.

Later, he awoke as her hair brushed his neck, their legs entwined. She looked up at him and her smile was that of total trust and gratitude, and they kissed again.

"I never thought I could feel this again," he whispered.

"I know," Hannah said.

And then, because he felt compelled, and because he wanted her to know, he told her the story of the accident and how Abby and Caroline died, and then they cried together again. This time, the lovemaking was fierce, more frantic, both holding onto each other like they both needed it, craving comfort from each other's touch. And when it was over, they both wiped away tears as she rolled over and sunk back against him, spooning, their bodies fitting perfectly—a warm comfort as they fell asleep yet again.

CHAPTER 21

JACK WOKE UP, Hannah wrapped around him, and fear, guilt, and uncertainty came rushing back. Panic set in. He reacted, wanting to run far and fast. He'd needed to go like he needed air. But he'd managed to fight off the urge 'til morning and help Warren with the chores, when Ellen appeared outside the lighthouse, looking even madder than she had the morning before at the diner.

"She's not ready," Ellen had said, striding up. The woman poked Jack in the chest, accusing him.

"I'm sorry," Jack had replied, taken aback and confused as to what Ellen was mad about.

"Hannah still pines for my Rob, and who's to say she'll never get over him?" Ellen said, "and the last thing she or Sam need is you forcing yourself into their lives to confuse their emotions."

Jack frowned. "I didn't force myself on anyone."

"She spent two nights with you," Ellen said. "Don't think I don't know what happened."

"Hannah is an adult. I can tell when she talks about Rob, they shared something special. I'm sorry, but your son is gone," Jack said. "She has the right to make her own choices."

"She's not thinking clearly," Ellen snapped. "So don't you go confusing her."

Jack raised his hands in surrender. "Whatever you say. I really think you should be having this conversation with her." He invited her into the lighthouse. "She's still asleep. Want me to wake her?"

Ellen scowled. "No. I'll talk to her when she gets home. I have to get back and take care of Sam. He's eating with Lou at the diner. Lou and Denise can't watch him long." She turned to march back across the beach.

Jack watched her go, wanting to blow it off, but then his mind started working. He thought about Caroline and Abby. His heart had already carried a tinge of guilt about what was happening between him and Hannah, especially after they'd made love. He realized he hadn't thought much about them for almost the entire day; not like he usually did. On top of that, he'd vowed his love to Abby forever, never planning to fall in love again. But Hannah was ... amazing. A great mom, so dedicated, way too smart for a diner waitress—she could do or be anything he believed. She'd opened his eyes to parts of himself he'd denied existed. She had caught him by surprise. But he'd always love Abby. She was his first love.

The next thing he knew he'd booked the earliest flight he could find, and he was upstairs packing his overnight bag as hurriedly as he could. Shortly thereafter, he rushed from the lighthouse with apologies to Warren and a request that he make sure Hannah saw the note he'd left for her. By the time he placed distance between himself and the Keys, he had convinced himself he shouldn't come back. Send movers to get his stuff, call the Coast Guard with some excuse and quit. Be done with the Keys. Rash? Maybe, but in that moment, he felt like he couldn't breathe if he stayed a second longer.

He hadn't wanted this. Things had gotten out of hand. Making love was something he'd only ever done with one person: Abby. He wasn't that guy. He didn't sleep around. Never had. To him, it was the culmination of so much that made couples work—trust and commitment, hopes, dreams, promises of forever. It wasn't something you did with someone without establishing all that first. Could he reach that point with

Hannah? He couldn't deny the possibility had entered his mind often the last few weeks. And he suspected, with time, they could and would get there. But they weren't there yet. It was too soon. And the fact that it had happened anyway because it felt right in that moment and seemed natural, didn't change the fact that in retrospect, it felt wrong.

Then he realized what he really needed was a talk with Abby. And for him, since the accident at least, that had always meant visiting her grave site. So he left and didn't look back.

HANNAH AWOKE FEELING like she'd had the best night of sleep she'd slept in years. Yawning, she relished the feel of the soft sheets against her skin and then gently reached out for Jack who was gone. The smell of his cologne still scented the sheets. She felt the need to go again.

Opening her eyes she glanced around. "Jack?"

The room was empty except for her, and no sounds of water or movement came from behind the bathroom door. She sat up and looked around for her clothes. He'd left her a bathrobe, draping it across the bottom of the bed. She slid it on.

"Jack?" she called again, taking the stairs down.

The kitchen was empty. Someone had made coffee in one of those old model coffee pots. As she reached for a mug, she heard footfalls on the stairs and turned.

Warren appeared, smiling. "Can I offer you breakfast?"

She suddenly felt flush. Of course Warren had been there to cover Jack's day off. She'd completely forgotten. Recovering, she forced a smile. "Have you seen Jack?"

"He hurried off early after making a couple of calls," Warren said, his eyes full of sympathy. "Said it was an emergency. Something about Kansas. He left a note on the table for you."

Hannah set the mug down and fought the urge to run as she made her way to the table.

"I have eggs or I can whip up pancakes if you're hungry," Warren offered again.

Hannah found an envelope with her name on it in Jack's handwriting. Picking it up, she opened the unsealed flap and reached inside for the contents. He'd left her a letter.

> Hannah,
>
> Thank you for a lovely night I'll never forget. There's something I have to take care of. Taking the Jeep. Kiss Sam for me.
>
>   Jack

No mention of contacting her. No details. They'd just made love and now he up and runs off somewhere without even a word or a goodbye kiss? He'd done it again! Treated her like a one night stand. She bit back a curse. What a fool she'd been to let him in, let him charm her. How could Abby have been happy with a man like this? What was wrong with him? Clearly the accident had broken more than his heart. She tossed the letter on the table and turned for the stairs, then went back and picked it up, crinkling it as she shoved it into the pocket of her robe.

"I'm sorry he didn't tell you. Are you okay?" Warren asked.

Hannah nodded, swallowing. "I'm fine, Warren. I really have to get home."

"Well, let me get you coffee and I have sweet rolls I can warm if you want to eat on your way."

"Kind of you, but no." And then she dialed Bert to arrange her pick up.

As she hurried up the stairs to find her clothes and dress, she went over the previous day and especially last night. He'd been

286

so at ease, so natural with her. Content, at peace. Even when they'd shared the stories of their mutual tragedies, he'd been with her, fully present the entire time, never seeming distracted or hesitant. Then there was that kiss. He kissed her with such passion last night. Made love like she meant something to him. Had someone called with bad news? Maybe something happened with his family? He'd mentioned a sister—what was her name? Was it financial? Warren had said Kansas. Who rushes off in the middle of the night to fly across the country?

She picked up her phone, dialing Jack. The phone started to ring, then she heard Jack's voice on voicemail. She waited for the beep, keeping her emotions in check, saying, "Jack, it's me. I missed you this morning. Hope you're all right. Please call me and let me know."

A few minutes later, she came back down to the kitchen to find a mug of coffee and plate of warm sweet rolls waiting on the table. The sweet spicy cinnamon reminded her of happy times, despite the hail storm inside her. She sat and sipped her coffee, thankful Warren had disappeared back downstairs, somehow sensing she needed to be alone. What had happened? What did this mean? She steeled her resolve to not over react, yet what rose up in her was that old fear of getting her heart broken again. She told herself to stay calm, whatever happened today. Yet waking up to his cold side of the bed made her feel ... abandoned; dismissed; used.

She finished her coffee in ten minutes then hurried downstairs where Warren kindly drove her to the pier to meet Bert. She told him not to wait with her, and after he said good-bye and headed back to the lighthouse, she thought about Ellen. She hadn't bothered informing her she wouldn't be coming home last night. What was she? A teenager with a curfew? She'd had it with Ellen and her problems. It's why she wanted to buy and renovate an old abandoned house that had just become available on Lower Matecumbe. She'd been about to make an offer, the week before, but had put off, despite Denise urging her not to tie up her life waiting on Jack to come around.

Her finger hovered over Ellen's number in her contacts. She would scold her again, of course. She couldn't help herself. Hannah briefly considered calling her to ask if she and Sam had gotten to bed okay and tell her she'd be home soon, but decided all that drama could wait. She had enough on her mind already.

When Bert arrived dockside, she sat up front with him and made small talk, since she was the only passenger, but her thoughts were elsewhere, lost in questions. Bert asked if her Jeep was still at the park, and when she said no, took her back to the pier near the diner so she could call Ellen for a ride or walk home.

All the way, the same questions and memories circled round and round through her head. And when she arrived at the house, after hugging Sam, who was excited to see her, she felt a pang in her heart again as he asked her about Jack. To her surprise, Ellen said nothing, just turning away to continue putting away a load of dishes from the dishwasher. Hannah managed to give a few nonspecific answers to her son before excusing herself to go shower and change. After that, she preoccupied herself with Sam's lessons before heading to the diner for her next shift, all the while wondering where Jack was and what he was doing and when he would call her back or see her again.

"WHAT ARE YOU doing here?" Josie demanded when she opened the door to her house in Salina, Kansas to find Jack standing on the stoop. Looking at his younger sister for the first time in several months, Jack was surprised at how much she'd come to resemble their mother in her thirties—with the same blonde curls, brown eyes, and long, skinny arms leading to slightly larger hands.

"Can't a guy visit his sister?" Jack said as Josie's boys Tyler and Blake ran to embrace their favorite uncle, while her daughter, Lizzie, hollered from the highchair because she couldn't get down and do the same.

"Totally unannounced?" Josie said as she grabbed a hug from her older brother. "No one in their right mind would come unannounced into this chaos." She ushered him inside and closed the door behind him. Her house on Starlight Drive looked as chaotic as it always had, or as Josie preferred to say, "lived in," the kids toys scattered about, some books and papers, shoes, odd bits of clothing. On the kitchen table remained half eaten bowls of cereal, besides other remnants of breakfast as he followed her into the kitchen. It didn't smell as lived in as it looked though, he pleasantly noted—the scent of air fresheners and fresh coffee overriding any unpleasantness that might be lurking around.

"Boys, go get out of your jammies and put on some day clothes," Josie ordered, shooing her sons away with both hands as she attended to her daughter.

"Something happened," Jack said.

Josie set Lizzie's half-eaten cereal bowl on the table as her daughter continued struggling to free herself from the chair, then wiped her mouth on her own bib and loosened the straps pulling her free. As soon as she did, Lizzie threw her arms out toward Jack and screamed so Jack took her and hugged her, then set her down to toddle off after her brothers.

"Lizzie, you go get clothes, too," Josie called. "I'll have to help her in a bit. What happened?"

Jack told her about the Island Fest and his night with Hannah and a few other details.

"Oh my God! You actually dated this woman and you wait until you sleep with her, and then what? Freak out and fly all the way here to tell me about it!" Josie was almost yelling from a foot away. "You are the worst big brother ever, Jacky!"

"You know, sometimes I wonder why I tell you things," Jack said.

"You had me thinking you totally blew this woman off.

That's why I stopped asking about her much when you called, but you are dating her! You cheated me out of a sister's right to all the juicy gossip." She calmed herself enough to say, "How was your flight over?"

"I'm so sorry my personal life carried on, duly neglecting to tittilate you and your gossipy friends," Jack said with a sigh.

"I don't tell them much," said Josie, calming down. "But Jack, this is me—Josie. After all, I am your only sister, and until now I thought my best friend. You tell me everything, but no, you make me wait until you sleep with her to know you're serious with this girl? From—Pete's sakes—Florida?" She stopped a minute, her face showing realization. "Wait. It's three o'clock. You were with her last night and you're here already. You left her, went to Miami, caught a flight...Oh my God! You left her in bed to fly off and whatnot?"

Her wide eyes told him she'd figured him out. God, she was like mom, the soothsayer of his childhood.

"What the hell is wrong with you? Oh my God! Are you trying to screw this up?"

"I needed to..." He could think of no better way to say it. "...talk to Abby." It was true. He told her about Ellen's visit to the lighthouse.

"Hannah must be hurt or going crazy or both," Josie scolded. "Jack, my God, I should never have bothered with kids. I should be raising you. Mom and Dad clearly weren't done with you."

"Her mother-in-law is right," Jack said. "We rushed into this. It's not right."

Josie scoffed. "Pure bullshit, Jack. You're grown adults. Falling in love is normal. Healthy. You were both widowed and have every right."

Jack shook his head. "What if Ellen's right? Then all I'm doing is not only setting her up for disappointment in me, but what of Sam?

Outside, they heard the rumble of thunder and then a light patter began on the roof.

"Oh great, rain, just what we need," said Josie, checking to see if the kids were inside.

Jack sighed. "I just came to see if I could leave my stuff in the spare room. But if you're going to beat me up like this, I'm better off at a hotel."

"You will not stay at a hotel!" she said, before she gathered herself to continue more softly, "Don't be silly. Of course the spare room is yours for the asking. How long are you here?"

"Two or three days until I figure stuff out," Jack said.

"Wow, new government job must be cushy if they can just let you take off last minute like that."

"I told them it was an emergency."

"So you lied, nice."

Jack sighed. "It's an emergency to me."

Josie reacted to commotion from the back bedrooms. "Pipe down," turning back to say, "Do what you gotta do. If you need me, you know where I am. I gotta go referee." And with that, she was off, hurrying down the hall and leaving Jack to fend for himself. He went back out to the rental car and grabbed his quickly packed duffel, depositing it in the guest room before grabbing a soda from the fridge and heading off to visit Abby's grave.

He knew he'd been lucky to even make the trip. Warren had been surprisingly happy and had told him a training class he was supposed to lead that week had just been cancelled, leaving him with a few days to either float around or report to headquarters in Miami and catch up on paperwork. So Jack had made his excuse, stressed the urgency, and Warren, reading his face, had been too polite to ask a lot of questions. He'd owe Warren a big apology when he got back for sure. But for now, he was just thankful things had somehow aligned in the universe as they had to allow him to come.

As he drove, he thought about Hannah. He knew he was being unfair to her; that taking off suddenly like this had to hurt her, scare her. And he hated that, but he couldn't stop himself. He'd been fine with what happened between them, totally in the moment, caught up in the emotion and passion as it happened. It wasn't until afterward that he'd woken up with paralyzing guilt and confusion and uncertainty compounded by Ellen.

It was undeniable that he had something special with Hannah. It was undeniable he cared about her, that what they had together was something unique and special of a kind he'd only experienced once before. Perhaps that was part of what was bothering him so much. If Abby had been his best friend and soul mate, how could it happen again? And did allowing himself to feel this way, to be this way with someone else mean he'd been fooling himself all those years with Abby? Did it mean what they had wasn't near as special as what he'd always thought it to be; that he didn't love her the way he thought had? The idea of that just tore him apart inside.

And he simply didn't know if he could live with that.

He paused to listen to the gentle tapping of the rain against the windows as he caught his breath. He reached the end of Claremont Drive observing the familiar water tower to his right. The fence lining the south end of Gypsum Hill Cemetery lay to his left and he turned parallel to the fence, heading east toward Marymount Road and the main entrance. Founded in the 1870s, Gypsum Hill had grown to forty-seven acres, and the Pace family had bought plots when Josie and Jack were in preschool. Jack had added some for his wife and child later, but they were buried there beside his parents, grandparents, and the empty graves still waiting for Jack, Josie, and her husband and three kids. The cemetery was old enough to hold plots rooted in history and as kids, Jack and Josie would walk down from their grandparents home on Starlight—where Josie lived now—and wander amongst the gravestones, inventing wild stories about the various inhabitants and their histories based on the information chiseled in stone.

Waiting the few minutes for the light to turn green at

Marymount and Glen, Jack glanced at the seat beside him, double checking he'd brought the towel and garbage bag he'd retrieved from his duffel before carrying it inside. He hadn't known it was going to rain, but Abby had instilled the habit in him when visiting her grandparents' graves. For her it was about not winding up with dirty hose or knees beneath a dress, but Jack found it just as effective for preserving his suit pants, jeans, or knees, so he'd adopted the tradition. Given the ongoing downpour, he was thankful he had.

When the light changed, he turned left and went north on Marymount Road, slowing to a stop halfway between Hillside and Knollcrest to turn left into the main entrance of the cemetery. From there he followed the winding maze of roads he'd long ago memorized to the cemetery's northwest corner, where he began carefully looking for the Oak tree and ancient mausoleum that served as landmarks for his family's plots. Within two minutes, he'd spotted them and the short side road that led to a circle with a fountain in front of the mausoleum. He turned right on the side road and stopped in the circle, turning off the car before grabbing the trash bag and towel as he readied himself for a walk in the rain.

Undoing his seatbelt and bracing himself, he reached for the handle and opened the door, taking a deep breath, then climbed out and lumbered across the lawn. For just a moment, he'd thought about running, but then realized it was pointless since the grave was out in the open with not even the nearby oak providing much cover. Reaching the marker that read: "Beloved Abigail Grace Pace," he bent and stretched out the garbage bag, then the towel on top of it and knelt before his wife's final resting place.

By the time he'd settled there, his clothes were already well on their way to soaked, but he had a ritual, so he started by first straightening the plastic flowers in the holder beside the grave followed by wiping the headstone with his palm. The faded flowers were red roses, Abby's favorite, and although he preferred real, he'd surrendered and purchased the plastic when he decided to move to Florida.

Pulling his hand away, he fluttered his fingertips, letting the rain water wash them clean., "Hello, baby, I missed you."

He forced a smile he didn't feel, and then leaned over to the right to gently caress their daughter's headstone. "Hi, baby girl."

Immediately, memories flooded into his thoughts of the time he'd spent with them—special moments, memorable conversations, important incidents and so on. He knelt there in the rain getting soaked and remembering, filling his girls in on everything that had happened since he last saw them. "I'm still screwing up. Still getting caught up in work. I guess I didn't learn my lesson yet, huh, babe? I'm so sorry." Then he told them about Hannah and Sam. He talked and talked, and he listened too, and then, when the rain got so heavy he felt a chill and couldn't take anymore, he told them he'd be back tomorrow. He trooped back to the car and headed back to Josie's.

CHAPTER 22

THE NEXT DAY it rained even harder, prompting Jack to spend the day indoors playing uncle to Josie's youngest until the older boys got back from school. All three piled on Uncle Jack. Josie loved his attention to them. She seized on the opportunity to catch up on a lot of things she was behind on like laundry, personal shopping, and even some sewing projects.

Jack checked his voicemail again this morning finding another message from Hannah like the two she'd left before. She clearly wanted answers, but the problem was he didn't know what to say yet, and he didn't want to call her back until he did.

What was troubling him was the tremble in her voice, now familiar to him. It meant he was upsetting her all over again.

"She's called three times," Josie said when he took a lemonade break. "She loves you. If you're not going to love her back, be a good guy and tell her, so she can move on."

"I do love her, but—"

"There's no but," Josie said, as she shot him a look like their mom used to do. "You either do or don't." She spun away from Jack, reacting to her boys bouncing on the living room sofa. "You break that sofa, your dad will beat you when he gets home! Get down! Now!" She said it in a way that should've scared the boys, probably didn't.

The boys shot her sheepish looks as they hopped down.

"And put it back where it was, too!" she added. The boys argued about how to adjust the sofa as Jack went on.

"It's complicated."

"Well, uncomplicate it."

That sounded great on paper, only Jack didn't know how to do it in real time. His feelings were still all over the place. One minute he missed Hannah and Sam, the next he felt guilty for thinking of them when he'd come here to see Abby and Caroline. Shouldn't his loyalties start shifting? He'd known it would be hard to leave their gravesites behind when he relocated, but partly he'd thought it would help him move on. Even though he planned to live out the rest of his days isolating so he could properly mourn their loss without every damn person knowing them and telling him how he should do it, Hannah was a living testament to how one goes on after all oxygen is sucked from life. So he'd thought he'd said good-bye to his Kansas angels, only they'd never left his thoughts or his heart. He carried them to the very damn tip of the country, still not knowing how to deal. And after what happened with Hannah, he felt like they were calling to him, so here he was.

"You know," Josie said, interrupting his reverie, "I have a friend named Maria who thinks you're hot. Maybe you need some perspective. Ask her out, see how it goes. It might help you clarify what you want at least."

"She thinks I'm hot?"

"She says you have a great butt," Josie whispered, then added, "And you should see her rack."

"Big boobs!" Tyler, the eight-year-old, shouted and then six-year-old Blake echoed like always. "Big boobs! Big boobs!" They chanted.

"Boys! Stop right now!" Josie said, glaring. "I've told you not to say that word."

Jack laughed, then Josie whispered, "She really does."

"No thanks," he said.

"Seriously. She's Italian and happily promiscuous," said Josie said, her hand aside her mouth to keep the boys from hearing. "Maybe sowing a few wild oats would unscramble your brain...and your heart."

"I'm not looking to sow my oats, that's the whole reason I'm here," he said, shaking his head, before Blake and Tyler rushed him, grabbing his arm, pushing him back into the living room to play. And as they did, he found himself wishing Sam was there to join in, and Hannah to watch and laugh.

"Everyone always says that's when you find someone," Josie said. "When you're not looking. Your problem is you're scared you'll get hurt again, but that's what happens with relationships. Sometimes you get hurt. But not always. Sometimes, they bring you so much joy, it's worth the occasional blip."

Jack didn't respond but knew she spoke from her heart.

After watching him wrestle the boys a moment, she went on, "You need to figure it out, Jack. Whatever it is."

He shook off the last kid, to cross toward her. "What if I can't? Maybe I just won't go back."

The way she looked at him didn't speak well of what had just come out of his mouth. It was as if she didn't know him. "That's crazy. Jack, whatever's bothering you, work through it, but sounds like you made a new life there. What if that's your future? Your past is what you leave here. And you can't move forward into the past."

Thoughts of Hannah and Sam wouldn't leave his mind. And he suddenly realized that even when he'd visited Abby and Caroline's graves, he'd spent most of the three hours he hovered there talking about Hannah and Sam. Not recalling memories with Abby and Caroline. And he'd talked about them like they were a family. In that moment, he realized he'd started thinking of them that way, too.

God, he hated it when Josie was so damn smart. Just like their mother. If only it was that easy and logical to him. As the boys and their sister jumped him again, he defensively became the tickle monster. Still, it didn't stop his mind racing with all the questions again. He couldn't compartmentalize what she meant to him. He loved Hannah. And Sam. That wasn't the question. It was how to be fair to them. And how to share a part of himself that would always belong to Abby and Caroline. Didn't Hannah and Sam deserve his all—the same all he'd given to his first wife and his daughter?

He knew he was probably overthinking it, but he also didn't want to let himself love someone else if it meant letting go of his love for them. Loving them was such a big part of who he was, who he'd always been. How did you let go, and move on, without forgetting and loving less those who came before? Was it possible?

"Why do you love me?" Abby had asked him once during their honeymoon trip to Niagara Falls.

"I just do," Jack replied.

"No cheating. I want an answer." She held him suspended in one of her body pinches.

He pulled away, thinking thought about it. "It's hard to find words. I just do. Seriously. The way those cute dimples form when you smile, your laugh and the way your stomach jiggles when you do your walk. I love the way you think about the world, the way you care about people—the way you love me."

"For me it's simpler," Abby said.

"It is?" Jack was surprised and he watched her, waiting for her to explain.

"I love you because I was born to love you," she finally said.

He thought about that one statement the most. Abby believed in soul mates, plain and simple. He wasn't sure because the universe bore variables. "So you don't think you could love anyone else?"

"If I hadn't met you, sure. Probably. Or if you were gone or dead."

"Wow, second day of our honeymoon and I'm already dead. So romantic," Jack had teased.

She pinched his arm hard enough to make him cry out, and then gave him a slobbery, noisy kiss on the cheek. "Stop that. You know what I meant. If I had to, could I find love with someone else? Sure. But it wouldn't be the same. The way I love you is special."

"That's exactly how I feel about you," he'd said.

"So why can't you say it?" She'd said, her accusing eyes locked intensely on his.

"You're better at words than me, you know that," he'd said and looked away, feeling trapped and at a loss for originality. Women can ask a lot of men.

She'd laughed and kissed him again, this time on the lips— gentle but passionate. "You're so fun to corner."

"Meaning you take pleasure in ..."

"Come on, Jack," she went on. "If you'd never met me, there'd be someone else."

"I don't like to think about it," Jack said.

"Would you really want to go through life alone?"

He'd thought about it more than she knew, and realized he wouldn't. "No. I don't think you would either. Who would wish a lonely existence on someone they love?"

She'd hugged him. "Me either. 'Cause you've got too much to give, and there's someone out there who needs it, so you've a reason to share out of that big goofy heart. There's nothing wrong with that."

"I'm sharing it with you," he'd said because there was no one else for him and never would be he thought.

She'd brushed a strand of her brunette locks from her eyes and smiled the smile that made him melt. "And I'm the luckiest girl in the world. Believe me."

He was coughing now, the wind knocked out of him, Josie scolding them again. "Tyler and Blake, you stop that! Jumping up and down on Uncle Jack's stomach is not okay!"

"He stopped tickling!" Tyler said.

"We were waking him up!" Blake added.

She hurried to pull them off to the side where they looked at him with sheepish amusement. "Are you okay?" she asked as she leaned over him.

He coughed again and nodded. "Fine. You know me, lost in thought."

"You've got too much to give, and there's someone out there who needs it, so you should share that gift. There's nothing wrong with that."

"What you need is kisses 'cause you miss Caroline and Aunt Abby," Lizzie proclaimed and then proceeded to give him slobbery kisses on his face and neck, giggling as she did.

Jack laughed and started tickling her again and then the boys jumped back in as Josie just shook her head and stared down at them. "I swear to God, if they won't go to bed tonight, you'll pay for this."

"This is us sowing wild oats to unscramble their brains and hearts," he said while Josie stuck out her tongue before marching back to the kitchen as the play resumed—furniture squeaking as it got bumped or pushed against. Jack yelped when he rolled onto a sharp toy or got thumped a little too hard, making the kids laugh. He'd forgotten how much joy there was in playing with kids. He knew he'd be exhausted soon enough, but it was from a level of joy that had been missing from his life for far too long. Except when he was with Sam and Hannah.

"You've got too much to give, and there's someone out there who needs it, so you should share that gift." Abby's words continued to nag and poke at him in the same way she had that day. He lay awake while the household settled for the night, reliving memories of the past few months he'd spent with Hannah and Sam.

"YOU'RE BETTER OFF anyway. He disappears the morning after you make love without any notice, leaves a generic note, takes the Jeep, and he won't return your calls?" Denise said over the phone after Hannah called her to vent. "I'm so sorry, hun. I hurt for you. I liked seeing you challenged, but in a good way. Not like this. I'm just sorry he turned out to be such a jerk."

That's when Ellen shouted from the hallway, "I warned you not to get involved with him. You should listen to me. I only want what's best for you."

"Oh, like you're wanting me to stay single for the rest of my life has anything to do with what's best for me!" Hannah yelled, throwing her hands up. She hadn't realized Ellen was listening from the hallway. She'd thought her mother-in-law and Sam were both fast asleep. Oh my God, she needed to get back to looking for her own place as soon as possible. Having her mother-in-law always in her business was exhausting. "You're concerned about what's best for you, Ellen, and we both know it! Anyway, it's his Jeep. He can have it whenever he wants."

"At least he could give you notice," Ellen said, coming around the corner and opening the fridge. "You know what I mean. I was on best behavior at the Festival. I didn't say anything that might embarrass you, took Sam off your hands. I feel responsible!"

"No one thinks that but you," Hannah said, knowing her mother-in-law wasn't unhappy one bit about the latest development. "His boss said he had an emergency. I'm sure he's coming back. Now, can you stop eavesdropping and leave me be?"

Ellen raised her hands in surrender. "I just wanted some milk to take my pills."

"Hang on," Hannah told Denise as they waited for Ellen to finish pouring milk and leave.

In truth, she was starting to wonder too. Jack's odd and inconsiderate ways considering last night's amazing sex left her to wonder why he would treat her with indifference today. Sure, he left a note but leaving that many messages left him no excuse to leave her hanging like this. Even if he felt they'd rushed a little on sleeping together—that was something you talked about. She would understand. Grief can make you do crazy things. There'd be time to talk about it, if only he'd stay in touch. It was his unreturned calls that bothered her most. As if she'd ceased to exist for him after he left the note.

Rob had never acted that way. He'd been sensitive and attuned to her. She realized the chances of finding someone else like that were slim to impossible, and she and Jack were technically still getting to know each other. She'd been with Rob for years. Denise was right, Jack was a challenge, but not the right kind of challenge. At the moment, neither was Ellen.

Ellen dawdled putting the milk away, and Hannah lost her patience. "Go. I'll put it away," she said as she hurried over and grabbed the milk, returning it to the proper shelf inside the door and shutting the fridge.

Ellen sighed. "I'm going, I'm going." She shot Hannah look of distaste as she carried her glass in front of her and shuffled away.

"Is she gone?" Denise asked.

"Almost," Hannah whispered, listening for the sound of Ellen's bedroom door closing down the hall.

"I don't care what kind of emergency it is," Denise said. "This is not how you treat someone you care about. It's selfish. And you need to think carefully about whether you want to further involve yourself and, more importantly, Sam with a selfish man."

It hadn't been easy the last two days at the diner either where Denise, Janice, and even occasionally Lou couldn't resist offering their advice and opinions on the matter as well.

"Bastard," Lou declared as he wiped down the counter one afternoon.

"Yep, a total loser," Janice said while she poured drinks.

"Guys, haven't you ever had an emergency?" Hannah said as she returned from delivering an order, already tired of defending Jack but feeling obligated, until she knew the facts.

"Girl, you can do better," Janice said.

"You are the best, honey," Denise added.

"Thanks, but I'm fine really," Hannah said. "He'll call me when he can." And she slipped into the kitchen to escape only to see Lou's sad face watching her.

Lou shrugged. "I like him, but I don't want to see you hurt. You're like one of my own."

"You should never have slept with the SOB," said Janice loudly through the order window.

"Booos!" and cries of "Loser!" and "You don't need him" came from several of the booths and Hannah blushed. Just what she needed—the customers getting involved, too.

"Janice," said Lou, training his eyes on her like he meant business. "Keep it down. This is Hannah's business."

Janice rolled her eyes. "I'm looking out for her, Lou. We women do that."

"Well, go look out for your customers for a while," Lou said and shooed her with a wave of the back of his hand.

Hearing Ellen's bedroom door finally click down the hall, Hannah leaned against the kitchen counter with a sigh. "Honestly, I don't know how I'd get through half of this confusing life without you and Denise."

"How's Sam?"

She shot him a puzzled look. "Fine. Why?"

"I thought he'd be upset about Jack abandoning you."

"He doesn't know what happened, and he hasn't asked," said Hannah said.

"What will you say when he does?"

She didn't know. But then it wasn't like they hung out with Jack every day. They'd had a streak here and there. There were stretches of days when they didn't see him. She figured when Sam asked and what he asked would help her decide what he needed to know. She knew for sure her sweet Sam didn't need to know everything. She regretted how she'd told Ellen and Janice so much.

The truth was what she really wanted to be left alone; to escape somewhere and exist in peace and quiet for a while and think things through. She was fine, really. Whatever happened, she'd survive. It wasn't like she was unacquainted with heartache. Between Rob's death and past breakups, she'd had all the experience needed to deal with men like Jack. If it came to that, she'd get through and she'd go on. But all this doting and talking and fretting was stressing her out. It was too much. She couldn't get a moment's peace, and although she knew she was lucky to have so many friends and people who cared about her, the truth was—they were driving her nuts!

She'd distracted herself for a few hours the past few days looking through rental ads, hoping for another break on a condo or even a two bedroom apartment that looked tolerable, but found nothing. She'd probably missed a once in a lifetime deal and needed to resign herself being stuck where she was until she'd saved up enough or her finances improved.

So ninety minutes later, when she finished her shift, she took her bike for a ride along the Overseas Highway. As she passed the Publix, she drove on through the intersection with South Hammock that led home. A Jeep sped past her causing her to strain her eyes to get a look. She missed Jack's Jeep—the one he'd loaned her. She'd gotten so used to having it, she'd hardly ridden her bike like this in weeks. God. She'd gotten a call the morning he left from Enterprise, the agent saying he'd arranged a rental car for her, but she hadn't bothered to go pick it up. She was scared to keep depending upon him if he wasn't coming back, and besides, what would she do when the rental ran out?

So much of her life connected her to him now. A guy she hadn't even known four months ago. How do these deep-seated troubles seep in and take hold? It had to be due to the first time he registered in her mind, and lingered. At the diner? No. The Publix? Maybe. He'd insinuated himself unintentionally or not into her life and her son's life, until the day he mattered to them. That's the way of men like him.

She wasn't going to make a pest of herself. God, how many messages did she leave? "Denise, you're better with technology than I am."

"That's not saying a lot."

"Beside the point. If I sent out some texts I wanted to get back, how could I do that?"

"You can delete them from your phone," she said.

A big wave of relief washed over her. "Can you show me later?"

"Sure, but if you're trying to delete messages you sent to Jack, his phone received them already. You'd only be deleting your side of them."

She should delete the pictures too, and maybe burn the letter. Anything that reminded her of him. Total clean break. The more she thought about it, the better it made her feel, but what wouldn't go away were the burning questions: why? What was going on?

When she woke up forty-five minutes late, Sam greeted her in the kitchen in his jammies. She saw his mostly empty serial bowl in the sink and a half-finished glass of orange juice on the table.

"You're late," Ellen said from across the table where she was reading a Jodi Picoult novel and sipping her evening decaf.

"I don't go in until three today and I was tired, so I slept in," Hannah said.

Ellen didn't bother looking up. "Sam has something he wants to show you in his room. He's been waiting the whole time, quite impatiently."

"You do, honey?" Hannah said.

Sam nodded.

She held out her hand. "What is it? Show me, baby?"

Taking her hand, he led her to his room and pointed to his desk chair.

"You want me to sit?"

He gave her a thumbs up and she did. When she looked up again, Sam had his iPad and he was holding it up with words on it. For a moment, it stunned her because she was so used to him using signs. It wasn't that he couldn't use words or didn't know them, but the signs had just been faster, easier. He'd gone to a lot of effort here. She read the words:

Is Jack okay?

"Yeah, baby, he's fine, I think," Hannah replied. "He had to make a trip to see... his family back where he's from."

Are you okay?

"I'm fine sweetie, why?" She smiled to try and reassure him but Sam was looking at her with a serious look and wouldn't falter.

Did you and Jack have a fight?

"No, what makes you think that?"

Grandma's mad at him.

"Yeah, well, Grandma gets dramatic. She shouldn't be talking to you about such things, okay? I'm sorry she did."

I miss him.

"I miss him, too," Hannah said.

When's he coming back?

She felt a pang in her heart at that one. "I don't know, baby. Soon, I hope. I left messages, but he hasn't called me back yet."

The next one stunned her with its insight: I like that Jack makes you happy.

At that, Hannah choked up, tears forming in her eyes. But she managed to keep her voice steady as she said, "I know, baby. Jack is a good friend." It was a hedge because she didn't want to share too much and confuse him. She had a feeling Sam had already deduced more than she'd realized. Had he imagined a future with them as a family the way Hannah had? She hoped not. Jack had been the first man since Rob with whom she'd been able to imagine a future. She didn't want Sam to hurt the way she was.

Suddenly, he ran over and hugged her, but there was more to it than his good-night hug. She wrapped her arms around him as her tears flowed.

Please, Jack, come back to us. Please.

CHAPTER 23

THE NIGHT HAD been restless and stormy, so it wasn't until Jack actually got up the next morning and looked out the window that he realized the storm outside had passed. Now the sun was shining and puffy cumulous clouds filled an idyllic blue Kansas sky. Robins fluttered and played amongst the branches of pines in the yard as neighbors walked dogs or watched children playing on lawns.

He'd lain awake until 4 a.m. reliving memories with Abby, but the same words had come back to him time and again: "You've got too much to give, and there's someone out there who needs it, so you should share that gift." He'd gone to bed convinced he needed to return home to Kansas and be with his family; spare Hannah and Sam the heartache he would undoubtedly cause them, and save them from being cheated out of the love and commitment they deserved. Only he couldn't seem to reconcile the decision with the longing inside. He missed them.

So he awoke conflicted yet again. He managed to shower and head down for breakfast in spite of his mind going a mile a minute, swirling with the same questions he'd wrestled with for the past two days. He'd come up with one clear answer: visit their graves and decide once and for all the path he would follow for his future. This time, wanting fresh air, he chose to walk down Claremont to cross the cemetery on foot.

The Lighthouse

It was the kind of pleasant spring day early Aprils in Kansas were known for. Jacket weather, if one chilled easily, sleeves only if one didn't. Jack wore a polo and jeans planning to warm up as he walked. He admired upgrades and additions made to several neighborhood houses he hadn't taken notice of on his drive two days prior. There had been turnover, obviously, and he wasn't even sure if the same neighbors owned the houses, but they'd all been around for forty to fifty years, some even longer, and it was nice to see them being maintained and refreshed over the years to keep the neighborhood looking vibrant and alive.

Crossing Glen, he ducked through a gap between two fence posts near the water tower, walking among the headstones—taking note of the various shapes and sizes as he showed particular interest in the older ones. Some of them told stories with revealing statements like "Taken by small pox," or "Beloved mother and grandmother," while others had scripture citations or left generic—Baby Boy Smith, leaving few clues about who lay at rest here or why they mattered to the world. He found those particularly sad. He found himself asking "is this all we come to" and hoping that somehow, someway, most people left more of a legacy people would remember. Especially Abby and Caroline. He didn't want that for them.

It took fifteen minutes to cross the thirty-some acres to his family's plots, a gentle breeze tousling his hair. The grass had a fresh cut smell, glistening under the sunlight. As he walked, he looked around and saw no other cars, not even maintenance vehicles. He seemed to have the place to himself. After crossing several sections of lawn and paved trails that wound through Gypsum Hill, he finally spotted the oak and the familiar mausoleum atop the next rise and headed straight for them.

He was about to spread out the towel he'd brought to kneel on beside the graves when he heard leaves rustling to his right and looked up to see an older woman approaching. May Pace would be seventy-five next month, her blondish brown hair now gray and showing signs of curls it hadn't had when she was younger. Her skin was growing prunish, in contrast to the brightness in her smile and her green eyes as she looked at him with the kind of love only mothers can give. It was better than a hug—the waves rushing to surround and embrace him, even as he stood to greet her with a real embrace.

"Mom? What are you doing here?" he asked as they parted.

"Josie said I might find you here," she said, then frowned, eyes narrowing. "Shame on you for being here for two days already without visiting your mother. I raised you better."

Jack's eyes found his shoes. "Yeah, I'm sorry. I've had a lot on my mind."

"I know. Your sister filled me in."

He sighed internally. Josie always as a big mouth, but he knew she meant well and wondered exactly how much she'd let slip.

His mother put a hand on his arm, gentle caressing it. "I know. You don't want to talk to your mother about these things. You're a grown man now, and you and your sister have always been close. But I wanted to tell you something, so I came to find you."

Jack's throat constricted, his stomach tightening. "What is it? Is it dad? Are you feeling okay?"

May smiled, shaking her head. "We're in perfect health. That's not why I'm here."

Jack took a deep breath, relaxing as he bent to position his towel. "What is it?"

His mother stood a moment, her face turning wistful as she remembered something. "It's the most wonderful feeling in the world falling in love. And the worst losing it."

Jack stood again, his forehead crinkling as he tried to figure out what she was trying to say, but she continued before he could ask, "I was in love before your father. I don't know if you knew that. Billy Pierson. So handsome. A real charmer, funny, well-mannered. We were high school sweethearts, so in love. I

311

was crazy about him. Grandpa was very worried when I started spending every moment with him I could."

"Wait. This was before dad?" Jack couldn't believe he'd never heard this story.

"Yes, just listen," she scolded gently. "I have more to say."

"Sorry," he said and closed his mouth as their eyes met.

"Then we invaded Iraq," May went on. "Under the first Bush, not the second. Young men everywhere signed up in patriotic fury, and several of Billy's friends were among them. I begged Billy not to leave me, and he stayed for a few months, but then his older brother died. After that, there was no stopping him. He was angry, blamed himself for not being there, wanted revenge—the whole gamut of grief. I don't have to tell you. He signed up the next morning after he heard, and when he came to tell me, I cried for three days." She took a deep breath and stared off into the distance a moment, and Jack knew she was revisiting memories, so he just waited, not daring to intrude. "He left two weeks later, and our last night together, he gave me a ring. Asked me to marry him."

"Really? Did you accept?" Jack was surprised. He'd never heard any hint of this in thirty-eight years.

"Of course, I did, and before you ask, your father knows all about it," May stopped a beat, staring off to the east, she sniffled a bit before continuing, "He's buried a few rows over. It was an IUD, I think they call it. An underground bomb buried under a road. Took out his entire Humvee. He died instantly, they said, and my heart died with him. I cried for weeks and swore I'd never fall in love again. I thought my life was over. It was all I could do to climb out of bed and take a breath. But Grandpa and Grandma doted on me for a month, then pulled out the tough love. They forced me to get back out in the fields and work, and told me if I wasn't going to go to college and use the music scholarship I'd been offered, then I could stay home and help on the farm. That was fine with them."

312

"Wait? Grandpa said that?" For as long as he was alive, Jack remembered his grandfather bragging every time he saw them about how talented Jack's mother was and how proud they'd been of her being the first in the family to finish college and become a teacher. His Grandma had always smiled and winked at him every time his Grandpa told the story, and Jack had known it was a sign of her own pride at their only daughter. Jack had seen awards and certificates proudly displayed on the walls of his mother's old room, yellowing and cracking from age, but kept all that time. And when they'd died a year apart a few years ago, Jack and Josie had taken them down carefully and packed them up for their mother as they helped their mother clear and prepare the old farmhouse for sale.

"He sure did," his mother went on, interrupting his thoughts. She tipped her head back, eyes closed, and allowed herself one more sniffle, then stood there silent for a minute or two before taking one slow, easy breath. When she opened her eyes again, there was no sign of tears. Instead, her voice warmed and her face took on a look of total contentment as she said, "So I went away to school and tried to forget. You never really get over it, I'm sure you realize. But I carried on and studied hard, and then one day I met your father, and he was so handsome and sweet and romantic. Quieter and more reserved than my Billy, but a hard worker and he loved me and courted me. Swept me off my feet. So we got married."

She looked at Jack a moment, then patted his arm again. "I've visited Billy's grave every year on his birthday, the anniversary of our engagement, and the day he died. Your father knows. Sometimes he came along, and others I came alone. I wanted to. It was like talking to an old friend, confessing my worries, sharing my joys—all the things I needed to tell someone and share with those I loved."

"You still loved him?"

"Of course," she said, her eyes widening as her eyes filled with a peaceful glow. "Always have, always will. But that doesn't mean I love your father any less. Because the way I loved Billy

313

and the way I love your father are not the same. Billy was amazing, and I loved him with all my heart for the time I had him. But comparing that love for what I have with your father is like trying to equate an apple with a grapefruit. They both have peels, they're both fruits, and they both have seeds. Beyond that, they seem completely different. Billy was Billy and your father is your father. It's not the same."

She took a deep breath then brushed back a few loose strands of hair the breeze had blown down across her forehead. "Jack, your father's a wonderful man. We've had a wonderful life together. Two amazing kids. God has blessed me so much. And I'm very, very thankful. That's what I came to tell you. It was a special privilege I had that few people have to fall in love with two amazing men twice in my life, and love them both. Completely. Not everyone can do that. Not everyone gets to. But if you're so blessed, and if you can find someone who can live with that, your life can carry on wonderfully. It doesn't mean you have to leave the memories or stop loving them or forget them. You just make room in your heart for someone else."

She sighed, touching her cheek as she glanced off toward Billy Pierson's grave again. "That's it." Her eyes met his again as she reached for his hand. "That's what I came to tell you. You make of it what you will, okay? I hope you find the answers you're looking for." She leaned forward to kiss his cheek and hugged him again, but pulled away quickly and turned back the way she'd come. "Come see your parents soon, all right?"

"I will, I promise," he called after her as he replayed their conversation, a wave of emotions rushing through him. After a minute, he looked down at the towel in front of Abby's grave. The plastic flowers in the holder beside the grave were pretty much as he'd left them yesterday, so he pulled a handkerchief from his pocket, and knelt on the towel, then wiped the headstone whispering, "Hello, baby, I miss you."

Next he leaned over to his daughter's grave and did the same, finishing with "Hi, baby girl."

An odd thing happened then. This time, when memories came, they were moments he'd spent with Hannah and Sam. Showing them the lighthouse, the trip to Island Fest, shelling on the beach, his dinners with Hannah, even how smart and confident she sounded when they argued. Instead of the guilt, he felt a sense of warm comfort as Abby's words came back to him one last time: "You've got too much to give, and there's someone out there who needs it, so you should share that gift."

And so, once again, he told his beloved girls about Sam and Hannah: who they were and what they'd come to mean to him, and how much he wished they could all meet each other, get to know each other. And it finally dawned on him the emptiness he felt being there without Hannah and Sam. It wasn't the same emptiness he felt at the loss of Abby and Caroline, no. It was a different emptiness. He hadn't realized that was possible. But he kept talking and remembering, remembering and talking, and by the time he'd finished, Jack knew what to do.

HANNAH HADN'T WANTED to go anywhere near the Key West Aquarium's annual fundraiser, but Ellen had insisted. She loved the place, and she was a vendor every year with her shell creations. She insisted Hannah come and help with her table. If nothing else, it would allow Ellen to mingle and drum up interest, she claimed. But Hannah knew what her mother-in-law really wanted was to get Hannah out of the house and get her mind off the situation with Jack. Maybe even introduce her to some eligible bachelor or two now that she was open to dating; show her her options.

Hannah finally relented because she was tired of moping at home, and a little activity couldn't hurt, but also because she wanted to support Ellen—the event met a lot to her. Besides, the weather service was predicting a storm that night, and although it wasn't a hurricane or tropical storm and was supposed to be fairly mild, she didn't want Ellen driving back alone at night when she was tired. So she agreed, and they got Sam a babysitter for the day and drove down together.

They arrived around eleven and set up Ellen's table in plenty of time for the 2 p.m. opening. The black-tie event drew a decent crowd, given Florida's local culture was made up of two roles—those who are served and those who serve. Key West Aquarium was lit up with candles and spotlights, smelling incense, hors d'oeuvres, and a cornucopia of colognes, perfumes, and aftershaves. Hannah hid herself behind her mother-in law's table, focused on greeting and selling her mother's wares to interested parties. Ellen mingled, occasionally stopping by the table to check in or dragging over some eligible bachelor Hannah "just had to meet." But mostly Hannah handled it alone, pleased to see Ellen having the time of her life.

And it really was good to get out of the house. She was polite, of course, to the two men Ellen introduced her too with salacious looks. They chatted for a few minutes, before the men each realized she wasn't that interested and excused themselves. The booth had steady business, and Hannah couldn't help feeling proud at how people admired Ellen's creations. After all, Sam had helped, too, at least collecting the shells.

Once or twice, she found herself wondering about Jack. Where was he? Was he thinking of her? Did he miss her too? Denise had showed her how to erase messages and photos and they'd erased a few, but Hannah had later Googled how to restore and gone back and rescued the photos. The rest she couldn't bear to delete on her own. At least not yet. She hated being in this situation, but she could only blame herself. She'd known Jack was still mixed up about losing her family. She should have stuck to her guns about being just friends, and then none of this would have happened. If only, she'd stayed away from the lighthouse...

JACK STAYED ONLY a short time at Abby and Caroline's

graves, even though part of him felt guilty that he couldn't stay longer. He'd come back once or twice a year; he promised himself he would, but today, he had another mission that was far more pressing—he would take a flight back to Florida, hoping Hannah would let him explain why he had taken off. And praying Hannah could somehow forgive him.

The Salina airport had a flight to Kansas City in two hours with room on it, and another call confirmed he could get on a flight to Miami an hour after that, so he booked both flights, and then he hurried to Josie's to say a quick "goodbye" to his niece and his sister, before leaving in a cab to the airport. He'd arrive in Miami just after 5 p.m. and he couldn't wait to get back to Hannah.

ABOUT FIVE, BECCA called. She rarely called when looking after Sam. The reliable high-school-aged daughter of a neighbor, she had been Hannah's go-to babysitter since they'd moved in with Ellen. Better yet, Sam loved her. So Hannah answered the call with a tad of trepidation.

"Hi, Becca, everything okay? Sam isn't playing video games all night is he?"

"I can't find Sam." She didn't sound like herself at all.

"What?" Hannah tensed, feeling a mixture of worry and confusion as she raised a finger to pause the woman who'd just approached the table.

"He went to nap earlier, said he wasn't feeling well. I checked on him a couple times, but this last time, he's gone. I don't know where he went, Mrs. Loaney. I never heard him leave. And he's not outside in the yard. What do you want me to do?"

Hannah's mind raced with scenarios, some not good. Instead, she focused on more positive possibilities first. She had to keep Becca calm, given home was two hours away. "Did you call the diner?"

"I still have your work number in my phone. Would he know how to get there?"

"Yeah, he sometimes goes there with me, and it's walking distance from the house."

"Okay," said Becca, calming a bit.

Hannah changed her mind, her temple starting to throb. "You know what, can you go drive around the area a bit?"

"Sure. I have my dad's car."

She felt some relief. "I'll call the diner and a couple other places I can think of and call you back if I find him."

"Okay. Has the storm hit there yet?"

Thunder rattled the above the center since they'd arrived.

"It's raining pretty hard."

"I want you to not worry, I'll handle this, Mrs Loaney. Try to have a good night."

"I'll get home as soon as I can. Go look and I'll call you back."

"Okay, I'm so sorry."

"It'll be okay, Becca," she said, reassuring her, although she didn't feel so confident herself at the moment. She hung up and looked at the customer who'd been waiting. "I'm very sorry, but can you come back in a little bit? That was my babysitter. My son is missing. I need to make a few calls."

The woman looked somewhere between disappointed and sympathetic but left. Hannah dialed the phone. Denise answered. Sam wasn't at the diner. She called the manager at the Publix who hadn't seen him either. The last person she called was Tim's mom, Judy, to see if Sam had gone there for some reason. No sign of him.

Hannah took a deep breath, looking around for her mother.

She needed to stay calm herself. Stay focused. She had to go home. Now. Finding Sam and making sure he was safe was her new priority. Ellen would just have to understand. Before tracking down Ellen, she rang Becca, who was crying.

"I can't find him, Mrs. Loaney."

"Okay, we're coming home."

"He wasn't at the diner?"

"No, or the Publix or his friend's house."

"My God! I feel so terrible!"

"Becca, kids do dumb things sometimes. It's unusual for Sam, but it happens. Try and stay calm. If you don't see him after driving around the area for a bit, go home and wait for him. We're on our way. It's not your fault. Stay in touch. We'll find him." She felt like throwing up as she ran to find Ellen, fighting the urge to call Jack. *Where are you?!* her inner voice cried out. *I need you, Jack!*

Ten minutes later, the rain started.

CHAPTER 24

JACK'S PLANE LANDED at 5:05 p.m. and he grabbed his bags from the overhead bin, apologizing as he gently squeezed past and around other passengers and hurried to the front so he could be the first to deplane.

He checked his cell phone for messages, but it was quiet, so he hurried to the parking shuttle and headed for his Jeep. Should he call Hannah on the way or just go straight to the diner? He didn't know if she was working tonight or off, so he called the diner to ask. The GPS calculated the drive at one hour and forty-five minutes, but even as he started the engine, he knew with traffic, it would take closer to three.

ELLEN DROVE AS Hannah worked the phones, calling her friends at the diner first, in case Sam had gone there, and then, when they said they hadn't seen him, the police. Ellen pulled onto the Overseas Highway headed north under a purple gray sky. Rain pounded the car roof. Hannah took deep breaths to keep her focus. Ellen stopped talking altogether. What could Sam have been thinking? And where would he go? This wasn't like him. He knew better.

She wished Jack was with her instead of Ellen. At least he

would have shown some emotion. Ellen's face was so solemn and focused as she drove that Hannah felt almost alone in the car. Her heart pounding, body tense, fear so overwhelming she had to remind herself to breathe. At least Jack would notice. Ellen seemed oblivious. The sad part was Ellen hadn't been like this before Rob died. She and Hannah had actually gotten along very well. They'd had their run-ins, sure, like any daughter and mother-in-law, but when Rob died, something had broken in Ellen. She'd never been the same. This cold, manipulative woman wasn't the mother-in-law Hannah had once loved.

Jack, I need you, she cried out silently. *Where are you?*

Lightning lit the night sky as the heavens boomed. Sam would be terrified if he was out in this alone.

Oh my God, please let my baby be okay.

JACK HIT TRAFFIC just south of Miami International Airport after picking up the Jeep in the short term lot. Janice had answered when he called the diner and said Hannah wasn't in, so he'd tried her cell but gotten voicemail three times. The phone at home was busy. His plan to go straight to Hannah wasn't working out because he didn't know where she was. So instead, he checked in by phone with Warren, who was manning the lighthouse. Warren suggested he wait out the storm and get a hotel, so Jack decided to go to the diner and decide what to do from there. Regardless, he worried Hannah might not be happy to see him. What did Josie call him? Oh yes, a rat. He knew he had to face it, but he hoped he could at least do it when she wasn't worried about Sam being frightened in a storm.

Traffic, fortunately, started to thin south of Miami proper, so he was making good time. He flipped on the CD player and listened to Keith Urban's Greatest Hits, the perfect bouncy music for a long drive. At least, it would put him in good spirits. The rest he'd figure out when he got to Islamorada.

HANNAH AND ELLEN were forty minutes out on Highway 1 when Hannah's phone rang and Bert's name appeared on the callerID. "Did you find him?!" she asked frantically as she answered.

"Did Sam make it home alright?" Bert asked.

"Sam? You've seen him? Where is he, Bert?" Hannah demanded, straining forward against the seatbelt in her seat as they passed signs reading "Cudjoe Key." Lights from resorts and homes punctured the raindrops through the thumping of windshield wipers as she glanced around, trying to pinpoint their exact location. Traffic was bad tonight and the usual drive of under two hours was clearly going to stretch out longer.

"I don't know," Bert said, his voice rising with concern. "He came by earlier asking for a ride to go meet you and Jack on Cristof's Key. I told him no. You know the policies about unaccompanied minors. I figured he came from the diner; tried to call Ellen but got no answer. Then I had an unruly customer hassling me and turned, and Sam slipped over the rail before I could stop him."

Hannah spun toward Ellen in the driver's seat as she cupped the mic on her cell. "Did you get a missed call from Bert earlier?"

"This afternoon around five," Ellen replied. "We were in the midst of the event, and I figured it could wait."

"Where did you last see him?" Hannah said as she returned the phone to her ear and glared at Ellen.

"Running back toward Chesapeake Beach Resort from the pier," Bert said, referring to the resort just off Highway 1 next the diner. "Is he missing or something?"

"Yes! Becca called about six. He snuck out and no one knows where he is!" Hannah was close to tears. Where are you, baby?

"In this storm? My God, I'm sorry. I should gone after him and kept calling. The customers were so antsy—How can I help?"

"The Police are looking but with the storm... can you check where you last saw him?" Hannah pleaded.

"Of course! Did you call Warren?"

"I can't get through," Hannah admitted with frustration. She couldn't reach either Warren or Jack after several attempts, but the storm was playing havoc with cell phone signals as they always did. She didn't know if the calls had even gone through.

"I'm on it," Bert said. "I'll call some others, too. Don't worry, we'll find him, Hannah."

But the thunder rumbling outside as he hung up was like a soundtrack to the hopelessness Hannah felt inside.

JANICE CALLED BACK as Jack was crossing the bridge from Key Largo to Tavernier. The heavy rain had started as he crossed Little Blackwater Cove south of Manatee on Highway 1 and the sky had quickly gone from indigo blue to black as night.

"What do you mean Sam's missing?" Jack replied when she told him there was no sign of Sam and everyone was out looking, even Denise, Lou, and several customers. Jack's throat tightened, a sudden pressure from his bladder signaling he needed a pit stop soon.

Janice explained what she knew. Jack's stomach hardened as hair stood up on the back of his neck. "Oh my God! Where's Hannah?"

"She was in Key West." Janice explained the rest.

"Sam's missing and she's not here?!" Jack hung up and tried to call Hannah but her phone was busy, so instead he texted her. I am here. Will find Sam. There would be a lot more to say later, but the message conveyed what mattered most for the moment. The message and the sudden crushing feeling in his chest as he became both weighed down and panicked at the thought of never seeing Sam again. He couldn't lose Sam like he'd lost Caroline. And he couldn't let Hannah experience that. He couldn't bear to think of life without either one of them now.

When he arrived in Islamorada fifty minutes later, he drove the Jeep straight past the diner toward the pier in search of Bert. He ran into him in less than a block, carrying a huge flash light, his rain jacket flapping around him in the heavy winds. Jack climbed out of the Jeep, getting soaked and hurried over. The air was filled with the smell of damp earth and the usual chemicals and odorants brought out by rain. The bar across the street was packed to the gills. Pedestrians hurried along the sidewalks with newspapers and umbrellas over their heads in vain attempts to shield themselves from the rain.

"Have you seen Sam?" he asked as soon as he and Bert were close enough to hear each other over the storm.

Bert's face took on a pained look, his eyebrows drawing together as he looked down at his feet. "I turned him away earlier. I feel terrible. I was arguing with a customer and he ran off—"

"Let's just find him," Jack said, putting a hand on his shoulder.

Bert nodded, shining his flashlight around. "I've been tracing the path he took. Nothing. I stopped at the diner earlier and they said he wasn't at home or Publix."

"Where was he wanting you to take him earlier?"

"He said Hannah was with you at Cristof, but I thought you'd said you were leaving town," Bert explained. "I couldn't reach Ellen or Hannah—"

"Did you try Warren?"

"Yeah, but I got an error message. Phone may be out on some islands."

325

"Shit," Jack said. "Okay, hop in. Let's work together."

Bert followed him to the Jeep as Jack unlocked it with the key fob. "I sure hope we find him," Bert shouted over the storm as they both climbed inside.

Jack restarted the engine and lit up the Jeep's floodlights before they began a slow drive back to the pier, checking every nook and cranny they could in the surrounding area. At times they got out and used flashlights, other times, the flood lights lit up the area enough to scan it with their eyes. The entire time, Bert shifted restlessly in his seat—pulling at his earlobes, scratching his neck, rubbing his arms. He clearly felt guilty, but it hadn't been his job to babysit, and Jack knew how busy things got around the water.

As they worked, Jack flashed back to a time when Caroline was four and Jack had taken her to Salina's Central Mall to buy a Christmas present for Abby. They'd done fine in JC Penney's and Books-A-Million—with lots for her to touch and look at. He'd even stopped to let her sit on Santa's lap and ride the Santa train. It was when he stopped at Bling! By Nicole, a jeweler, that she'd wandered off.

He'd been distracted looking at diamond earrings he wanted to get for Abby. The saleswoman was bringing him various designs to examine and he'd let go of Caroline's hand a moment as they discussed each pair. It only took three or four minutes, but when he looked down again, his daughter was gone. He felt the adrenaline surge as an overwhelming feeling of dread started to swell and he called her name. "Caroline!" over and over to no response. The saleswoman and her cohorts helped him search but Caroline was nowhere in the store. He glanced back to the opening into the mall and couldn't breathe, a tingling in his chest. *Oh my God, baby, where did you go?*

He thanked the sales people and ran out the door, his body twisting and turning as he searched both ways frantically, He saw a little girl down the way with blonde hair and started running toward her, when a woman called out, "Sir?"

For some reason, he turned to see who it was and heard,

326

"Daddy!"

An older woman in his fifties with curly brown hair and rosy cheeks was approaching with Caroline, and they were both grinning ear-to-ear as Caroline sucked on a candy cane.

"Is this your daughter?" the woman asked calmly and Jack fought the urge to yank Caroline from her hands.

"Yes, thank you," he said, catching his breath. "Where did you go, baby?"

"She was snatching a candy cane from Santa's tree," the woman explained. "It's okay. They're free. When I saw she was alone, I talked to her and got her to come with me until we found you."

Caroline reached for him then and Jack swept her into his arms, hugging her tight and kissing her forehead. "Thank you, so much," he said, his body so tense he had to think to move or breathe.

The woman merely smiled and walked away, but Jack had never forgotten the feeling.

As he remembered it now, he thought about what Hannah must be going through. Caroline had been missing less than five minutes, but Sam had been gone for two hours now. His heart ached for her. And he realized he couldn't breathe.

"He's not here," Bert confirmed as they searched another parking lot near the pier. "I guess we should check the neighborhoods."

"Well, the police and Denise and others are searching those," Jack reminded him, forcing a breath. "Let's go back to the diner and check in, then decide where to look next." Time was precious, but searching the same places over and over was wasting time. So he turned the Jeep right at the next intersection and headed back for Highway 1.

ELLEN DROVE TOO fast to suit Hannah. The rain was coming down in sheets and visibility was cut down to a few feet in front of the car. But Hannah said nothing. Sam was in danger. All her focus was on getting home to him. They were still at least an hour out, though traffic had cleared quite a bit. The only ones still on the roads seemed to be emergency vehicles and a few others trying to get home from Key West, like them.

"You're too quiet," said Ellen said, glancing over at her.

Hannah kept staring at the text from Jack—I am here. Will find Sam. A million questions popped into her head but she fought them back. She'd been longing for him, and Jack had known what she needed of him most right now without her asking. She'd feared she'd never see him again, but here he was. The rest could be worked out later.

"Hannah," Ellen said, turning to tug on her sleeve.

Hannah frowned. "Keep your eyes on the road, Ellen."

"There's not much to see with this rain."

"My turn, pull over."

Ellen sighed. "Stop mothering me."

"I don't think I asked Becca if Sam ate his dinner. I'm calling her back." She pointed to an orange grove stand. "Pull in there. I'll drive."

JACK AND BERT rushed into the diner to find only Lou and Janice and a few first responders who'd stopped to get coffee and snacks. Most of the booths were empty, and the usual smells of grease and bacon weren't coming from the kitchen.

"Any luck?" Janice asked as Bert headed for the coffee.

Jack shook his head. "No. We've checked and rechecked the areas around where Bert saw him. Is Hannah back yet?" He looked around for any sign of her.

Lou shook his head. "She went with Ellen down to a fundraiser in Key West. They're on their way, but it can take hours in sunny weather. In rain like this—"

Jack took a pained breath and closed his eyes, saying a silent prayer for Hannah. Then asked Lou, "Any luck in the neighborhood?"

"No," Lou replied, looking harried. His hair was disheveled and his shirt collar sticking up. He looked exhausted. "And the police have checked the resorts and other shops and restaurants around here. We're at a loss where he could be."

"Probably hiding somewhere frightened by the storm," Janice said, stating the obvious, "Poor little guy."

Jack wanted desperately to go back and change what he'd done. He should never have left, especially not without telling Hannah. He couldn't help feeling responsible for the nightmare she was living now. The words were coming out so fast he was surprised anyone understood him, and he couldn't seem to stand still, shifting back and forth on his legs and not knowing what to do with his arms. Then he thought of the shells, wondering why he hadn't thought of it before. "Has anyone checked the beaches?" Jack asked.

Bert frowned as he returned with his coffee. "We can't go down there in a lightning storm." He shifted his legs around in a clumsy dance as he shook his head.

Lou added, "Florida isn't called the Lightning Capital of the World for nothing. No one goes near the water when there's a storm."

"It wasn't storming when he disappeared," Jack said. "You know how he loves shells. We have to go look."

"Several units are supposed to be making their way there," a sheriff's deputy said from a both where he was finishing a donut and looking at a plate with two more.

"Well, I'll help," Jack said, turning to Bert. "You can stay here if you're uncomfortable, but I know Sam and it seems a likely place."

Bert shook his head, grabbing a couple donuts. "No, I'll go."

"Good luck!" Janice called as they raced out the door again.

JACK DROVE THE Jeep too fast down onto the beach behind the diner, slowing as he squinted, looking for lights at either end where first responders might already be. "I don't see anyone."

"Let me check in on the radio," Bert suggested. As he fiddled with his handheld radio, which he'd now set to the police bank, Jack looked out the window at debris blowing across the beach. If Sam was out there walking somewhere, he was in big trouble.

Bert tried raising the police, but the signal was staticky from the storm. When he finally got through, he reached a unit searching beach on the opposite side of the island.

Jack took a deep breath. He really couldn't afford to wait. It had already been raining for two hours. They had to find Sam right now.

"I'm going for it," he called to Bert, and before the other man could object, opened the door and flung himself out into the rain. He shut the door behind him and headed onto the beach, his police issue flashlight piercing the darkness as he panned the area in front of him. Visibility was so bad, he could barely see the hand in front of his face. The rain and wind pounded him so hard he had to move slowly, weaving back and forth to stay upright. Someone small like Sam though, wouldn't stand a chance.

He was hurrying so fast, his eyes focused across the sand

ahead of him, that he didn't even see the old cannon until he was right on it. He almost tripped, barely dodging and saw a few more. Ripples of electricity pierced the night sky, illuminating an inlet to his right with docks for several yachts and boats of all sizes. Next to it was the parking lot it shared with a nearby restaurant. Lining the beach on his left, white rocks were piled, leaving only a little bit of sand down below touched by the waves. Not the best place for shelling, so he turned and hurried back to the car, knowing they needed to move on further down the beach. As he went, he stumbled and fell, looking down to see potted small palms—palmettos the locals called them— lined up in a row. Warren had referred to them as a born nuisance, and at the moment, Jack certainly didn't see the appeal. His knee hurt as he climbed back to his feet, thunder pounding overhead, and ran back toward the Jeep.

Two minutes, later, driving past the Chesapeake Resort, which Bert had now confirmed was thoroughly searched, he left Bert to monitor the radio, and stepped out again, spotting what he thought might be a lifeguard stand or two down the beach. The beach here didn't stretch all that wide, with buildings bordering it, but there were rows of tall palms and other plants, and a few white beach chairs spread around for beachgoers, but here there weren't white rocks lining the shore, so the sand stretched down to the water, uninterrupted. Jack panned his flashlight and began shouting Sam's name as he resumed his search.

HANNAH DROPPED ELLEN at her house because she insisted, saying, "Someone should be here in case he comes home." Then Hannah hurried on toward the diner to find her son...and Jack. Before she'd gone a block, her cell rang with Denise's number in the caller ID. "Hello?"

"Hun, are you back yet?" Denise asked.

Hannah's attempts to remain calm failed her. "Did you find Sam?"

"No," Denise's voice cracked. "But we're searching everywhere."

"Oh Jesus! He wouldn't go that far. He knows better." Hannah searched her mind for any ideas. "Did you check the beaches?"

"The police have and Jack and Bert headed there as well," Denise said.

"Jack's back?" Hannah felt a sudden surge of hope.

"He got in an hour ago," Denise said. "Been searching since. The storm's messed up phone signals. I tried reach you."

Lightning light the sky as several bolts landed on either side. "Oh my God! Where could he be?!" Tears burst from her eyes as she pulled into the parking lot beside the diner and put her head in her hands.

"We'll find him, hun. I promise," Denise said, sniffling on the other end.

But Hannah was losing hope. She'd already lost Rob. She couldn't bear to lose Sam.

Jack, find him, please!

CHAPTER 25

BERT FOLLOWED JACK in the Jeep as he made his way south along the beach at a turtle's pace. He refused to stop looking and ride, fearing he'd miss Sam if he did. The storm had been raging now for over four hours—a long time for a young boy to be out in it, especially one who was terrified of storms. Worst case scenarios flooded Jack's head. Please God, let him not drown. Sam would be cold and wet for sure.

He crossed an access road and saw buildings painted in rainbow colors. Familiarity tugged at the back of his mind, and then he saw them—an ice cream shop and donut vendor's trailer. Sam's favorite shelling beach! He made his way forward through limited visibility, calling Sam's name. He heard the rush of a large tide rolling in and saw the shadow of the water rushing across the sand toward his feet. During a storm, the tides were stronger and covered more area. But Jack ignored the water as it soaked his feet and kept panning his flashlight. What else was here? There was something he wasn't remembering?

Several beach chairs blocked his path and another row of palmettos—though he dodged around them without trouble. When his light first hit the old lifeguard stand, he noticed something strange underneath, up against the pilings that made up the frame. He panned the area between as he made his way toward it, but the night was ink black, so it wasn't until he was right up on it and a bolt of lightning lit the night that he realized it was a boy.

"Sam?!" he called as he moved closer. The boy was sprawled against a corner of the undercarriage. He'd wrapped himself in a tarp from the lifeguard stand and one arm was swung up, desperately holding two large fronds over his head. The tidewater rushed back out to see from underneath them both as Jack gently reached down to touch him and hollered, "Sam?!"

He got no response but the boy's skin felt cold to the touch. Jack carefully pulled the palm fronds away and immediately realized it was Sam, his head lolled to one side, his mouth open. He was soaked and disheveled, and it looked like he might have taken on water, so Jack parked the mower and ran over, laid him flat on his stomach, and patted his back, trying to drain any liquid. Then he felt for a pulse. It was there but weak.

Pulling Sam into his arms, and ignoring his own shivering, he covered him with his own rain gear and ran back to the mower. Laying him across his lap to keep him covered, he shifted the machine into gear and took off running back down the beach as he could safely manage, trying to spot Bert and the Jeep.

The moment he came into view of the Jeep's headlights, Bert hurried out to meet him, and together they laid Sam across the back seat as Jack climbed in beside him to do what he could.

"Mariner is closest, though it's a bit of a haul in this mess," Bert said. "I'll radio ahead and see if we can meet an ambulance somewhere."

"Okay." Jack nodded as Bert slammed the back door and raced around to the driver's side again.

As Bert drove, Jack focused his attention on Sam, constantly monitoring his breathing and pulse, and praying for him to wake up. He flashed back to the first time he'd seen Caroline's body in the hospital morgue. She'd been so pale and lifeless. He'd never seen her look that way and it was surreal and frightening at first, before he was overcome again with sorrow. He'd been told they were gone before he'd arrived, of course, but seeing them there was something no one could prepare you for.

Oh God, he prayed silently now, Not this one, too. Please. Let him be okay.

If only he hadn't run off. If only he'd stayed and dealt with his feelings directly. Jack had so many "If Onlys" he had to live with and now he had another. God damn it, Jack. Not again.

He wasn't going to lose Sam the way he lost Caroline. Hannah couldn't go through that. He would fight with his last breath to prevent it.

He steeled himself and kept monitoring Sam as the jetty boat bounced across the waves and Bert finished on the radio.

"They ambulance will meet us at Marker 88 restaurant," Bert said. "Ambulance and police."

"Good. Thanks, Bert. For everything."

"I just hope he's okay. I feel responsible."

"Me too," Jack whispered. Me too.

And then Sam grabbed his phone and dialed Hannah.

"IS HE ALIVE?" Hannah cried as soon as she answered and heard Jack's voice. Her hands gripped the wheel so tight they were turning white. "He's unconscious but alive for now," Jack said glumly. "Soaked to the bone, cold to the touch, shivering. We're meeting the ambulance at Marker 88, and they'll get him to Mariners as fast as they can."

"Okay," Hannah said, choking up as she drove through the downpour. She'd been headed to the beach where Jack found him, the idea popping in her head it was a place Sam might go. "I'll meet you at Marker 66 in two minutes!"

She hung up and dialed Denise as tears covered her face and

she focused on breathing. Sam needed her. Now was not the time to breakdown.

"Hey, hun, I'm at your place with Ellen."

"They found him!"

"Where? How is he?" Denise put her on speaker so Ellen could hear.

"Down off Bonefish Point," Hannah replied.

"Oh my God!" Ellen exclaimed.

"Get to Mariners. I'm meeting the ambulance." And then she hung up and wrapped her arms around herself as she rocked in her seat, her seatbelt flinging her back. Her temple throbbed and she had to remind herself to breathe.

"Oh Jesus. Oh Jesus," she mumbled over and over.

JACK RODE WITH Hannah and Sam in the ambulance as Bert followed behind in the Jeep. The police escorted them, clearing traffic as needed, and they arrived at the hospital in under five minutes, despite the storm. The paramedic wrapped Sam in blankets and warm packs to heat him up. His body temperature was 89.6 and Jack' heard the words "hypothermia...lethargic..." and "semi-comatose" as the paramedic spoke with doctors at Mariners. At one point, he tried to find a vein, but failed so there was no IV for now.

"We need to warm him up first," the paramedic explained.

Doctors, nurses, and orderlies rushed out to meet them with a cart and Jack and Hannah followed them in. The air smelled of ammonia and antiseptic, fluorescent lights glaring over the small, crowded waiting room. He sat waiting at the end of a row of metal-and-vinyl chairs that filled the room in rows. In the corner outside the Emergency Room, a short line had formed at the intake counter as people filled out forms and asked questions. As Hannah continued into the ER with Sam and the

ER staff treated him, Jack filled out as much as he could, answering any questions they had. It was half an hour before Bert, Denise and Ellen appeared, out of breath, and soaked.

"Where is he?" asked Ellen.

"ER One," Jack said and looked around for a nurse.

"Where did you find him?" Denise asked and Jack quickly told the story. They listened but said nothing, not that Jack expected them to.

Ellen nodded to him curtly and said, "Thank you for getting him here."

Jack simply nodded.

It was another twenty minutes before the doctor came out and explained what was going on, "He's hypothermic, lethargic, cold to the touch. And that's why he's semi-comatose, but the warm packs and blankets helped enough that we found a vein and he's on fluids. He took on some water, but we've pumped his stomach as a precaution and we're giving him oxygen," the doctor said. "He's not out of the woods yet, but he should wake up once his body temp normalizes."

"Will he be okay?" Jack asked, before anyone else could.

The doctor smiled and nodded. "With a few days' rest and solid fluids, yes." He asked Ellen to finish the paperwork. Hannah was too distraught, and wanted to stay with Sam. Then Hannah, Jack, and Ellen thanked him as he hurried off to tend to Sam and then the nurse escorted them to a larger, more comfortable private family waiting room to continue their wait.

Jack knew Ellen wished he would go away, but he couldn't bring himself to leave. She'll calm down with time, he told himself. Besides, he was here for Hannah and Jack. He really needed to clear the air, and he couldn't bear to leave until he knew Sam was okay, so he leaned against the wall nearby to wait.

WHEN SHE WAS sure Sam was okay and settled in a room to sleep, Hannah came out to join Jack and Ellen in the private waiting room. It was almost 11 p.m. and Bert and Denise had already headed home.

After Hannah brought them up to speed, Ellen said, "Well, we just have to wait now," as she settled onto one of the waiting area couches and pulled her Kindle out of her purse.

Hannah sighed, too restless to sit and relax, but knowing there was not much else for her to do. Jack was there, leaning against the wall, and for seeing him now, despite what he'd done for Sam, brought a rush of emotions. On the one hand, he'd done exactly what she needed—rushing off to look for Sam the moment he returned and found out what was happening. And he had texted her and tried to call, even if the signal and her own frantic calling had kept him from getting through. And he was here waiting like a worried parent, while Ellen pissed her off by sitting there reading as if it was just another ordinary day.

Ellen glanced up for her Kindle and looked at Jack, snapping, "Well, you found him and got him. Your job's over. This is a time for family. You can go now, okay?"

Jack stiffened, looking somewhere between hurt and shocked, but Ellen just glared at him. "I'd like to hear from Hannah," Jack finally said, ignoring Ellen and looked at Hannah. "Hannah, I'd like to stay. His tone was sincere, genuine, and his eyes showed real concern.

But suddenly, Hannah felt her anger rising. If he'd cared about them so much, he wouldn't have left the way he did. Especially without any notice or discussion. "You abandoned us! You made love to me, got what you want, and then just disappeared. With just some generic note to say goodbye!"

Jack winced, shuffling his feet, and refusing to meet her gaze.

"We started to care about you. You mattered to us. But you

chose to leave, and I chose to let you go. I have to think of Sam. He's so sweet and he loves you so much, but he almost died."

"I know, and I'm sorry. I made a big mistake."

"We're a mistake? Is that what we are?" Hannah turned away, scowling. She should have never trusted him. Never let him matter.

He shook his head. "That's not what I meant."

"What did you mean?"

Jack stared at her a moment, his eyes glistening with pain, his lips cracked as if he was about to speak but his mind working to find the right words. Finally, he breathed deeply and said, "I went home to say goodbye to Abby and Caroline. To clear my head." His eyes met hers. "I needed to sort through feelings, but I always intended to come back. I'm sorry."

"Sometimes, sorry doesn't cut it!" Ellen snapped.

Jack ignored her and went on, "Hannah, when I met you—"

"You made a choice," Ellen said, looking up from the Kindle to glare at him. "Did what was best for you. But this isn't about you. It's about Sam. So go home. Leave us be."

Jack kept his eyes locked on Hannah's, taking a step toward her, his eyes filled with yearning. "I didn't plan on falling in love with you," he said. "And I don't think you meant to fall in love with me."

"Oh please. She was better off without you, enough is enough!" Ellen scolded.

"Ellen! Stop!" Hannah spun and said. "I can handle my own life just fine." She returned her mother-in-law's glare before looking at Jack and leading him across the room to the other side. "You disappeared. Do you know how much that hurt?"

Jack nodded, looking down at his feet. "I should never have done that. I was overwhelmed. But I should have talked to you."

"Why?"

"I just needed some air," Jack said. "That's why I left at first, but then I got to thinking and Ellen was there, and I needed to sort my feelings. I used to visit their graves to do that. It always helped me figure things out—"

Hannah's heart pounded and her forehead creased as she realized what he'd said. "What was that about Ellen?"

Jack stopped, taking a deep breath while continuing to stare at her. She kept waiting for an explanation, but instead he just watched her a moment. What had Ellen done? And just when she thought she couldn't stand it and was ready to explode at him—

Ellen grunted. "It's his fault Sam was out there in the first place. Both of you have been acting crazy ever since he showed up. I knew when you saw him for what he was, you wouldn't want him here. You just needed a push."

As Ellen went back to her Kindle again like it was nothing, Hannah ran over those words in her mind. You just needed a push. Something about those words, knowing her mother-in-law's nature, bothered Hannah. Sure, Ellen was pushy, but she also had been very helpful with Sam, and Hannah couldn't have made it the past few years without her. But then Ellen had never wanted Hannah to date Jack in the first place. She'd been trying to interfere since it started. You just needed a push? "What did you mean by 'a push?'"

Ellen kept reading a moment ignoring her, while Hannah continued staring. After a few moments, her mother-in-law sighed and lowered the Kindle until their eyes met. "Well, I just meant you were distraught over Sam, as we both are," Ellen said, barely looking up from the book she was clearly now engaged in reading. "And he was making things uncomfortable at home. You weren't in a space to ask him to leave so I did it for you."

"You had no right," Hannah said, stunned and feeling dizzy. Was that why Jack had left?

Ellen sighed. "We don't need him. You deserve better. So does Sam. If he hadn't always been intruding himself, none of this would have happened. So I went to that lighthouse—"

"'Intruding himself?'" Hannah repeated. "We had an attraction. And one thing led to another. He wasn't pushy or intrusive, like some kind of stalker. It was very casual and natural."

Ellen grunted. "It was a mistake, Hannah. You couldn't see it at the time maybe, but I knew."

Now, the burst of anger Hannah had felt at Jack was rising again, this time aimed at Ellen. "You came to the lighthouse and spoke with Jack?" Hannah said, growing more alarmed as it dawned on her: Jack hadn't left because of her. He'd left because of Ellen. "My God, Ellen! It wasn't your place!"

Ellen just stared at her, shaking her head. "I just did what was best for you. You'll see that in time. You don't need him."

"Ellen, just shut up! Or you can leave!" Hannah screamed, losing it. She turned to find Jack had disappeared while she was arguing with Ellen. She hadn't even heard the door open. Where could he have gone? She'd missed her chance. My God, who knew what he might be thinking after what Ellen had said! Whatever it was, it might have cost Hannah the best thing that had happened to her since Rob, and as she realized she'd probably lost Jack for good, her shoulders sank as she reached for the door and opened it.

But here he was. Standing in front of her. She stared at Jack, who was holding a flower arrangement he must have purchased at the gift shop. At the same moment she saw him, he saw her, and as she yanked open the door, he started toward her. In a few seconds, they were face to face, Hannah searching for words. He looked sad and worried, but his eyes were filled with such warmth and compassion. He loved her.

"Hannah, I love you," he said they stopped cold, their eyes meeting. "Something rare and beautiful happened between us, and I wasn't expecting it so it caught me off guard, but it wasn't planned or something we could control..." His words faded off as he searched for what to say, and Hannah couldn't find words either. His sincerity, the genuine emotion of it was unexpected, but it was clear he was trying to apologize, and he really meant what he was saying.

Finally, he cleared his throat and continued, "Hannah, I'm in love with you, and to be honest, it scares me to death. I don't know how I could survive going through what I went through with Abby again. If I lost you—"

Then she realized what had happened. He hadn't rejected her or walked away because he didn't want her. It had been just the opposite. They'd gotten too close too fast. And then Ellen had interfered. Whatever she'd said had been the final straw. Jack had been scared and worried he'd gotten ahead of himself. He'd pushed her away trying to protect himself.

Jack swallowed, tears forming at the edge of his eyes, and continued, "She was my greatest dream; she made me who I am, and holding her in my arms was like coming home. I think about her all the time, and maybe I always will."

And suddenly, she understood him exactly. She knew what he'd been feeling and wrestling with, and she knew why, and the wall she'd put up around her heart melted, a wave of compassion and caring filling her, as she reached out and set her hand gently on his arm. "I understand. I feel the same way about Rob."

"You deserve someone who can love you with all they have," Jack said. "I wasn't sure if I could give you that. What you deserve. Sam, too."

"I've struggled with the same thing thinking about Rob. I'll never forget him either, or stop thinking about him—the memories," Hannah said.

"I thought if I forgot them, I was betraying their memory. But if I held on to them, would there be enough room to love you and Sam?" Tears streamed down his face now, but he ignored them and took her hand. "It scared me, but I didn't know how to explain or what to say. But I needed to see them so sort it out. And I'm sorry I hurt you in how I did that."

"You should have told me," Hannah said, squeezing his hand. "I would have understood."

"I'm sorry."

"I'm sorry, too," she said, closing her eyes as they started at each other, the emotions overwhelming. "But I know how Ellen gets; how you must have felt." Then she reached up and gently put her hands on his cheeks, wiping at his tears with her thumbs. "You loved Abby and Caroline with your whole heart and part of you always will. They're part of you and you're part of them. I'll never ask you to give that up. I wouldn't give up Rob if you asked me."

And they stood there, close to each other, his breath on her face as her words sunk in.

JACK STARED AT Hannah a moment, hardly believing what she'd said yet seeing in her eyes that every word was true. Could she really love him so much? He'd never met anyone who seemed to have it all figured out...until now. But Hannah did, and it filled him with admiration and longing.

Then she went on, "I won't promise to love you the same as I loved Rob, but that's because you're different people. We have to make our own love, but we can do it...together."

Her words struck his heart like arrows of truth not to be denied and he believed every word. Gathering himself, he leaned in to kiss her and this time as she kissed back, their lips stayed together for a long time before they came up for air.

She smiled and they both wiped at their tears.

"You're sure Sam won't mind?" Jack joked.

"Not one bit," she said, and they kissed again. This time it was as if time stopped and the world paused its spinning around them. In that moment, it was just them. And no one else. And nothing else mattered as long as they were together, side by side—they could get through anything.

It was then that the nurse stuck in her head. "Ms. Hannah, Sam's awake."

THE NURSE LED Hannah and Jack down the corridor and back down the hall past the nurse's station. The nurse opened the door to the PICU, the pediatrics' ward for children in health crises. "Sir, are you a family member?" she asked Jack.

"He certainly is," Hannah insisted. "Can't you see the resemblance?"

The nurse's face took on a funny look but she stepped aside. Hannah bolted past, looking up and down the smallish beds until she saw Sam—sitting up in bed and smiling. Tears filled her eyelids, as tension drained from her body and a lightness replaced it. It was as if her senses suddenly sprang to life—the smell of ammonia and antiseptic, the beeping of machines, the hissing of oxygen lines, the bright overhead lights—everything more vivid and overwhelming at the sight of her son. As she moved toward him, there was that slightly crooked smile, but then his eyes darted away as he reacted to something behind her, and she turned to see Jack and Ellen standing just inside the outer curtain.

Instantly, Sam leaned forward, his arm outstretched and she heard a voice she hadn't heard in two years as he said, "Jack, please don't go."

For a moment they all stood there, not believing Sam had spoken. Then as he moved closer, coming up on the opposite side of the bed from Hannah, Jack grinned and said, "I'm here, right where I belong, buddy. And there's nowhere I'd rather be."

"Good," Sam said and then he hugged Jack as Hannah and Ellen looked on with a cornucopia of emotions.

"We were so scared, Sammy," Ellen said.

"I did what daddy taught me; found shelter," Sam said. "I love you."

Hannah's heart surged along with her tears as she rushed forward to wrap him in her arms and held him to her. Then Ellen was beside her, caressing his arm, unable to hide her own tears.

"I love you, too, Gramma," Sam said as Hannah released him and he hugged Ellen, too.

Hannah still couldn't believe her son was speaking again, almost like the past two years hadn't happened. "Oh baby, hearing you speak helps more than words could ever say," she said.

Sam chuckled. "I found something I had to say, mama."

"You sure did!" Hannah said and hugged him again. And Hannah thought about his first words in two years—Jack, please don't go—and wondered if they had anything to do with his leaving. Those questions would have to wait.

They doted on him a moment before he coughed and then asked for Jack again.

JACK APPROACHED, taking Sam's outstretched hand.

"Thanks for saving me," said Sam. "I did my best to hold back enemy forces, Keeper Jack."

Jack spoke into his invisible shoulder mic: "Commander Gregg, Lt. Sam secured the fortress, driving back the enemy forces."

"Not bad for a noob," Sam teased, and Jack and Hannah

laughed. Then he rubbed his throat. "I need a drink. Can we go home?"

Jack felt tears forming at the corners of his eyes again as he leaned down to let Sam give him a hug. Just like the first hug, Sam's touch filled Jack with a wave of euphoria, reminding him of how it felt to hug his daughter. The grief and pain he'd been living with for so long, seemed to fade, replaced by wholeness and a sense of rightness with the world.

"I love you, Jack," Sam whispered.

"I love you, too," Jack whispered back.

"Thanks for saving my mom, too," Sam added loudly, looking past him at Hannah. "Gramma will get over it." He looked at Ellen now, who used the backs of her hands to wipe away the remnants of tears on her cheeks and refused to make eye contact with any of them.

Jack and Hannah exchanged a look, and, to Jack's surprise, Hannah reached for his hand; their fingers entwining.

"Can you teach me to drive your cart?" Sam asked.

Jack looked at Hannah. "You just focus on getting well first, okay? Maybe later."

"I'll think about it," said Hannah, who reached across Sam to touch Jack's arm.

Sam grunted. "Typical."

And they all laughed, including Ellen, maybe for the first time since Jack had come into their lives. Then the nurse returned.

"Don't wear him out," she warned. "There'll be plenty of time to chat later. He needs his energy to heal." She injected a needle into his IV. "He'll be asleep soon."

Taking that as a cue, they said their "good nights" to him and headed back out toward the waiting room. A group of nurses rushed past, pushing carts and talking back and forth about some emergency down the hall, and Jack's eyes were drawn after them to see a worried father pacing outside a door.

They all sat together for a while in the private waiting room until he doctor gave them another update, before loading in the Jeep and heading for Hannah's. Jack would head back to the lighthouse when the storm let up. For now, he was overcome with gratitude that the storm between him and Hannah was over and everyone was safe.

For the first time in two years, Jack actually looked forward to the future with a sense of hope and anticipation. As he drove them back south along Overseas Highway, he caught the slow, rhythmic flapping of a great blue heron gliding over its domain. Sailboats bobbed off shore in the distance, the peaceful, easy Florida life rolling on as if the storm had never been. The faces of Caroline and Abby flashed into his head, and they were smiling. A flood of warmth and contentment filled him as he smiled, and he knew everything would be all right.

THE END

ACKNOWLEDGMENTS

Authors work alone in a room, but no book comes to be in isolation, and *The Lighthouse* was no exception. A lot of people accompanied me on this journey, so it behooves me to give them my great thanks for their support and encouragement.

To my editors Patricia Hickman and Claire Ashgrove, both successful authors themselves. Thanks for your patient guidance of a man exploring a new genre and approach, for your gentle nudges and the not so gentle ones, too! For great conversation and attention to detail. I am so proud of what you helped this story become, and I hope you are too.

To Ramon Schmidt, Guy Anthony DeMarco, and Anthony Cardno for proofing and other notes. To Jennifer Barnhill, Stacey Elliott, Patricia Hickman, and a few Facebook friends who answered my post helping me get the details right about life in the Florida Keys. To Leslie Bennett and her family, who introduced me to the Keys years ago and have hosted me back there a few times, inspiring my love of the area and desire to set a book there one day.

Thanks to Audra Redington for a superb cover and ebook formatting and support and friendship.

And big thanks to you readers for giving me a chance.

Thanks to my kids, Kishi, Kenjie, Louie, Amara, Ernie, and Phantom (pets are kids, too) for their support, love, and teasing. Keeping my sense of humor is vital to my writing and breathing both. I love you.

Last but not least, thanks to May, the love of my life, who is my second chance, and for moving 8000 miles to a strange place just to take a chance on me. I love you, and this one's for you.

MA Lanham

Ottawa, KS August 2024

350

AUTHOR'S NOTE

Thanks for reading *The Lighthouse*. I hope you enjoyed the story as much as I enjoyed writing it. To find more of my work, you can follow me on my socials:

https://www.facebook.com/malanhamauthor

https://www.x.com/malanhamauthor

Or on my website at https://www.malanham.com.

My next book, out soon, is *The Last Wish*. With more to come.

In the meantime, please take the time to spread the word. Posting your review to Amazon and Goodreads is a huge boost and, of course, tell your friends.

With sincere thanks,

M.A. Lanham

www.ingramcontent.com/pod-product-compliance
Lightning Source LLC
Chambersburg PA
CBHW010732130726
47899CB00015B/3189

* 9 7 8 1 6 2 2 2 5 6 8 1 5 *